Murder in Millbrook

Loren Schechter

ISBN-10: 1481004557
EAN-13: 9781481004558
Library of Congress Control Number: 2012922920

CreateSpace, North Charleston, SC

For Dotty and Susan

ACKNOWLEDGEMENTS

Writing fiction is a wonderful adventure, and I've had the good fortune to share parts of my journey with a lot of very fine people. I learned much of what I know about writing from the late Professor Arthur Edelstein, who taught in the Brandeis adult education program, and from the spirited discussion of my classmates, none finer than Art's wife, Tima Smith. Many years later, after starting this novel, I participated in three workshops at Grub Street, a center for creative writing in Boston, where I benefited from the knowledge of two published writers and excellent teachers, Michelle Hoover and Jeff Talarigo, as well as from the candid feedback of other unpublished writers.

Three of my former classmates and I still meet regularly in our own writing group, and these colleagues – Kristin Knutrud, Laurie Nordman and Holly Raynes – have been exceedingly patient and entirely constructive, even when encouraging me to kill the "little darlings" that seemed wonderful in my head but bombed on the page. If any of those poor creatures survived in the manuscript, it is my fault alone.

I was inspired to write this novel after the death of an elderly friend in a small Massachusetts town in which she'd lived her entire life. Other than raising her children alone, Dorothea Foster had no remarkable achievements and chose to live quietly, or as quietly as her cat would permit. She didn't like socializing or traveling, and she hated to be in the spotlight. She loved her children and grandchildren, and she enjoyed reading, playing the piano and, much to my surprise, watching professional football She never would have gotten involved in a murder investigation, but I believe she would have vicariously enjoyed Addie's gumption and adventures.

As the behavior of our cat Betty has always been exemplary, the character of Flash, the delinquent cat in this novel, came not only from Dotty's cat, but from anecdotes told to me by cat owners Roslyn Kaplan, Karla Ritcey, Geraldine Ryan, and Joanne Woodworth. The names of those cats are being withheld to protect their privacy.

Noreen Auterio graciously allowed me to use her family's name, but the Auterios and all other characters in this novel are fictional. I also thank mystery fan Katsch Belash and gallant members of my extended family, Cristina Pierce, Lowell and Judy Schechter, and Marilyn Schechter, who volunteered to critique a later draft of my manuscript. I found their feedback and support very helpful.

Finally, I am truly blessed to have a wonderful wife. Susan writes fiction in lyrical prose, paints abstracts with acrylic, and makes the best apple cardamom pancakes I've ever tasted. Her suggestions, criticism and editing were invaluable to this novel, and she is invaluable to me.

Week One

CHAPTER 1

Friday Morning

Flash squeezed through the cat-door sporting what looked like a handlebar moustache.

"What've you got this time?" Addie dropped her wet nightgown back into the washer and wiped her hand on her overalls.

The gray tom strutted forward and dropped a black object at her feet. It clinked as it bounced once on the mudroom's linoleum tile, then lay still.

She peered down through her bifocals. Oh, crumb. Herbert Elwood's pipe. There was no mistaking the rustic bowl and tapered stem he'd thrust toward her so many times in the forty-two years he'd owned the big Colonial next door.

"How many times have I told you not to bring things in? I don't need more trouble with Herbert." She scowled at the cat. "I don't suppose you're going to go back there and apologize."

Beneath unwavering yellow eyes, Flash's nose and whiskers offered one twitch.

"I didn't think so." Addie picked up and inspected the tooth-scarred stem and empty bowl. Of course, no tobacco. Herbert had given up smoking after Janet was diagnosed with cancer. "Don't know how to talk any more without holding the damn thing," he'd said. Nothing was safe from Flash, outdoors or in.

"You keep doing this, I'm going to take you back to the shelter. And you can wipe that smirk off your face."

Addie placed the pipe on the narrow shelf above the dryer, finished transferring her clothes and started up the machine. Flash sprang onto the dryer and settled down as if preparing to nap.

"You'll kill yourself jumping up there, one of these days. We're not getting any younger you know." Addie took the pipe from the shelf and stuffed it into the pocket of her overalls. "Now I have to go make excuses for you again." She gave Flash the look her children had dubbed "the MAHIB," for Ma's-Had-It-Big-Time. "You could have the grace to look ashamed."

Flash yawned.

I've lost my touch, she thought as she went for her windbreaker. Well, at least the children had turned out decently.

* * *

Addie rang Herbert's front doorbell. Good apple picking weather, she thought. Have to get to Hammett's Farm early tomorrow. Being Columbus Day weekend, half the town would go there to pick apples. She rang the bell again, then rapped the door knocker against its brass plate and waited. Maybe Herbert was working out back.

"Herbert?" she yelled. Stupid. He'd never hear her if he was in his tool shed. At 70, she was eight years younger, and she'd already lost some of the higher tones. How could his hearing be much better?

She started around the cedar-shingled house. His lawn was still damp from Wednesday's rain, the sod thicker and greener than hers, and his rhododendrons looked a lot healthier. Give credit where credit was due, but – "You are such a pain in the ass, Herbert Elwood," she muttered. "In my face when I don't want you, gone when I do. You'd think you were my husband." Thank

God he wasn't. Her ex had shown her the folly of catering to men. How did Bella put it? "So? You picked a bad apple and he ran off with a tart. It's not the end of the world."

In back of the house, the bulkhead gaped open, its rust-pitted green door as inviting as the upper jaw of an alligator's yawn. Probably airing out his basement workshop. "Herbert!"

She glanced back at the shed where he kept his riding mower and garden tools. Padlocked. Behind the shed, the trees were ablaze with fluttering orange and red leaves. No sign of Herbert on the path into the woods. Perfect day – she'd leave work early enough to take a walk.

"Herbert!"she called. A blue jay darted up and away. Addie shook her head and turned back toward the house. To the right of the bulkhead, she saw glass sparkle on the top step to the back door. She walked toward the steps. Did he break a glass, cut himself, run to the bathroom? She looked up at the bathroom window. "Herbert!" she yelled. What if he'd fallen upstairs, or in the basement, or had a stroke? "Herbert, it's Addie – I'm coming down!"

She stooped and extended a hand to the side of the bulkhead, then carefully descended the steps. "Herbert?" The overhead fluorescents were on; one emitted a barely audible hum. Next to the bulkhead entrance, the faded sweatshirt he wore when gardening was draped over the chair on which he sat to change into his gardening shoes. No socks or shoes on the floor today. The fresh air drifting in behind her hadn't fully eliminated odors of sawdust and something like lacquer or paint thinner. She glanced at his workbench, saw a pair of birdhouses styled like red barns, an electric sander, and a few paint brushes sticking out of a coffee can. The only other hand tools visible were neatly hooked to the wall.

Addie moved around the table saw and stopped short. "Herbert!" At the bottom of the steps to the kitchen, he lay face down, his arms extended as if he wanted to rise. She rushed forward, then saw dark blood and bits of brain around an opening in Herbert's bald head. She clutched her belly, collapsed to her knees. "Oh, my God! Herbert!"

* * *

"I hate throwing up," said Addie. "I haven't done it since I was twelve and had appendicitis."

"Drink the tea, Ma," George said. "It'll be good for you."

She felt comforted with her son sitting next to her at the kitchen table. He was dressed in the dark blues of the Millbrook police department, concern on his craggy face, holstered gun at his side, clearly ready "to serve and protect" his mother. George had placed his cap on top of the refrigerator, where it was safe from Flash. The cat was sunning himself on the folded towel she kept on the radiator next to the side window. Still, the sunlight streaming through the café curtains had done nothing to chase away her chills.

Addie picked up the bone china tea cup. "It was so – sudden." Her hands were trembling, so she set the cup down on the saucer. "I'm sorry that someone will have to clean up my mess."

"It's okay," said George. "The state police techs are used to cleaning up worse. Drink the tea."

"Techs? Like CSI? I didn't mean to contaminate the crime scene."

"Ma, it's not like on television. You didn't harm the crime scene." He leaned forward. "You didn't touch anything. You got out of there and called me – you did all the right things."

Addie nodded. There was comfort beyond words in her son's blue eyes, all the more because they were the only facial feature he had from her. The years had turned his blond hair a lusterless brown, furrowed his brow and even thrust out his chin like his father's, but George's concern for her was no less fervent now than it was after Dave abandoned them.

"Drink the tea," he said.

"Could you pour it into a mug, George? There are only four of these cups left from my mother, and I'm so shaky right now."

"Sure." He got up and took her cup and saucer to the counter between the stove and refrigerator.

"I just can't believe that Herbert's dead. Not that way." Addie closed her eyes and tried to focus on her breathing, but images of Herbert's bashed-in head were overpowering. Her eyes popped open, her body trembled, her fingernails dug into her palms. "Horrible – so horrible."

"It is," said George. He set a white NPR mug down in front of her, then moved behind her chair to gently massage her neck and shoulders. "I'm really sorry you saw that."

"So am I. At least he didn't have to lie there until his cleaning lady came on Tuesday." She grasped George's hand. "Who'll tell his children? This will be awful for them."

His mouth tightened as if he didn't trust himself to speak. He patted her hand, then cleared his throat. "Don't worry. Detective Barker and I will tell them personally."

Of course George was hurting, she thought. Herbert's three kids had grown up playing with her four, and George, the eldest and most serious, had always been their protector. "It's so hard to believe," she said. "I mean people may have wished Herbert dead at times, but to kill him? In

Millbrook, Massachusetts? When's the last time this town had a murder?"

He shrugged his broad shoulders. "Maybe ten, twelve years ago. Remember that convenience store guy?"

She snuffled and reached for the napkin holder. "He was trying to resist a hold-up." She wiped her nose with a napkin. "They said the killer was on drugs. To me, this looked deliberate."

"Just drink your tea, Ma. Let us get the facts and draw the conclusions. That's how we earn our pay."

"At least it's Sergeant's pay now. That must help."

He sat down next to her. "Mostly it helps Luisa's orthodontist. Please Ma, drink some tea."

The tea was hot and bracing. "You sure you don't want some?"

"Uh-uh." He rubbed his temple with his middle three fingers, his telltale sign of a worry he was trying to spare her.

"So?" she asked. "Let's have it."

"When you're ready, you're going to have to talk to Detective Barker."

"Do I know him?"

"He's Rona Barker's nephew."

Addie sniffed. "He has my sympathy."

"You mean the choir?"

"I'm not the only one who left the choir because of her bossiness. But not only there. That woman comes into Auterio's every week, fills up her shopping basket, then decides at the register she doesn't want two or three items. Good thing for her I'm not the one who has to put them back on the shelves. The cashiers say she never even apologizes."

"Detective Barker isn't like his aunt."

"You sure?"

"He doesn't shop at Auterio's. And I once heard him apologize to the Chief."

"Herbert told me he was very offended by her."

"By Rona? Herbert was in the choir?"

"No. He attends – attended a fundamentalist church. But two weeks after Janet died, Rona started calling him to sell his house. He said she asked him, now that he was a widower, why did he need such a big house? As if it was *her* business."

"Ma, real estate is her business."

"She could've waited a decent interval. She has no sensitivity and no tact. And she pestered him about it every few months. I surely hope her nephew's very different."

"He's not pushy like Rona. But play it cool, anyway. With Marbury out on disability, Barker's our only detective."

"I never met him at one of your barbecues, did I?"

"No. We just work together. He doesn't live in town because he doesn't want his kids hassled. So, you ready?"

"No, but let's get it over with." How do people ever get over something like this? she thought.

George took out his cell phone and speed dialed a number. He cocked his head toward Flash. "Maybe you should put the beast in the bathroom."

"He won't like it."

"Detective Barker won't like his shoelaces used as dental floss – Hello, it's George. My mom's ready... No, in the kitchen. Use the back door." He pocketed the phone.

Flash was licking a paw. "I hate to disturb him," she said. "He's so comfortable there."

"Ma, this is a murder investigation. Detective Barker doesn't need distractions."

"You're right. I can't let Flash out, either, or next thing you know he'll be down that basement again." She pushed back from the table. Flash jerked his head toward the sound of chair legs scraping the worn oak floor. "That's where he must've gotten the pipe, don't you think?"

"We'll know better once they put it under a microscope and see what's on it."

She stood up. "I probably messed it all up by handling the pipe."

"You didn't know he was dead, Ma."

"I still can't believe it." She remembered Herbert's face lighting up with appreciation of her pies, his rage when he felt betrayed by her ex-husband, his grief and confusion after Janet's death. She shook her head. "Poor Herbert." She walked to the radiator. "Come for a ride, Flash."

In her arms, the cat was a purring bundle of warmth. "See, he's on his good behavior today."

"You should've been a public defender, Ma. I hear the little beast bit Robert hard yesterday."

"No harder than usual. Robert shouldn't have sat down on the couch. Flash knows you and your brother don't like him."

"You're wrong. It's Bess and Joanne that don't like him. Robert and I hate him."

"Oh, dear." She sighed. "I have only myself to blame."

"For adopting him?"

"For failing to teach you how to be tactful. But I don't think the police department succeeded in that, either." She left the room before he could reply, walked down the hallway to the powder room under the steps, closed the door behind her and gently deposited Flash on the mat. "You stay here." She scanned the surfaces for errant socks or other potential playthings, picked up her comb and hair brush and scowled at the white strands that were once red. Even cut short, it was her hair, not her face, that gave away her age. Maybe Bess was right about trying a mild coloring.

She put the comb and brush in the medicine chest. Who did she need to impress at this late date? A homicide detective? My God! Her thoughts were all over the place, today.

"Take the toilet paper out of there," George yelled from the kitchen.

Addie took the toilet paper off its roller. Flash regarded her with angelic calm, as if all this fuss was unnecessary. "Sorry, sweetie, I can't have you tearing it up again. You probably wouldn't like Rona's nephew, anyway." She closed the door securely and returned to the kitchen, brandishing the roll of toilet paper. "You didn't have to remind me. I'm not dotty, yet." She put the toilet paper on top of the refrigerator. "But do remind me to put it back in before you go – I mean leave."

"I know what you mean," said George. A double knock on the back door brought him quickly from his chair. "I'll get it."

She heard a muffled exchange and then they were back, the detective ducking his head as he followed George through the doorway. "Ma, this is Detective Barker. Harris, this lady, I'm proud to say, is my mother."

"George says that when he wants me to be good." She offered a polite smile and her hand to the burly, gray-haired detective. As he reached down for her hand, the jacket of his brown suit opened enough for her to see a holstered gun.

"Pleased to meet you, Mrs. Carter." His voice was husky.

She smelled lime and cigarette smoke, felt engulfed in his hand and withdrew hers quickly. She'd not felt so dwarfed by a man since childhood. Barker was at least six inches taller than George – a good six-seven, maybe six-eight. She wondered if he'd ever played football.

Barker's small mouth stretched into a teasing smile. "George always raves about you."

"I'm sure he does." She didn't like the way Barker's dark eyes shifted away to assess the old ceiling fan, fading paint and worn appliances. "Almost as much as he raves about my cat."

"Ma –," warned George.

"Would you like to sit here or in the living room, where it's more comfortable?" she asked, even while recognizing it was an unfair test. He had no way of knowing she preferred the informality and comforting memories of her kitchen.

"Here's fine." Barker pulled a maple chair out from the table. "Okay, George?"

Maybe he's smarter than he looks, thought Addie.

"It's your show," said George. He signaled Addie to sit.

She turned to Barker. "Would you like some tea or a glass of juice, Detective?"

"I'm afraid we need to get right down to business, you know what I mean?" He smiled with lips sealed. A faint scar linked the center of his upper lip to his oversized nose.

"Yes," said Addie. She reclaimed her seat. "About the murder."

As the men sat down, Barker's chair squeaked like a piglet in pain. Addie wondered how long the re-glued joints would hold him.

"First off, Mrs. Carter, I want to assure you that you are not suspected of doing anything wrong. But if you feel that you need an attorney present – "

"Not at all. I generally don't like attorneys. In my experience, most seem to charge double for being too clever by half."

"Okay, no attorney. So then, what makes you think Dr. Elwood was murdered?"

"He –" She swallowed hard. "He was face down and the back of his head was bashed in. His wooden steps aren't hard enough to do that. I broke a leg on steps like that about five years ago." She reached below her right knee. "I was in a cast for – how long was it, George?"

"We're talking about Elwood, Ma."

George was right – she needed to focus. "Yes. I suppose the cement floor could do it, but if the back of his head smashed onto it that hard, I doubt he'd have lived to turn completely over."

"That's an interesting theory." Barker rubbed his ear as if it bothered him. "Say hypothetically – you know what hypothetically means?"

She glanced at George. He sat poker-faced. "Yes, I *imagine* I do," she said.

Barker acknowledged her sarcasm with a tight smile. "Right. Well, assuming that Dr. Elwood was murdered, do you have a theory of who might have done it?"

"I haven't the foggiest. Some of the neighbors didn't like Herbert, but I never heard anyone out-and-out threaten to kill him."

Barker's eyes lit up. "But you heard some kind of threat?"

"I think it was merely a stupid remark from a hot-tempered young man. You remember the controversy over the ice-cream truck, George?"

"Ray Miggens?" asked George.

"I think I know him," said Barker. "He's been down the station a few times, hasn't he?"

"Yup. Drunk and disorderly. One DUI that I know of. Way before that, he served a little time in a juvie lock-up for assaulting a store clerk and a mall security guard who tried to stop him from shoplifting. You went to his trial, didn't you, Ma?"

"His mother asked me to go with her. They had a public defender."

"There wasn't much he could do," said George. "We also thought Ray spray-painted the high school after he dropped out, but we couldn't prove it. I'm not aware of any trouble in the past year or two. Must be about 35 by now, but still lives across the street with his mother."

"He has his rough side," said Addie. "But he's always been nice to me. And devoted to his mother. When he was young, he used to help us shovel snow from the driveway, and I'd give him some hot chocolate and cookies."

"And pay him," said George. "Ray always liked money."

"Who doesn't?" said Addie. "I think we got along so well because Raymond had an alcoholic stepfather, and I let him know I'd survived one, too."

"So what was this loser's connection with the deceased?" Barker stared at her, his face expectant.

This man has the sensitivity of a garbage disposal, she thought. "Two summers ago, Raymond bought a used ice-cream truck and started driving around town selling ice cream – you know, like popsicles and ice cream sandwiches. He had some old freezers in his garage to keep some stock there, but one or two mornings a week – usually early – a big refrigerator truck from Deighton's Dairy would come up the street to deliver cartons of ice cream. Living right across the street, Herbert didn't like the noise, and he complained about the pollution from the diesel fuel. It really wasn't that bad. I think it was Herbert being Herbert – trying to control, like with the hedge."

"The hedge?" asked Barker.

"That awful privet hedge down my driveway. Herbert had them plant it a foot beyond his property line. In the winter there's no room to push the snow to that side. It's not as if he needed more space for his cars. His driveway is all the way on the other side of his house."

"Ma – We know. We're parked there."

She flashed him a MAHIB look. "And when he cuts the hedge, he cleans – cleaned up his side, but not mine. He would just smirk and say 'what falls on your property is yours.' You were right, George. I should've taken him to Court years ago."

"Too late now," said George.

"How angry did you get at Dr. Elwood?" asked Barker.

She stiffened. "Enough to give him what for, not to kill him."

"Were you ever his patient?"

"No. Root canals are bad enough as it is. I certainly didn't want his face smirking over mine."

"They've been feuding on and off for forty years," said George. "But a lot less since his wife got sick, right Ma?"

"Janet and I always got along fine – we were close toward the end. And Herbert wasn't always a curmudgeon. Now and then he'd act like a human being and talk with me about gardening or lend me a tool or a helping hand. And I'd be sure to bring over a casserole or something to show I appreciated it. But you're right – he wasn't the same after she got sick."

"In what way?" asked Barker.

Addie picked up the mug, cradled it in her hands. "He was much more – solicitous of her – all of us were. Janet told me he had a lot of difficulty seeing her in pain. Until she got very sick, she tried to hide it from him. Herbert really did love her – and it ate him up inside that he couldn't do anything about her cancer, or the fact that he was going to lose her." Addie took a sip of tea, then put the mug down on the table. "I remember once, when Janet was worrying about how Herbert would do after she was gone, I told her he'd do okay – he was as stubborn an old donkey as I am." She smiled at the memory. "She told me Herbert was older, but I was more stubborn. She said – " Addie shook her head. "That's not important. What did you ask me?"

"How Dr. Elwood wasn't the same," said Barker.

"What did Janet say?" asked George.

Addie looked at her son. "She said there was a bigger difference. Herbert got stubborn to contain his anxiety; she said I got stubborn to survive." Addie shifted her gaze to Barker. "At the end – it'll be two years this coming January – he was really overwhelmed. Grieving, but not coming out of it. In a lot of ways, she was his compass." She rubbed her forehead. "I can't believe he's dead. Who on God's earth would do that to an old man?"

"We're going to find out," said Barker. "What happened between him and Ray Miggens?"

"Herbert complained to Raymond about those big trucks coming up the street, but Raymond didn't have the money to rent commercial space – he was just starting up the business. So Herbert went to the Zoning Board, and there was a hearing which I didn't attend. They both asked me to go, but I didn't want to be put in the middle. Legally, Herbert was right, this area is strictly residential. On the other hand, we only have ten houses on the street, so it's not like he was inconveniencing a lot of people. Raymond was trying to turn his life around and that should've mattered to his neighbors – especially me, because I once worked with his mother. After that hearing, Delia – that's his mother – stopped talking to me for almost a year." Addie looked down at her hands. "Not that it would have changed the outcome, but I should've gone and spoken in support."

"They shut down Ray's business?" asked Barker.

"They gave him thirty days to find commercial space, after which the town was going to impose fines for every day he operated out of his house. I don't know that his ice cream truck ever made a profit, but once he couldn't build the business from home, he couldn't – or at least he didn't – go on with it."

"And he blamed Dr. Elwood."

"Yes. I was weeding out front one morning before the thirty days were up – it was one of the last times the big delivery truck was there – and Herbert had come out to watch. You know how some people can gloat without saying a word? Raymond must have felt that, too. He ignored the ice cream cartons in his driveway and walked over to Herbert's front lawn and ranted about people who didn't mind their own business ruining his life."

"And you heard some kind of threat in his rant?"

"I think he was merely blowing off steam."

"What did he say, Ma?"

"Raymond yelled 'I'll fix you, you old blankety-blank.' Except it wasn't blankety-blank. He used the mother of 'f' words."

"What happened after that?" asked Barker.

"Nothing. I didn't hear Herbert say a word. He just turned around and went into his house, and Raymond went back to getting his ice cream into the freezers. And I never heard any more about it. Toward the end of the summer, Raymond got a job at Doyle's Autobody, over on Route 111. Frankly, I think he's better off."

"We'll see," said Barker. "Do you know of any other arguments Dr. Elwood had – or possible grudges against him?"

"No, but that doesn't mean there weren't any."

"Was he upset or angry at anyone lately?"

"Lately?" Should she? Well, it was true. "He was upset by that realtor."

Barker's eyes narrowed. "What realtor?"

"Rona Barker." She tried to look innocent. "Oh, is she related to you?"

"She's my aunt." He glanced at George, but her son's facial expression was impenetrable.

Barker turned back to Addie. "You've been in that basement before?"

"Yes." Why had he changed the subject?

"Aside from the dead body, notice anything different, anything out of place today?"

She bit her lip. Is that all Herbert was now – just a dead body? "I'm afraid Dr. Elwood's – condition – blew everything else from my mind."

"Naturally. But be sure to let us know if anything else occurs to you."

She tried to recall her entry into the basement. "His shoes – "

"He wasn't wearing shoes," said George. "He was wearing slippers."

"Yes, but he usually kept his gardening shoes and a pair of socks under the chair near the bulkhead. They weren't there. That's why I thought for a minute he might be outside."

"What color were the shoes?" asked Barker.

"Dark brown, but quite worn. They were ankle high lace-ups. He had heavy brown socks to go with them. Maybe they're in his closet."

"We'll look. You know anything about the birdhouses?"

"You mean who he was building them for? I've no idea."

"Was he interested in birds before he retired?" asked George.

"Not especially – at least as far as I know. I suppose like all of us he enjoyed looking at them."

"He didn't know squat about birds," said Barker.

"How do you know?" asked George.

"Bird lovers around here wouldn't use bright colors. They attract predators. Most people who know birds wouldn't paint a birdhouse – they'd leave it natural or stain it. And Elwood cut the entrance holes too big – starlings or house sparrows would've taken over."

"You like birds, Detective?" asked Addie.

"I generally find them prettier and more predictable than people," said Barker. "But let's go back to last night."

"I told George. Flash and I went to bed at nine. I didn't see or hear anything after that."

"Then take us through today from the time you got up."

Addie sighed. "Are you sure you wouldn't like a mug of tea first?"

"No, thanks. I'm not much of a tea drinker."

"I'm not surprised," she said. "I've never seen an American detective on television asking for tea. Of course, all I know about detective work is made up by someone. I'm very curious about how it really is. Have you uncovered any clues next door?"

"That's police business, Ma. You know all those yellow tapes that say 'stay out?'"

"I've already been to the basement, George. From now on, all those yellow tapes will say to me is 'too little, too late.'"

CHAPTER 2

Saturday Morning

Addie slipped out the back door at sunrise, closing it quietly so as not to announce her departure to the two reporters who were drinking coffee at the bottom of her driveway. She locked the door, tucked her purse into a pocket of her windbreaker, then crossed her back yard to the path through the woods. The cool air was invigorating, the silence a blessing.

What a miserable night. Reporters, neighbors, the phone ringing off the hook, then the nightmares – yes, she'd be better off at work. The walk through the woods and a talk with Bella would clear her head. How lucky to have always had both a place of refuge and a trustworthy friend. Poor Herbert. He'd lost his best friend when Janet died and neither his basement workshop nor the garden seemed to give him much solace.

She dawdled along the path, listening to the birds. Against the dark background of pine and spruce, the autumn leaves danced in spotlights of sun. She missed the elms with their drooping branches. She never thought they'd all die before she would.

That huge detective seemed an unlikely bird watcher. She hoped he wouldn't think to do that here. Not that she'd ever seen many strangers in these woods. Herbert had often walked here, and the abutters, of course. It had always been a great place for hide and seek, and a paradise for dogs. And thanks to the Herbal Woodland Trust, there'd been no development to ruin it.

The maple under which she'd discovered Nancy Drew welcomed her under its multi-colored canopy. Addie kissed two fingers and touched the furrowed bark. "That's for being more wrinkled than I am." A squirrel scurrying along a branch reminded her she needed to get to work.

She passed the modest houses on Parsons Street, stopped to allow a delivery van to pass, then crossed diagonally onto Juniper. Andy Marston's brown terrier barked at her from behind his picket fence.

"Oh hush up, Rigby. You know who I am."

Rigby wagged his tail, but he chased and scolded her until he came to the end of the lot.

Alongside a garage, a tractor peeked from beneath a tarp. Already the stacks of wood were covered and bushes were wrapped. Everyone was buttoning up for the winter.

As she crossed the Main Street Bridge, the wind nipped her cheeks and ears. The water level alongside the bankrupt Sawmill Museum was only half-way up the retaining wall. She missed seeing blue-roofed cottages upstream and wondered where the children of the workers in the paper and shoe mills ended up after those industries died and the cottages were sacrificed for a power plant. Not that Millbrook ever had a chance once the giant mills of Haverhill, Lowell and Lynn got rolling. Now those giants were dead, too.

"You're the hope," she whispered to the renovated factory downstream. Yes, everyone in town was hoping, but few had faith. How could a start-up like Nascent Technologies compete with the giants of I-495 and Silicon Valley? Still, it was lucky for Millbrook that Erik Cortland made it through MIT and wanted to bring his company home. If only Ruthie had lived to see her son and the Governor cutting the ribbon.

Across Main Street, Robby Smith was sweeping up in front of his Shell station. Addie waved but he didn't look up. She hurried by the red brick monstrosity that had been rehabbed into senior housing, then the row of offices and stores. Out on the Common, an old man was walking his chihuahua across the grass, defying the PLEASE KEEP PETS ON THE PATHS signs in full view of the brick police station across the street. George hadn't liked her arguing at Town Meeting about the stupidity of that ordinance. Bella had suggested having her friends stand up and chant "Save our sidewalks! Save our shoes!"

"It's one of your saner ideas," she'd told Bella. "But it really would make me uncomfortable."

"You're such a prig."

She couldn't really disagree, so she'd said, "Why should I believe the opinion of an insane friend?" Then they'd had another glass of wine.

As she approached Auterio's Supermarket, Addie saw Carlo taping bargain signs in the front windows. His silver hair, moustache and wire-rimmed glasses made him look more like a retired professor than the fruit peddler who'd built a thriving business by dint of street smarts, determination, and equal effort from his wife. Their son Anthony once joked that his parents split their work fifty-fifty: his father always wore a white shirt and tie to deal with employees and customers, while his mother always wore the pants to deal with Carlo.

Carlo acknowledged Addie's wave by raising his thumb. She understood he wasn't indicating that things were fine – it was that Bella was waiting upstairs.

* * *

"And that was it?" Seated at her desk, Yoplait cup in hand, Bella paused between spoonfuls of yogurt. Her black trousers and cardigan were topped by a pink and yellow striped scarf. "What did you leave out?"

"Nothing I can think of," said Addie. She shook her head at the jumble of letters, memo slips, food magazines and recipe cards competing for space with Bella's laptop. Her own desktop, back to back with Bella's, was clear except for her computer, a box of tissues and a mug. She saw Bella's lips twist into the same skeptical smile she'd flashed as a chubby, outspoken little girl in elementary school. Only now Bella's dark hair was permed with chestnut highlights and her lips were primed hot-pink – to divert attention from her jowls and age spots, she'd said.

The clang of a shopping cart slamming into others reverberated up to their office from the supermarket floor. Bella looked to the door. "I hope it's not

Anthony doing that. I can't fire my son." She turned to Addie. "I don't want to have to worry about you, either. Why did you throw half your toast away?"

"I'm not hungry this morning." The odor of chickens roasting on the spits downstairs in the deli had made her queasy. No, the real problem was with her nerves. Too much excitement in the last 24 hours. "Detective Barker did come back in the afternoon, without George, but he kept repeating the same questions he'd asked in the morning. After a while, I was saying things like, 'No, I didn't hear anything go bump in the night. No, I haven't seen suspicious gypsies lurking in the woods.'"

"He asked you about gypsies?" Bella's gravelly voice broke on a note of incredulity.

"He asked about strangers. I didn't actually say gypsies."

"You did in fourth grade."

Addie looked up at the wall clock. Oh, crumb. She'd never get all the vendor checks out this morning. "I don't remember."

"Oh, you do so. You remember everything. You just hold out on me, sometimes."

"It's not personal. There are times I need to think things through before sharing them with anyone, even my best friend."

Bella leaned back in her chair. "If I recall correctly, your best friend has helped you think through some very tough things."

"That I will never forget." Bella had always been there for her – Carlo, too, once he came to Millbrook. They'd supported her through her divorce, given her a steady job, and backed her as she struggled with Bess' drug addiction. She could never repay all they'd done for her. When she'd run out of the stamina needed to manage the store's front end, they'd insisted she stay on as a bookkeeper, paying her more than she was worth. Without that money, she would've had to sell the house, move into senior housing and share cat chow with Flash.

"So what are you remembering?" asked Bella.

"Nothing. Everything. Don't you have to get down to the deli counter?"

"Why? You think I own this place to work here? If I wanted to work, I'd go home."

"You and Carlo still work harder than anyone."

Bella's plastic spoon waved the compliment aside. "Stop trying to change the subject."

"I wasn't."

"See! Another lie." Bella's eyes danced. "I remember what you said. You told Miss Sayers that gypsies wouldn't let you cut through the woods unless you gave them your homework."

"Book bag and lunch."

"Same thing." Bella chuckled. "The gypsies ate your homework."

"I couldn't say my stepfather was drunk and threw them into the furnace." Her muscles tightened as if to resist his grip and his image as he dragged her toward the furnace. She'd been terrified he'd go through with his threat to incinerate her along with the book bag over which he'd tripped.

"But gypsies?" said Bella.

Addie leaned back in her chair. "It worked out okay. I had to stay in for recess and write 'I will always tell the truth' a hundred times, but then Miss Sayers gave me half of her sandwich."

"You never told me that." Bella sounded aggrieved.

"She swore me to secrecy. Not that it makes any difference now – she's gone, too." That entire generation and more and more of their own. Now Herbert. "At least Miss Sayers passed away in her sleep. I remember she made me do a report about gypsies. Stories about them fascinated me. I guess that's what comes of living in one town my whole life."

"I lived here since I was six. I never once thought of a gypsy until you came out with that ridiculous story – and I certainly didn't give much thought to them afterwards."

"You were always very practical. Speaking of which, I need to get the checks done." She hit the spacebar and the computer awakened, bringing the Moonstone Bakery account onto the screen.

"It won't kill them to get paid a day later, Addie. This is the biggest thing to happen here since the hurricane of '38. Didn't you watch the news on TV last night?"

"No. Flash and I went to bed early."

"'Murder in Millbrook' was the lead story. Didn't you see the TV people on your street?"

"I wouldn't talk to any of those vultures."

"That nifty reporter should have interviewed you instead of Walter Highsdale. Walter's a blowhard. You could have described finding the body."

Addie reached for her mug. "I don't even like to think about that. And George told me not to talk about it. That way only the murderer is aware of the details, and not those people who confess to everything." The tea was cold. She got up and went to the printer table, where she set the mug on the electric warmer and glanced down at the traffic. Most of the cars were heading toward the rotary and the highways beyond. "I don't need to be on TV. Let Walter have his fifteen seconds of fame. I want fifteen more years of peace and quiet."

Bella snorted. "At our age, peace and quiet are going to come all too soon. A little excitement let's you know you're still alive."

"So does sciatica. That doesn't mean I prefer it to a football game."

"You and your football. I bet if Herbert's murderer came to kill you during a Patriots game, you'd ask him to sit down and wait until the game ended."

Addie smiled. "No, I'd just ask him to let me record the game for later. Seriously though, Herbert's murder has been a terrible shock. And I have my doubts about this detective."

"Because he's a jerk?" Bella dropped the plastic cup and spoon into her wastebasket. "What did you expect from a relative of Rona's?"

"I didn't expect him to be handsome and smart like the detectives on TV. But I also didn't expect him not to ask one follow-up question when I said that Herbert had been angry at Rona's attempts to get him to sell his house. For some reason, he seemed fixated on Raymond Miggins."

"Maybe Detective Barker already knew about the house issue from Rona."

"So why didn't he say he was aware of it? He sure had more than enough questions about everything else."

"You think he's covering something up for Rona?"

"I don't like to think he is, but it's possible."

"Listen, everything's possible. For all you know, he could be the murderer. Have you talked with George?"

Addie shook her head. "I'm sure he'll tell me I'm still in shock and my imagination is running wild, and maybe that's right. Also if I start raising doubts, it puts George in a difficult position."

"So are we going to investigate?"

"Don't be so dramatic. This isn't TV and I'm not a detective. I just want to make sure the one we have is on the up-and-up."

Bella lifted her hands from her lap. "And how are we going to do that?"

"Stop with this 'we' business. I have a few doubts, that's all. And the quickest way to get rid of them is for me to hold my nose and talk to Rona."

"You think, if she was up to something shady, she'd admit it to you?"

"I think all she's guilty of is being overeager to get another listing. She might admit to that."

"Why bother when there are no buyers in this neck of the woods – although come to think of it, I did see her driving a Chinese guy around in her car last week."

"Chinese?"

Bella shrugged. "Maybe Korean. I only got a quick look as they passed me. But it's the Chinese who are buying everything these days."

"Probably some engineer who's come to work for Nascent Technologies. Although why he'd want to live out here where there's no Asian community is a mystery."

"You could ask your nephew."

"Marty? Ask him what?"

"To talk to Rona – you know, interview her for the *Millbrook Messenger*."

"No, if she won't talk to me about why she was pestering Herbert, she's not going to want a story like that in the town newspaper. Besides, Marty's all caught up in covering Herbert's murder. He wanted to come over last night, but I was exhausted. I had to promise not to speak to any other reporter before I talked with him."

"I'll bet lots of reporters were here. On Channel 7, they said that one or more thieves broke in through the back door, and it was possible Herbert got killed because he tried to stop them."

"That sounds right. I did see glass on his back steps. His back door has glass panels like mine, and his storm door has glass." Addie saw the warmer's green light go on. She picked up her mug and headed back to her chair.

"You should get an alarm system," said Bella.

"Thanks, but I don't have anything anybody would want to steal."

"You have a TV, don't you? And a nice piano."

"Nobody breaks into a house to steal a piano. And my TV is ten years old."

"So what was in Herbert's house that was so special someone would want to steal it?"

"I haven't the foggiest. His furnishings are pretty worn. And Herbert wasn't a fool. I doubt that he kept much cash at home." She tapped the spacebar to awaken her computer.

"He probably had plenty somewhere," said Bella. "Root canal dentists make a bundle, and he was at it a long time. He certainly didn't spend it on Janet."

"Janet wasn't one to ask for expensive clothes or jewelry. Her life was in doing for her kids."

Bella slapped her desk. "It just hit me – what if the murderer comes back to the scene of the crime? Does that really happen?"

"How should I know?"

"You read a lot. Doesn't that happen in a lot of books?"

"Books aren't real life," said Addie. She heard footsteps coming up the stairs.

"You definitely need to put in a burglar alarm. If it's the money, Carlo and I – "

"No. It's not the money. The kids are grown now and I'm just responsible for myself."

"Still, Carlo and I would – "

"Carlo and you would what, Bella?" Carlo's deep baritone preceded him through the doorway. Addie was always surprised by how such a big voice could emanate from such a short, slim man. He walked toward his wife. "You think the store can run on a Saturday without you downstairs?"

"Addie needs a burglar alarm."

"No I don't."

"Because of the murder?" asked Carlo.

"Yes," said Bella.

"No," said Addie.

Carlo stepped toward Addie's desk. "Addie." His tone was fatherly. "How many years have you known my wife? You know her longer and better than I do, right?"

"Longer, but not – "

"Listen, my dear friend. If Isabella Maria Bavarone Auterio says you need a burglar alarm, you need a burglar alarm. I learned long ago, if she says the Pope is wrong, the Pope is wrong."

"That was only twice," said Bella.

"With this Pope, twice. And the one before?"

"She needs the money, Carlo."

"I don't!"

"She says there've been gypsies lurking behind her house."

"Bella!"Addie glared at her.

"Gypsies? A murderer's not enough? Write her a check," said Carlo.

"I won't cash it."

Carlo dismissed her refusal with a wave of his hand. "So post it on the refrigerator where the murderer can see it. But later, Bella, later. For now, please, may we all go back to work?"

CHAPTER 3

SUNDAY AFTERNOON

"I can't believe it!" said Addie, hearing the doorbell ring again. She gripped the arms of her rocker. Her gaze remained fixed on the TV. The Patriots were on the Colts' eight yard line, threatening to score a go-ahead touchdown. "What nit-wit visits me on a Game Day without calling?" she asked Flash, who was grooming himself on the green hassock, his reserved seat for all football games. Not family, she thought, and not Bella. Even church friends knew better than to interrupt her on Sundays during a Patriots game.

"Quarterback sneak to get the first down," she told Flash. She glanced over to see if he agreed. Flash was licking his privates. "You could wait, you know. That's what commercials are for."

The doorbell rang again. "Go away," she muttered. The quarterback rolled out in an option play. The Colt linebackers came up and smothered it. "Idiots!" she said. "Didn't I tell you a sneak?" She saw the field goal team coming in, then heard someone pounding on the door. An emergency? "Oh, crumb." She rose from her chair. "Hold your horses!"

Flash beat her to the front door.

"Who's there?" Addie demanded.

"Ray Miggens. Open up, Mrs. Carter. I need to speak to you." His voice was muffled by the door, but there was no mistaking his insistence.

Let him in? She bit her lip. Maybe it was safe – Sunday afternoon. No, better safe than sorry.

She raised her voice. "I'm not dressed for visitors." Well, the khaki slacks and thrift-shop sweater she'd put on after Church had certainly seen better days. "And I'm watching the Patriots. Come back tomorrow."

"I can't. I have to work."

"Then come back at four-thirty."

"I can't! I need to see you right now!"

She frowned. No way to put him off. "Give me a few minutes, Raymond. I have to get presentable." She walked down the hall to the kitchen telephone and dialed George's cell phone. After the second ring, she began worrying. Four rings before he picked up.

"The Patriots losing, Ma?"

"Yes. I'm sorry to bother you on your day off, but Raymond Miggens is banging on my front door. And how did you know it was me?"

"My phone is smart. You be smart, too. Don't let him in."

"I'm going to. I don't want him hammering on my door."

"I'll send a cruiser."

"No, don't. He probably wouldn't hurt me anyway, but he certainly won't if I tell him you know that he's here."

"Detective Barker was going to have another talk with him this morning. I doubt that Ray's in a good mood."

"I'm not either," she said. "He's interrupting my game. I'll let you know what happens."

"I'm coming over."

"Don't. He won't talk freely in front of you."

"That's not my main concern."

"Give me fifteen minutes," she said. "I'll know what's upsetting him by then."

"I'm leaving now. You have ten minutes. Be careful."

"I will be. I want to see the second half." She hung up the phone, went into the living room and took a blank tape from the cabinet under the TV and VCR. Flash jumped from windowsill to floor and padded quickly over to rub against her legs.

"Not now, Flash." Addie inserted the tape, pressed the VCR's record button and turned down the volume on the TV. "Just in case this takes longer than I expect," she said.

Flash meowed as if his pleasure was being interrupted, too. When she started for the door, he scooted ahead of her. She nudged him aside with her foot and opened the inner door.

"It's about time." Still holding the storm door open behind him, Raymond inched forward. Beneath a mass of dark hair that spilled onto his forehead, his face was taut with anger.

"I'm sorry to keep you waiting. Please come in. Be careful of the cat." She stepped aside, inhaling a whiff of machine oil as his jeans and gray sweatshirt brushed by her. Still, if he shaved more, scowled less and did something about his beer belly, many women might consider him a handsome young man. Flash had backed off, eyeing the visitor with suspicion. Addie heard the storm door click shut. "What can I do for you, Raymond?"

He glared at her. "I want to know why you sicced the cops on me."

"I'm sorry I had to mention your name. But the detective asked me if anyone in the neighborhood had quarreled with Herb – Dr. Elwood."

"Fuck that! You said I threatened to kill him."

She felt a rush of blood to her face. "I did not. As a matter of fact, I said I knew you since you were a boy and I believe you would never kill anyone. I did repeat what you said when you confronted him on his lawn that day the ice-cream truck came, but that wasn't a threat to kill, and I never said it was. Who's telling you such – things?"

"Who do you think? That fat fuck, Barker. I knew he was lying." His face and voice moved from anger to bitterness. "He's trying to pin it on me."

Her tension eased. Beneath his adolescent bravado, Raymond was afraid. Still – "That's two 'fucks' since you walked in, Raymond. You may've forgotten, but in this house the rule is 'three fucks and you're out.' I know you're perfectly able to talk like a reasonable adult with your mother. So be reasonable with me. Why would Detective Barker want to pin a murder on you?"

"How the fu – hell should I know? The cops in this town have had it in for me ever since they couldn't get me for spray-painting the high school. Which I never did, by the way. I knew who did it, but I wasn't about to rat him out. So why did you have to tell Barker anything about me?"

"He asked me direct questions. I try not to lie."

"Bullshit."

"Don't be rude, Raymond. I'm not saying I'm virtuous. I just know I'll get caught."

"You must be a lousy liar. But I told Barker the truth on Friday, and he didn't believe a word. This morning, he came back and tried to connect me to Pedro Serrano. You got to fix this before it gets out of hand."

She raised her eyebrows. Fix it? What was he talking about? "Let's go to the kitchen where we can sit while we talk this over." Without waiting for a response, she walked right by him. "Who's Pedro Serrano?"

"A kid I knew in juvie. I haven't seen him for twenty years. Where do you want me to sit?"

She indicated the closest of the six chairs at the kitchen table. "I'm going to make myself a cup of tea." At the stove, she hefted the kettle and turned on the gas. "Would you like something to drink?"

He flopped into the chair. "You got any beer?"

"No, I'm afraid not."

"You don't drink?"

"Once in a while, when I'm out." She took a teabag from a canister and placed it in a mug. "My ex-husband – do you remember Dave?"

"No."

"He had a love affair with alcohol. I refused to keep his lover in my home." She walked back to the table. "I have milk and juice – cranberry, grapefruit, or prune."

"No thanks. I'm not old enough for that stuff."

"Just wait a few minutes," she said as she sat down. "Aging doesn't take long. How is your mother doing. I didn't see her outside all summer."

Raymond's face became grim. "She was feeling so good in the spring, she stopped her medicines. It was all downhill after that. When she gets that depressed, she doesn't want to go out of the house, even to the doctor. She thinks everybody's out to get her, even me. A couple of weeks ago, I had it up to here." His hand rose an inch or two above his head. "I had to threaten to move out to get her to start taking her medicine again."

"And she did?"

"I watch her do it every night. She was getting a little better, but then someone had to go and kill Elwood. You know how hard something like that is on depressed people? She's saying Elwood is the lucky one, that the Angel of Death picked the wrong house. Then Bad News Barker shows up at my door this morning. If I say 'I don't want to talk in my house,' he'll think I've got something to hide. And if I go outside with him, my mother will be sure I'm planning with the cops to put her away. So I have to say, 'Sure, man, come in.' Right away, he hits me with the time I yelled at Elwood, and I know you and the truck driver were the only ones around to hear that. And then he hits me with Pedro – I mean the bastard's really out to fu – foul me up."

"What does this Pedro Serrano have to do with Dr. Elwood's murder?"

"I don't know. It seems some of the stuff they stole from the old man included a laptop. The sneaky bastard had a LoJack in it. Somehow the cops found out and traced the signal to Pedro's apartment up in Lowell. Barker's trying to connect me with Pedro." His hands spread wide in a show of innocence. "I didn't know he lived in Lowell. I swear I haven't seen him or talked with him or anything. You've gotta get the cops off my back."

"And how am I supposed to do that?"

"Convince your son I had nothing to do with that murder. Tell him to convince Barker."

"George doesn't talk, much less listen to me about police business." She suppressed a pang of guilt. George seldom listened to her suggestions, but he'd stop sharing completely if she ever repeated anything about his work. "Why don't you tell George yourself?"

"Because he won't believe me, that's why. But he will believe you. And you know I always worked hard for my money. I never stole a dime from you."

She nodded. "I believe that, Raymond. And George will believe the truth. Tell him the truth."

"I told Barker the truth. You think he believed me? That dumb bastard – You know, when me and my friends were in tenth grade, we'd go out at night to tip cows at Tey's farm. Compared to Barker, those cows thought faster and smelled a lot cleaner. The only reason he got this job was that his father served in the MPs with Chief Considine."

"Really? Who told you that?" The tea kettle began whistling. She rose from her chair.

"Doesn't matter. I don't rat on my friends."

"Yes, you've made that point." She went to the stove. "What did you tell Detective Barker?"

"Like I said, the truth. I was tired after doing an 8 to 6 at the shop that day, so I went to sleep early. I didn't see or hear anything. And I haven't seen or heard from Pedro in twenty years. Don't you think if I did kill the old man, I'd have arranged a better alibi?"

She poured hot water into her mug, then turned down the flame under the kettle. "Did you point that out to Detective Barker?"

"Sure I did."

"And he said?"

Raymond puffed out his chest and dropped his voice. "Listen shithead, either you're too dumb to invent one, or just dumb enough to think no alibi is the best alibi of all."

Suppressing a smile, Addie returned to her seat. "It is hard for me to believe he's a detective. Whatever happened to Columbo?"

"Who?"

"A TV detective."

"He was a clever cop who played stupid," said George from the kitchen doorway.

Addie looked up. Raymond's head and body jerked in an effort to see who was behind him. His knee hit a table leg; the table shuddered.

George was dressed in a plaid flannel shirt and boot jeans. In one hand, he carried a pie box. On one ankle, she knew, he carried a handgun.

"Why George, what a lovely surprise," she said.

"Hello, Ray." George placed the pie box on the counter nearest the door. "Long time, no see."

"Hi, George. I was just leaving." Raymond turned back to Addie. His brow was furrowed, his eyes doubting.

"Oh, stay and have some pie," she said. "What kind did you bring, George?"

"Coconut cream. We had it in the house. I figured you and Flash might like it."

"We love any cream pie. How about you, Raymond?"

"No thanks." His distress was obvious. He looked over his shoulder at George. "You come in the front way?"

"The inside door was open. I saw a couple of flies buzzing around inside, Ma, so I hooked the storm door back so they'd fly out."

"Very thoughtful of you, dear." But not likely that Raymond would believe it. "Raymond and I have been having a very nice chat." She offered an encouraging smile. "Why don't you tell George what you told me?"

"Maybe another time." He started to get up.

"Stay in your seat, Raymond." Her tone was quite firm.

Raymond glanced at George, then sank back in his chair.

"George is going to take what you say very seriously. You talk, he'll listen, I'll cut the pie. In this house, I'm the top cop. Right, George?"

George sat down at the table. "That's the way it's been and always will be, Ray. Ma doesn't let anyone get away with anything."

CHAPTER 4

SUNDAY EVENING

She was into her third attempt to get through playing *Dance of the Sugar Plum Fairy* without her fingers going astray when the doorbell rang. Addie took her hands from the piano. Damn those reporters! She rose from the piano bench and went through the living room to the front door. "Go away!" she called out. "I'm a blind old lady. I didn't see anything."

"Ma, let us in."

"Joanne?"

"And Marty, Granny."

She flipped on the hall light, undid the deadbolt and chain, then opened the door.

Wearing her padded hiking jacket, purse slung over her shoulder, Joanne clutched a quart-size Tupperware container. Her dark curls, still a genetic mystery, had either run from the hair brush or driven it to distraction. Seeing the flash of appraisal in her daughter's eyes, Addie stepped forward and kissed Joanne's cheek. "I'm fine, sweetie."

Marty was right behind his mother, his shaggy brown hair, long nose and good-natured smile visible above Joanne's head. Addie backed up to let them in.

"Quite a weekend, huh?" said Joanne.

"I told you I was okay on the telephone."

Joanne grimaced. "You'd say that if you were dying. Besides, Fred has the flu and we had to get out of the house. You know how he carries on when he's sick."

Marty stepped over the threshold, eyes opening wide, lips a straight line, a facial expression so innocent, Addie knew he had mischief in mind.

"She neglects to mention that Uncle George ordered her to come. He was worried about you being alone this evening."

"Marty!" Joanne cast a narrow-eyed glance at her son.

"Where's the blind old lady?" Marty made a show of looking for her. "Oh, hi Granny." His long arms swept her into a hug. "Blind as a sparrow hawk and twice as lethal. Why did you go and kill old Herbert?"

She laughed. Despite his boney frame and the doggie odor of his Boston Marathon sweatshirt, she cherished the playfulness and love her 22 year-old grandson was unashamed to shower on her.

"Marty!" said Joanne. "Death isn't funny. And the least you could do is find out if Granny's feeling okay before you pounce on her."

Addie looked up at Marty and winked. "If that's a pounce, I rather liked it." She gave him a final squeeze, then faced her daughter. "Raymond never had any intention of hurting me."

"You didn't know that when you let him in," said Joanne. "Next time you might not be so lucky." She held out the Tupperware container. "I brought some chicken soup. Fred wanted it, so I made extra for you." Joanne's body squared up as if daring her to refuse the gift.

"You worried about my soul?"

"I pray for it constantly."

"Dad uses it to wash down his Tylenol, antihistamines, and Viagra," said Marty. "It's a good thing Uncle Robert is a pharmacist."

"It's a good thing I am a forgiving mother, Marty. Otherwise you might have to crawl out of here without kneecaps." She dropped her purse under the small telephone table and headed straight back toward the kitchen. "I'll put this in the fridge. You can eat it tomorrow."

"Thank you," Addie called after her. She turned to Marty. "We'd better go see she doesn't reorganize my kitchen. I'll make some tea, and I have a package of Oreos tucked away for emergencies."

"Is the emergency our visit or the murder?"

"Well, Herbert died of one, don't let me die of the other." In the kitchen, she found Joanne rearranging items in her refrigerator.

"There's hardly anything in here," said Joanne. "No wonder you stay so thin."

"Now there's plenty of chicken soup. Remember, sweetie, you're feeding three kids and a husband – I only have Flash. And I eat my lunches at work." Addie put a hand on the door of the refrigerator. "Excuse me."

Joanne backed off. "You'd think working in a supermarket, you'd have more to show for it."

Addie closed the door. "What I have to show for it isn't found in my refrigerator. As Bella and Carlo's godchild, you know that better than anyone."

"Where's Flash?" asked Marty as he entered the kitchen.

"Outside. I'm hoping some curiosity seeker will be foolish enough to pet him. You want tea?"

"Sure," said Joanne. "I'll go hang up my jacket." She raised a finger toward Marty. "Don't push," she said on her way out.

Addie picked up the empty kettle and headed for the sink. "Push what?"

"Push you." Marty sat down at the table. "I know you've had a hard weekend and that you've talked to the police and Uncle George and my parents and Aunt Bess and God knows who else. But I need to talk to you, too."

She started filling the kettle. "Haven't we been talking?"

"Sure, but not about the murder."

"Your father wants you involved in this – crime?"

"At least 'til he feels better. It's a much juicier story than Tuesday's finance committee meeting or the next game of the Millbrook Marauders."

"I don't think they'll beat Ayer. Their offensive line is too big for us to get to Monroe Gates."

Joanne came in. Her blouse looked like she'd slept in it. "Who's Monroe Gates?"

"Ayer's quarterback," said Marty. "Granny would rather talk football than murder."

"So would I." Joanne opened a cabinet and took out three mugs. "As much as your father and I would love to make money out of the paper, we won't let the *Messenger* sink into sensationalism."

"How about letting it rise to life?" said Marty. "Between Uncle George and Granny, we have the inside track on the biggest story to come out of Millbrook in decades."

"Bigger doesn't mean better," said Addie. "I thought your father's story about why those two couples volunteered to be foster parents was a lot more valuable than writing about a murder."

"I'm not knocking Dad's writing. But let's face it, ever since Cain and Able, murder has been mankind's most compelling story."

"Another good reason for women to run the world," said Joanne.

"How are Nick and Wendy?" asked Addie.

"Doing fine," said Joanne. "Nick's got a report due on global warming, so he's on the computer. And Wendy is supposedly studying with Rachel Harding."

Addie opened the cabinet above the stove. "What kind of tea would you like?"

"Granny, please. If I can get a scoop here, maybe the Worcester Telegram and Gazette or even the Globe might pick up my story. Maybe I can put something on the Net. It could be good for my resume. I don't want to stay with a community weekly forever."

"Ginger tea, if you have it," said Joanne. "Your dad and I don't want you to stay too long, either, Marty. And you're doing the story. But there's no need to drag your grandmother onto page one."

"I don't want to be on any page. What kind of tea, Marty?"

"Anything with caffeine. I'm not asking that you be the focus of the story, Granny. But you lived right next to him for what – forty years?"

"Forty-two." She extracted three teabags from their boxes.

"I don't have to use your name," said Marty. "I can use a phrase like 'a neighbor said' or 'an anonymous source.'"

"It's a small street and a small town. People will figure it out."

"Marty, why don't you get the milk and lemon," said Joanne.

He rose from his chair. "Even if I don't use any quotes, over forty-two years you must have gathered some stories or insights that could help me write a good article."

"I suppose I remember a few things, but Herbert was a very private person."

"Any idea why?"

"I'll have to think about it. I also have to talk to his children."

Marty opened the refrigerator. "You don't have much food in here, Granny."

"That should make it easier to find the milk."

"I'm sure Herbert's kids will appreciate hearing from you," said Joanne. "I called Leslie a couple of times, but all I got was the answering machine. Did you get through?"

"I'm holding off. I want more than a phone conversation to express my condolences." She brought a package of Oreos to the table. "Also, Herbert's children may have some ideas about who might've had it in for their father. The detective in charge – a man named Harris Barker – seems to be focusing his attention on Raymond Miggens. I've known Raymond since he was born, and I can't believe that he'd murder anyone."

"Is this detective related to that woman in the choir that you couldn't stand?" asked Joanne.

"She's his aunt. Except for appearance, the resemblance is striking."

"Did you talk to George about him?" asked Joanne.

"Not yet. He'd get defensive and tell me to stop poking my nose into police business."

Marty stood in front of the open refrigerator. "I talked to Uncle George. He wouldn't tell me any more than Chief Considine said to the media. It's a robbery-murder that's under investigation. The Chief spouted the usual stuff about all leads being vigorously pursued... Where's the lemon?"

"Can't find a lemon in a nearly empty refrigerator?" asked Joanne. "And you want to be an investigative reporter? Try the fruit drawer."

Marty bent to the task. "I asked Uncle George whether he was personally involved in following up a lead or two, and he just laughed and said I shouldn't believe everything I see on TV, especially the news."

The kettle whistled. Addie went to turn off the burner. "It sounds like the police are still clueless. So what are you going to write?"

"I don't know." Marty placed the milk and a lemon in the center of the table, scooped up the package of Oreos and sat down. "Maybe the bigger story is how the police in small towns can't catch murderers once they leave the scene of the crime."

"If you write that," said Joanne, "your loving uncle will personally beat the – stuffing out of you. And I would probably be there cheering him on."

"You would?"

"It would be encouraging murderers," said Addie, bringing the kettle and tea bags to the table. "And one in this town is too many."

"You think the murderer lives here?"

"I haven't got the foggiest...You know, there are a couple of things that might be interesting for you to pursue. There's a man by the name of Pedro Serrano who was arrested in Lowell because he had some of Herbert's possessions."

"Really? Chief Considine hasn't said a word about that to the media. How did you find out?"

"George tell you that?" asked Joanne.

"No, not George, but I can't say who. Raymond Miggens told me never to rat out my informants." She tried to sound naïve. "Don't you reporters have a similar ethical code?"

Marty grimaced. "C'mon, Granny, be real. What's the second lead?"

"I wouldn't call it a lead. Call it a hunch. See what you can find out about Detective Barker."

"You think he's crooked?" Marty's eyes widened. "Involved in the actual murder?"

"Oh, no. I've no reason at all to believe that. Think of it as getting background information."

"Wow, you keep feeding me ideas like this, I'll scoop all the dailies."

Joanne frowned. "Please, Marty, we have a bare-bones local paper and, as talented as you are, you're not Bob Woodward. So don't push Ma into playing Deep Throat."

Addie reached over and took her daughter's hand. "He's not pushing me – and I'm not playing here. Herbert's murder has left me with great sadness – but also with lots of fear and doubt. You know Janet was a very good friend. For her sake and mine, I need to feel confident that there's a proper investigation." She gave Joanne's hand a gentle squeeze, then withdrew her own. "Now why don't we talk about something less upsetting, like the weather – even global warming or bird flu – so we can just relax and enjoy our tea."

"I really need you to tell me about Herbert," said Marty.

"Not tonight. And I have to work until five tomorrow. Come over at six and we'll have supper together. I always record the Monday night game, anyway."

"My favorite meat loaf?"

"Did I say I'm cooking? You bring Chinese take-out. And good stuff, not fried and oily. No MSG."

"Chopsticks?"

"Forget chopsticks. Bring a nice fish for Flash."

CHAPTER 5

MONDAY EVENING

Addie closed the curtains of the windows flanking the fireplace, then went to do the same for those behind the sofa. Marty had chosen well, she thought. They'd feasted on General Gau's chicken and lo mein while Flash had devoured a Beijing Bass. But instead of settling right in for a nap, the big tom was circling warily on the plaid blanket that overlay the sofa cushions.

"Nobody's sat there since your Uncle Robert," she assured him. She reached behind the table lamp and drew the curtains closed.

A sneeze came from the powder room. Flash's head jerked up. He began clawing at the blanket.

"It's only Marty," she said. "You're going to wear that to a frazzle. If I have to cover the sofa with plastic, you won't like it one bit."

Flash cocked his head at her, then settled down into hunting posture. Addie took her burgundy and gold afghan from the back of the rocker, unfolded it and seated herself with the afghan across her lap. Too bad Marty's visit to the police department in Lowell hadn't been as successful as his visit to the Chinese restaurant, she thought. Pedro Serrano was being held on the charge of receiving stolen property pending a bail hearing, but neither the police nor Pedro's public defender would say more.

As for Detective Barker, the information Marty had been able to gather was still sketchy. She liked his middle name – Mayfield – for it reminded her of a spring meadow, and she liked that he'd played left tackle for the Red Raiders of Fitchburg High. It was certainly commendable that he'd enlisted in the army and later got a bachelor's degree from Worcester State College. But those positives didn't offset the fact that he'd left the Worcester Police Department not long after his partner had been convicted of stealing money from the home of a murdered drug dealer. There was no evidence that Barker had participated in the theft or even known about it, but the reporter who'd followed the story doubted that Barker left Worcester simply because his wife wanted to live close to her family in Groton.

She heard the toilet being flushed, the sink being used. Flash meowed his annoyance.

"You start anything, I'll put you in that toilet," she warned as Marty's footsteps came up the hall.

"Do you want to turn the floor lamp up?" she asked as he came through the archway. He looked at Flash and headed for the nearer of the two small armchairs she'd found in a secondhand furniture store. "Light's okay," he said.

Good. Flash's sheddings didn't need more exposure, and she didn't need a higher electric bill.

Marty pulled over the green hassock Flash used when she watched TV. "I appreciate your doing this." He took a mini-recorder from the pocket of his sweatshirt and stretched his long legs out on the hassock. "You mind if I record this?"

"I certainly do. There are things I may say that I wouldn't want talked about in the family, much less recorded or in a newspaper."

"Okay. I didn't forget how to take notes." He pocketed the recorder.

"No. God gave you two good ears and a brain. That's all the equipment you need to talk with me."

"But I don't want to misquote you."

"Then don't quote me at all. Focus on Herbert. Consider me part of the wallpaper."

Marty's face took on the look of an injured puppy. "You can trust me a hundred percent, Granny. Whatever you want off-the-record will stay there."

She sniffed. "I don't even trust myself that much. Not that I don't believe you, but sometimes life has a way of corrupting our best intentions. Don't take it personally."

"Alright. So what was Herbert like when you first met him?"

"Young." She told him they were all young then, and raising little children. She and Dave and Janet were in their thirties, Herbert past 40. He was focused on building his dental practice and on making and investing money, but then he was a professional and he'd worked his butt off to get there. Herbert didn't like to talk about himself, but over the years, especially after she got cancer, Janet had worried and talked about him.

"What worries about him?" asked Marty. "She was the one with cancer."

"His relationship with the children, mostly." Addie pushed her bifocals a bit higher on her nose. "Herbert was a very demanding father. Larry once told me how he came home with a 98 on a math test and Herbert asked him what happened to the other two points. Herbert wasn't joking."

"Not very sensitive."

"Far from it. But you need to understand." She explained that Herbert came from a working-class family that didn't value education. They lived in Saratoga, and his father preferred the race track to an honest day's work. But Herbert was bright, and in those days you could get a scholarship if you were a bright, white boy and your parents were poor. And he worked after school to help put himself through. She told Marty she only had the house they were sitting in because it was handed down from her Grandfather Chandler, who was a rich man in Millbrook before the Great Depression wiped out his bank, but Herbert never had those kinds of advantages. He got the Army to put him through dental school, and then put in several years in the service after that, squirreling away as much money as he could to go on with his training.

"Janet worked as a dental assistant at Tufts, that's how they met."

"What did she like about him?" asked Marty.

Addie fingered a panel of her Afghan. The wool had become fuzzy but it was a job well done. "She said he was serious and stable, not just out for sex like some men she'd met. When Herbert said he loved her, she knew he meant it. And he wasn't puffed up with himself like other dentists and doctors she'd known. He really cared about his patients. She felt she could help him go easier on himself, relax and enjoy life more. I think she did – to the extent it was possible."

Marty sniffled. "Excuse me." He withdrew a wad of crumpled tissues from his pocket, peeled off one and wiped his nose. "So they moved here after he finished at Tufts?"

"No, he worked for a few years in Worcester. Janet stopped working during her pregnancy with Leslie. By the time they moved here, she had her hands full with Larry, who was in his terrible twos, and she was pregnant with Gloria. Leslie was five, the same age as your mother."

"Really? My mom and Leslie grew up together?"

"They were friendly in elementary school, but they were different kinds of kids. Once they started junior high, they pretty much went their own ways and had different friends."

"I thought my mom could get along with anybody."

"Oh, Joanne could – she does. It's not that the girls didn't get along. But your mother was interested in exploring the woods, and in going over to Tey's farm and asking if she could help rub down a horse or milk a cow. Leslie was more interested in teen magazines and nice clothes and boys. It was your Aunt Bess and Gloria Elwood that really grew up as best friends."

Marty used his feet to push the hassock away. He stuffed the tissues into his pocket. "Do you have any idea why someone might have wanted to kill Dr. Elwood?"

"No. I've asked myself that over and over. I just wish I hadn't slept so soundly that night."

"Maybe it's better you were completely out of it. Who knows what would have happened if the murderer saw your light go on. Did Herbert have any peculiarities?"

"He was a coin collector, although I don't know if that qualifies as peculiar. He'd buy rare coins, but he was cheap in other ways. They'd seldom go out to dinner, much less take an expensive vacation – but Janet didn't seem to mind. She loved being at home, reading and gardening. I once asked why she didn't get out more with people and she reminded me they did go to church on Sunday and, other than that, she'd looked into enough foul mouths and heard enough dirt from others to last a lifetime."

"As a hygienist? Wait –" Marty leaned forward. "– did she mean there was gossip about them?"

"Not directly about them. About Gloria."

"Gloria?"

"When she was sixteen, Gloria came out as a lesbian."

"Really?" Marty straightened. "My mom never told me that."

"Why should she? In this family, we don't consider somebody else's sex-life any of our business. It's horrible how they – they celebrate that kind of gossip on TV. But you asked what was peculiar. I sometimes thought Herbert's turn to religion was peculiar."

She described how Herbert suddenly changed from Sunday morning gardener to regular church-goer after he threw Gloria out of the house, within days after she and Bess graduated with honors from high school. But it was Bess, not Gloria, who came crying because she was so angry, asking, then pleading, that Addie let Gloria move in. Bess was too young to understand the difficulties, not the least of which would have been Herbert's fury. He would've believed Addie was trying to embarrass him publicly. And if Janet wouldn't stand up for a daughter she loved, what support would she give her neighbor? Gloria understood, probably better than anyone. She'd grown up with the handwriting on the wall.

"Still, it must've hurt her a lot," said Marty.

"She was crushed. Mostly that Janet didn't put up a fight. Gloria was always a fighter. I remember one day when she and Bess were in seventh grade, three boys were beating on Charlie Rendell in back of the school and Gloria dove in to rescue him.Your Aunt Bess tried to help, too."

"The girls got beat up?"

"No. The girls were suspended from school for a week, and Herbert and I had to pay one boy's hospital bills."

"Really?"

"Oh, yes. Gloria had a rock in each hand when she started swinging. After the first boy went down, Bess tried to pull Gloria away, but the boys blamed her, too." Addie shook her head. "No, Gloria wasn't about to let her parents see how crushed she was. Fortunately Janet's sister in Milford took her in – that wouldn't have happened without Janet's blessing."

"I still don't see what was so odd about Herbert going to pray every Sunday."

"Prayer should be based on love, Marty, on our love of God, our love for others – and our own needs for improvement and redemption. I don't think Herbert ever felt guilty about throwing her out. At least that's my opinion. I think he prayed for Gloria to come to her senses and see being lesbian as sinful, or maybe even that God would change her – I don't really know. Maybe he thought he was being punished through her. Even when Janet knew she was on borrowed time, she wouldn't talk about it. That was in the past and all she wanted toward the end was reconciliation in the present and hope for the future."

"So it was after he threw Gloria out that you and Herbert began fighting?"

Her mouth suddenly went dry. "No, earlier than that. Almost 40 years ago. When I was pregnant with your Uncle Robert."

"What started the fight?"

"Would you please get me a drink of water? All this talking is drying me out."

"Sure." He rose from the chair using only the power of his legs, a marathoner's legs, strengthened in a sport they loved, generations apart. Flash looked up, too, and she thought he almost smiled as Marty left the room. "How much do I tell him?" she asked softly. Flash's whiskers twitched, then he turned his head toward the sounds of the kitchen faucet being turned, water hitting the sink. "A big help you are."

What could have helped? She recalled Herbert's angry face when he stormed over to their house, accusing Dave of trying to seduce Janet while he was away at a dental convention. Dave looking surprised, indignant, denying any dishonorable intention, saying with all the sincerity a security chief could muster that his arm going around Janet's shoulder when he went over to help with a leaky boiler was merely a show of support, how uncertain Herbert must be in his marriage, how dare he accuse Dave of betraying their friendship, of trying to screw Janet and fuck-up two good marriages. And she, seven months pregnant, refusing to believe, defending her man, defending him even when Janet tried to tell her the truth.

"You okay?" asked Marty as he came in with her glass of water.

"Yes." She'd been too stupid, too fearful, too proud to admit that she'd chosen wrong and on the rebound, that her husband had the appetite of a wolf and the integrity of a weasel. "Thank you, Marty." She took a drink as he sat down again.

"You looked kind of glassy-eyed."

"Remembering can be hard work." She put the glass down.

"I won't keep you much longer. So what started the fight between you and Herbert?"

"This is the part that's off-the-record. To the family, as well. Agreed?"

"Forever?"

"Until I tell you otherwise. Or until I'm as dead as Herbert."

"Don't say that. You're going to be with us a very long time."

"I hope so. But those are my rules. Agree?"

"Sure."

She closed her eyes to collect her thoughts, then opened them. "Almost 40 years ago, Herbert planted that privet hedge outside, planted it a foot over the property line."

"I know that."

"Well, rightly or wrongly, Marty, other than my friend Bella who helped me through the hardest times in my life, you're the only person I've decided to tell why."

She tried to tell it as matter-of-factly as she could, tried not to insert her anger, her opinions about Dave, or her recollections of the disastrous year that followed his leaving. As she finished, she wondered whether she'd sanitized her account to protect Marty, his absentee grandfather, or herself.

"Wow." Marty ran a hand through his hair. "But what I don't understand is how you got so friendly with Janet after all that."

Addie pulled the Afghan up to her chest. "What do you know about your grandfather?"

"Mom said the trucking company fired him for drinking on the job and he took off for California – and that he really wasn't a family man."

Addie sniffed. Too bad Dave hadn't figured that out before they had four children. "Your mother left a few things out."

"What things?"

"The blonde secretary that Dave took with him, along with most of our bank account."

Marty's eyes widened. "Does Mom know that?"

"I'm sure it's not something she likes to think about. She was – yes, she was nine when her father ran off. I'm telling you this because you asked about Janet and me. And because there's no chance your grandfather will ever come back here."

"It would be an interesting family reunion."

"I can't joke about it."

He bowed his head. "Sorry."

"After Dave ran out on us, it took me a long time to stop feeling numb. But I had to keep going. I had to do things I never thought I would do." She remembered the gold cuff-linked idiot at the bank, the homeless men at the food pantry, the sympathetic black woman at the Welfare office. "I had to eat a lot of humble pie, and that included going over to apologize to Janet and Herbert. We hadn't talked except for an argument I had with Herbert about that hedge – an argument he won because he threatened to tell the judge, jury, and all of Millbrook why he'd planted it. Dave and I could have won in Court, but we'd have been ridiculed in town. Back then, what people thought of me seemed important." She grimaced at her misguided self. "Anyway, I expected a cold shoulder or an I-told-you-so from Janet. But that's not the kind of woman she was. She said, had she been in my shoes, she wouldn't have done any different. Against one accusation, she would have defended her husband, protected her marriage. And if she had four small children, she would have put up with a lot more."

"I can understand that."

"Yes, but she even said she'd worried about whether she and Herbert had somehow contributed to Dave's leaving. If so, she was sorry. Either way, she wanted to help me. I just hugged her and walked out of that house in tears. But within an hour, I was numb again. If it wasn't for Bella and Carlo, I wouldn't have gotten through it."

"Yes, you would've."

"Thank you."

"No, thank *you* for trusting me with that story."

She shrugged. "I'm afraid it's a different story than the one you wanted to write. That's what you get when you talk to an old lady."

"You're not old yet. And your story is more important to me than the other one. Because you're more important. To the whole family."

She swallowed hard. "You, your brother and sister and cousin Luisa are my bridge to the future. Someday, you'll all be telling your grandchildren about our family, and about me."

"I hope so. You know, a bridge goes in both directions, so would you mind if I asked you about something else? It won't take long."

She glanced over at Flash. He was already asleep. "Okay, what?"

"How do you know that you're really in love?"

She looked at him sharply. Better to keep it light. Men generally didn't like heart-to-heart talks. "You mean in love with something more than General Gau's chicken?"

"You know what I mean. You meet someone, you're attracted to each other – how do you know you really love that person? That she's the right one for you?"

She leaned back in her chair, started rocking slowly. She'd met Dave in the Sports section of the Nashoba Valley Bookstore. He couldn't believe a woman loved football. She couldn't resist his charm or his invitation to a Patriots game. "That's a good question, but with my record, I'm a poor one to ask. I take it you've met a girl you really like."

"Yeah. But 'really like' and 'love' are two different things, aren't they?"

"Yes." She'd liked Dave's looks, loved his energy and humor. He wasn't Cletis, and he'd got her laughing again. "Although sometimes where one stops and the other starts is hard to tell," she said. "Is that the problem?"

"Maybe it's that. I don't know. I asked my father how he first knew he loved my mother, and he said he knew the first time he saw her in freshman orientation that she was the girl he loved and wanted to marry. I mean isn't that a little bit crazy?"

"More than a little bit. Yet it seems to have worked out very well."

"Oh it has. But what kind of example is that for me? I really like this girl I've been dating. I like her a lot. But I haven't been bowled over, if you know what I mean. I don't know whether I'm not capable of the certainty that Mom and Dad had, or whether this girl isn't the right one."

"Then give the relationship more time. Your Uncle George lived with Aunt Marjorie for three years before they got married."

"Even living with someone is a big commitment. How long did you know Grandpa Dave before you two got married?"

Three months, she thought. "Obviously not long enough." She stopped rocking. "I'm afraid I'm not a good example of anything."

"Don't tell me you blame yourself for Grandpa Dave running off like that."

"I got over that a long time ago. Still, I think there was something in me that picked very charming men who couldn't make long-term commitments."

"Men? You mean it happened before?"

"Only once before, and that was in my first year of college."

"I thought you only went to one year of college."

"I suppose I should have said my first and last year. But enough of that." She put her hands on the arms of her rocker. "Who is this mystery woman that you've been dating?"

Marty rubbed his jaw. "If I tell you, I don't want you to make a big deal of it, okay? I don't want my parents to know because they'll be giving me the third degree every time I turn around."

So young, she thought. "I promise to keep it in confidence. I won't twist your arm for progress reports."

"I know that. It's really good to have someone I trust to talk to about this. Her name is Cassandra Adams, but she goes by Cassie."

Addie's hands tightened around the arms of her chair. No, don't even go there – it's a common enough name. "Cassie Adams?"

"You wouldn't know her – she never lived here. I met her down in Amherst. She just graduated from Mount Holyoke in May and came to Boston to work."

"For CDA International?"

"Yes, how did you know that? You mean you've met her?"

"No. I've never met her. I know her grandfather."

"She has a grandfather here? You mean that developer, Cletis Adams? Oh, shit!"

"You didn't know? CDA is Cletis Desmond Adams." Oh, shit, indeed, she thought.

CHAPTER 6

Tuesday Evening

Too many funerals, thought Addie, as the two-story clapboard building came into view down Main Street. Her mother, her stepfather, two aunts and a cousin had all started their final journey from Rendell's Funeral Home. So many aching farewells there to family and friends. And now Herbert.

Joanne braked as the Jeep's headlights picked up two teenagers darting across the street.

"Jerks!" said Joanne.

"Be careful," said Addie as the Jeep accelerated again. She looked up, saw the lights of an oncoming car and braced her hand against the dashboard as Joanne swung the Jeep into a sharp left turn and braked just before the car bumped over the curb-cut to enter the crowded parking lot.

"Jesus!" said Bess, from the back seat. "Who the hell taught you to drive?"

"Ma," said Joanne, slowing the Jeep to her version of parking lot speed.

"Not like that," said Addie. She saw a few young men out back, the glow of cigarettes in the dark. "Slow down. Herbert isn't going anywhere – and if he is, I don't want us going there, too."

Joanne turned the Jeep into an empty space. "Don't worry, I'm careful."

"Last time you said that, you came home pregnant," said Bess.

"I was very careful. Fred wasn't." Joanne turned off the headlights and motor.

"I've heard all this before," said Addie, unfastening her seat belt. "And I'm thankful for every one of my grandchildren." Amazing how it never changed – Bess picking, Joanne pretending to be unflappable. "Let's go to the viewing."

Bess opened her door. "Yes, let's get it over with."

Addie got out of the car, reached between the buttons of her woolen coat to straighten her skirt, then closed the car door. Her daughters were waiting for her in front of the Jeep. Quite a pair, she thought. Bess, two inches taller and two sizes slimmer than her older sister, was already shivering in her camelhair coat, while Joanne looked ready to change a tire or milk a cow in her hiking jacket. "Thank you for coming with me."

"No problem," said Bess. "Let's go in. I'm cold."

"We would have come anyway," said Joanne as they started to walk toward the floodlit portico. "He wasn't such a grouch when we were growing up. Remember the birthday parties he and Janet did for their kids, Bess?"

Bess nodded. "And soccer in the back yard. You think Gloria will come? I haven't seen her since Janet's funeral."

"I'm sure she will," said Addie. "If not tonight, then certainly to the funeral."

"He was a jerk with her, that's for sure," said Joanne.

"Herbert couldn't accept what he couldn't control," said Addie. How would she have reacted had either Joanne or Bess been lesbian? Certainly not by throwing her daughter out.

Rendell's ornate front door opened and a woman emerged buttoning her coat. Under the portico light, her gray helmet of hair, pinched face and iridescent quilted coat were clearly visible.

Rona! Addie's lips tightened.

"Addie Carter! I thought you'd be here." Rona Barker descended the three steps, blocking Addie's progress. "Where have you been hiding yourself lately?"

"Hello, Rona. You know my daughters."

"Of course. Hello, girls. Bess, that's a lovely coat. I used to have one just like that thirty years ago."

"Thank you," Bess muttered.

Joanne cast an amused glance at her sister. "I knew you had good taste. Hi, Ms. Barker."

"How have you been, Rona?" said Addie.

"I can't come out of a funeral home complaining, can I? The good news is that my daughter Ann delivered a seven pound boy last Saturday. The bad news is in there." Rona jerked her thumb toward the funeral home. "Murdered – it's terrible. Not only for the family. The value of every house on your street will drop."

"Congratulations to you and the new parents. As for my house, I'm not planning to sell."

"But Herbert's children will have to. Who'd want to buy with this all over the news? It's so sad. If Herbert had only listened to me, this wouldn't have happened."

"Listened to you?"

"Ma, I'm cold. We'll meet you inside," said Bess.

"Okay." Addie waited while her daughters said their proper good-byes and were going up the steps before she asked Rona, "You advised Herbert to sell?"

"Of course. If he'd done that, he would've been somewhere else. I had a very good buyer.

Instead, I have to deal with Cletis Adams, and you of all people know what he's like."

Of all people? Addie bit her tongue. She needed information, not confrontation. "I really don't know what Cletis is like, these days. How's he involved with Herbert's house?"

"A leopard doesn't change his spots, Addie. It's not the house. Cletis wants to develop the property, but I'm sure my client will pay more for it. Anyway, I have to run."

Did Herbert own more than an acre lot? "What property?"

"It's a long story. Cletis is inside, ask him." Rona started to walk away.

"Has your nephew made any progress in the murder investigation?"

Rona glanced back but didn't stop. "I'm sure Harris is doing his best. See you at the funeral."

Not one straight answer, thought Addie as she headed up the steps. And Rona knew she'd have a tough time asking Cletis. Once a man humiliates you, you don't go back for crumbs.

Charlie Rendell, in black suit, tie and well-shined shoes, greeted her in the reception area. "Good evening, Mrs. Carter."

A maitre d' for mourners, thought Addie. "Hello, Charlie. You look very spiffy." Certainly more manly than the nerdy adolescent who'd found every excuse to study with Bess and Gloria.

"Thanks. May I take your coat? I'll hang it downstairs."

Addie started unbuttoning. "Thank you. You see which way my girls headed?"

"Parlor A, but we opened up the dividers to B, so they might be in either one. The guest book is on the pedestal." He pointed down the center hall where almost a dozen people stood in line beneath a large oil painting of the 18th century sawmill from which Millbrook drew its name.

"I'll sign the book later," said Addie, handing Charlie her coat.

"It's so good of you all to come. Bess looks amazing. You look lovely, too."

"Thank you, Charlie. It's good of you to say so." She walked away regretting that Bess had always resisted Charlie's advances.

The viewing parlors were comfortably warm but uncomfortably crowded. Ignoring the buzz of conversations, the flower arrangements and funeral wreaths, Addie focused on the black coffin. It was open. Her hands clenched as she recalled Herbert's bloody brain peeking through his skull. A long line of people moved in fits and starts toward the coffin and Herbert's three adult children who stood beyond it. Addie turned away, took a deep breath and looked for her daughters. She recognized neighbors and a few people that frequented Auterio's, but she was surprised at how many people she didn't know. Sport jackets, dresses, skirts, pant suits, even some young people in jeans. Well, she was no fashion plate in her pleated blouse and too long skirt.

She found Bess in front of a long table displaying family pictures. "Where's Joanne?"

"Restroom," said Bess. "Look, Ma." She pointed to a wedding portrait of Herbert and Janet. "Hard to believe he ever looked that handsome."

"Harder to believe they're both gone," said Addie.

"Good evening, ladies." The man's voice was pitched low, the tone faintly mocking.

As she turned toward the man, Bess brushed a lock of auburn hair back from her forehead. Under the picture spotlights, her hair glistened as it fell below the collar of her chocolate brown dress. "Hello, Mr. Adams."

Addie forced herself to smile. "Why Cletis, how nice to see you." How many lies would God tolerate before he slammed the Gates shut in her face? Cletis' face hadn't surrendered to age, but its asymmetry had become more prominent and less attractive. His right eyebrow still arched higher than his left, but the right side of his lips no longer turned upward as if quietly amused, while the left side of his mouth was cast further down. Behind rimless glasses, his green eyes were still intense. "Too bad we have to meet. Under these circumstances," she added.

As Cletis studied her, his expression seemed to soften. "Yes, I wish the circumstances were different. Ah well, life marches on – " He glanced toward the coffin. " – for some of us."

Addie sniffed. Maybe he'd take the hint and march on to someone else. He looked thirty pounds heavier and more stoop-shouldered than when he played wide receiver for Millbrook High. Not fair that *his* hair had improved with age, his awful high school crew-cut and restrained Harvard pompadour replaced by a pure white mane. No doubt he'd taken one look at her colorless hair and dowdy clothes and thanked his lucky stars he hadn't married her.

"It was a horrible way to die," she said.

"Yes. Even for an endodontist."

"You didn't like him?" asked Bess.

Cletis looked around, lowered his voice. "Frankly, I don't think he liked me." He caught Addie's smile. "I know. That's not unusual. As for Herbert, I believe such friends as he had were friends from his church."

"True," said Addie. "But Janet really loved him. And the children did – for the most part."

Bess frowned. "Gloria had – Excuse me. I'll get on line, Ma. Save you a place."

"You still at the bank, Bess?" asked Cletis.

His question brought Bess back a step. "Yup. You ready to buy it?"

Cletis chuckled. "Not yet. But if I do, I'll let you run it."

"Thank you very much, but I run it now."

"She was promoted to branch manager," said Addie.

"I know," said Cletis. "But I wasn't talking about the Millbrook branch. I meant the whole New England Savings and Loan."

Sure, thought Addie, promise the pretty ones anything. Her jaws clamped shut. Three marriages, and now he'd dare come after Bess?

"Hello, Mr. Adams," said Joanne, rejoining them.

"Hello, Joanne," said Cletis.

"The entire bank?" Bess said. "I'm good, but I'm not that good."

Cletis chuckled. "And I'm rich, but not that rich. But let's not underestimate us, either."

"No, no. It's wonderful that you're both modest, but not that modest," said Joanne. "Oops. Sorry." Above the open collar of her blouse, her skin turned pink.

"Touché," said Cletis. His smile seemed genuine.

Addie remembered him caressing her at Archer's Pond. The warmth in her cheeks competed with a bitter taste in her mouth. "Where's Marty?" she asked Joanne.

"Downstairs, talking to that detective."

"Marty's my son," Joanne told Cletis. "He works for the *Messenger.*"

"Ah, *The Millbrook Messenger,*" said Cletis. "The champion of tree huggers. Perhaps your son might talk with me before the paper comes out against my next development here. We do need jobs."

"And we do need truth," said Addie. "Why do you want Herbert's property?"

Cletis looked at her sharply. "Are you asking as a neighbor, a reporter, or a friend?"

"Marty's the reporter. What's so great about Herbert's acre of land?"

"Acre? You don't know? I thought Elwood would've at least told *you*. But I guess it's not that surprising."

"Know what?"

"Your grandson is going to have a field day with this, but it's bound to come out now, anyway. It's always been on the public record had anyone cared to look."

"What has?" asked Joanne.

Cletis smiled at her. "A little scoop for your son, eh?" He refocused on Addie. "You know that fifty acres behind your house owned by the Herbal Woodland Trust? The trustee was Herbert Elwood. It was all Herb El-wood's land. Now his children have to sell it."

Addie felt the breath go out of her. Herbert's land? "Did Janet know?"

"She was the alternate trustee, should Herbert die first."

"So that's what Rona Barker wanted him to sell."

"That woman doesn't take 'no' for an answer," he said. "Maybe the word doesn't translate into Chinese."

"Chinese?" asked Addie.

"Ma, we have to pay our respects to the family," said Joanne. "You want to get in line with us?" she asked Cletis.

"As my granddaughter says, 'been there, done that.'" Cletis looked at Bess. "Perhaps I'll stop by the bank one day so we can talk."

"Good customers and good friends are always welcome," said Bess.

Cletis hardly qualifies as either, thought Addie. "Are you going to the funeral?"

"No, I have another engagement. I came tonight out of – respect – for his daughter."

"Gloria?" asked Bess.

"No, Leslie. Many years ago, she worked for me."

"I didn't know that," said Addie.

"How little we know of each other. Although – " Cletis smiled.

"End of story," said Addie. "Good-bye, Cletis."

"The story of my life," said Cletis, raising his hands chest high in a gesture of surrender. "Dismissed by beautiful women. Good night, ladies."

He's impossible, thought Addie. He turns everything around. "Life is full of little disappointments," she said as he walked away. "Come on, girls."

She made her way around Charlene Glavin who was saying something about "not safe in our beds" to the Baptist minister, and then noticed Detective Barker looking about. What did he expect to see here? Addie joined the queue behind two middle-aged men who were quietly grieving the collapse of the Red Sox.

"You certainly dissed him," said Joanne from behind her.

"Cletis? I am unfailingly polite to that man."

"We noticed," said Bess. "Someday you'll have to give us the low-down."

Addie turned around. "He is the low-down," she said softly. "But this isn't the time or place to discuss it."

"That's what you always say about Cletis," said Joanne.

"Maybe I'll ask him when he comes by the bank," said Bess.

"If you want the truth, don't bother," said Addie. "It'd be like asking a Turk to write Armenian history."

"Then you tell us the truth," said Joanne.

"Another time." Maybe on my death-bed, she thought. No, she'd have to warn Bess.

As she came up to the casket, Addie fought back tears. Thank God the pillows concealed the back of Herbert's head. His face looked waxy, his cheeks too pink. Herbert wouldn't have wanted to be on display like that. Good thing she'd told the kids to keep her casket closed and to cremate her – let them remember her full of life.

She turned and stepped into a needy embrace from Herbert's eldest child, Leslie, slim and elegant in black, her dark hair falling to her shoulders.

"Oh, Aunt Addie – thank you for coming." Leslie released her grip and stepped back. Her angular features had sagged and become puffy. Her nose looked raw. Her eyes were dark pebbles beneath a veil of tears.

"I'm so very sorry, Leslie. So very sorry."

"Thank you. I know you care. It was such a shock – "

Addie took Leslie's hand between her own. "Terrible. Let me know what I can do to help."

"Everything's arranged, but thank you." With a parting squeeze, Leslie withdrew her hand. "I understand you found him. It must have been awful for you, too."

"Shock is the right word."

"All of us are blown away. I'd like to talk to you later. I mean after the funeral and all."

"Any time. Feel free to call or stop by – whatever's better for you."

"We're having a luncheon at Dad's house, after the cemetery. I hope you'll come."

"Of course, dear. What can I bring?"

"Don't worry, it's catered. We'd do it at Larry's house, except – you know, his separation – "

"Cheryl didn't come?"

"She called me. Everyone's having a hard time. Talk to you later." Leslie's eyes shifted to Joanne. "Hi, Joanne." As the two women hugged, Addie offered her hand to Leslie's husband Todd, whose thick glasses, high forehead and receding gray hair suggested wisdom and experience.

"We're grateful that you came," said Todd. It sounded like a recorded message.

Burned out greeting people he doesn't know, thought Addie. No way he could be that wooden with clients at his investment firm. "Herbert and I go back a long way," she said. And then Herbert's son, Larry, grabbed her for a hug.

"My favorite Jack O'Lantern and pumpkin pie maker," said Larry. "She's the best, Todd, even after what – 40 years?"

"I'm not keen on pumpkin," said Todd.

"He's not from among us," said Larry, setting her free. "He's a Nebraskan. An alien species."

"I'm terribly sorry about your father, Larry."

Tears welled in Larry's eyes. "Thank you, Addie. It's awful the way he died. I hope they catch the bastards that killed him. Has George said there's any progress on the case?"

"What's that?" asked Gloria, Larry's younger sister, next on the receiving line. Gloria turned away from the petite brunette next to her. "Hi, Addie." She extended her hand. "Thank you for coming."

Shortest of the three Elwood children, Gloria had been the most athletic. Even tucked into a black pants suit, it was clear she'd kept herself in good shape. Physical therapists had to set a good example, thought Addie. Although why Gloria had decided to cut her wavy hair short and then dye it blonde was a mystery. "It's good to see you again, Gloria. I'm so sorry it's like this."

"It's okay," said Gloria. Her hand was warm, her grip firm. "We'll live through it."

Gloria's hazel eyes and high cheekbones were almost identical to her mother's. No earrings, no makeup. Her only adornment was a gold brooch.

"Of that, I'm sure," said Addie. "I'm so sorry he died in such a terrible way."

"It was nasty – awful – no doubt about that. But he had a long life before – "

"A good life," said Addie.

"As good as it gets making other people feel miserable," said Gloria.

Larry shot Gloria an angry look. "Longfellow wrote that 'There is no grief like the grief that does not speak,' dear sister."

"Life isn't poetry, Larry, or haven't you noticed?"

Larry turned to Addie. "Excuse us. Death makes fools of us all. I was asking about George."

"He's not allowed to talk police business with me," said Addie. What on earth possessed these two smart people to squabble in front of their father's dead body. "Besides, it's Detective Barker who's leading the investigation."

"He's talked with us," said Larry. "He's not the brightest bulb on the Christmas tree."

"He's Rona Barker's nephew," said Addie.

"That explains it," said Gloria.

"I'm glad you're here, Gloria. Bess was really looking forward to seeing you again."

Gloria looked down the line, saw Bess and smiled. "It was good of you all to come. I want to introduce you to my wife."

Wife? Addie tried to keep her surprise from showing.

"April?" It was a gentle summons to the slim brunette whose attention had wandered from her duties on the receiving line. "This is Addie Carter, our next-door neighbor as I was growing up. Addie, this is my wife, April Brelland."

"Pleased to meet you," said April. Her voice had a musical lilt. Beneath a fine spray of freckles across her cheeks and pert nose, April's smile was broad and engaging.

"Congratulations, both of you. I didn't know you were married, Gloria."

"My family seems to have lost the announcements."

Addie shook her head. "Maybe the gypsies got them."

The women looked puzzled.

"Don't worry, girls. It's how I explain mysteries."

CHAPTER 7

WEDNESDAY, NOON

This weather doesn't help, thought Addie. Even though the Elwood kids had hired a cleaning service to scrub and vacuum their parents' home the day before Herbert's funeral, the musty odor of Janet's long illness, of her cancerous body and Herbert's self-neglect, seemed to defy pine-scented disinfectant and air freshener. The cold rain had reduced the number of acquaintances and curiosity-seekers. Even her own children had made their apologies and gone back to work, Joanne and Robert after church, George and Bess after the interment. Poor Marty was home in bed, having awakened feverish and congested.

Still, too many people and too much food here. She tuned out the chatter and watched the tangle of damp and hungry bodies pressing toward the buffet in Herbert's dining room. The returnees were balancing full plates of canapés and salads with one hand, drinks in plastic cups with the other, eyes searching in vain for an empty chair or window seat. Was it worth giving up her cushioned chair near the fire for a cup of hot tea in the kitchen? It didn't seem right that she was weighing her comforts while Herbert was lying out there in drenched earth, his house overrun by people he'd never cared about.

"I thought the world of Dr. Elwood," said a plump woman from an adjacent chair. A double strand of pearls and matching earrings complemented the woman's silver hair and black dress.

"I'm sure you did," said Addie. How long had it been since she bought a new dress? No, nothing wrong with her wool skirt and black cardigan. Better to be warm than stylish.

"He did all four of my root canals," the woman said. "I don't know how I would have gotten through any one of them without his encouragement. Did he do yours, dear?"

"No. I wasn't that –" Friendly with him? "– fortunate," she said.

"But you said you live next door. I always thought there was great advantage in having your dentist or your doctor as your next door neighbor."

"Not when they get murdered."

"I tried to get down to the basement to see where it happened, but they've locked that door."

"I think that's to keep the – "

"And that killer is still out there," the woman interjected. "If I lived next door, I wouldn't sleep without my gun under my pillow."

"Excuse me," said Addie. "I still feel chilled from the cemetery. I need of a cup of hot tea."

She stood up and threaded her way through a crush of mourners, some visibly happy now that they were dry, warm, and eating. Did any of these people feel as odd as she did, walking around this house with both Janet and Herbert dead and buried?

The large yellow kitchen was brighter and less crowded, although a half-dozen people clustered in front of a countertop bearing silver urns of coffee and hot water. Two young women in white shirts and black trousers were hustling trays in from the dining room to be refilled from pans on the stove and sink counter. Larry Elwood, Dr. Traver and two men she didn't know were seated at a small table, where Larry was holding forth a bit too loudly about his frustration with insurance companies.

"Addie!" Styrofoam cup held high in a bejeweled hand, Bella advanced like a flag-waving battleship plowing through the cluster of people waiting their turn for coffee. A poncho-clad man coming through the back door carrying two covered pans from the catering truck had to stop abruptly lest he be rammed.

"Be careful," Addie said as Bella came near. "They're running in and out."

"I can see that," said Bella. "I'm not totally blind without my glasses." Her voice dropped to a whisper. "The caterer is Le Carré Cuisine."

"So?"

Bella took a quick sip from her cup, then whispered again. "From Worcester. Carlo is miffed. He thinks the children should have had us cater this lunch – keep it local."

"Where is Carlo?"

"At the store – where else? I had to run back there after the church service, so I missed the interment. Anything happen?"

"I cornered Rona Barker. She didn't want to say too much about her clients. She told me she was contacted by an attorney who represents people interested in developing some kind of Chinese-American spiritual retreat. Rona thinks it's for the Falun Gong."

"The who?"

"Falun Gong. That spiritual group that's being persecuted in China."

"And they want to come to Millbrook?"

"Apparently there are many Chinese-Americans who follow their precepts."

"But why Millbrook?"

"I had the same question. Rona said it's the peaceful setting, and we're close enough to Boston and even New York."

"I don't know how people around here will take to a bunch of Chinese camping out in our woods. You think they'd buy from our store?"

"Don't jump the gun, Bella. Cletis wants the land, too. Rona said his company had a purchase and sale agreement with Herbert that she's been trying to get them to back out of. Her client is willing to compensate Cletis and pay a premium for the land, but Cletis is being stubborn."

"That's nothing new. Anything else happen at the funeral?"

"Just the usual."

"Other people's funerals can be so boring."

"You think you'll find yours more interesting?"

"At least I won't have to sit through it."

"You could wear your glasses, you know. They don't look bad on you at all."

"I don't have your perfect features, Addie. And you don't have my age spots. You could pass for Jessica Tandy's daughter. People look at you and think, 'I wish I could look like that when I'm older.' When they look at me, they think 'I'd rather die than get old.' So where's the bathroom?"

"You going to cut your wrists? If so, I want to have my tea first."

"My bra is pinching. I need to readjust. But I don't suppose my best friend cares about that, either."

"If I find her, I'll ask her. You can invite her to your next pity party instead of me." Addie stepped aside and pointed. "There's a bathroom at the end of the hall, and another one upstairs."

"Thank you. I'll be right back. Don't have any fun without me." Bella brushed by her, leaving a hint of orange scent in her wake.

As she moved in behind the people waiting for coffee or tea, Addie was still smiling. Bella was always 'on.' Yes, until serious reflection, a keen mind and a big heart were needed to solve a problem or uplift a friend. The intimacy that they'd evolved through sixty-four years of playing, going to school and then working together, was the greatest gift life had brought. Except for the children and grandchildren. But with no one else had she ever shared such real intimacy, such fun in conversation, such understanding and compassion.

"Excuse me," said a stocky, bald man, easing by her with a cup of coffee in each hand.

"Certainly." Poor Herbert. He'd never enjoy another cup of coffee, another spring flower or autumn walk. Soon it would be her turn. Who'd take care of Flash? Certainly not any of the kids.

"Hi, Addie." Larry Elwood was suddenly at her side. "Have you eaten already?"

"No, I'm not very hungry. I'm just waiting for a cup of tea."

Beneath his brown moustache, Larry's lips turned down with disapproval. "You need more than that to keep going. Listen to your favorite doctor. After your tea, dig into that buffet and find something interesting. We have the best caterer in Worcester."

"You look like you've lost a few pounds," said Addie. "Do you take your own advice?"

"Not always. But I've sampled a bit of everything except the desserts. Too rich for my cholesterol level. I'm a little thinner because I've been running again. Who knows, I may even try the Boston Marathon next spring."

"I ran some when I was younger," she said. "Girls weren't supposed to, but I enjoyed it. Still, I could never run a marathon." Ah, finally. She took a paper cup from the counter and chose a chamomile teabag.

"I'm not saying I can do it, either," said Larry from behind her. "And I'm certainly not the spring chicken you must have been back then. What did you like about running?"

She glanced at him. He'd reached the coffee urn. "You mean besides being young and physically able?"

"Yes, what else?"

"I enjoyed the freedom – and the solitude." She filled her cup with hot water. "The country roads – that was before things got so built up, of course – were beautiful. I loved to run along them – especially in spring and autumn." She smiled. "It was also a good excuse to be away from home a lot. Speaking of homes, what are you and your sisters going to do with this one?"

"We have to see what Dad's will says before we make any decisions."

Addie turned to face him. "Didn't he ever discuss it?"

Larry grunted, then gestured toward the pedestal table. "My colleagues have gone for second helpings. Let's grab the seats while we can."

"But they'll be coming back."

"Maybe." He took her arm and gently led her forward. "But they're younger and less charming than you, and you need a place to sit down and eat."

"I'm not that hungry."

"So sit here and have your tea." He pulled out a chair for her.

He emitted a heavy sigh as he sat down next to her. Dark semicircles underscored his bloodshot eyes.

"You look very tired," she said.

"I'm sure this hasn't been easy for you, either."

"It was so unexpected, especially the way he died." No, telling him about her nightmares wouldn't be appropriate today.

"I want to find out who killed him," he said quietly. "Did you see or hear anything unusual that night?"

"No. Flash and I turn in early. He's free to come and go, but I didn't feel him get out of our bed. Sometimes I wake up hungry around one or two in the morning and I make myself a peanut butter sandwich or some cereal, but that night I slept right through." She gazed down at her cup. "Funny how simple things like a cup of tea or a peanut butter sandwich can be so reassuring."

"In dark times we all need whatever comforts us. It must have been hard for you to find Dad like that. But thank you for going over to check on him."

"If any credit is due, it should go to Flash. If he hadn't come in carrying your father's pipe, I might not have gone over there at all."

"Your cat carried Dad's pipe?"

"I know it sounds weird, but Flash is half pack rat. He's brought in dead birds, tennis balls, children's shoes – and that's only the stuff I see. I caught him outside with a neighbor's silver necklace last spring, although how he got into her house is a mystery."

"He went into her house?"

"Not only hers, I'm afraid. It's hard to know, because people do misplace things, but because of the necklace theft, my neighbors blame Flash for every small item that goes missing. He does like shiny and tinkly things." Addie shook her head in disapproval. "He knows I take everything away, so I'm sure he tucks his prizes into a hidey-hole somewhere. But he still brings some things in. I swear he likes to provoke me. He once dragged in a live snake and the sneaky thing slithered behind my dryer. That was quite a day. Of course, Friday was far worse."

Larry brushed his lips with the back of his forefinger. "I keep wondering who did it, and why – why would someone kill my father?"

"Has Detective Barker kept you informed?"

"All he'll say to us is, 'We're working on it full-time. We'll let you know when we know more.' To tell you the truth, I don't have great faith in Detective Barker. He asks the same questions three times over. I don't know whether he has faulty hearing or faulty wiring upstairs."

"I saw him at the viewing, and again at the church and cemetery this morning."

"Oh, he's been poking around our lives enough. He even wants to be there when the attorney reads us the will tomorrow. Not that I mind – who cares if he hears – but he should be out there looking for the stuff that was stolen, which might lead him to the killer."

Addie covered her mouth and coughed to conceal her astonishment. Did Detective Barker not tell the family about finding Herbert's laptop in Lowell? Should she tell Larry? No, Barker must have his reasons. "I still can't believe Herbert didn't talk to you about how he'd leave things. I don't have much more than my house, my Social Security and what I make at Auterio's, but I've certainly discussed my finances and final arrangements with my kids."

"You're a wise woman, Addie. And you have four good children to show for it. Dad only talked about his will when one of us made a life decision that aggravated him: Gloria's coming out, Leslie's affair – before she met Todd, of course – my separation from Cheryl. I wouldn't be surprised if he carried through with his threats and all of us were written out of it."

Leslie – an affair? "I know your father could be difficult, but I find it hard to believe he would be vindictive. Your mother told me that he really loved all of you, that even his great disappointment about Gloria was – how did she put it – 'the inverse measure of his love.'"

He cracked a smile. "Mom was a great one for words – you sure she didn't say 'perverse'?"

She raised her eyebrows.

"No, no, nothing like that," he said. "Nothing obscene. Forgive me, I've been a lot more cynical lately."

"No need to apologize. You've done nothing wrong."

"I wish my wife thought that. As for Dad, I really believe that he loved us. He just had a tough time showing it. And actions often speak louder than words."

"Larry!" The alto voice and tone of command were unmistakably Leslie's. Addie looked up as Leslie bore down on them, her thin face anxious, but her body moving fluidly in high heels and another black dress. An antique cameo pendant framed by tiny pearls adorned her long neck.

Janet's favorite piece of jewelry, thought Addie. An heirloom from Janet's Austrian grandmother.

"You look lovely, Leslie."

"Thank you. And thank you again for seeing us through all this." Her face hardened as she shifted her attention to her brother. "Larry, I'd appreciate it if you were out and about, not holed up here in the kitchen. The Kellermans are leaving and want to say good-bye, and they certainly haven't been the first."

"Sorry." He stood up. "I am always on call to those who need me. I was trying to convince Addie that eating should be a daily exercise."

"You mean you haven't had anything?" Leslie's face registered her concern.

"I'll try something after I finish my tea. You two go on and do what you need to."

Larry moved his chair under the table. "I'll take that as a promise, Addie. Excuse me."

As he walked away, Leslie said "I'm sorry your children couldn't come for lunch."

"Me, too. They all had to go back to work."

"Yes, so they said. But I'm glad you're here. You were such a reassuring presence when Mom got sick. And I still remember the fun we used to have at your house."

"Those were good days," said Addie.

"I want to do some catching up, but I can't now," said Leslie, looking over at the bustling waitresses. "All these arrangements with the funeral home, the housecleaners and the caterer have me frantic. Is it okay if I give you a call once things settle down?"

"Sure. That would be nice."

"And forgive Larry if he was being a twerp. He hasn't been himself since Cheryl demanded he move out."

"I saw her with Cara and little Janet in church. The girls are adorable."

"Aren't they precious? We wanted them to come here directly. There was no need for the little ones to go to the cemetery. But Cheryl didn't feel comfortable here. I don't blame her." Leslie withdrew her hand. "Listen, I do have to run. Some people are leaving already. Get yourself a good lunch. And take a snack home for Flash. We have loads of food."

"I will. Thank you."

Addie was debating whether to finish her tea or go get something to eat when Bella appeared in the doorway, raised a glittering hand in greeting, and came to join her. "You wouldn't believe the line," she said. "By the time I got in there, I had more than one need." She looked down at the tabletop. "You know, you don't have to boycott the food on our account. Carlo will forgive you if you eat a few of Le Carré's canapés."

"I had an interesting conversation with Larry," said Addie.

"And I bumped into Gloria on the loo line. You know that she and her – her – "

"Wife," said Addie.

"If you say so. Anyway, they're thinking about adopting a baby."

"Really?"

"She'd like you to come upstairs for a tête-à-tête. Not about the baby – something else, she said. What fun we're going to have dishing all this, tomorrow."

"What are you, one of Charles Manson's girls? How can you have fun discussing a real murder? I mean, you know the victim."

"Knew," said Bella. "Remember that Susan Hayward movie, *I'll Cry Tomorrow*? For me, it's still today, and right now, I'm hungry enough to eat the competition. Let's go get some goodies."

Addie stood up. "You do that. I'm more curious than hungry. I'm going up to see Gloria."

"Suppose I make up a plate for you and we meet back here."

"I'm sure someone else will grab the table if we leave it."

"Don't worry. I'll take care of everything."

"A small plate of salad will be fine," said Addie.

"It won't be enough to help your hypoglycemia."

"I don't have hypoglycemia."

"You will by the time you get here." Bella gave a broad wink. "That's how we're going to get our table back."

CHAPTER 8

WEDNESDAY, 12:30 P.M.

The open door to the master bedroom revealed a mountain of coats overlapping the beds, with only the edge of Janet's green comforter visible. The door to Gloria's old bedroom was closed, so Addie knocked.

"Who's there?" said a female voice.

"Addie Carter. Is Gloria in there?"

"Yes. Just a second," said the woman.

Addie heard indistinct words, then Gloria's raised voice saying, "I know what I'm doing!"

A frowning April Brelland, her dark hair in an updo, opened the door, slipped out and closed it again without letting Addie by. "Give her a minute," said April. One hand reached down to smooth the skirt of her burgundy suit. "She's having a real hard time."

"I understand. I'm sure only coming back to this house for funerals makes it harder."

"She's been back before," said April.

"She has?"

"Yes. After her mother's death, she tried to patch things up with Herbert. I'm afraid our marriage put an end to that. You knew him – he was a 'class A' homophobe. Gloria says you're a very understanding woman. How do I say this – - I know you'll take what she has to say seriously and that's good. But don't take it too seriously. Don't encourage her, okay?"

Behind April, the door swung open and there stood Gloria in a black, mock turtle-neck dress. Her eyes were swollen and smudges of mascara had not been completely wiped from her cheeks. Still, she managed a smile as she extended her hand. "Come on in, Addie, before April convinces you I'm rabid. April, my love, please move your ass."

"I'll be downstairs."April started down the hall. "Ring the servant bell when you want me."

Gloria shook her head. "I'm sorry, Addie. I've dragged you into a lovers' quarrel." She stepped aside so Addie could enter, then shut the door. "I really do love her, but she has the annoying habit of trying to protect me from me."

Addie raised her eyebrows, less in response to Gloria's comment than to the decor of the bedroom. The maple dresser and desk paled against dark lavender walls. A painting of a black horse bucking in a corral competed with posters of Sigourney Weaver facing down an Alien, Charley's Angels in flying kick formation, and Billie Jean King serving up a tennis ball.

"My rebellious adolescent phase." Surveying her posters as if seeing them now through other eyes, Gloria ran a hand through her short blonde hair. "I admit I was a jerk, but I decorated like that to stick it to Herbert. I think my mom kept my room like this after he threw me out for much the same reason – although it may also have been her way of holding on to a part of me."

"Why didn't your father change it after she died?"

"I don't know. Stinginess, maybe. They didn't need the room. He had his basement workshop to putter around in. And they'd converted Larry's room into his study and Leslie's into a room where mom could do her watercolors. They could just shut the door and ignore my shit."

Addie looked about. The bookshelves looked forsaken: a handful of old books, a picture puzzle, and a game of Boggle, unwanted relics of Gloria's childhood. The scarred desktop was almost as forlorn, holding only an old clock-radio and an open box of Kleenex.

"Your mother said she saw you frequently," said Addie.

"If you call once a month frequent. As much as she loved me, she had to keep him from finding out. Otherwise, there'd be war, maybe even a divorce. Listen, if you don't mind, I have a few questions. Why don't you sit in the desk chair and I'll plop here." Gloria indicated the wrinkled white bedspread and exposed pillow.

Addie moved to the swivel chair and sat down. "I hope I can help you."

"Yeah, me too." Gloria perched on the side of the bed. "Forgive my directness, but who do you think might have wanted to kill Herbert?"

Herbert? Was Gloria so bitter she needed to disavow her relationship? "I don't know. I have no idea why he was killed other than what the police said. You don't think it was a robbery?"

"Did he say anything in the days before he died that made you think he was worried or frightened?" asked Gloria.

Addie had thought about that and come up empty, but for Gloria's sake she took a moment to reconsider. "I don't remember him saying or doing anything unusual. But we were hardly on good terms. I mean he did his yard work and I did mine. Occasionally, when he was in a better mood, I borrowed a tool from him or he accepted a morning cup of tea. Some mornings when I said 'hello' or 'lovely day,'he answered or waved. On other days, he pretended he didn't hear."

"What about the night of his murder?"

"I slept like a log." She rested a hand on the desk. "Have the police checked the other neighbors?"

"Of course. The people in the house across the street from you – "

"The Hillermans," said Addie. "They were visiting their daughter in Arizona."

"Yes, Detective Barker said they were out of town. And directly across, the Miggenses said they saw and heard nothing. Apparently they still roll up the sidewalks here after sundown."

"They never even built sidewalks on this street," said Addie. "The Planning Board promised but never delivered."

"You'd think a dog would have barked or something."

"I'm sorry that I can't be of more help."

Gloria reached forward and patted the air. "Let's not give up so easily. Do you remember when my mother was in the last stages of her cancer?"

Addie frowned. What was Gloria after? "I remember some things, but that was two years ago."

"You often brought food over here, came over to talk to her, right?"

"A few of her friends did."

"But you were the most faithful. At least that's what my mother told me. That's what Leslie and Larry said, too."

"I tried to be helpful. Your father seemed overwhelmed."

Gloria nodded. "He may have been a good dentist, but he was a lousy nurse. When we kids got sick, he withdrew and let her do everything. When she got sick, he – well, Leslie took the brunt of it. Anyway, when you were visiting my mother, did she ever say she wanted to die?"

"No. She wanted so much for your father to make peace with you. She said she wasn't going to die until she saw that happen."

"I hope she saw what she wanted to see. After her doctor said no more chemo was possible, that the goal was to keep her comfortable, I began visiting her two afternoons a week. I felt so good being here with her, but I had to clear out before Herbert got home from the office. Then one evening he called and invited me to come over to talk. I was shocked, but I figured she'd pushed him into it. Whatever his faults, he did want her to die in peace."

"So what happened?"

"I don't think I should – " Gloria's clear fingernails withdrew into a fist. "Fuck it! You want to know? We had about two minutes of polite conversation. Then he told me again what a tremendous disappointment I was to him and that my sexuality was an abomination in the Holy Bible and in the sight of the Lord, and I told him what a bigoted s.o.b. he was and how he'd abdicated true Christian values and his responsibilities as the father of a 16 year-old daughter he said he loved. And why?" Her hand slashed through the air in front of her. "Not because I was screwing around like some of my heterosexual classmates, but because I had the guts to come out. I told him it was a lot easier for him to curse his bad luck and throw me away than to admit it was his twisted genes that created me." Gloria bowed her head, lowered her voice. "Believe me, we left nothing hurtful unsaid. Including that I wished him dead." She took a deep breath, then looked up. "Be careful what you wish for, right?"

Addie's face offered agreement and sympathy.

"Anyway," said Gloria, "in the end, we both loved Mom, so we promised to be civil to each other in her presence and he said he'd pray for me and he'd put me back into his will provided I gave him my word that none of his money would go to support homosexual causes other than me." Gloria's expression indicated how ludicrous a bargain that was. "Hey, I thought that if I used his money to support me, I could give more of my money to any cause I wanted. Besides, he'd be dead, so who would be the wiser? Anyway, we made that agreement, composed ourselves over a snifter of brandy and went upstairs to tell Mom, but she was zonked out on morphine." Gloria's eyes brimmed with tears. "She died two nights later."

"Did he tell her?"

"He said he did. I may find out a lot more when the will is read tomorrow."

"You think he went back on his word?"

"You know, whether I get a penny from him or not isn't what concerns me. I was more upset when he refused to give me Mom's diamond wedding ring, which she promised I could have to give April. I mean he bloody well heard her promise it, and didn't say a fucking word." Gloria's hands rose in exasperation. "Then when I asked him for it after she died, he said he'd have to think about it." She raised the finger on which she wore a plain gold wedding band in a gesture that was almost obscene. "I guess he's stopped thinking, but I have a pretty good idea of what he must've thought – no ring that he bought would ever touch a lesbian finger. It was like he saw homosexuality as an infectious disease. How could a bright man be that stupid?"

Addie just shook her head. "He gave the ring to someone else?"

"Maybe we'll see in the will. Anyway, he told me Mom didn't want to die except when she was in great pain. But she had the morphine for that, and it mostly did the job. The point is, you never heard her say she wanted to die, and neither did I, but both Leslie and Larry say she begged them to end her suffering."

"Couldn't everyone be telling the truth?"

"Sure. That's what I thought until Herb – until my father got killed." Her right hand grasped a piece of the bedspread. "You'll probably agree with April that I'm completely delusional. I know that's what that dimwit detective would think if I told him."

"Told him what?"

"As much as I hate to think it, I believe my brother or sister killed both of them."

CHAPTER 9

WEDNESDAY, 12:45 P.M.

"You okay?" Gloria leaned forward from her perch on the bed, her face registering concern.

Addie felt her stomach right itself, her breathing resume, but her thoughts still skittered out of reach. "Yes. It's – it was a shock to think that." She straightened up in the desk chair.

"Your face got so pale. Maybe we should stop talking about it."

"No. It's just that I've known you all since you've been children. I'd never think any of you would murder anyone – especially your parents."

"You never know people until you live with them. Sometimes not even then." Gloria eased herself back on the bed. "I mean my parents never suspected my sexual orientation. After sixteen years of living together, they went from not knowing me to not wanting to know me." She glanced at her Sigourney Weaver poster. "In my last two years of high school, I lived here as a stranger. Honestly, I felt a lot more at home in your house."

Had the childhood friendship between Gloria and Bess ever turned sexual? Addie gripped her chair. She'd certainly missed Bess' drug abuse for too long. No, whatever happened, Bess was okay now. Herbert wasn't. "But even at your angriest, would you have thought seriously about killing one of your parents?"

"Not Mom, certainly. And I didn't kill Herbert, if that's what you're asking. If I had, I wouldn't be raising this issue."

Maybe, maybe not, thought Addie. "What proof do you have that Larry or Leslie killed them?"

"That's the thing – I don't have real proof. If I did, I'd be talking to the police."

"I think you should still – "

Gloria raised her hand. "No. I can't go to the police and accuse my brother and sister – I mean even April thinks I'm wacky on this one, and she really loves me." Gloria lowered her hand to her lap. "But you know my family better than anyone outside it. So hear me out and then tell me what you think, okay?"

Addie hesitated. Gloria's story could lead down a nasty road. But she couldn't just turn her back on Gloria. That's what Herbert had done. "Okay."

"Let's start two years ago. We knew my mother's cancer was terminal and despite the opiates, she was in a lot of pain at times. But no one expected her to die that suddenly. After her death, I asked Larry if he was surprised by how quickly she died – I mean he's a doctor and should know more than us, right? And I also mentioned it, separately, to Leslie. Larry gave me some b.s. about no one being able to predict the day or time of death, and Leslie said she was stunned, which seemed over-the-top considering Mom was terminal. But both of them said that Mom must've felt her work on this earth was done after Herbert and I declared a truce."

"Isn't that quite possible?"

"Yes. Except Mom wouldn't have wanted to die without saying good-bye to me."

"You're assuming your mom had a choice," said Addie. Gloria was also ignoring how pain or drugs might have altered Janet's priorities. "Did you ask whether she'd left you a good-bye message?"

"Yes, and she hadn't. Even then, I doubted that she'd just turned over in her sleep and died without help, but I didn't push the issue. Leslie and Larry always resented me, and Herbert had just cut me in for a third of the estate, so I was walking very softly in this house. What bothered me even more was that on one of my last visits to Mom, I went to the medicine cabinet to get her a morphine tablet, and I saw an almost full bottle of antidepressants that Larry had prescribed."

"Wouldn't anyone with terminal cancer be depressed?" said Addie.

"I suppose – although as a physical therapist, I've seen a lot of people handle their pain and disabilities with grace and humor. But the thing is that Larry shouldn't have been prescribing for Mom at all. The State Board has regulations about doctors not prescribing for their families. Anyway, after Leslie called that morning to tell me that Mom had died, I drove right over here. For a while we all sat around boo-hooing and trying to wrap our minds around the loss. But when I couldn't pull myself together, I went to Mom's medicine chest to see if I could find a tranquilizer – and that bottle of medicine Larry prescribed wasn't there. At first I thought she'd overdosed herself. But the bottle wasn't in her room, either." Gloria pointed a finger at the door. "And no one I asked – Herbert, Leslie, even Larry, who's bleeping name was right on it – said they saw or remembered that bottle."

"They all denied it?" Had Gloria's grief and anxiety caused her to misperceive?

"Yes. I just thought they didn't want to get Larry in trouble, and neither did I. Back then, I couldn't believe that any of them would have killed Mom."

"Frankly, I still can't," said Addie. "I remember there was some gossip at the store about her dying of an overdose. I shut it off. I hate gossip that puts people down or magnifies their tragedies. And I loved your mother."

A liquid sound came from Gloria's throat. She put a hand to her neck. "That was my fault. I poured out my heart to a nurse – not April – I thought was a close friend. The next thing I knew, rumors about Mom's suicide had spread through the hospital like a virus. Thank God I didn't mention Larry or that antidepressant bottle. As it was, I had to take a truckload of shit from him. He wouldn't admit he wrote a prescription for her, much less that he destroyed the evidence."

No, thought Addie. That wasn't the Larry she knew. "You said Larry and Leslie always resented you?"

"I thought that was obvious – the way they picked on me when I was little. You know, the baby gets all the attention thing. I'm not saying I didn't like attention, but what little kid doesn't?

"And as I got older, I turned out to be a good athlete and got very popular in school. Leslie was more intelligent, but she was so boy-crazy and jealous that she didn't have many friends."

"Larry had lots of friends," said Addie. "I remember the tree house they built in the woods, and the games of 'capture the flag.' My kids loved those summers."

"Sure, Larry played, but he was a wuss. He depended on his jokes and big, smarmy smile to get by. At the first sign of trouble, Larry would disappear. Like the antidepressants did. And get this – that day Mom died, we're making funeral arrangements and calling our friends or taking calls as the word spreads, and Larry is out on a food run. But as I'm coming downstairs, I hear Leslie say 'It's your fault. You and your fine son.' And then Herbert says, "Well, you wanted out, didn't you? Now you're out. So if Larry and I are guilty, so are you.'"

Gloria leaned forward. "So of course, me and my big mouth, I pop right in and ask, 'Guilty of what?' They practically jumped out of their skins. Herbert recovered first and said, 'Of not calling you to come see your mother in the last two days, when it was clear she was getting worse. I asked Larry to do it, but it slipped his mind.' I said 'You expect me to believe that bullshit?' And Leslie, always the rational one, said 'Mom's dead. Isn't that enough grief for one day?' So I dropped it. And for more than a year, that was that."

"Until – ?"

"Until four months ago, when Larry told me he and Cheryl split up. He said it was a mutual decision. Anyway, I called Cheryl to say I was sorry they'd split, but I wanted to stay a friend to her and a loving aunt to their kids. I really meant it – I've always liked Cheryl and she always accepted me. If she ever had qualms about lesbian cooties rubbing off on her girls, she never let on. And this time was no different. She said she was glad I still wanted to be part of their lives. She asked me not to take sides, that she and Larry would work things out if it was possible. But then she said that Larry did need help, and that maybe he'd listen to me or Leslie." Gloria's mouth turned down to indicate she thought otherwise. "Cheryl had tried to get Larry to go to a therapist, but he'd refused any professional help and finally she had to ask him to leave. Of course I asked what issues he needed help with, but she wouldn't get specific."

"Did you talk to Larry?"

"You bet. The next day, I cornered my charming brother and said I wasn't taking sides but I wasn't pulling any punches, either. Why did some people think he needed professional help, and why was he avoiding it if it could save his marriage? Could you pass me a tissue, please?" Gloria pointed to the box on the desk.

"Oh – yes." Disconcerted, Addie handed her the whole box. "What did Larry say to you?"

Gloria extracted a tissue, then put the box on the bed. "He said Cheryl always saw everything as his fault. And that he was overworked what with all the insurance forms and reviews, not to mention the medical needs of his patients, the time he needed to be with his daughters, the financial strain of running two households – I mean the list of what he was dealing with could've filled a parking garage. His conclusion was that he probably needed a practice management consultant, except he didn't have enough money for that, either. Excuse me." She turned her head away and blew her nose.

Yes, Larry had looked tired and unhappy downstairs, thought Addie. But kill his parents? Unbelievable. Yet Gloria believed it. "What motive would Larry – or Leslie for that matter –have to commit murder?"

Gloria leaned forward and placed the used tissue on the desk. "I think with Mom it was that they couldn't stand to see her suffer any more. To tell you the truth, if Mom wanted it, I wouldn't have approved, but I wouldn't have stood in the way. This murder is different. I know both Larry and Leslie needed money, and Herbert had threatened to change his will."

Addie shook her head. "Leslie and her husband work – they have good jobs."

"I don't know what they make. I do know she likes good clothes, and they take lovely vacations twice a year. But who knows? The stock market's been awful and I know Leslie hates to have Todd go anywhere near a gambling casino. A couple of months ago, Larry told me he'd asked Leslie to lend him some money, but Leslie said she was having financial problems, too. I suggested he try to borrow from Herbert, but Larry said he had more than enough problems without getting our father on his case. The old man was afraid of losing his only grandchildren, so he was already siding with Cheryl."

Was it that simple? thought Addie. Was one of these kids greedy enough to commit patricide? No, it didn't seem credible. Such things did happen, but not in Janet's family. "Larry needed money for a practice consultant?"

"And a divorce lawyer," said Gloria. "Maybe even a psychiatrist. Over the last few months, April has nursed a couple of patients in the hospital who told her they were going to change doctors. They said Larry seemed disinterested and preoccupied, wasn't returning phone calls. I mean that's not unusual for doctors, but this was beyond their tolerance. And April also has a friend, another nurse, who was laid off by Larry. He told her there was nothing wrong with her work – he was having financial difficulties because of his marital separation. She wondered whether Larry had Bipolar Disorder, because he was up and down in mood so much. Then, about ten days ago, I went to ask Herbert for a loan. April and I want to adopt a baby."

"Oh, how nice," said Addie.

Gloria's hand made a dismissive gesture. "Herbert didn't think so. He said he wasn't going to support bringing a child into a house in which sinfulness and perversion flourished. I told him the real sinfulness was his, for he'd made it impossible for relationships in his house to flourish. That's when he hit the roof and said he wished he'd never had children, that even his 'normal' kids couldn't keep their marriages together, and that all we ever wanted from him was money. He'd been hit up for money by both Larry and Leslie, and now here I was, hat in hand. He said he'd be damned if he was going to support any of our vices. He threatened to redo his will and leave all his money to charity." Gloria shook her head. "That man always thought money gave him control. So I told him to stick his will up his ass – sorry, Addie – and forget his children and grandchildren, and see if that made him any happier."

So mean spirited, both of them. Janet wasn't like that. Addie rubbed her forehead. "I still don't see how that shows who killed your father."

"Wait. After that, I'm so hot under the collar, I called Leslie to sound off. That night, I get a call from Larry. He wants to know exactly what Herbert said about changing the will. Do I think he's going to do it? I tell him his guess is as good as mine. What about the fight he had with Herbert the week before? It really wasn't that big a deal, says Larry. He'd asked Herbert to front him some money for a divorce if it came to that, and it got a little heated, but not out of hand. Larry said to me, 'You know he's been a bastard to you for years. I guess it's my turn now.' Then he said, 'Don't worry, Gloria. It won't be long before he's going to have to answer for the way he's dealt with his children.'"

"Oh, dear. Larry really said that?"

"Yes. And get this! On the night Herbert was murdered, I was in bed with April, watching TV but thinking about all this, and I decided maybe it was best if Larry, Leslie and I met to plan a strategy for how to smooth things out with Herbert. It was about ten-thirty, but I called Leslie and then Larry. When I got voicemails at their home, I tried their cell phones. No answer, no answer. Eleven o'clock, the same. Eleven thirty – " Gloria's hand came up empty. "After that, the news was over and we went to sleep."

"And you've since asked them where they were?"

"Leslie said she was at the movies, so she turned off her cell phone. Larry said he was fast asleep and didn't hear anything."

Addie felt queasy. "Clearly you don't believe them."

"Why would someone who doesn't much care for movies be out seeing one, alone, on a Thursday night? And since when does a doctor who's used to taking calls in the middle of the night sleep through a half-dozen calls, three on his land line, three on his cell? You bet I don't believe them. I believe both of them are lying, and at least one of them is a murderer."

CHAPTER 10

WEDNESDAY, 1:30 P.M.

"I'm glad Gloria's not my sister,"said Bella. "Do you believe her?" Seated at the kitchen table with a yellow blanket around her shoulders, Bella still looked waterlogged. Her hair was frizzy and damp, her eye makeup had smeared from toweling, and her expressive hands hadn't left the hot water bag on her lap.

"I don't know. She seemed sincere," said Addie, warming her own hands around a mug of tea. "Are you sure you don't want anything hot to drink?" She still felt guilty she'd pulled her friend away from the funeral luncheon into a downpour. And while she was able to change into a housedress and slippers, she had nothing to fit Bella other than a pair of dry socks.

"No thanks. I had too much coffee next door. So Gloria's sincere, so what? Do you really think Leslie or Larry murdered their parents?"

"Of course not, but her accusations are very disturbing."

Bella nodded. "Murder should be disturbing. I'd hate to think you dragged me away from those canapés through a nor'easter for the sake of idle gossip."

"This is certainly not for gossip. You can tell Carlo, and I have to tell George, but that's all."

"Did Gloria swear you to secrecy?"

"Even that was odd. She said I should do what I thought best. She's smart enough to know I'd tell George." Addie frowned. "I think that's what she wants. Telling me was her round-about way of getting the information to the police without going to them directly and accusing her brother and sister. If I tell George without her asking me to, he'll be more inclined to give her accusations serious thought, and she'd have some deniability. To her brother and sister, Gloria can deny she went to the police. She'd say they came to her."

"Oh," Bella scoffed, "that should make Larry and Leslie feel lots better."

"I doubt Gloria wants them to feel better. I think she's trying to protect herself while sowing doubt about them – or seeking justice – I don't really know."

"I'm sure I know even less." Bella's hands came off the hot water bottle. "But how did Gloria know that Herbert died Thursday night, not during the day or early Friday morning?"

Addie cocked her head. "You know, it's good you caught that. I just assumed it was Thursday night. Perhaps she did, too. I also wondered about her persistence in calling Larry and Leslie. And why Larry would lie about writing a prescription for his mother."

"Gloria said he lied. She could be the one lying."

"Yes, but the record of a prescription could be checked so easily. It's hard for me to believe that Janet committed suicide – on the other hand, I can't believe Herbert or the children deliberately overdosed her."

"I can understand the idea of mercy killing, but I think it's not only criminal, it's against God's Commandment," said Bella. "And I can't buy that Leslie or Larry beat their father's head in."

"Neither do I. But Gloria does."

"Or says she does."

"It gives me a headache," said Addie.

"That's because you haven't eaten. You should've brought some of those goodies back here."

"I was so upset by what Gloria told me. All I wanted to do was get you and get out. I needed to talk this through."

"What's in your fridge?" Bella pushed her chair back from the table. "I'll make you a snack."

"You don't have to do that. I can get something myself."

"What, cold cereal?" She placed the hot water bag on the table and stood up. "You call George and get him over here. I want to be in on that. Meanwhile, my shoes will dry out and I'll amuse myself by making lunch for the two of you." She headed toward the refrigerator.

"Don't you have to go back to the store?"

"Why? To sell more prosciutto and bologna? All the juicy meat is right here."

* * *

"I don't like that she told all this to you and not to us," said George. Seated between the two women at the kitchen table, he leafed through the notes he'd written in his spiral pad. A plate of macaroni and tuna salad garnished with sliced tomatoes lay untouched in front of him.

Addie cut a small piece of tomato from a slice on her plate. "You interviewed her?"

"Detective Barker did. That's his job."

"Doesn't sound like he did it very well," said Bella. "You want a different lunch?"

"No, thanks, Aunt Bella. I told you I wasn't hungry."

"You're just like your mother. You let everything come before food. I'll bet there's not a Mediterranean gene in your bodies." She gestured toward his plate. "Try it."

George sighed, hesitantly took up a forkful of salad, put it in his mouth and began chewing.

"I don't think it was Detective Barker's fault," said Addie. "Gloria probably answered his questions. She may not have wanted to volunteer her suspicions until she was ready. But we were wondering, George, how did Gloria know exactly when Herbert died?"

"I'm sure that's no secret to anyone who was questioned in the days after the murder, because Harris was trying to establish where everyone was around 11 p.m."

"And did Leslie and Larry tell Detective Barker they were where Gloria said they were, one at the movies, the other home asleep?" asked Addie.

George waggled his fork. "That's police business, Ma. I can't discuss it."

"Of course you can," said Bella. "We won't tell a soul."

Addie leaned forward. "Whatever her reasons, Gloria made it my business, too. Just like Raymond Miggens did."

"Look, Ma, I'm in the middle here. What you learned may be real helpful, but I can't give you information that's not already in the public domain. We have a murder investigation going on."

"Better than ours?" asked Bella.

"Bella! Detective Barker is the investigator." Addie turned to her son. "But I'd have to be a turnip not to be curious about a murder next door. Has Detective Barker told you that Herbert owned all this land out back and that his Aunt Rona was trying to get him to sell it?"

"Yes. Surely you don't think Rona Barker had anything to do with Herbert's murder, do you?"

"I'm just wondering how objective Detective Barker can be, that's all."

"Look, Harris doesn't even like his aunt. He thinks this — thing she's into is crazy."

"What thing?" asked Addie.

"I'm not at liberty to say. Stay out of it, Ma."

"He thinks you are a turnip," said Bella. She put on a tragic face. "It's so very sad. He doesn't trust his own mother."

"It even worse for you," said Addie. "He doesn't like your tuna salad."

George's hands shot upward, one holding his fork, the other a stop sign. "That's enough, ladies. I've had plenty of practice being double-teamed by you two as I grew up, and I have plenty of it at home with my wife and daughter. This interrogation is over." He lowered his hands, put his fork on the plate. "Detective Barker will want to talk with you about Gloria, Ma. And he and the Chief are the only ones that can release information. Do you have any questions about that?"

"Does this mean you don't like all my salads, or just tuna?" asked Bella.

George smiled. "I love your deli salads, Aunt Bella, but I ate two donuts before Ma called."

"Talk about alibis," Bella said.

"I only have one more question," said Addie. "And you don't have to tell me anything new. Do you have any reason to believe that Gloria was lying in what she told me?"

"No."

"Good. I'm glad," said Addie. "I really like Gloria."

"Don't like her too much," said George. "She didn't tell us everything. Why should we believe she told you everything?"

CHAPTER 11

Thursday Morning

Addie walked down the aisle between vitamins and food supplements on one side, and antacids and laxatives on the other. At eleven in the morning, the Millbrook CVS had few customers, but two white-jacketed young women were busy behind the pharmacy counter. An older gentleman in a ratty black coat sat in the waiting area. The man's face was weathered, his eyes were closed. Addie stepped up to the counter. A young Asian woman, her black hair glistening under the lights, looked over from her computer.

Someone new, thought Addie, placing her purse on the counter. "May I please speak to Robert?" she asked.

"Certainly." The girl turned toward a rear workspace. "Robert, please?" It was a melodious summons.

From behind a counter, Robert glanced up from the stream of tablets he was pouring from a jar into a counting machine. "In a minute, Ai Linh." His red hair was worn just long enough to be neatly parted. Rimless glasses sat forward on his slightly upturned nose. He beamed when he saw Addie, looked down until he completed his task, and then came to greet her by leaning over the counter and planting a kiss on her cheek.

"Hi, Ma," he said softly. Looking back over his shoulder, he saw his crew watching. "Did you see what I just did?" he asked them. "That's what is known as superior customer service."

Addie caught Ai Linh's eye. "Doesn't the customer have to decide what's superior?"

"Yes," said Ai Linh. "The customer must always be given great respect."

Robert turned back to Addie. "Shall I have each of them kiss you so you can decide?"

"No!" said the man seated behind her. "Have them kiss me. I'll decide."

Addie laughed.

Robert joined in. "Sorry Mr. K, not without a doctor's prescription."

"I'll have him phone it in," said Mr. K.

Addie turned to face the man. "I think I'd like your doctor. Hi, my name is Addie Carter. This young man is my son Robert." She heard the pharmacy phone ring.

Mr. K. struggled to his feet. "Pleased to meet you. I'm Joe Kearney." His face took on an unexpected liveliness as he extended his hand toward Addie. As they shook hands, he asked, "Is it Addie from Adeline, then?"

She smiled. "Adelaide. But I much prefer Addie."

"Your ride is here, sir," called the pharmacy tech.

"God bless the Council on Aging," said Kearney. "A pleasure meeting you, Addie. You have a good son there, but truth to tell you're a lot prettier than he is." He waved in farewell. "No offense, Robert."

"None taken."

"Good-bye," said Addie. She watched Kearney limp toward the front of the store. Yes, her ex had that affable manner, that same ability to charm and make people laugh. How sad that Dave was so hollow inside. Even sadder for the children that no one could fill that space.

"Good guy," said Robert. "So how have you been feeling, Ma?"

"Good enough, but disturbed by what happened next door." She glanced at Ai Linh, who was typing at her computer, then at the chunky blonde arranging boxes on a shelf. Addie lowered her voice. "I need some professional information along with my atenolol. Can a person die from an overdose of antidepressants?"

He looked puzzled. "Sure, but some can be a lot more lethal than others. Which person and which antidepressant are we talking about?"

"Janet Elwood. I'm not sure which antidepressant."

"Janet?" Robert looked over his shoulder to see if he'd been heard, then spoke more softly. "But that was – it was Herbert who got – you think Janet committed suicide?"

"It's possible she was murdered, too. Could that sort of medication be introduced without a person's knowledge?"

"Not likely. It would take a lot of pills or liquid – she'd surely have tasted it if someone slipped it into her juice or coffee."

"What if she were taking other drugs?"

The pharmacy telephone rang. Robert turned his head but Ai Linh was moving to answer it.

"Then yes," said Robert, "in combination with alcohol or strong sedative or blood pressure medicine, some antidepressants could be lethal. Was she a drinker?"

"I think she liked a glass or two of wine now and then, but she told me she stopped drinking when she started the first round of chemotherapy."

Addie rested a hand on her purse. "What if someone knew what medicines she was taking. Could they have mixed her a lethal combination?"

Robert grimaced. "Anything is possible. If you knew what someone was on, you probably could go to the Internet and figure out how to produce a very bad drug interaction. But it would be hard to predict for sure it would be fatal."

"What about a doctor?"

"You mean doing that?" Robert's eyes went wide. "Larry?" he whispered.

"It's not likely. I'm just trying to piece things together, and I may have been told things that aren't quite true."

"Why are you piecing things together? That's the police's job. Talk to George."

"I have." She saw Ai Linh return to the computer. Oh, to be able to move like that again. "I wish all this had never happened, Robert, but it has, and people are pulling me into it. Besides, he was my neighbor for over forty years and Janet was my good friend for most of that. I have to do whatever I can."

"I don't want you getting hurt."

"I'm not about to do anything foolish. I'm too old to run fast and too wise to tempt fate." She pointed to the baskets of medication waiting to be picked up. "May I have my atenolol, please?"

"I love you, Ma, but sometimes you're too deaf for your own good." He turned and went to look for her medication.

Addie sighed. Robert needed to get married and have children of his own. Maybe then he'd stop trying to be her parent.

Robert returned with a small white bag. "You know, if Janet's death looked suspicious, the medical examiner would've done an autopsy and tested for drugs."

"It didn't look suspicious. Janet had terminal cancer. It's likely her own doctor put her on the antidepressants. By the way, how long does a pharmacy keep records of a prescription?"

"You mean us?"

"No, not in a big chain store. Probably some out of the way apothecary."

"The rule in Massachusetts is to keep them two years on site, but many independents keep them longer, sometimes seven years, like tax records. Why do you ask?"

"I'll tell you another time. How much do I owe?"

Robert scanned the bar code on the bag. "Six dollars and sixty-four cents."

Addie handed him a ten. "You haven't been to the house for almost two weeks. Flash won't bite if you stay off the couch."

Robert rang up the sale and gave her the change. "Are you kidding? That beast would attack if I even looked at the couch. I wish he'd go play under an eighteen wheeler."

"That's cruel, Robert." Addie tucked the bills and coins into separate compartments of her wallet. "You know I could put Flash in the bathroom or the basement. Is there another reason why you haven't been around?"

"I've been very busy."

She put her wallet in her purse. "Aside from work, with what?"

Robert glanced over his shoulder at Ai Linh, then turned back. "Like you said, I'll tell you another time." His face was pinker than a moment before.

Oh Robert, thought Addie, you've already told me. She picked up the bag of medication. "Remember," she said, "we have a family music night a week from tomorrow."

"I remember."

"Feel free to bring a guest."

Addie was still smiling as she walked out the door.

CHAPTER 12

THURSDAY EVENING

Addie looked up from the frying pan she was scouring in the sink to admire the play of light and dark on the trees. "It's a lovely sunset," she said. Flash was much too busy lapping water from his bowl to respond. Smiling, she returned to her task.

She was wiping up around the sink when she glanced out the window again.

"Oh, my."

A man had come out of the woods and was heading for Herbert's house. No dog, no back-pack. She moved away from the window. Should she turn off the light? No, that would catch his attention. Maybe it was a policeman in plain clothes. But a week after the murder?

Flash's ears perked up. He bolted for the mudroom. "Flash, don't go out!" Stupid cat! She hurried to the phone and dialed George's cell number.

"What now, Ma?" He sounded a trifle annoyed.

"George, there's a man who came out of the woods, headed toward Herbert's house. Is he one of your policemen?"

"Is he wearing a uniform?"

"It's too dark for me to see clearly. But I don't think so."

"Did you call 911?"

"No. I thought he might be a policeman in plain clothes, like Detective Barker. Or maybe he's someone who got lost on a walk."

"Are your doors locked?"

"I think so. I'll check."

"I'll send a cruiser."

"If he's the murderer, he'll just run back into the woods."

"Hell with that. Go into the bathroom, lock it, and don't open it until I tell you to. I have my key to get in."

"Flash ran outside."

"I hope he mauls the asshole."

"George!"

"Sorry, Ma. Gotta get moving."

The click on the line spurred her to action. She opened a kitchen drawer and grabbed a wooden rolling pin, tucking it under her arm before hurrying to the mudroom. Yes, thank God, the back door was locked. She started to go check the front door when she heard a gentle knock-knock behind her. She turned quickly. "What do you want?" The double-glazed panels quartered her view. Tall, long face, bulky dark jacket.

"My name is Steven Mars. I'm a private investigator. May I come in?" His tone seemed polite, his voice nasal, without any accent.

She couldn't make out his features. Not young, though. Put on the porch light? No, don't go near the door. "I don't think so. My husband is – indisposed."

"You don't have a husband. I mean you no harm. And I found your cat." The man held Flash up to the glass panels. "Actually, he found me. We'd like to come in where it's warm."

My God! Flash looked absolutely docile in his big hands. None of her children ever dared pick Flash up. She pointed downward. "There's a cat door."

"I know. It's too small for me."

"What do you want?"

"Evidence. And a cup of hot coffee, if you have one."

"You're a private investigator? You have a license?"

"Of course. Do you have a key to Dr. Elwood's house?"

"No, I don't," she lied. "Put your license through the cat door."

"I never let my license out of my hands. I'll show it to you inside."

What's taking George so long? "If you won't trust your license with me, I have no reason to trust you. Go to the police. They can let you in."

"The police wouldn't believe me. They're ignorant or corrupt, sometimes both."

"I doubt that. My son's a policeman."

"Maybe he's an exception to the rule. Do you think the higher-ups will ever admit the real reason Dr. Elwood was killed?"

"Once they know it, I'm sure they will."

"No, they'll have their orders. They won't tell us anything. A random robbery-murder, perpetrators unknown. Isn't that what the media people are saying?"

"And you know the real reason he was killed?"

"Certainly. The problem is I don't have any hard evidence."

"So why was he killed?"

"It's a long story. I won't tell it standing out here."

If she said no, would he break in or hurt Flash? No, Flash would sense the threat. "I'm sorry, Mr. – " The roar of a car charging up the driveway was music to her ears.

"You called the police. You shouldn't have done that!" The man bent and propelled Flash through the cat door, then turned and ran for the woods.

* * *

By the time George returned, she was on her second cup of tea. Her mother's white china cup and saucer were more comforting than the tea itself.

"Did you find him?" Addie asked.

"No, but Westlake and Parker are still searching." George pulled a chair out from the table and sat down. "We don't have enough guys to do it properly."

"The water is hot if you want some tea."

He looked over at the kettle on the stove. "No, thanks."

"I wish he'd told me his thinking on why Herbert was killed. You don't think he could've been a private investigator?"

George's hand brushed the notion aside. "Not approaching you that way. It's possible he's the killer."

"I don't think so. Flash liked him."

"What difference does that make? Flash doesn't like any of your children."

Addie sniffed. "Sibling rivalry. You weren't too nice to Joanne, as I recall. Nor to Robert." She rested her fists on the table. "Maybe it wasn't evidence Mr. Mars was looking for. If he is the killer, it's possible he didn't get what he was after in the first place. Or maybe he thought he left something incriminating behind. Did you and Detective Barker find anything over at Herbert's?"

"Not really."

"That's what you said when I asked you whether you punched Billy Parker in the face."

"C'mon, Ma."

"And it turned out you'd punched him in the stomach and elbowed him in the face."

"For Christ's sake. That was in the sixth grade."

"So what does 'not really' mean this time?"

"It means it's police business, a murder investigation. I could lose my job if I tell you things and they get out."

"Don't be so melodramatic. I've kept more secrets than you can possibly know." Addie took a sip of tea and set the cup down carefully. "Look, the murder was right next door and this Steven Mars – I doubt that's his real name – came to my house. I feel very vulnerable without information."

"I'm sorry you're being dragged into this, but right now you have more information about this guy than I do."

She pointed a finger at him. "Don't play games with me, George. It's not just about Steven Mars and you know it. I'm still smart enough to be your mother."

She saw him considering his options.

George sighed. "Okay, but this is between us – no one else, understand?"

"Yes."

"Not even my sisters and brother. And certainly not Aunt Bella."

"Not anyone. I promise."

"We're thinking it's a robbery that Dr. Elwood interrupted. The presumed entry point was the back door, where a glass panel was broken. Elwood either fell or was pushed down the cellar steps, then killed by blows to the head."

The image of Herbert's battered head made her shudder. "Who would do such a thing?"

"I'd give a week's pay to know."

"Did you find his gardening shoes?"

"No, and all the footprints out back were Herbert's shoe size. We think the killer – or one of the killers - used Herbert's shoes and socks to go in and out, taking the stuff to the car. But there were no fingerprints in the entire house other than those of the Elwood family and Herbert's cleaning lady." George rubbed his forehead. "I hate to think of those guys as suspects. Anyway, the prints don't mean much, because they all admit being in the house within a few days before the murder. Samples of hair and blood from the basement are being processed for DNA, but we expect it's all Herbert's because the crime scene and autopsy didn't show any signs of a struggle."

"What about his pipe?"

"A little cellar dirt, a little grass, and a fiber that turned out to be from Elwood's pocket. The only clean fingerprint was your right thumb."

Addie frowned. "And from where, may I ask, did you get my fingerprints?"

"Off the tea mug you drank from, the morning you found the body."

She pushed the saucer and teacup aside. "You should have asked me."

"We didn't think we'd need a complete set, and you were in tough shape at the time."

"You still should've asked me. Do I have fewer rights because I'm your mother?"

George took a deep breath, looked up at the ceiling, then met her gaze again. "I'm sorry. I didn't think you'd mind."

"I wouldn't have, had you thought to ask. Well –" she tapped the tabletop. " – what's done is done. Catching the murderer is more important than my sensibilities." She looked at her thumb. "Are my fingerprints going into some national database?"

"No. Like you say, we didn't get your permission. And as far as I know, the only crime you've committed is harboring a delinquent cat."

"Seriously, did you find any other clues?"

"Not really."

"Again, not really?"

George sighed. "I got to stop saying that."

She raised her eyebrows with expectation.

"Okay, okay. The presumed murder weapon was a mallet or small sledge hammer missing from its place on Elwood's tool board. And one of the birdhouses had what looked like a finger mark in the paint, but there was no print."

"The killer must have worn gloves," said Addie.

"Sure – but why touch a recently painted birdhouse? That impression in the paint might not have had anything to do with the murder. Herbert could have worn gloves or touched that spot through a rag when he painted the thing. And his kids didn't know when that was. According to Leslie and Larry, a stereo system, a bedroom TV, his cell phone and his laptop were stolen. His wallet and wristwatch are gone, too. What else? Oh, no prescription pills were left in the medicine cabinet. You satisfied now or do you want it in triplicate?"

"When I was over there after the funeral, the big TV was still in his living room."

"Maybe too big to transport easily, or maybe they didn't have time to detach it from the wall."

"Was the wall safe opened?"

George looked surprised. "You knew about the safe?"

"Janet showed it to me years ago. Wasn't it clever the way they hid it? The portrait of their children would have no value for a burglar."

"Did she tell you what was in it?"

"Not specifically. She said they kept their important papers and some jewelry there. Does this Pedro person that Raymond talked about have a history of robbery or home invasion?"

"Pedro Serrano? He may be involved, but he's not the killer. The Lowell police traced the laptop to his apartment. They got a search warrant and not only found the laptop but also a baggie of cocaine hidden in the kitty-litter. Pedro told the officers he found the laptop and the bag of cocaine lying on the street, like someone had put it out with the garbage." George's face registered his disbelief. "When the officers stopped laughing, they read him his rights and told him he was suspect *numero uno* in a murder case. I hear Pedro started crying and quickly gave up his brother-in-law Hector, who was enjoying the TV and stereo three blocks away. Hector gave pretty much the same story – they found the electronic stuff on the street walking home from a bar that closed at 2 a.m. But no wallet or credit cards, no cell phone, and no pills or jewelry. At least that's what each of them said independently. When Hector was asked about finding a baggie there, he said he didn't know anything about that. If Pedro found it, Pedro never told him."

"Perhaps Pedro didn't want to share the cocaine."

"Or Hector is distancing himself from drug charges. The problem is that the bartender and a couple of regulars swore Pedro and Hector were there from about ten Thursday night until two o'clock Friday morning. If the M.E. is right about the time of death, those two couldn't've been down here."

Addie moved the cup and saucer aside and put her fists on the table. "So either Pedro and Hector were telling the truth about finding Herbert's things on the street or someone gave or sold those things to them."

"And that someone could be Ray Miggens."

"I don't believe Raymond would murder anyone," said Addie. "He acts tough, but he's really soft-hearted."

"You think that because he's still taking care of his loopy mother. But Ray might be a little loopy, too. Or it's quite possible he brought a friend along to steal a few things and the friend got mad and shoved Herbert down the staircase. Then they had to silence him."

"It was more than one person, then?"

George shrugged. "Harris thinks Ray Miggens is involved, even if he wasn't the guy who bashed Herbert."

"And you?"

"I have my doubts. I mean if Ray was going to get back at Elwood for the ice cream truck thing, why did he wait so long? And why not have a good alibi?"

"And now that you've heard what Steven Mars had to say?"

George rubbed his temple. "All bets are off. We're going to have to find this guy and have a long, heart-to-heart with him."

"I wonder what Detective Barker will think about Steven Mars."

"I'm more concerned about what he'll think of you. First it's Ray Miggens, then it's Gloria, now the man from Mars – you have some kind of magnet that pulls forth confessions?"

"It seldom worked with you."

"Yeah, like tonight, huh? I'm pretty sure Harris will want you to come down to the station to look at some pictures tomorrow. I'll give you a ring in the morning to let you know."

Addie's eyes widened. "The ring!"

"What?"

She extended her hands toward George. "At the viewing, Herbert was laid out wearing his wedding band. Was that an extra ring?"

"What man married fifty-odd years to the same woman has an extra wedding ring?"

"I remember seeing it when I found him. Don't you find it odd that it wasn't taken?"

"It's a simple gold band. Maybe the perp thought it wasn't worth much."

"Still – "

"Hey, it could have been overlooked or hard to dislodge, or maybe the killer didn't want to risk messing with the body because of the risk of leaving DNA evidence."

"You certainly know more about these things than I do. But if someone who came to rob Herbert saw a gold ring on his finger, is it likely he would leave it there? And leave that big TV on the living room wall?"

"No, not really." George smacked his thigh. "Shit! I said it again."

Addie offered him a reassuring smile. "Don't worry. This ends up as a very good night for both of us. Not only did I learn a lot, but I didn't hear a word you said."

Week Two

CHAPTER 13

FRIDAY MORNING

The phone rang while Addie was spreading orange marmalade on her toast. Flash looked up from his water bowl.

"That's probably my invitation to go look at mug shots," she told him. "So much for getting any work done this morning." Let the phone ring? No, Detective Barker would call her at Auterio's or show up there. She pushed her chair back from the table and went to the phone.

"Hello?"

"Good morning, Miss Addie. I hope you slept well." The voice was male, the tone lighthearted.

"Who is this?"

"It's Joe Kearney, of course."

"Who?"

"Don't tell me you forgot our fateful meeting in the drugstore yesterday. I'd be sorely disappointed."

"Life is full of disappointments, Mr. Kearney. I have to go to work this morning. What is it you want?"

"Why to brighten up this cloudy day. No more, no less. I wondered if you'd have time today to meet me for a cup of coffee."

Selling something? A date? Ridiculous. "No, thank you. I have to work."

"Certainly. Would you join me for lunch, then?"

"I'm sorry, I'm otherwise engaged."

"Surely you get a wee bit of time to eat lunch."

What was he after? "As I said, I'm otherwise engaged."

"Do you mean engaged as in a romantic way then?"

"That's none of your business, Mr. Kearney."

"Indeed it's not, Miss Addie. So perhaps I can explain my business at dinner tonight?"

"Certainly not. Look, to be blunt, I don't go out with men I don't know. As a matter of fact, I don't go out with men at all. My engagement today is down at the police station. I have a son who's a policeman here. And he won't look favorably on anyone pestering me. Is that clear?"

"Yes, and what a relief it is," he said.

She eyed the receiver. "Relief?"

"Yes. Relief that you already know me from yesterday, that your son Robert can tell you I'm not a pest, not selling anything in my retirement, and most relieved that you have a son who's a policeman. That murder next door to you must have been very alarming."

The breath caught in her chest, put a croak in her voice. "What do you know about it?"

"Only what I saw on TV and read in the newspaper. How about if we do coffee tomorrow?"

"Please. Go away. And don't call again." She hung up before he could reply. "The nerve!" Just nerve, or something worse? She'd have to ask Robert about this man – and tell George.

The phone rang, louder than before. She snatched it up. "I told you not to call again," she snapped.

"Aunt Addie?" said a female voice. "It's Leslie."

"Oh, I'm sorry. I thought you were someone else."

"Clearly. Are you alright?"

"Yes." How could she explain? "You know these telemarketers bother me day and night."

"I know. You ought to get on the no-call list."

"Yes, definitely." Whatever Joe Kearney's business was, she wanted no part of it. "I'm sorry I had to leave so abruptly the other day. But the funeral and luncheon were done very tastefully."

"Thank you. You're feeling better?"

"Much better."

"Good. I was worried. I wonder if I can come over to talk with you later this morning."

She glanced at the wall clock. "I'm sorry. I need to work today. I took Wednesday off for the funeral, so I have to get out some checks. And this afternoon I have to go to the police station."

"The police station?"

"You wouldn't believe what happened here last night. A man showed up at my back door and asked for keys to your father's house."

"Keys? You have keys?"

"Your mother gave them to me when she was sick, then later when I tried to return them, your father told me to keep them because he was living alone. I'm sorry, I should have brought them back to you the other day."

"It's best you keep them while the house is empty. You didn't give them to that man, did you?"

"Of course not."

"Any idea who he was?"

"No. But that's why I need to go to the police station. Detective Barker is going to show me photos to see if I can recognize the man."

"I hope you do. He may be connected to my father's murder. Are you safe enough at home?"

"I don't see why not. I don't have anything anybody would want."

"I suppose that's good. But maybe you should consider putting in a burglar alarm."

"Bella suggested that, too. But I'm okay. I call George when scary things happen. He responds a lot faster than any alarm company would."

"It must be great to have that kind of son. What say we get together sometime soon, alright?"

"Certainly. Do you want to arrange something now?"

"No, unfortunately I have to go day by day managing these properties. I have to show empty condos on weekends and I never know what the tenants or a super will consider an emergency on any day of the week. I'll give you a call next chance I can."

"Okay. I promise I won't snap at you like I did when I answered this time."

"No problem. Let me know if you come up with anything at the police station, okay?"

"I will. I want your father's murderer found as much as you do."

"I'm sure you do, Aunt Addie. I'm sure you do. Bye now."

* * *

"I'm afraid I can't do it," Addie told Barker. She pushed away the mouse. "I don't think I saw him clearly enough to distinguish his features." After an hour in the detective's small office, she was sure she couldn't identify Steven Mars, no matter how many computer files she looked through. She was equally certain her clothing and hair now reeked of stale cigarette smoke.

On the other side of the desk, Barker looked up from his magazine. "Please finish those out," he said. "We need to cover all the possibilities."

We? She was the one doing the work. He'd sat alongside her while she looked through the first two files, but then he'd retreated to his swivel chair and pulled out a copy of BirdTalk magazine. Maybe he talked to birds better than to people.

She glanced at the picture frame that faced Barker. A photo of his wife, his family? "I spoke with your Aunt Rona at Herbert's funeral."

He looked up from his magazine. "So?"

"Did she tell you who had an interest in purchasing Herbert's land?"

"She told you?"

"We've known each other since high school." And never liked each other, she thought. "Do you think the Woodland Trust property had something to do with Herbert's murder?"

"You have any reason to believe the land was involved?"

"No. I just find it strange that Herbert was willing to sell the land rather than keeping it as a

Trust. I'm not surprised Cletis was interested in it because he grew up here. But a Chinese spiritual retreat in Millbrook? Doesn't that seem strange to you?"

"No stranger than all the Japanese and Korean cars being made down south. My aunt said there are over 50 spiritual retreats spread out from Cape Cod to the Berkshires. Why is it strange that a bunch of Falun Gong or Buddhists or Tai-Chi nuts want their own place?"

"It's just hard for me to believe Herbert was killed for what he had in the house. Are you going to investigate that Chinese group?"

"I'm looking into it. But people get murdered for a pair of sneakers these days. And some perps just kill for fun. So how about finishing the pictures."

Reluctantly, she opened the next file and scrolled down the first page of sullen male faces. "Somehow I doubt the man who came to my door is a career criminal."

He didn't bother to look up. "You never know. Maybe we'll get lucky."

She'd be lucky to get clean. She'd have to return to Auterio's smelling like an ashtray. "We can't count on luck. Perry Mason never depended on it."

He frowned and stopped reading. "Who's Perry Mason?"

Chowderhead! thought Addie. No, she was being too hard on him. Not everyone read mysteries or watched television. "A lawyer for the defense."

"Those guys don't need luck." He offered a waggish smile. "Most of the time, they just lie."

"Do they? Well, live and learn. By the way, speaking of lawyers, how did the reading of Herbert's will go?"

Barker straightened up in his chair. "How did you know I was there?"

"Larry – young Dr. Elwood – told me you were going to be." Should she tell a white lie? Why not? She'd just been told Perry Mason lied. "Larry was worried they'd end up fighting."

"He had good reason to worry," said Barker.

"Gloria didn't get anything, then."

He tapped his fingers against the edge of the desk. "I can't give you any specifics." Again, the waggish smile. "On the other hand, I can't say you're wrong."

"Did you learn anything helpful to the case?"

"You sure do like to ask questions."

"Can anyone learn without them?" She managed to smile. "I'm sorry, I'm afraid that's another question. You must think I'm a nosy lady."

"No, that's okay. I see where George gets his curiosity from." He placed the magazine on his desk. "What was your question?"

No, she thought, he knew what she was asking. Okay, no specifics. "Hypothetically speaking, does the reading of a particular will add to your knowledge of a case?"

He looked away as if thinking, then turned back. His expression was serious. "Let's say that a will could always introduce a motive for murder."

"By the one left out of it?"

"What would she have to gain by the death?" he asked.

"Revenge?"

"Probably not in a hypothetical case where the person left out didn't know she was odd-one-out again until the will was read. Anyway, that's last week's dirty laundry. It may stink but it's not lethal. I'm keeping my eye on the prize – the real murderer."

"Raymond Miggens, I suppose."

His head inched upward, his eyes seemed to bore into her. "Who told you that?"

"Raymond did."

Barker looked incredulous. "He told you he did it?"

"No, he told me you thought he did. He denied it to me."

"What does George think?"

"Why don't you ask him? George never talks to me about his work." No, no twinge of conscience about that one. Scary how lying came easier the more one did it. "What about Steven Mars?"

Barker shrugged. "We've run his name through the National Crime Index files. Either the name is phony or he's not been in trouble with the police."

"So where will you look?"

"I tried all the computerized phone listings, and an Advanced People Search site off of Google – you know what Google is?"

"I was one of the original stockholders." She saw his eyes widen. "No, I'm only teasing. Anyway you tried Google and – "

"I struck out. Over two million references. The People Search site was more manageable. Two in Massachusetts, one in Rhode Island, none in New Hampshire or Vermont. I wasted most of my morning calling them and the people they told me they were with yesterday. All three had iron-clad alibis."

"So how will you find him?"

"I'm not. I'm the only detective here. I don't have time for that."

"You're giving up?" How could he? Could he be in cahoots with Steven Mars?

"No. It's just more practical to let Mr. Mars find you again. Then you'll call 911, or George."

"Wonderful. But what if he catches me when I'm out gardening? Or what if he doesn't come back and we never find out what he knows?"

"You have a better suggestion?"

She leaned back in her chair. "You'd really like to know what I think?"

"Why not? Sometimes good ideas come from concerned citizens like you."

"If I were doing the search, I'd start with veterinarians and animal control officers."

"Why is that?"

"Because Flash let him hold him so easily."

"I see." His smile didn't soften his sarcasm. "Nobody else could pick up your cat."

She squeezed her fingers tight. "Not without getting bitten. If you don't believe me, ask any of my children."

"What would that prove? My children agree with me so long as their mother's not around."

"I'm not here to prove anything. You asked me where I'd start. I told you."

Barker's smile was apologetic. "Look, I didn't mean to hurt your feelings. And I don't want to ignore any leads. But I have too much on my plate to visit all the vets in central Massachusetts. What am I going to do, say 'Excuse me, doctor, are you Steven Mars?'"

She bit her lip. He did have a point. "I suppose that wouldn't work. Unless I could go with you. I'd certainly recognize his voice."

"It would take too much time and effort. And for what? As far as we know, the man's committed no crime. I have to focus on the real investigation." He pointed at the computer. "So, please, will you finish up?"

"Yes. But I don't think it's going to help."

"Please look. You never know."

"Yes." She took hold of the mouse. "You're right. If we don't look, we may never know."

CHAPTER 14

Friday Afternoon

As soon as she opened her front door, she heard the muffled yowls and thumps. "Flash!" She dropped the day's mail on the threshold and was inside listening for the direction of his howls before her eyes took in the chaos in her living room. Lamps, chairs and end-tables were overturned, the contents of drawers were strewn on the floor among couch pillows and sheet music from the open piano bench. "Oh, my God." Flash's screech and another thump snapped her into a frantic run down the hall, through the vandalized kitchen and into the mud room. The week's dirty clothes were scattered everywhere. From inside the dryer, Flash shrieked as he hurled himself against the metal. She opened the dryer door expecting him to leap out, but his cries became louder, his contortions wilder.

"Flash, stop!" she yelled as she kneeled down to extract him, then saw a rear toe caught in one of the small holes. Damn! "Shh, I'll get you out." She reached in toward the squirming body, jerked back as sharp nails raked the back of her hand. "Ow!" She plunged her arm deeper into the machine and grasped the trapped leg. "Easy, now." Flash yowled close to her ear. She lifted and moved the leg gently side to side but met resistance, so she tried a back and forth motion and the foot popped free, toenails ragged and bloody. With a hoarse cry, Flash sprang forward, barely missing her face as she recoiled, and he raced away. Addie pulled herself shakily upright against the drier and looked at the blood welling up from the gouges on her hand. "You'll live," she muttered. She took a clean rag from the laundry shelf and pressed it against the wound.

Kicking aside the dirty clothes, she headed for the kitchen sink. "Oh, God." The kitchen looked as if a horde of vindictive teenagers had rampaged through her drawers and cabinets, throwing their contents to the floor. Even the refrigerator and the stove had been pushed away from the wall. Her mother's china! Tears rolled down her face as she angrily kicked over a stepstool to rid it of the fragments. No, not now. She needed to wash her wounded hand, then she needed to call George, take off her coat and attend to Flash. There'd be lots of time to grieve later.

* * *

She sat in her rocking chair, one arm wrapped firmly around Flash's restless body, the other gently pressing a washcloth to his injured paw, trying to ignore the noise and chaos that had replaced the security and order of her home. She couldn't avoid hearing the technicians tramping upstairs and down to the basement, calling out as they searched for fingerprints and other clues. She focused on keeping Flash calm and George in view. She hadn't seen George's features so grimly set since the day he realized his father had abandoned them. Reassuring George that she was okay and that her wound was from a panicked Flash and not from the vandals had softened his expression only momentarily. But he'd seen through to her fear and she worried what he might do to the people who'd caused it.

"I'm sorry they hurt your cat," said Barker, approaching like a bear on its hind legs, uncertain where to put his paws.

"Now will you look for Steven Mars?"

Barker shrugged. "Did you go into the upstairs bathroom?"

"Is someone dead in there?" She saw George stepping over the clutter to get to her.

"No, no," said George. "Nothing like that."

"They used your lipstick to write on the mirror," said Barker. "They drew a picture – the open jaw and fangs of a snake. Does 'Los Reyes Víboras' mean anything to you?"

"It sounds like Spanish."

"It is. Never heard the name before?"

"No. Why would someone leave me a message in Spanish?"

"It means 'The Viper Kings,'" said George. "It's a gang out of Lowell. At least that's one of their cities."

"But why would they come here and wreck my house?"

"That's what we need to know," said Barker. "You have any ideas?"

"Not about that. Do you?"

Barker frowned. "Your neighbor's laptop was found up in Lowell in the apartment of one Pedro Serrano, presumably a member of the Viper Kings. Pedro is still in jail, but some of his friends may have visited your house today. Perhaps a warning of sorts."

"I've never laid eyes on Pedro Serrano." She'd only asked Marty to look into his background – and

Barker's for that matter. "And I never heard a sound the night of Herbert's murder. What would they be warning me about?"

"I wish I knew," said Barker.

"Did Elwood ever give you anything to keep for him?" asked George. "A letter, a package, a safe deposit or locker key?"

"Only his house keys. That Steven Mars person wanted the keys last night. Maybe he wrote the name on the mirror to divert suspicion to that gang."

"Which may be why your TV, VCR and microwave are still sitting pretty," said George.

"Where do you keep Elwood's keys?" asked Barker.

"They should be in the drawer next to the stove. They're on a ring with a green plastic tag."

As the detective moved away, George stepped closer and put a hand on her shoulder. "You and Flash holding up?"

"I'm furious that someone would come in here and hurt my cat. I can forgive them for trashing the place and breaking my mother's china, but not for torturing Flash like that."

"Has he stopped bleeding?"

Flash squirmed as she gently separated the damp cloth from his paw. "Yes. But there's still swelling around those toes. And I know he hates ice. How did these people get in?"

"Broke the window on the back door. Same M.O. as with Herbert. Lucky you weren't home."

"No, I think not. If they wanted to kill me, they would've waited until dark. They wanted to do this when I was out."

With a gloved hand, Barker slid her white garbage pail out from under the sink. "Did anyone know for sure you were going to be out this afternoon?" He lifted the cover and peered in.

"My friend Bella." And you, she thought. No, he wouldn't make extra work for himself.

"Bella Auterio?"

"She was at the store with me all day, and she wouldn't – " The telephone calls! "Two other people knew. They called me this morning."

"Who?" asked George.

"Leslie Elwood, and a man I met in Robert's store yesterday. His name is Joe Kearney. He invited me out for coffee. I said no, but then he asked about lunch, then dinner, then tomorrow. He was terribly persistent."

"Was he selling something?" Barker had squatted and was searching through debris on the floor by the stove.

"No, he was clear about that."

"Maybe he likes you," said George.

Addie grimaced. "Don't be absurd. I'm too old and too smart to start dating."

"I'll check him out, anyway. See if he's a vandal, a murderer – " George offered a small smile. "– or a suitable beau."

She frowned. "This is hardly the time for that." Oh, crumb. She was turning into a biddy.

"Are these Dr. Elwood's keys?" said Barker, holding them up in a gloved hand as he high-stepped over the clutter.

"Yes. Where were they?"

"On the floor with a lot of other junk – sorry, I mean kitchen stuff."

"You'd think he would've seen the keys as he dumped the drawer out," said Addie.

George looked at the mess on the floor. "Whoever did this wasn't interested in keys. They trashed the whole first floor and the basement. Who looks for house keys in a basement?"

"There goes your Steven Mars theory," said Barker.

Was he that stupid? "Not if Steven Mars wanted something else, and asked for the keys as an excuse. Are you going to find him, Detective?"

"I'll find him. But first things first. I think I have to have another talk with Pedro Serrano and his boyfriend across the street."

"You think Ray Miggins did this?" asked George.

"Maybe. Or maybe he knows who did," said Barker. "Or why it was done."

The man has a one-track mind, thought Addie. "I don't believe Raymond would be part of something like this."

"Nobody ever believes their neighbor is capable of awful crimes," said the detective. "But the fact is that every murderer or rapist has unsuspecting neighbors. Maybe we should brand scarlet letters on people's foreheads."

He'd read *The Scarlet Letter*? Not surprising he'd missed the point of it. "Yes," she said, "M for murderer, R for rapist, B for bigot and U for uncaring. Everyone in the world could wear their own letter. What would yours be, Detective?"

"Ma!"

She saw the shock on George's face, but Barker only looked as if he was confronting a difficult problem on an algebra test.

"Hmm." The tension left his face. "I think I'd choose S for steady. There are always smarter guys and flashier guys coming up and going down, sometimes even running rings around me. But I'm like that old Timex ad – I can take a lickin', but I keep on tickin.' It does take time, Mrs. Carter, but most folks learn they can rely on me."

CHAPTER 15

Wednesday Afternoon

"What do you want, Addie?" From behind the barely opened door of her split-level home, Cordelia Miggens squinted against an invasion of afternoon sunlight.

Snug in her parka, Addie cradled the pan of lasagna against her chest and leaned sideways to get a better look inside. Delia was still in her nightgown. Her feet were bare. "Sorry if I wore out your doorbell, but you and Raymond haven't answered my telephone messages, so I got worried." She's thin as a rail, thought Addie. Probably hasn't eaten all day.

"I was going to call back. I just haven't been feeling well."

"I'm sorry about that. I was making lasagna, so I thought I'd make extra for you and Raymond." Addie offered up the pan.

Delia didn't move. "Thanks, but I haven't had much of an appetite, lately. And Ray mostly eats out. Give it to your church's meal program."

"Raymond might like it. Why don't you freeze it, then you both can defrost a piece whenever you do get hungry."

"Hungry?" Delia seemed puzzled by the word. Vertical creases formed between her shaggy eyebrows. Her gray hair looked wild, her eyes terribly sad.

"If you let me in, I can cut it into separate portions and help you wrap them for the freezer. That way, I can take my pan home so you don't have to clean it."

"I'm really not up to company today." Delia's gaze fell. "And my house isn't – you know."

Addie put a foot on the threshold. "My house was even more of a shambles. Joanne, Bess and I spent all weekend putting it together."

"It must've been terrible. I saw the flashing lights, the police cruisers – two Fridays in a row, and bad things come in threes." Delia wrapped her arms across her chest. Her fingers burrowed into the sleeves of her nightgown. "I was worried the murderer had killed you, too. Or Raymond. I always worry about him. The police gave him a hard time until his boss swore he was there all day. I just couldn't get myself to call you. Or do anything. I'm sorry."

"You needn't apologize. After my husband Dave ran out on me, I was paralyzed, too. I didn't want to see anyone or do anything for a long, long time."

Delia looked up. Her eyes welled with tears. "Raymond said he's going to leave me."

"Oh, Delia. I know he loves you. Young men often say things in anger they don't really mean. Why don't you at least let me put this heavy pan down in the kitchen."

"I'm sorry." Delia backed away from the door.

Addie entered the living room. She wrinkled her nose at the mixture of odors from spoiled food and neglected bodies. Magazines, comic books and soiled dishes competed for space with compact discs and dusty knickknacks. Across from an old sofa, two sagging chairs flanked a video game console.

"I haven't felt up to it," said Delia.

The kitchen was even worse. The few surfaces visible under the multitude of beer cans, fast food boxes and unwashed dishes were as filthy as the linoleum floor. Addie looked about for a place to put the lasagna. How could Raymond let it get this bad? Delia obviously needed a doctor, but that wouldn't help this mess. The Board of Health? No, that would alienate both Delia and Raymond, and they might be forced out of their house.

"Why don't you clear enough space on the table so I can put the lasagna down."

Delia looked around the kitchen as if lost, a stranger in her own home. Addie cleared her throat. "Delia?"

"Oh – where should I put the dishes?"

"For now, over there, on the stove. We'll get to things a little at a time."

It took Delia two trips to clear enough space for the lasagna pan. Addie set it down with a sigh, took off her parka and hung it on the back of a chair. "Do you have a radio in here?"

"Over there." Delia pointed to a mound of plastic bags on a counter.

"Could you put on some music?" Addie rolled up her sleeves. "And find a dish towel. I'll need your help."

* * *

After twenty minutes of standing at the sink washing pots and dishes, Addie's back was aching. She turned off both taps, looked in vain for paper towels, then shook both hands over the sink. "Do you have a small stool I could rest a foot on?"

Delia clutched her striped dishtowel as if it offered protection. "I – I don't think so."

"What about a telephone book?"

Delia seemed to shrink under the weight of another question. "You want to call someone?"

A doctor, thought Addie. Have to find out who her doctor is. "No. I want to put the book under one foot to take the pressure off my back."

"You should go home and lie down if it's hurting." Delia put two fingers to her eyelid to stop it from twitching. "I should go back to bed, too."

"It's just pain. I won't die from it. But I do need to see a doctor. Who do you use?"

"I haven't gone in a long time."

"That's not good, either. Maybe a doctor could help you with your depression."

"I'm okay."

And I'm the Queen of England. Addie reached out and gently touched the dishtowel Delia was holding. "May I share this for a minute?" Delia reluctantly let it go. Addie used it to dry her hands. "Which doctor did you used to see?"

"Dr. Elwood. Not the one across the street that died – the other one."

Good. They shared the same doctor. "I know – Larry Elwood. The way Herbert died was very upsetting." Addie offered the towel back.

Delia made no move to accept it. "Not really. We didn't like him. He ruined Raymond's business. And dying isn't so bad. It stops the pain."

Oh crumb. "You think a lot about dying?"

"Maybe Dr. Elwood was the lucky one."

"Lucky?" Addie dropped the towel on the pile of clean dishes and took Delia's hands in her own. "Delia, have you been thinking about killing yourself?"

Delia sighed, then stood mute.

"Delia…"

"I told Ray I wouldn't do it as long as he stays with me."

She gave Delia's hands a sympathetic squeeze. "What makes you worry he'll leave you?"

"He said he would. And he goes out a lot. He thinks I don't know because he goes out after I'm in bed. But I hear his car start. Then I wait up until I hear him come in."

"Why not ask him where he's been?"

Delia shook her head. "He lies. He says he goes out for a pack of cigarettes, or to meet a friend at a bar. But he's out for hours. Every Tuesday, Thursday and Saturday night."

"Young men do go out. He's not a child any more."

"He always went out Friday and Saturday nights. I don't mind that. But he's out every Tuesday and Thursday night, too."

"Raymond told me he was in bed fast asleep the Thursday night Herbert got murdered."

Delia's eyelid twitched.

"That's true, isn't it?" said Addie.

"I don't remember."

"That's what he told me. That's what he told the police. Didn't they ask you about that?"

"I said he didn't go out. I said I heard him snoring."

"Is that true?"

Delia bit her lip.

"Delia?"

"With those police cars outside, that big detective in here? What would you say for your son?"

WEEK THREE

CHAPTER 16

FRIDAY NIGHT

Bess came up the stairs and closed the basement door behind her, but the family band's rendition of *Back in the USA* beat against Addie's kitchen floor and blasted through the holes cut for water and steam pipes. "So, what's up?"

Addie turned on the tap and started filling the coffee pot with water. "How do you mean?"

"C'mon. You almost always do the coffee yourself. You wouldn't've asked me to help unless you wanted to talk."

"True enough." Addie glanced at her daughter. In jeans and a UConn sweatshirt, with her auburn hair drawn back in a ponytail, Bess looked more like a grad student than a bank manager. "But I do appreciate your help." Addie turned off the water. "Would you get out the coffee? There's a can in the freezer from last time."

"What do you want to talk with me about?" Bess opened the freezer. "There's hardly anything else in here. You expecting a power outage?"

"Cletis Adams."

"I'm really not in the mood for serious. Music night's supposed to be a fun evening."

"There are more important things. Your mood's been okay until I just spoiled it?"

Bess took off the plastic lid and sniffed the coffee. "It smells okay."

"Bess?"

"Hey, I'm fine. I take my little pills and life is bearable again – sometimes even enjoyable."

Addie put the pot on the counter. "I'm glad." Glad that it was now, not then, with both of them sinking in the quicksand of Bess' teenage tantrums and drug abuse before her depression was recognized. Thank God their love survived the battles to keep Bess in treatment, the relapses, and her own despair as Bess abased herself in promiscuity and then married another addict.

"Why don't you count out the scoops," said Addie. "You know how strong you like it." Sure, Bess was stronger and wiser now, but she was still no match for Cletis Adams. "Has Cletis visited you at the bank since the funeral?"

"Yes. I was going to tell you about that."

"Oh?" She'd heard those same words from her mother whenever an antique dealer carted away another piece of Grandfather Chandler's furniture or a pet was given away without warning. "Were you going to tell me before or after you made your decision?"

"Before." Bess covered the coffee pot and plugged the cord in. She turned back to Addie. "How do you know he made me an offer?"

"Cletis was always a fast worker. In high school, he would walk out of forty-five minute tests ten to fifteen minutes before the next person finished."

"That much faster?"

"Bella timed him. She was in awe of Cletis."

"Were you?"

"Will you put this conversation in one of those secret Swiss bank accounts?"

"Done. Those guys torturing music downstairs will never get me to give up your account."

Addie opened her mouth, closed it, tried to swallow away a bad taste.

"So?" asked Bess softly.

"I was in love with Cletis."

Bess's mouth popped open. "You were?" Bess clapped her hands with delight. "Amazing!"

"What? That I was in love?"

"No, that you told me. Wait a minute!" She walked to the basement door and opened it. "Hey, down there!" she shouted.

The music stuttered to a stop. Addie stiffened. She felt betrayed, angry enough to scream.

"Anybody besides Ma want tea?" Bess yelled.

There were a few moments of consultation below, then Joanne's voice floated up. "One tea, one hot chocolate, and three decafs."

"Okay." Bess closed the door, turned back to Addie and winked. "That's for keeping us in the dark all these years. We Swiss can really play dirty."

Addie tried to smile. "I see."

"Only half the picture." Bess opened the refrigerator. "Should I take out the baked apples?"

"Yes. What do you mean, 'half the picture'?"

Bess extracted a large Pyrex dish of apples. "Cletis told me his side the day before yesterday."

"He what?" Addie eased herself onto a chair.

Bess followed her to the table and set the dish down. "Really, Ma, it's not like Joanne and I hadn't guessed you were star-crossed lovers or something. I mean the way you reacted every time his name came up. We knew it wasn't just because he was a greedy developer."

"What did he say to you? And for God's sake, why now?"

"Because he offered me a job as a project controller and knew you'd hit the roof. He wanted me to evaluate it on its merits, not on the basis of your history. Do you have hot chocolate?"

"My history?" Addie shook her head. Hot chocolate? Bess was acting like she was discussing the Fed's interest rates.

"I mean the history between you two," said Bess. "And Cletis didn't say that you loved him. He said he loved you, but he didn't want to speak for you." She put the teapot on the stove and came to the table to sit down. "So tell me – what happened?"

"It's not anything special." Addie took a napkin, coughed into it, then crumpled it in her hand. "We both grew up in Millbrook. Cletis had his family troubles, I had mine. His parents had divorced when he was four – maybe five. He lived over on Pine Street with his mother. She was a well-meaning woman, a hard worker, but she wasn't what you'd call a warm person. She felt life had been terribly unkind to her and expected the world to either apologize or make her lot easier. She was a waitress over at Captain's Catch on route 111. It's now Gianetti's."

"Yeah, I know."

Addie took a deep breath. If only Cletis had stayed away from Bess, all this wouldn't be necessary. "Cletis' father was a chauffeur for a wealthy family in Carlisle and lived there in an apartment over the garage. He only saw Cletis when that family was away. The truth is that Cletis never really felt wanted by either one of his parents. So we were thrown together by being bright in school, and by not really trusting our parents' intentions or their love. Which of course made us need love and family all the more. So we would talk about everyday experiences, our ideas, our frustrations, our hopes. And we both loved the outdoors. Cletis loved hiking, to walk the land, and I loved to run." Addie heard the family band launch into *Don't Be Cruel*. "But it was much more than sharing the countryside. We knew where the other was coming from and escaping to. It's not surprising that we fell in love. The surprise was that it lasted all the way through high school, even with him becoming captain of the football team."

"I'm sure you were his best catch," said Bess.

"I think his buddies wondered what he saw in me. I wasn't the prettiest face in our class, and I certainly wasn't cut out to be Miss Congeniality."

"So the jocks thought it was sex?"

"Isn't that where they're at, at that age?"

"Did you and he – ?"

"What did Cletis say?"

"I didn't ask and he didn't tell."

Addie offered a tentative smile. "Now I see the value of that policy."

"Hey, you always told us kids we could talk about anything with you. If I'm to decide about this offer, I want to know all the facts."

Not a chance, thought Addie. "My sex life, then and now, is not relevant."

"Now?"

"Now and forever." She mimed locking her lips and throwing away the key, but she remembered the excitement she'd felt with Cletis. Knowing she was loved made her feel whole, proved her stepfather wrong, freed her to be herself.

"The least you can do is tell me how you two broke up," said Bess.

The least? "You of all people should realize how painful the past can be." Addie saw anger flash in her daughter's eyes, the ghost of adolescent resentment devouring Bess' face, then a silent struggle for facial equilibrium, for self-control. How stupid to bring up Bess' past. Tit-for-tat never helped anyone see anything.

Bess seemed to draw in on herself. "Believe me, I feel the pain every time I think about the stuff I did. But I've had therapist after therapist tell me to talk about it, that acceptance from others breeds acceptance from oneself. I don't know if it's done you harm keeping your stuff locked up inside, but it certainly hasn't done you any good, Ma."

"That's for me to decide. You asked how we broke up? Cletis got a scholarship to Harvard, and I went to UMass. He met girls at Radcliffe who were brighter, prettier, more sophisticated, wealthier. Wealth was always Cletis' prime mover. A couple of times, when that millionaire family was in Europe, Cletis' father took him to their summer mansion in the Berkshires. Guess who owns it now?"

"Cletis."

"Yes, who's been married three times. He's probably had enough mistresses to fill a bordello."

Bess lifted her hands from her lap. "So if he's that kind of man, why aren't you glad you got rid of him years ago? Why are you still so angry with him?"

"I'm not angry with him. But I don't trust a word he says. I don't want him lying to you, humiliating you in any way."

"Hey, I'm a big girl, now. Believe me, I don't put any trust in princes. But it's more than just me. You positively seethe every time someone mentions his name. What happened?"

"Nothing remarkable. It was the first time I was truly in love with someone." It was much more than sex, she thought. It was intimacy. He was her companion, her counselor, her lover, her best friend. "All my hopes and dreams for the future were about us together. We talked about getting married after college, what kind of careers we might have, and how many children we wanted." She felt sadness welling up. She looked down at the tabletop, focusing on the gouge she'd accidentally made years ago, carving a pumpkin. "To feel all those – to feel everything in me slowly disintegrate as his calls became less frequent, as he kept making excuses why he couldn't come back to Millbrook, why I couldn't visit him, that was bad enough. He always had a reason why it couldn't work that weekend, maybe in a few weeks time, but oh how he loved me, oh how he missed seeing me." She ran a finger over the gouge. No polish had ever filled it in.

"But then he didn't come home for the Christmas break. A rich buddy had invited him to spend the month skiing out in Colorado, all expenses paid. Cletis said it was too good an opportunity to pass up." She swallowed hard. "I tried to tell myself that it really was a unique opportunity for him, that loving someone meant making some sacrifices for the good of one's partner. Still, it was – I remember I tore the Christmas card he sent to shreds. It was one of those Hallmark 'missing you at Christmas' things you'd send a cousin, signed 'Love, Cletis.' Not even 'I Love You.' I threw the little box he sent into a drawer without unwrapping it. I told myself I'd open it the next time I saw him."

"And did you?"

Addie was suddenly aware of the silence. She turned her head to the basement door. Were they on their way upstairs?

"Did you?" asked Bess.

"What?"

"Did you open the box Cletis sent you?"

"Yes. He came back for spring break for a few days, before going off with another friend to Florida. Cletis could always charm his way into getting what he wanted."

"What was in the box?"

"A gold locket. I only put it on that one time. It was a lie."

"The locket?"

"Yes. He'd had it engraved on the back. It said 'I love you, Cletis.'"

Bess shrugged. "Maybe he did."

"I'm sure in his own mind he did. But not in the way we'd been in love, or at least the way I'd thought we'd been in love." Addie grimaced. "Even so, I could have handled losing him, tough as it was, but it was the way he – humiliated me – that's what stuck in my craw."

"Humiliated you?"

"Right after my mother died. I'd called Cletis soon after she had her stroke, but he wasn't at school. I left a message with his roommate. I didn't know what else to do. I didn't have any brothers or sisters, and my stepfather was determined to stay drunk." So drunk, she recalled, she'd had to help him button his shirt and pants before the funeral. "I didn't see or hear from Cletis until the day of the funeral. After it was almost over. He'd gotten in touch with Bella the night before, said something about being away, not getting the message, he couldn't get through to me because my phone was always tied up. So he finally showed up at Rendell's and pretended to be oh so sorry, oh so comforting – "

"Pretended?"

"Pretended. Because after the funeral, the neighbors had fixed a snack here for the mourners. Cletis didn't want to come, but I was at such a loss, I begged him to. It was one of the few times in my life I begged anyone for anything."

"But he didn't come?"

"No, he – " She raised her fingers to form invisible quotation marks. " – dropped in. But after twenty minutes or so, a young woman shows up at the door and asks for him, and someone – I don't know who – someone let her in. And she comes into the kitchen where Cletis and Bella and some of my other friends are standing – this blonde china doll in a blue traveling suit with a diamond lapel pin in the shape of a butterfly – and she goes right up to Cletis and says, 'You've certainly led me a merry chase. Now we're going to be late.' And he turns a little red and he introduces Eleanor, and says she drove him down from the Berkshires, and they had to get back there, and he starts to excuse himself. But people look at me, and Eleanor says 'you must be Addie. I'm sorry for your loss. I know you mean a lot to Cletis, and I'm sorry to have to drag him away. But my parents need us back tonight.' And Cletis calls out 'Ellie!' trying to stop her, but she says, 'They have some important friends coming for dinner.' And Bella says 'Cletis has some important friends here.' Then Eleanor says, 'Yes, but we're announcing our engagement to them.' And she puts out her hand to show us her ring."

"What a dreadful bitch! What did you say to her?"

"I wish I had said something. I was in shock. I really don't remember it after that. Bella told me later the room went dead silent, so finally she said 'Congratulations, I'm sure you two deserve each other.' Bella said I turned to Cletis like a zombie and said 'Good-bye Cletis,' then I walked upstairs to my bedroom."

"Oh, Ma." Bess covered Addie's hand with her own.

Addie placed her other hand on top and squeezed gently. "That's more than fifty years ago. I just felt I needed to warn you about Cletis."

"But it still hurts," said Bess.

Addie sighed. "It doesn't matter. I'm a big girl, now."

CHAPTER 17

SATURDAY AFTERNOON

"Not so tight – we don't want to choke the life out of it," said Addie, embracing the wrapped rhododendron so that Marty could secure the sacking with gardening twine. She wrinkled her nose at the odor of peat moss which emanated from the burlap.

On the other side of the large bush, Marty eased the tension in the twine. "This okay?"

"That's good." Yes, good to be tucking her plants in for the winter. Sure, it was disappointing Marty'd been unable to flesh out Pedro Serrano's connection to the Viper Kings, but it was reassuring that nothing he'd uncovered about Detective Barker suggested he was a dirty cop. She'd tell Barker that Raymond wasn't at home the night of the murder as soon as her church friends began helping Delia. Arresting Raymond would be a mistake. He wasn't a killer, and he wouldn't have trashed her house. No way that Herbert's children would've done that, either. Who did that leave? Steven Mars?

"That'll hold the top," Marty said. "We need another tie for the middle."

She wiped her hands on her overalls, turned back toward her house and retrieved the ball of twine and scissors from the deck of the front porch. "I've got it."

Brushing dirt from his UMass sweatshirt, Marty came around the bush and met her half-way. "That burlap is filthy."

"It's from last year." She gave him the ball of twine, but held the loose end. He started back, unwinding twine as he went. Then he stopped. "You've got a visitor."

Addie poked her head out from behind the bush. The street was still lined with parked cars owned by people trying to get a memento or a bargain at the Elwood's estate sale next door. Apparently Gloria was not one of them. Dressed in a beige turtleneck and neatly pressed slacks, she was striding up Addie's driveway like a woman on a mission.

Addie draped the loose end of twine on the bush and stepped around it to hand Marty the scissors. "I'll be right back. Stay here."

"Why?"

"No reporters allowed." She walked across her lawn to meet Gloria.

"Hi," said Gloria. Her hair was a golden cap above a tight face and thin eyebrows.

She's gloomy as a damp winter's day, thought Addie. "You didn't go to the estate sale?"

"I dropped in. It's a zoo. My darling protective April was right, there's nothing in that house that matters any more. All I really wanted was my mother's wedding ring, and my dear old dad left it to Cheryl in the will. She's to give it to one of her daughters, someday." Her facial muscles tightened as she blinked back tears. "I do have a few family pictures I liberated after Mom died. My father didn't want me to have anything."

"He left you out of his will entirely?"

"No surprise there." Gloria snorted. "He left me a dollar to show he didn't forget me."

Addie's gaze darted away and back. "I'm very sorry. That was mean." Had she misremembered their previous talk? Hadn't Gloria hoped Herbert would keep his word about including her? One dollar and no wedding ring. "It must've felt like a slap in the face you didn't deserve."

Gloria's head jerked as if dodging sympathy. "Well, that's life." She indicated Herbert's house with her thumb. "How come you didn't go?"

"Leslie called to invite me, but there's nothing there now I would want."

"Nothing there can replace my mother, that's for sure. Listen, you told George I thought Leslie or Larry killed them?" It was less a question than an accusation.

Addie stiffened. Had she misunderstood Gloria's intent? "Yes, wasn't that what you wanted?"

"I just wanted proof that's what happened – or didn't happen. Believe me, I don't want to go the rest of my life thinking my brother or sister is a murderer. I shared my suspicions with you because you know all of us. I thought maybe you'd help me see things in a different light. Or maybe you saw something the night of the murder that the police told you not to talk about."

Addie rubbed her forehead. "I'm sorry I disappointed you on all counts." She tried not to let anger creep into her tone. "When I asked you what you wanted me to do with the information you shared, you told me to do what I thought best. I thought telling George was best."

"It's not George. I don't mind him knowing anything. It's Barker. All that oversized lump of – detective has done is to hassle me about where April and I were that night and how much I had it in for my father, and what I might gain by pointing my finger at Leslie and Larry."

"Did you really expect George to keep what you said from the detective managing the case?"

"He might've, had you told him it was important. He could've made his own inquiries, then talked to Barker once he had proof either way."

Addie grit her teeth. No sense arguing against romance-novel logic. "So Detective Barker has talked to Leslie and Larry?"

"You bet. With such candor, my dear siblings now have a better reason to disown me. That idiot asked them why I had accused them of murder."

"Oh dear."

"'Oh dear' is right. I'm going to end up without any family at all." Gloria's hazel eyes brimmed with tears again. "I know it's my own fault – I never should've shot my mouth off to you. But I was grieving, I was angry – and they always got so much more from my parents. I have lots of reasons, but that doesn't mean shit to Leslie and Larry. You're the only one who can help me out."

"Me?"

"Please, I need you to tell them you misunderstood what I said to you, or that George misinterpreted what you told him – like that game of telephone, where the message gets more and more distorted as it's passed down the line." Gloria's hands came up, palm facing palm. "I was worried that they *could* be blamed for the murder because they didn't answer their cell phones that night, not because I thought they actually did it."

What nerve! Or desperation. And how sad. "You expect me to lie for you?"

"I never expect much from people, but you've always been good to me." Gloria clasped her hands as if pleading, but her tone was slightly challenging. "I'm asking you to tell a white lie to save my relationship with my family. If not for my sake, then to honor my mother's wish that we be reunited as a family, such as it is."

Addie took a deep breath. Gloria was laying it on too thick. "I'm sorry – "

"There you are!" said a male voice. Both women looked toward the mouth of the driveway.

"Not now, Todd," Gloria called out, shaking her head. But her brother-in-law kept coming, his maroon tie swaying between the unbuttoned margins of his suit. "Todd, this is private."

Addie's muscles relaxed. A reasonable person and a change of subject were welcome. She glanced back toward her house, saw that Marty had finished wrapping the rhody and had moved to the flower bed around the red maple. Pretending to deadhead the marigolds, but clearly listening.

"Privacy is something we've had damn little of since you made us murder suspects," said Todd, coming to a full stop in front of Gloria. Dark glasses and a suntan didn't soften the anger in Todd's expression any more than it diminished his ski jump nose.

Addie stepped took a step back.

"I don't mean you, Mrs. Carter. I'm sure you did what you had to. And if Gloria would've talked to me in the house instead of bolting, I wouldn't be here bothering you at all."

"Thank you. If you don't mind, I'll go back to my gardening."

Gloria reached out with a hand that stopped well short of Addie. "No, please stay. I need a witness to what's said. Todd is Mr. Reasonable in public, but he can be pretty nasty one-on-one."

"Gloria likes telling tall tales that get other people in trouble," Todd said.

"I never liked refereeing these kinds of arguments between my children," said Addie, "and I certainly don't have to do it for you two." She turned away.

"Wait!" said Todd. "Please."

Oh crumb!

"I want you to witness that I'm telling Gloria quite civilly but firmly that I want her to stay away from my wife." He fixed his eyes on Gloria. "Leslie is very upset about the accusations you've made and all the fuss about the will. She wrote you a note saying she wants no further contact with you, and yet you keep trying to call her, and then you show up here trying to embarrass her in public."

"I wasn't trying to embarrass anyone. She won't take my calls. You'll read my notes, so there's no privacy there. What am I supposed to do?"

"Just leave us alone. Go enjoy your little lesbian wife. Have a great life or a miserable existence. I don't really care."

Gloria's face flushed, she thrust her jaw forward. "Well I do, you homophobic asshole." Her intensity compensated for the foot she gave away in height. "I care about my sister. I speak out about what I see, things that stand out, like bruises on my sister's face. That's who I am. If someone shows me I'm wrong, I apologize. But at least my tall tales, if that's what you want to call them, don't cause people to lose their shirts in risky investments. And I don't take my frustrations out on my wife." She turned to Addie, her face suddenly contrite. "I'm sorry, Aunt Addie. I'd better leave before I really lose my temper. I apologize for dragging you into this again. My family is a bloody mess."

The image of Herbert's battered head crashed through Addie's mind. A bloody mess, a bloody mess. Addie closed her eyes to repel dizziness, put a hand to her mouth to stifle a wave of nausea.

"Are you okay?" Gloria sounded frightened.

"See what you've done," said Todd. "Shall I call a doctor?"

Suddenly Marty had his arm around her shoulders. "You okay? You want to lie down?"

Addie took a deep breath, exhaled slowly and opened her eyes to three concerned faces. "I'll be fine, I'm okay. I had a flash of – a hot flash, that's all. I'd appreciate it if you two took your quarrel elsewhere."

Gloria nodded. "I'm really sorry." She looked at Marty. "Take care of her. She's one fine lady." She turned and headed down the driveway.

"I apologize, too," said Todd. "If I can be of any assistance, please let me know."

"We can handle it," said Marty. "You want to go back to the house, Granny?"

"I want to finish what we set out to do."

"Forgive me," said Todd, "but I don't want to leave accusations on the table that I haven't responded to."

"Accusations?" asked Marty. His arm tightened around her shoulders.

Little reporters have big ears and bigger ambitions, thought Addie. "Marty, we have gardening to do." He hesitated before removing his arm.

"I won't keep you but a minute," said Todd. "I just want you to know that I'm very careful and conservative in advising my clients, but no one can always get the stock market right. It's a risky business."

So is murder, thought Addie. "Thank you for clearing that up, Todd."

"As for that nasty bit about bruises on Leslie's face, Gloria's out to cause trouble. Leslie got up one night to go to the bathroom and walked smack into the door. That happened months ago."

"Then it hardly matters now," said Addie. "Consider the tabletop clear and have a more pleasant afternoon." She turned on her heel and walked toward the house, conscious of Marty following her. She stopped at the second rhody in front of the porch. "Has Mr. Reasonable left?" she asked without a backward glance.

"You mean Todd? Yes. He's headed back next door. What was all that about?"

She turned to watch Todd disappear into the Elwood house. "It was about guilt. I'm not at all sure who killed Herbert, but I think the murderer isn't the only one with reasons to feel guilty. Now please get the burlap – we still have a job to do."

CHAPTER 18

TUESDAY, 6:30 A.M.

The wind nipped at Addie's ears as she walked the short distance from her house to her Corolla. The frost on the car's windows glistened beneath the floodlight. As long as the roads stayed dry, it was no burden to open the store. The important thing was to have Carlo come out of this colonoscopy with a clean bill of health.

Addie deposited her purse on the passenger seat, started the engine and defroster, then retrieved her long-handled scraper from the floor. As she scraped and chipped ice from the windshield, her breath floated away like smoke.

She glimpsed headlights before she heard a car come up the street. Who this early? A dark sedan turned into her driveway and stopped behind her Corolla. The visitor cut his engine but not the headlights, then stepped out of the car.

What in the world did Cletis' stepson want with her? Michael Planchette was dressed in work boots, jeans and a plaid sweater-jacket. Only his driving gloves seemed a concession to the cold. She put the scraper down on the hood of her Corolla.

"Good morning, Michael."

"Good morning, Mrs. Carter." He brushed a wave of dark hair back from his forehead and approached with a good-natured smile. "It looks like Jack Frost is here to stay for a bit."

"Yes, he's an annoying guest." Like you are, when I want to get to work. "How have you been?"

"Real busy. Our New England crews are rushing to get foundations in before winter hits. That's why I'm here so early – my guys start at sunrise. We're also building some condos in Mexico and a big hotel on Vieques."

"Vieques?"

"An island off Puerto Rico."

"Sometimes I think how nice it would be to live in a warmer climate for the winter. Why this unexpected visit?"

"Cletis sent me. I don't mind the cold. And Cletis needs me to supervise things around here."

"I'm sure." She hadn't been the only one surprised when he'd returned to the area three years ago. Before he'd been packed off to boarding school, Michael had been in her younger son's English class at Millbrook High. According to Robert, Michael had made no secret of feeling trapped in the "boonies" with a bunch of "hicks." If he still thought that after twenty years away, he hadn't shown it on the few occasions he'd shopped in Auterio's.

"How have you been, Mrs. Carter?"

"Fine. But if you'll excuse me, I have to open up the store at seven."

"Let me help you, then." He stepped forward and held a gloved hand out for the scraper. "Here, give it to me. I'll get it done faster."

No, no way to refuse gracefully. "Thank you." She handed him the scraper and backed away. Perhaps Michael had outgrown the adolescent arrogance spawned by his doting mother and his stepfather's wealth.

"How is your wife?" Claire? Donna? Oh crumb. Her memory for names was becoming a black hole.

"Good, I suppose. Didn't you hear? We were divorced over a year ago." He started scraping the windshield. Shards of ice flew as he delivered short powerful thrusts.

"I'm sorry. I didn't know."

"That's okay. I'm poorer but a lot wiser. As for Gail, what with her soaps, eBay and a big alimony check each month, it's like she's died and gone to heaven." He glanced above the car to the dark Elwood house. "Terrible what happened there, isn't it."

"Yes, it was."

Michael walked around the front of the car, and held the scraper poised an inch above the passenger's side of the windshield. "You hear anything unusual that night?"

Gypsies playing tambourines, she thought. "No. I slept right through everything."

He turned his attention to scraping. The defroster was making his task easier.

"How'd you hear about what happened?" she asked.

"Cletis told me. He's why I'm over here."

She looked at him sharply. "Yes, so you said. But you haven't said why."

"Because of the land." He moved to get at the car's back window.

They'd better not try any tricks with that land. What a mistake, to let him help, surrender control. She stamped her feet to get blood moving. Michael finished the back window, then took a few seconds to clear the ones on the driver's side. "All done." He wore a pleased smile as he handed her the scraper.

"Now, you have a message for me?"

His smile disappeared. "Cletis asked me to tell you not to worry about anything."

"And in particular, about what?"

He dropped his gaze. "We're going to have a surveyor in the woods out back of your house today, and probably a geologist and a hydrologist out there later in the week."

"Look at me, Michael!"

He raised his eyes reluctantly. "I'm just the messenger, Mrs. Carter. Cletis said not to worry – no one's going to mess with your property or your view back there."

"That's very thoughtful of him. Why didn't he come tell me himself?"

"I asked him that. He said you'd probably shoot him."

"Tell him I probably will next time I see him."

Michael flashed his good-natured grin. "I'll tell him. I certainly will."

She tried to stay angry. "And tell him to bring a gun, because I don't own one."

"Maybe you should get one. Not for Cletis, but for your protection. I mean the murderer is still out there."

"I have a burglar alarm now, for whatever good that does." At least it reassured the children and got Bella and Carlo off her neck.

"Does George say the police have any idea who did it?"

"George never talks to me about police business. I'm always the last to know anything that goes on. Where are you living?"

"Down in Worcester. It's got a lot more stuff going on than here in the Valley."

"You were down there the night of the murder?"

"Yup. I have every Thursday night and every other weekend with Sally. Eight year-olds love princesses even more than us grown-up guys do, so I took her to a Disney movie at the Multiplex." He shook his head. "It really is awful about Dr. Elwood. I heard you found him because your cat dragged in his pipe."

"Yes."

"Strange cat."

She knew he expected something more but decided to remain silent. She was a bit surprised that he did, too. Maybe this visit was what he'd said, a messenger run. "Thanks for your help."

"No problem. Good seeing you again." He started toward his car.

She raised her voice. "Michael, how did it come about that CDA get the land back there? I mean I assume that it's not you and Cletis personally, that it's CDA."

He turned back. "It's the company. Cletis doesn't touch anything personally. But CDA doesn't own the land yet. We got permission from the Elwood children to see what's out there."

"The Elwood children?"

"Yes, Leslie and Larry. All I know is that Dr. Elwood and Cletis signed a Purchase and Sale more than twenty years ago. Apparently Elwood didn't tell his kids he did that."

"Good heavens, that long ago. Isn't that unusual?"

"I suppose. But a contract is a contract."

Why didn't he tell his children? she wondered. "Why did Cletis wait so long to buy it?"

Michael shrugged. "As I understand it, we had to wait until Herbert's 85th birthday, or if he wanted to sell sooner. Or if – "

Her guts jerked as if yanked by a drawstring. "He died?"

"Yes. What's wrong?"

"Nothing."

"You look like you just saw a fly in your soup," said Michael.

"Did Detective Barker question Cletis about the Purchase and Sale agreement?"

"Sure. Me, too, except I didn't know much about that. Mostly he asked me about where we were the night of the murder."

"And where was Cletis?"

His lips twitched, he looked down. "Don't you know?"

"How should I know?"

When he looked up, his face was apologetic. "He said he was sleeping with you that night."

"He what?" she shrieked.

Michael offered a rueful smile. "Sorry. Don't shoot. He told me to say that if you asked. He actually did have a good alibi."

Had Cletis really become such a shameless old turd? She tried to restrain her temper. "And that was?"

"He was with the Governor."

"Sleeping with the Governor? Another sick joke?"

"No, really. It was one of those campaign fundraisers in Boston. A thousand dollars a plate. Quite an event. Probably two hundred people saw Cletis there."

"We only had a small event here. And nothing the Governor would want on his plate. As for today, tell Cletis a grown-up would've delivered the message himself. Tell him he's become a lot older but not a drop nicer in the past fifty years."

Michael looked very unhappy. "You really want me to say that?"

"You bet I do. I know he's your stepfather and you work for him, but you should have the spunk to stand up to him."

"I'm not afraid of him."

"Then what's the fly in your soup?"

"I'm wondering how you two got too old to pick up the phone or write each other an e-mail – or a note – you remember notes?"

"You're right. But it's not the technology. It's the history. Now please back your car out of the driveway. I have to go to work."

"Yes ma'am. Have a good day."

Addie watched him walk to his car. What were they going to do to her glorious woods?

As Michael's car started up, she opened her car door, flung the scraper into the back and got into the driver's seat. A contract they'd kept secret for twenty-plus years, activated by Herbert's murder? How in the world was she going to concentrate on invoices and orders when Michael had unleashed a pack of hounds in her head. She took a deep breath, then fastened her seatbelt. Only one thing Michael said – no implied – was absolutely true. She and Cletis needed to have it out, face to face.

CHAPTER 19

Wednesday Afternoon

"The light's yellow," warned Marty.

Sitting behind her grandson, Addie saw his hand reach up to brace himself as Bella's Cadillac accelerated past a Gulf station and a row of small stores. Addie clutched her shoulder restraint with one hand and used the other to stabilize the cat carrier. "You don't have to drive so fast, Bella. The appointment isn't until four-thirty."

"It's how I drive," said Bella. "You know I don't like to be late."

"That's why I wanted Marty to drive."

"In his sardine can? No offense, Marty, but I'm a big woman. I like big comforts."

"No offense taken," he said. "Sometimes reporters have to risk their lives to get a good story."

"Who's risking here? It's my car."

Better not let Bella get going, thought Addie. "Don't get ahead of yourself about any story, Marty. We're not even sure this doctor is Steven Mars."

"Sure enough to drag me into it," said Bella.

"Drag you?" Addie leaned forward as much as her seatbelt would allow. "Didn't you say that if I made the appointment, he'd recognize my name and cancel it – or skip out at the last minute?"

"And he would, too, if he's Steven Mars," said Bella. "But even if he is, the chances this doctor – what's his name?"

"Simon Warley," said Marty. "Granny told me to Google local vets and animal control officers and look for names like planets, the Roman god of war, or science fiction writers."

Bella took one hand off the steering wheel to adjust her rear view mirror. "Even if this Dr. Warley is the man who came to your back door, what makes you think he'll fess up to anything?"

"I hope he'd rather talk to us than to Detective Barker," said Addie. "Besides, it's possible that – ouch!" Pain stabbed her buttock as the car jounced over the tracks of a railroad crossing. "Bella, please."

"Sorry. I hate train crossings and tunnels, so I go through them as fast as I can."

"Yeah, minimize the risk," said Marty. "How are you doing back there, Granny?"

"I'm okay. I still think about Herbert a lot. Why would he create a trust for fifty acres of woodland only to sell it for commercial development when he died?"

"Maybe he didn't care what happened to it once he was gone," said Marty.

"That's the obvious answer, but is it right? Herbert never mentioned Cletis to me. Were you aware they knew each other, Bella?"

"No. But Cletis knows everyone who's anyone."

"You know Cletis, too?" asked Marty.

"Of course. Your granny and I went to school with him. We were the grade school ABCs, Adams, Bavarone and Chandler. I was the marshmallow between two sharp cookies."

"Don't listen to her, Marty. She got the best grades."

"Only in elementary school. That's because I cheated from you in spelling and from Cletis in arithmetic."

"You cheated, Aunt Bella?"

"Only when I didn't know the answers."

"Which wasn't often," said Addie. "Bella was like a sponge."

"Unfortunately, I still have the same shape."

"Did you cheat, Granny?"

"No. But if I had, I wouldn't boast about it."

"Who's boasting?" Bella demanded. "Anyway, I never did it after seventh grade. I got caught on an algebra test with a few x's and y's inked under my bracelets. My father ended my criminal career that night."

"How?" asked Marty.

"Looky-looky! Dr. Warley's place is coming up on your right. Another time, Marty, okay?"

A white sign with black lettering announced the Care Hill Small Animal Clinic. Standing alone on the hill, the one-story, brick building was neatly landscaped with bushes and groundcover but devoid of trees except for a few saplings that still hung on to tired leaves. Bella parked the Cadillac away from the half-dozen cars already in the lot. "Welcome to Care Hill," she said.

Marty's seatbelt retracted with a thump. "The name sounds more like a nursing home."

"Or a cemetery," said Bella.

Addie unbuckled her seatbelt and opened the rear door to a clamor of barking from behind the building. Flash wailed and scratched the walls of his carrier. Addie patted the black nylon. "It's okay, Flash. Those big bully-dogs are all locked up." She got out of the car and reached back in for her purse and the carrier. Flash was crying. "Calm down, Flash. No shots today."

"Let me carry him," said Marty.

"Thank you." She handed Marty the carrier, then followed Bella up the cement path alongside the building. A tiny red light betrayed a security camera set under the eaves. "Bella!"

As Bella turned to look, her crocheted handbag thunked lightly against the side of the building.

Addie tilted her head up toward the camera, then quickly away, moving past Bella, who came back a few steps, then smiled and waved at the camera.

"I feel safer already," said Bella.

Opening the front door, Addie was assailed by barks and the sharp odor of disinfectant.

"Be quiet, Duffy." A young man in a ski-jacket sat with his jean-clad legs wrapped around a squirming beagle. "Don't mind him, he's nervous," the young man said.

Addie looked about. The waiting room was a yellow rectangle, with a coat rack close to the front door and five people already seated. Unoccupied plastic chairs created safe distances between their apprehensive pets. Vaccination advice and disease warnings shared the walls with photos of children holding their pets. At the far end of the room stood a receptionist's booth and a door marked Treatment Suite.

"Move in," said Bella from behind her. "I want to see."

Addie stepped forward and Bella followed. Marty's entrance with Flash set Duffy to barking again. Marty struggled with the carrier as Flash jumped and hissed wildly inside.

"Shut up, damn you," a grating voice commanded from the other side of the room. A grey parrot in a small cage occupied the chair next to a beefy man in a New England Patriots sweatshirt.

"Knock it off!" the man said.

"Shut up, damn you," the parrot insisted.

Closer to the reception desk, a giant schnauzer stood like an aging king eying the fools in his court. A gray-haired woman in overalls sat with one hand on the dog's collar. Between Duffy and the schnauzer sat a pre-teen and her mother, obviously unhappy about the anxiety Duffy's barking was causing a mewling kitten in the girl's lap.

"Sit over there with Marty," said Bella, pointing to three vacant chairs between the rack of coats and the parrot's owner.

Marty set the carrier down in front of the vacant chairs. "Let me hang up your coat, Granny."

Bella headed for the receptionist's booth, in which a shovel-jawed woman in a white jacket sat behind a barrier. The receptionist used one hand to smooth down a cowlick of brown hair, the other to open a small window in the barrier.

"I'm Bella Auterio. I've an appointment for my cat."

The receptionist consulted her computer. "His name's Scrabble?"

"Yes."

Addie grimaced. Bella still thought of their search as a game.

"First visit. If you'll please fill out these forms – " The receptionist handed her a clipboard of paperwork.

Bella put the clipboard under her arm. "Good thing I brought my reading glasses," she called back to Addie. She opened up her handbag.

Marty sat down next to Addie. "Looks like a long wait."

"Patience, dear." She leaned toward him. "Camera here, too," she whispered.

He followed her gaze to the ceiling above the receptionist's booth, from which a small camera monitored the waiting room. Marty brought his lips close to her ear. "You think they can hear what we say?"

"Why don't we find out?" she said softly. "Do an interview."

Marty looked puzzled. "You?"

With a smile, Addie turned toward the parrot's owner. "Excuse me. My grandson Marty is a reporter for *The Millbrook Messenger*. He's doing a story on veterinarians and the interesting animals they treat. Would you mind if he interviewed you about your parrot and Dr. Warley?"

"Why not? Beats waiting," said the man. "Shot Glass is an African Grey."

"Shot Glass," said the parrot, claws gripping a rope perch. "Shot Glass kicks ass."

"Oh," said Addie. The black beak of the small parrot certainly looked delicate enough to fit into a shot glass. The man's nose looked like it had spent more time in a beer mug.

"Could you put a cover over him," said the mother. "My daughter's only ten."

"Sorry," the man said, but he made no effort to comply. "His former owner taught him some nasty words."

"How old is he?" asked Marty.

"I want to see," said Bella, coming back from the desk.

"Doc thinks he's about thirty," said the man. "I've only had him ten years."

"What's wrong with him now?" asked Marty.

"He's okay. He's here for a calcium check."

"I hope his calcium is better than mine," said Bella.

"Bella, come sit down," said Addie.

Bella glanced over and winked, but she didn't move away from the parrot.

"Dr. Warley's been taking care of him for the past ten years?" asked Marty.

"No, only about four. He got Shot Glass through a terrible spell of feather plucking."

"Plucking," screeched Shot Glass, fluffing his feathers. "Stop plucking, bird brain!"

Duffy barked. Flash hissed. The giant schnauzer growled. "Remember your manners, Tillie," said the gray-haired woman.

"Shot Glass gets upset when he thinks about it," the man said.

A buzzer sounded at the reception desk. The receptionist left her post and went into the treatment suite.

"I like his red tail feathers," Bella said. "Did he go after them, too?"

"Yeah. He was really a mess until I brought him to Doc Warley. He's great with animals."

"Does Dr. Warley live around here?" asked Marty.

"I don't know. Why don't you ask him?"

"I intend to. What's Dr. Warley like?"

The receptionist came through the doorway of the treatment suite and approached Bella. The young woman's expression was apologetic, but her lips were pressed thin with determination. "I'm sorry," she said. "Dr. Warley is running late today. He won't be able to see your cat."

"But we have an appointment," said Bella.

"We don't mind waiting," said Marty. "I'm Marty Howard from *The Millbrook Messenger*.

Would you mind if I interviewed you for a story I'm writing?"

The woman looked flustered. "I don't really – "

"No, Marty," said Addie. She got up and looked directly at the camera. "We don't want to burden Dr. Warley's practice if we can avoid it. If he can't see us today, perhaps my friend Detective Barker will stop by with his own pet problems tomorrow."

"To-morrow, to-morrow, bet your bottom dollar," sang Shot Glass. Duffy howled.

"For God's sake," the woman with the schnauzer said.

"He likes to sing," Duffy's owner explained.

"Like Mick Jagger on steroids," said Bella.

The buzzer at the desk sounded. "Excuse me," said the receptionist. She scurried back into the treatment suite.

"Detective Barker?" asked the parrot's owner. "Harris Barker, down in Millbrook?"

Marty nodded. "You know him?"

"We used to play poker together. That's who I won Shot Glass from."

"Detective Barker owned Shot Glass?" asked Addie. It was hard to imagine the big detective playing with a parrot. Much less difficult to imagine the language lessons.

"Yeah, he's a big birder," said the man.

This time the receptionist returned with a smile on her face. "Dr. Warley has cancelled his evening engagement. He'll be able to see everyone after all."

* * *

"We can talk more openly in here," said Simon Warley, ushering Addie and Bella into a windowless examining room.

So far, he's been anything but open, thought Addie, as she placed the cat carrier on a stainless steel examining table. But his voice left no doubt that they'd found Steven Mars.

Warley had not made an appearance in the waiting room until all his patients had been treated and gone home, and then he'd excluded Marty from any further conversation, saying he would not discuss anything in front of a reporter and what little he had to say was for Addie alone.

The doctor's white coat, his ramrod posture and vulturine face had discouraged argument, but Bella was a tank that would neither stand idle nor retreat. She barraged Warley with reasons she needed to be included: her status as Scrabble's owner, her lifelong friendship with Addie, the sacrifices made by leaving work to attend to Scrabble's needs, and as her final shot, her concern for the safety of any woman left alone with strange animals in a back room. Warley had gazed down on her as if she were troubled by some malady he'd never encountered, but he'd remained silent until she'd spluttered to a stop. Then he'd simply said "No."

It had taken another threat to go to Detective Barker for Warley to change his mind. Now he stood in the examining room, arms folded across his white jacket, his gaze so piercing that Addie wanted to look away.

"You shouldn't have come," he said. "I can't guarantee your safety."

Flash continued to yowl and claw the carrier. Bella placed her handbag on the counter. "I guess I don't need reading glasses in here." She opened the bag to tuck them away.

Addie glanced at the instruments behind the glass of a cabinet, the box of latex gloves on a counter. "What sort of danger are we in?"

"Fleas?" asked Bella.

"This is no joke. You're both in terrible danger. The people who killed Dr. Elwood won't hesitate to kill again to cover up what they're doing."

"Kill?" Bella jerked back, leaving her handbag undone.

Addie tried not to sound skeptical. "And what is it that they're doing?"

"Illegal surveillance, murder, making a mockery of our judicial system, undermining our national security, you name it."

"In Millbrook, Massachusetts?" scoffed Bella.

"Millbrook is unimportant. It's just the tip of the iceberg."

"Please," said Addie. "Will you simply explain what's going on and how Herbert fits into it?"

"Isn't it obvious? There's a small group of influential people who are selling this country piece by piece to the Chinese." Warley stepped over to the counter and withdrew a pair of latex gloves from the box. "The politicians and the media are – forgive me for being blunt – the politicians and media types are whores who protect those people's treason in order to safeguard their own positions. Willingly or not, Elwood worked for the traitors." A puff of talc emerged from the glove he was putting on. "They disposed of him once he no longer was of any value."

"Value?" asked Addie. "What value could a dentist offer?"

"He wasn't just a dentist. He was an endodontist. Once he retired, he was of no more use to them." Warley flexed his gloved fingers. "But they didn't kill him right away. That would've aroused too many questions about the link between what he did and why he died."

"But what did he do?" asked Addie.

"Besides root canals," said Bella.

"Root canals were a pretext." Warley came forward. Addie backed away. Warley reached into his pocket, withdrew a brown nugget, then zipped open the cat carrier. "Okay, tough guy. You're getting paroled." He fed Flash the nugget and reached down to scoop him up. Flash squirmed to break free. Warley raised Flash up so they were eye-to-eye. "Hey, tough guy," he said in a soothing voice, "forget the gloves, it's me." Flash stared at him, went limp, purred, then licked Warley's nose. The vet rewarded him with another nugget.

Addie was dumbfounded.

"Amazing," said Bella. "How did you do that?"

"He knows I like him."

"Addie loves him. She can't get him to do squat."

"Bella!" Addie turned to Warley. So much for any pretense that this was Bella's cat. "What's in those pellets you're giving him?"

"Catnip and a few secret ingredients. Don't worry, it's not harmful. I call it Doc Warley's Wondernip." As he smiled, Warley's teeth clicked. Mouth open, he used his tongue to resettle his dentures. Then he set the cat on the table and began petting, gently poking and prodding him. He lifted a rear paw. "What happened here?"

Addie looked at Bella, who shrugged. Well, thought Addie, it was clear that Warley had recognized Flash the moment he looked at him. "He got stuck. I had trouble freeing his paw."

"Freeing it from what?" Keeping one hand on Flash, Warley reached behind him to a drawer and took out a nail clipper. "Can you hold him, please. Two of these nails are jagged."

Addie stepped forward and tried to hold Flash firmly.

"What was he stuck in?" Warley's clipper bit down and Flash jerked but didn't cry out.

"The clothes dryer," said Addie. Flash squirmed to escape her hands. "Stay still! It's okay."

The clipper bit again. "You should never leave the door open."

Addie looked to see if he was mocking her, but his expression was serious as he bent to examine Flash's paw.

"She has a burglar alarm now," said Bella.

"Good." Warley released Flash's leg. "You can't be too careful, these days. The cut's healing fine." He turned to Bella. "Do you use a heart-worm preventative?"

Bella looked about wildly for inspiration. "For me?"

"For Scrabble." Warley smirked. "That *is* his name, isn't it?"

"No, it's not," said Addie. "I'm sure you're aware Flash's visit is a pretext, Doctor. Like root canals were for Dr. Elwood – or so you say. How did you catch on to what he was really doing?"

"Ah," said Warley, pulling an ophthalmoscope from his pocket. "Now the tough part of the examination. Would you please hold his head still?"

"You don't have to examine him further," said Addie. "Flash is okay."

"And you don't have to examine me," said Warley. "But apparently you feel it's the right thing to do. Anyway, how else could I bill for a complete examination? Would you please hold his head?"

Addie put her hands to Flash's head, and Warley bent over to examine the cat's eyes.

"It started with a toothache," Warley said. "My regular dentist referred me to Dr. Elwood for a root canal. Now the other eye, tough guy. But despite my pain and my Percocet, I noticed some strange things in Elwood's office."

"Like what?" asked Bella.

Warley straightened. A quick twist of his hands transformed the ophthalmoscope into a tool for examining ears. "Like the super high quality of Elwood's X-ray equipment, and the radiation warning sign on a door that said 'Authorized Personnel Only.' And Elwood's receptionist was Chinese."

"So are a billion other people," said Bella. "So what?"

Flash cried out and squirmed in Addie's grasp as Warley used the instrument to examine the cat's ears. "Easy, now," said the vet. He came up glaring at Bella. "So what, you say? Nothing to worry about, right? So why don't you go home now and forget everything I've said." He redirected his anger toward Addie. "Go home and forget you've ever been here. And don't ask any more questions. You'll be a lot safer."

Addie put on her MAHIB face. "Look, if Herbert was doing something very wrong, and there's evidence in his house and some kind of conspiracy going on, I need to know. I lived next to him for over forty years and I don't think I misjudged his character that much. But if I did, I need to know exactly what danger I might be in, and if there's any risk to my children and grandchildren and my friend here."

"Right," said Bella.

Warley's eyelids fluttered, his mouth twitched. He appeared to struggle to control his face. "So be it," he said. "It started with the phone call. I was sitting in the dental chair, almost done, when Elwood got a call on his cell phone. He moved into the next room, but I could still hear him plainly. Like this cat, I have two good ears." Warley lowered a hand and Flash ducked his head under and against it, as if getting petted was the goal of his visit.

"When did all this happen?" asked Addie.

"Almost two years ago, but I remember it like yesterday." Warley shook his head as he stepped away from the table. "It was so weird I even wrote his remarks down as soon as I left his office. I puzzled over what he said for weeks." He took a stethoscope from a basket on the counter.

"What did he say?" asked Bella.

"The first thing Elwood said was 'You shouldn't be calling me here. I've got Simon in the chair right now.' I was startled by that because I wondered who and what he was telling about me, and how anyone else might've known about my appointment. Anyway, Elwood must've been asked a question because there was a pause before he said, 'Yes, I did.' And then whatever was said must've annoyed him, because he sounded very impatient. He said 'I know what you want, but I can't change the contract.' And then, after a few seconds, he said, 'No, bad as it may be, it's a done deal. Tell your Chinese friends it can't be changed.' The next time Elwood spoke, he was definitely angry. He said 'You're listening to the wrong people. Try listening to this.' And then he hung up and came back into the room shaking his head at me. 'I'm sorry,' he said. 'That woman will be the death of me.' Of course I asked, 'Who was that? What woman is giving you such a hard time?' Elwood didn't answer any of my questions. He just said something about finishing up and getting me out of there quickly. And believe me, I wanted to be gone."

"And that was it?" asked Addie.

"Of course not. That was only the beginning of my troubles." He put the head of the stethoscope against Flash's chest and listened.

Bella moved aside and turned her head so only Addie could see her puzzled frown.

Addie waited until Warley took the stethoscope from his ears, than asked, "What troubles?"

"Your cat's in good health." He handed Flash to her. "Three pellets of Wondernip daily should keep him that way."

Flash squirmed and snarled as Addie tried to place him back in the carrier. "Flash! Stop that! You said that call began your troubles."

"Specifically, what troubles?" asked Bella.

Warley replaced his stethoscope in the basket and began to strip off his gloves. "You're not going to believe me. After that visit to Elwood, people – strangers, even – knew little things about me that I'd not told them. I got calls on my unlisted cell phone, warning me about identity theft." Warley dropped his gloves into a waste can._"My broker told me I wanted to sell a certain stock before I said a word. I started to lose patients for no reason. Then I took my suit into the cleaners and the woman said 'you must be a Capricorn.' Now why did she say that? How did she know?"

"A lucky guess?" said Addie.

"No, it was because I talked to my sister in California the night before and she asked whether I still believed in horoscopes. Then she read me Capricorn's from that day. You know what it said?"

"Take your shirts to the cleaners?" asked Bella.

Warley shot her a malevolent look. "It said that I should listen very carefully to those who listened to me. Clearly, my sister was trying to warn me. Piece by piece, I put it together."

"Put what together?" asked Addie. "What does this have to do with Herbert Elwood?"

"When he did my root canal, he implanted a radio transmitter in that tooth. That's what he did to me, and to God knows how many others. That's how they listened in to what I was saying, to what I was thinking, trying to control my mind. That's why I need the evidence from his house."

"Oh," said Addie. The man was crazy as a loon.

"You see to what extremes they'll go? Yet no one will believe me, including the two of you." He glared at Addie, then turned to Bella.

"You thinking what I'm thinking?" asked Bella, gathering up her handbag.

Addie nodded. "Thank you for talking to us, Dr. Warley. And thank you for examining Flash. Please send me the bill. You know where I live."

"I do. I plan everything very carefully now. I even had my teeth out to be certain. You sure you don't have a key to Elwood's house?"

"So when you had all your teeth taken out, did you find the radio transmitter?" asked Bella.

"Of course not," said Warley. "It's all nano-technology these days." He turned to Addie. "A key to Elwood's house?"

"I gave it to George."

Warley's expression turned grim. "That's bad, very bad." He put his hands above his head, interlocked his fingers and took a deep breath. The tension in his face eased and he brought his hands down. "Well then, how about buying some Wondernip?"

CHAPTER TWENTY

Wednesday Evening

They drove back to Millbrook in the dark. Addie told Marty of their conversation with Simon Warley. Bella barely said a word, apparently concentrating on the twists and turns of the country road.

"So why couldn't he be the killer?" asked Marty. "He's a shoo-in for Time magazine's 'Paranoid of the Year.'" The lights of an oncoming car illuminated them in passing.

"Because he's still trying to prove this conspiracy exists," said Addie. "Killing Herbert would've done away with the only person that could prove there is a conspiracy. If he'd been my housebreaker, he would have taken the keys to Herbert's. He could've pacified Flash with Wondernip or just put him outside. He certainly wouldn't have put him in the dryer."

"Crazy people don't necessarily think rationally," said Marty.

"Even rational people don't think rationally," said Bella. "It's Flash, isn't it? Fess up, Addie. That's why you think Warley wouldn't kill anyone."

Addie smiled. Bella could read her thoughts even without the aid of an implanted transmitter. "That, too. Flash has never accepted anyone that way."

"Bingo!" said Bella. "Case closed."

Addie looked out at the houselights and dark shapes of trees speeding by.

"So this was all a big waste of time?" asked Marty.

"We bought two bags of Wondernip," said Bella.

"It wasn't a waste," Addie said. "Remember that conversation Dr. Warley overheard in the dental chair? Clearly Herbert did or was obligated to do something the Chinese wouldn't like. And it had nothing to do with radio transmitters in teeth."

"James Bond had one inserted under his skin," said Marty. "I bet the C.I.A. can do that, too."

Bella lifted one hand from the steering wheel. "Even better. No static when you chew."

"This is Millbrook, not Beijing," said Addie. "Let's not get carried away by Dr. Warley's paranoid fantasies. If there's a nugget of reality in what he said, it's that a woman called and made Herbert angry, and he told her he couldn't change the contract. I bet the woman was Rona Barker, pestering him about selling his property to that Chinese spiritual group, which he wouldn't or couldn't do because he already had a contract with Cletis. Remember, Bella, you said you saw Rona with a Chinese man in her car a few weeks ago?"

"Yes, but you better ask Rona. It's more likely the man was looking for a restaurant site or a family home rather than a hideaway for the Falun Gang."

"Gong," said Addie. "Falun Gong. I looked them up. They don't rent or buy physical places, and they don't distance themselves from the world. They don't even have a formal membership, so Rona can't be representing them."

"So ask. Maybe she'll tell you who her client is. Not that I put much stock in Dr. Warley's story. He was probably a nutcake before he took Percocet and whatever anesthesia Herbert gave him for the root canal. I think he heard what he wanted to hear."

"Yeah," said Marty. "That business of saying 'I have Simon in the chair right now –' No dentist would do that, would he?"

"Not unless the person on the other end of the telephone knew them both very well," said Addie.

"My guess is that Herbert said 'someone in the chair,' not 'Simon in the chair.' We should have asked Dr. Warley whether Herbert gave him an anesthetic."

The car's interior was lit up by the vehicle behind them. Bella reached to adjust the mirror. "Turn down your brights, you idiot."

Addie looked behind her and blinked against the onslaught of light. A black pickup truck was tailgating them. She felt the Cadillac accelerate. "Bella, let him pass."

"Road's too narrow – cars are coming."

"Why would the Chinese stay interested in Millbrook for two years?" asked Marty. "They could've bought in a lot of other places once Herbert said no."

"Maybe they have," said Bella. "Warley isn't all wrong about them buying up this country."

"Let's not get caught up in his paranoia," said Addie. She looked behind her. The truck was staying right on their tail. "I'll talk to George about what Dr. Warley said. I wish he'd heard that conversation first hand."

"He can hear it," said Bella. "I recorded every word."

"What?" Addie was dumbfounded.

"I recorded it."

"Bella! That's illegal."

"I'm not using the recording in court," said Bella. "Consider it Homeland Security."

Addie grasped a support handle. "Bella, slow down, let the pickup pass."

"How did you do it?" asked Marty.

"The tape recorder was in my bag. I left it open on the counter."

"You could have gotten us both in big trouble," said Addie. "God knows what Dr. Warley would've done if he thought we were recording him."

"Why didn't you tell us you were going to do it, Aunt Bella?"

"Because my best friend would've said no, and her grandson doesn't have a poker face."

"You weren't being fair, Bella. To Dr. Warley or to us."

"Addie, I love you, but sometimes you're a self-righteous prig. Your next-door neighbor gets murdered, your house gets ransacked, and you're worried about being fair to someone who – I know Flash thinks otherwise – someone who might be the murderer?"

"So that makes what you did okay?"

"It didn't cause any harm, did it? I can destroy the cassette and that'll be the end of it. But our whole trip up there was done under false pretences. What's different about what I did?"

Addie sat back in her seat. "I'm not sure. I just think it is. And it's a slippery slope."

"Maybe it was wrong not to let you two have a say in it, but honestly, I'd do it again. I won't lie or cheat to pass a test any more, and I certainly wouldn't ever cheat a customer at the store. But when it comes to helping someone I love, I'm pretty far down that slope."

The Cadillac's interior suddenly darkened as the pickup pulled out in the left lane to pass. Addie glimpsed the driver in a baseball cap as the dark pickup raced by.

"Watch out!" yelled Marty.

"Jerk!" Bella stamped on the brakes. Addie was thrown forward against her seatbelt, then felt something slam against the front of the Cadillac, heard the grind of metal as Flash's carrier rammed her and the airbags whooshed open. She grasped the carrier with a howling Flash inside as the Cadillac careened off the road, brakes locking and unlocking, the tires scrabbling over gravel, then hitting softer ground. Time seemed to slow as she was flung up and down, back against her seat and forward again as the car spun about, careened into a ditch and slammed to a stop.

"Jesus, Mary and Joseph," said Bella.

"Are you okay? Are you both okay?" asked Marty.

"It wasn't my fault. He cut back into my lane too soon."

Addie pushed the deflated side airbag away. Her heart was racing, her back hurt and she felt nauseous. But alive. "I'm alright." She unzipped the carrier just enough to peek at Flash, who jumped toward the small opening with a snarl. "It's okay, Flash, it's okay." She zipped the carrier closed. "Flash isn't hurt, he's frightened. What about you, Marty?"

"Banged my knees, that's all. Let's get out of here."

"Help Addie first," said Bella. "I need a few seconds to stop shaking."

"Okay, Granny, you first."

"What about Flash?"

"Don't try to carry him. I'll come right back and get him."

As Marty was helping her out of the car, Addie saw a man in a down jacket huffing and puffing toward them. About half a football field away, the emergency flashers of his car blinked from the opposite side of the road.

"Anyone hurt?" the man shouted. "I called 911. Told them to send an ambulance."

"Thanks," Marty shouted back.

Addie winced as she tried to stand up straight. Pain from her lower back shot down her leg as she took a few trial steps. At least nothing is broken, she thought. They could've died. She shook her head to clear it of instant replays. "Go see to Bella, Marty."

"Aunt Bella's out. Maybe you should sit down."

"If I do, I won't want to get up. Help me to the road."

Leaning heavily on Marty, Addie picked her way up the grassy slope.

"Did the driver of the pickup stop?" Marty asked as the Good Samaritan came close. Beneath a mop of gray hair, the man's expression was indignant.

"He just kept going. Crazy bastard. He was coming right at me. I didn't even have time to get his plate number." The man bent at the waist, put his hands on his thighs and took a deep breath.

Addie touched her grandson's arm. "Go help Bella get up here."

"Sure." He headed back down the slope.

The man looked up at Addie. "It was the other guy's fault – he was going too fast. Came right at me until he tried to pull back in front of you. He was either drunk or crazy."

Or he knew exactly what he was doing, thought Addie. Whoever it was, he didn't look as tall as Simon Warley. Radio transmitters aside, maybe there was more truth than paranoia in the doctor's story. "Thank you for stopping." She started to offer her hand, noticed it was trembling and dropped it against her side. "Would you be so kind as to get the cat carrier out from the back seat?" She mustered a smile. "Right now, it's a little hard for me to do anything."

"Sure." He hiked up his trousers, then started toward the car.

Addie closed her eyes, took a deep breath. Hard to think clearly. House ransacked, now this. If there was some kind of conspiracy out there, she was in big trouble. She felt like a fly that had nearly been swatted. Her peaceful, quiet life had died with Herbert. If only George were here. But what could a small town policeman do against a conspiracy? Well, George would try. And so would she. Even a fly could bite.

CHAPTER 21

Wednesday Night

Addie lay on her side, pillows under her head and between her legs, feeling chilled despite the sheet and thin blankets that covered her. The wrinkles in the jonnie and those of her body had gone separate ways, and the paper crackled each time she moved.

Waiting in an emergency department was always an ordeal, she thought, but this was one scream away from torture. Not only was her gurney harder on her shoulder and spine than an inquisitor's rack, but her hand hurt from the IV needle in her vein, Bella was fretting to beat the band, and the aides outside their curtained cubicle seemed to have nothing more important to do than chat about a new reality show called "Exposed."

Leaning forward in her wheelchair, Bella unwrapped the ice pack from her swollen knee.

"This is useless; it's warmer than piss." She tossed the pack onto the floor. "They probably sent our X-rays to India to be read. I hope the boat gets there before we die of starvation."

"April said there's a radiologist upstairs," said Addie. Better to focus on the credit side of the ledger, starting with the fact they'd all survived. Would Flash settle down without her at home? Surely Joanne and Marty would be able to comfort him until she got there. They'd be more useful there than sitting here twiddling their thumbs.

"The radiologist is probably in the cafeteria, eating a seven course dinner," said Bella, "after which, he'll lie down for his nap with a pretty nurse. Tell me, how does April Brelland keep that figure?"

Addie tried to ease the pressure on her shoulder by rolling off it a bit, but that made her back hurt even worse. She wished they'd given her something stronger than ibuprofen. "Come again?"

"I said how do you think April Brelland keeps her figure?"

"I suppose that as a nurse she knows what she needs to do to stay slim, and she does it."

"I do, too," said Bella. "But it's never worked for me."

"She's a lot younger." Yes, finding Gloria Elwood's wife working as a nurse in the emergency department was another piece of good luck. Without April's active involvement, it probably would've taken even longer for the resident to examine them and for the attendants to wheel them down to Radiology and back.

"No, really," said one of the aides outside the curtain. "On that TV show, the contestants get stark staring naked."

"That's never worked for me either," said Bella. "How about you Addie?"

"No comment." With her free hand, she tugged the edge of the blanket up to her neck. "I shouldn't've let you talk me into that ambulance."

"You must have hit your head. It was you who talked me into coming here."

"Bella, there's nothing wrong with my memory – not about this. You could barely stand; you couldn't put any weight on that leg."

"Nonsense. I've always been able to put weight on any part of me. Hello, out there! Anybody home?" She lowered her voice. "I should've asked to be towed home with my car."

A black aide with hoop earrings pulled the curtain back. "You folks need something?"

"Our X-rays, or else dinner and a bottle of Pinot Grigio," said Bella.

"I'd like something stronger for pain," said Addie.

"Didn't you understand Dr. Do-Little?" asked Bella. No narcotics until they know what's with your back. How about bringing us a couple of shots of Tuaca?" she asked the aide.

"Sorry, I'm not the bartender. I'll get the nurse."

"Not as sorry as I am," Bella said to the curtain as it closed.

It took a good five minutes before a scrub-suited April Brelland slipped into their cubicle. Her dark hair was pinned back, her expression was apologetic. "I got to him. It won't be long now." She saw Bella's bare knee. "What happened to your ice pack?"

"It got so old, I retired it," said Bella.

"Let me get a new one." April turned to leave.

"Don't bother," said Bella. "I trust we'll be getting out of jail soon."

April did an about-face. "Unless something is broken. How are you doing, Addie?"

"I need something more for pain."

"If you're not admitted, the doctor will send you home with something. I'm pretty sure both of you will be going home. May I have your permission to tell Gloria you were here tonight?"

"Fine with me," said Bella.

Addie tried to ease off her shoulder. "Yes, it's okay to tell Gloria. How is she?"

"She's having a hard time," said April. "I'm sorry she unloaded on you after her dad's funeral. It wasn't the time or place to do that."

"No, but Gloria's been carrying a heavy emotional load for years. I'm sure she's told you everything she told me – probably even more."

"Did she tell you how he didn't give her the diamond wedding ring her mother promised her?"

"Yes, that wasn't right."

"Actually, it was a bigger deal for Gloria than it was for me. I don't need a diamond to show I'm loved. And who cares if he wasn't making us a bird house?"

"That's truly romantic," said Bella, "about not needing a diamond to prove you're loved. I have to tell that to my son's girlfriends."

"I actually saw Gloria this past Saturday," said Addie.

"You did? Oh, the estate sale. You must think she's always popping off. It's just that she doesn't take any crap any more. Believe me, despite all she's been through with that family, she really has a very sweet and loving nature."

"That's wonderful," said Addie.

April bent and picked up the ice pack. "Has there been any progress in the investigation?"

"Not as far as I know."

Bella snorted. "Someone ran us off the road tonight. If that's progress, I can do without it."

"Did you recognize the driver?"

"No," said Bella. "It happened too fast."

"I didn't get a good look at him, either" said Addie. "And we don't know whether he wanted to harm us or was in too much of a hurry and too scared to stop."

"Massachusetts drivers are awful," said April. "We get survivors of some awful accidents in here."

'It must be terrible to see them in real life," said Bella. "I have a hard enough time watching it on the local news."

"I don't even watch TV news, any more," said April. "Accidents, fires and murders are all you see. I certainly don't need TV to show me more tragedies. And now we have this terrible murder right in Millbrook." She looked pained. "I just can't believe it."

"That's because you weren't there," said Addie. At least I hope you weren't, she thought. "I may not be remembering correctly, but I thought Gloria told me you two watched the late news together the night Herbert was murdered."

"Oh, we did. I didn't mean that I never, ever watched the news. That was one night we did."

"Do you recall what the lead story was?" Addie asked.

April flushed. "No. Surely you don't think Gloria or I killed Dr. Elwood, do you?"

"No, I'm sorry. I don't know who killed him. But I can't just sit back and wait for the police. Judging from tonight, I may be next on the killer's list. So forgive me, but it's safer for me to suspect everyone."

Week Four

CHAPTER 22

FRIDAY, 4:15 P.M.

Addie sat at a window table in the Main Street Coffee Shop, enjoying a lemon square and a cup of tea as she waited for Leslie Elwood. The antique photos of Millbrook and the aromas of ground coffee and home-made pastries always evoked memories of Hannah Lankins – energetic, loyal, mercurial Hannah, so frantic and hopeless before every final exam, so radiant as she strode forward to accept the Home Economics prize at graduation and, twenty-five years later, the first in their class to die of breast cancer. From Hannah, her daughter Carole had inherited the coffee shop and a collection of recipes that were unsurpassed.

The only other customers, two middle-aged men Addie recognized as teachers at Millbrook High, dawdled over their coffee. Outside on Main

Street, the twin spires of Town Hall stood out against the darkening sky. Pedestrians hurried by bundled up in sweaters and jackets. Not so the thinly-clad adolescents loitering on the Common's bandstand, demonstrating their freedom with cigarettes, smart phones and jeans sagging like loaded diapers. Addie frowned. The country had become too rich in toys, too poor in discipline.

Addie finally spotted Leslie Elwood, her black coat topped by a multicolored scarf, her evening bag swaying from a shoulder strap as she hurried toward the coffee shop. Leslie smiled in recognition, then waved. Addie signaled Leslie to slow down. An additional thirty seconds didn't matter. But Leslie entered as if it did, rushing over to the table with a "Sorry I'm late, it's great to see you," a peck on the cheek and a musk perfume that made Addie inch back.

"I'm glad to see you, too." Leslie looked so much better than at the funeral. Her dark eyes were free of tears and accented by mascara and green eye shadow. Lipstick enriched her rosebud lips, while a cascade of brown hair softened her face.

Leslie hung her beaded bag across the back of the chair opposite Addie and took off her scarf. "Our attorney went on and on," she said. "I didn't realize settling Dad's estate would be such a complicated business. Anyway, I'm glad you could meet me here, because I have to drive all the way into Boston for the symphony." She shed her coat, revealing a moss green dress and figure that hooked the eyes of the teachers.

"You look lovely," said Addie.

"Thank you." Leslie pulled the chair holding her bag out from the table and sat down. "I hope I haven't put you out too much."

"Not at all. I walked down from Auterio's. It was no bother."

"Still, I appreciate it. I've wanted to come talk with you, but I've been snowed under at work. We're preparing a bid to build a casino resort. Meanwhile, I'm still clearing stuff from Dad's house and trying to find the records we need to settle his estate. Actually, this is the first evening I'll have out – and I wouldn't have gone except that it's a benefit for Children's Hospital."

"It's okay. You did call to stop by, the day I was going to work – was that two weeks ago?"

"I'm sorry that I didn't get back to you."

"No. I know it's been a difficult time."

Leslie sighed. "You have no idea how difficult. I feel I haven't had a free moment to grieve Dad's – passing, much less do anything for myself."

"I know. There's never enough time. That day you called and wanted to see me – did you happen to mention it to anyone that morning?"

Leslie's brow furrowed. "Oh. I'm terribly sorry your house got broken into. I felt awful when I heard about it." She reached across the table to take Addie's hand. "It must've been a lot worse for you. As I told Detective Barker, I mentioned it to Todd and Larry, and also to Rona Barker."

"To Rona?"

"We'd planned to meet at Dad's house after my visit with you. But after I spoke to you, I decided to skip that and go straight to my office. Did they take anything valuable?"

Addie managed a smile. "Other than my sense of security? No, not really."

"But you think because I – "

"No, certainly not." Addie used her free hand to give Leslie's a reassuring pat, then withdrew her own hands to her lap. "I'm asking everyone with whom I spoke that morning. The timing is probably coincidental, but after what happened to your father, I feel much more vulnerable. Rona is handling the sale for you?" She let her tone convey her misgivings.

"I know, she's a bit of a flake. But she works hard and knows everyone in town. And between you and me, she's a client of Todd's."

"What do you know about this Chinese group that wants to buy the Elwood Trust property?"

"Only that Rona says they'll offer a much better price than Cletis. Our lawyer says we can't sell to them unless Cletis lets us out of the contract Dad signed. I worked for Cletis many years ago and we didn't part on good terms, so I've let Todd handle it. He says Cletis won't budge."

No surprise there, thought Addie. "I'm sorry. How is Todd?"

"He's okay." Leslie gave her wedding band a slight twist; her engagement diamond sparkled. "Unhappy about how the stock market is going, but who isn't? He's so busy pacifying clients and revising portfolios that he hasn't had much time for all this nonsense going on with my family."

"It's hardly nonsense."

"Don't I know it. It's just that Todd tends to see things in black and white. But that's the field he plays on. To manage people's money, you have to stay in the black and appear lily white."

"And that's difficult?"

Leslie shrugged. "At least the scorecard is right there at the end of every day. Family problems and personal relationships involve too many grays for Todd." Her lips hinted at a smile. "He doesn't like any game where his scorecard can be kept in someone else's pocket."

"That must make it harder for you."

"I'm used to it. After twenty-two years, there aren't many surprises. So tell me, how are you doing with all this – nasty mess?"

"I'm okay. It's still hard for me to believe your father's gone. Every time I go into the back yard, I look over, half-expecting to see him."

"I know." Leslie's eyes glistened. "I think about him every day. If your cat hadn't brought in his pipe, Dad could've lain in that basement for days, and rats or raccoons could've gotten at him."

"Thanks to Flash, nothing like that happened. What did happen was terrible enough."

"Larry told me Flash is an aggressive cat, that he's even bitten a couple of your kids. Was he there when they broke into your house?"

"Yes. He must've put up a fight, because someone stuffed him in the dryer."

Leslie winced. "What an awful thing to do. I hope Flash wasn't hurt."

"Not too badly."

"Do the police have any leads on who did it?"

"Not yet. Detective Barker seems to think it's the same people who murdered your father."

"I can't believe how incompetent Barker is. He's been bumbling around for three whole weeks and, as far as I know, he's not one step closer to finding Dad's killer than he was the day after it happened. Are you sure you didn't see or hear anything the night he was killed?"

"Quite sure. That's what I told the police and I said as much to Larry the day of the funeral. Didn't anyone tell you?"

"Barker may have mentioned it afterward. I couldn't take everything in. I don't think Larry told me. He's been really out of it, lately."

"Out of it?"

Leslie's face reflected both concern and annoyance. "He's withdrawn, moody, unwilling to talk about things. I know Larry's grieving Dad and depressed about his break-up with Cheryl, but he's so up and down and defensive, I have the feeling something else is going on."

She wants me to ask, thought Addie as she reached for her teacup. Oh crumb. Curiosity was a nasty itch. "Something else going on?"

"Larry and Cheryl only gave me fluff about why they separated. I thought I had a close relationship with both of them." Leslie shrugged. "I don't know – maybe I worry too much about Larry."

"Why don't you ask him what else is going on?"

"I have – I've called and called. He fends me off. Larry plays the omnipotent doctor so well. He says nothing's wrong that he can't fix. He tells me to get off his case and stop trying to replace Mom. His whole attitude has changed since the separation. His practice isn't going well, either. In my worst moments, I worry he's fallen into something awful, like gambling or drugs."

Addie felt the lemon square turning sour in her stomach.

"I can see you're not comfortable with this," said Leslie, "but who else can I share this with? You've always been there for our family. I thought perhaps you might ask George to check in with Larry."

Addie straightened in her chair. So that was it, another end-around to George. "Surely Larry has doctor friends. He and George haven't been close for years."

"But George protected him in school and Larry never forgot that. Until Larry got so high and mighty in medical school, he looked up to George like an older brother. I think he still does, and Larry really needs a friend right now. He's alienated Cheryl, he won't talk to me, and Gloria's pissed off and accusing us of murder because she's been cut out of Dad's will."

Had Larry really looked up to George that much? Addie wondered. If so, she hadn't been aware of it. What older boys felt and did out of sight most often didn't get told to mothers. Still, Leslie was gilding the lily. No doubt George had defended Larry a few times, but George had always protected younger children, starting with his brother and sisters on the day their father had abandoned them. What made a twelve year-old boy turn his devastation into responsibility, while so many others buried theirs in anger?

Leslie leaned forward. "So will you ask George?"

"Shouldn't you check with Larry to see if it's okay?"

"Larry's besides himself with grief. Right now, he'd say no to anything I proposed."

"Okay, I'll ask, but I can't guarantee that George will do anything."

Leslie reached over and gently squeezed Addie's hands. "Thank you. I know your kids. If you ask, it'll get done."

"Hi there, Leslie. Long time no see." Carole was approaching with a carafe of coffee in one hand, a white mug with spoon in the other, and a smile that lit up her broad face. A Boston Bruins cap failed to contain her scraggly brown hair, and her apron was a reminder of a long day's baking and serving. "Still drinking your high-test straight?"

"Hello, Carole. It's good to see you." Leslie's hand gestured toward the tabletop. "Please. I'd be lost without caffeine."

Carole set down the cup and poured the coffee. "I'm sorry about your father."

"Thanks."

"The police come up with anything yet?"

"Not that they're telling me. But Addie may have some idea of what's going on."

"Don't look at me. George never talks to me about police business."

Carole looked down her nose. "What's the use of having a policeman in your family if he won't give you the low-down on your neighbors? Oops

– sorry, Leslie. You want something delicious to go with your coffee?"

"No, thanks. I'm going out to dinner."

"Hey, Carole," one of the men called. "How about bringing that over here for a refill."

"On my way. Take care, Leslie. Give my condolences to your family."

"You bet." Leslie watched Carole walk away, then turned back to Addie. "Speaking of family, Larry said you had a long talk with Gloria the day of the funeral."

Addie nodded. Apparently communication between the Elwood children hadn't broken down completely. "Has Gloria talked with Larry?"

"Not as far as I know." Leslie took a sip of coffee, then put the mug down. "At the luncheon, Larry went looking for you, to make sure you'd eaten. April told him that Gloria was talking to you in her bedroom. What did Gloria want?"

Did Leslie really expect her to repeat what Gloria had said? "Has it really been three weeks since the funeral? Time goes so fast as I get older. I can hardly remember one day to the next."

Leslie smiled and raised one eyebrow. "I doubt that you've lost it yet, Addie. Anyway, Larry said he'd go upstairs and join in, but April said he shouldn't, that Gloria wanted to talk with you privately. The next thing he knew, you'd gone home in a downpour."

"I think I did say good-bye to you and Todd."

"Yes, you did. Did Gloria say something that bothered you?"

Addie pulled a napkin from the dispenser and wiped her lips. "She was just grieving. Mostly for the relationship that might have been."

"I think mostly for the inheritance she missed out on." Leslie thrust her hand halfway across the table. "Look, I don't deny that Gloria got a lousy deal from Dad from the moment she came out as lesbian. She went from Daddy's Darling to Daddy's Devil in five seconds, and the fall from grace was excruciating. But instead of using her smarts – and believe me, Gloria has plenty of smarts – she fought back tooth and nail, flaunting her gayness – it wasn't gay pride, it was adolescent entitlement. You saw what Gloria's bedroom looked like. My mother begged her to change it, but Gloria was as stubborn as Dad. She wouldn't back down or let things go. She couldn't resist taunting what she saw as Dad's religious hypocrisy. And if Larry or I said anything about it, she'd pop off like a firecracker. Believe me, she knew she wasn't going to get a penny from Dad, alive or dead."

Addie crumpled her paper napkin. First Gloria, now Leslie, bad-mouthing each other. Had there ever been any love between these kids? Maybe greed destroyed what little was there.

"Leslie, forgive me – I don't understand. If Gloria truly knew that Herbert wouldn't leave her a penny, why would she be grieving being disinherited now?"

"I suppose because the probability has become real. Not that Larry and I won't give her something, but I can assure you, she won't see it as enough. She's always resented Larry and me."

"What a pity." Addie pushed her cup aside. Enough sympathy. She was letting herself be squeezed like a napkin ball by these sisters. Would Larry try to get to her, too? "There seems to be so much hurt and anger among you three. Is it true you and Larry will no longer talk with Gloria?"

Leslie's eyes narrowed. "She tell you that?"

"The day of the estate sale. She walked over while I was gardening."

"Did she tell you how belligerent and insulting she was? She twists what we say and makes accusations – it's impossible to have a normal conversation with her. Believe me, I've tried, and so has Larry. Despite what she says, Gloria doesn't really care about us. She only wants revenge and reparations for getting kicked out by my father."

My father, not *our* father, thought Addie. Oh crumb. What would Janet have wanted her to do? "That's not my impression of Gloria. I know she's hurt and angry and she gets very feisty, but she does want the love and acceptance of her family. I doubt she's driven solely by money. She really does want respect – or at least acceptance – from you and Larry."

"Oh, sure. Give me one example of Gloria showing she cares about me."

"I don't live with her. She says she's called you many times to try to sort things out."

"Because she wants a share of the money, nothing more."

Addie shrugged. "She seemed concerned about your accident."

"What accident?"

"When you bruised your face."

Leslie's lips broke wind. "That was months ago. I rushed into the kitchen to answer the telephone and ran into the side of a cabinet. It was no big deal. Gloria's concern was a big show."

Addie tried to keep her face still. Todd had said Leslie had bumped into a door. Confront her? Not likely she'd tell the truth. "That's too bad. Tell me, before your father's will became an issue, why did Gloria resent you and Larry?"

"We had more privileges, more friends – she felt we excluded her. That's why my father did more with her. He felt sorry for her."

"Did you and Larry exclude her?"

"It wasn't malicious. I was five years older, Larry had four years on her. She wasn't our peer, and she was a terrible tattle-tale. She'd go to Mom with all kinds of stories to get attention."

"Your mother could separate the wheat from the chaff."

"That's why Gloria found my father an easier mark – until she came out, that is. You wouldn't believe the stories Gloria told. After Mom died, Gloria told her friends that Mom had died of an overdose. Now she's accused Larry and me of killing Dad. Mom would turn over in her grave if she knew the misery Gloria's caused."

"Perhaps." Addie dropped the napkin ball onto her plate. "Forgive me for saying so, Leslie, but I doubt your mother would be proud of the way any of you have behaved toward each other. Knowing Janet, she'd be blaming herself. She wasn't perfect – none of us are – but my guess is she'd be looking in the mirror before she threw stones. I think part of the tragedy of losing your parents is that you kids have smashed your mirrors."

Leslie shook her head. "I haven't smashed mine, and I don't think Larry broke his. Maybe you as an older person can understand. It's always easier not to look."

CHAPTER 23

MONDAY AFTERNOON

Sun-glazed autumn leaves crunched under her shoes as Addie walked past the row of white houses opposite the Congregational church. The well-groomed front yards of the Historical Commission's clapboard homes were picketed by trees refusing to surrender the last of their leaves. Snug inside her black woolen coat and gloves, with the hat she'd knitted years ago pulled over her ears, she was enjoying the walk from Auterio's despite qualms about having lied to get a same-day appointment.

If only Larry had returned her calls, he'd surely have fit her in, and then she wouldn't have had to lie to his receptionist. Oh, crumb. She was making excuses for herself again. She'd tried so hard to teach her kids that lying was never right.

She'd apologize to Larry – but after she talked with him about Delia. Her second visit to Raymond's mother had gone a bit better, but there was no way she could provide Delia with the care she needed. Nor would Delia open her door for any of the women from the church's outreach ministry.

She stopped at the corner to allow two cars to pass, then crossed Birch Street despite the red hand in the pedestrian light. Too bad the birches hadn't survived as long as she had. She remembered running around the thicket and across this street with Susie Lester, determined to beat her to "the Indian path" through the woods. No traffic light back then. Sad that the Lesters were gone.

She focused ahead on the white signboard bearing the names and specialties of Lawrence Elwood, M.D., and three other doctors, testing how close she had to come to see the smaller letters clearly. No worse than last year. Good, no need for new glasses. As she turned up the walkway toward the large house, the door to the vestibule opened and a tall, grizzled man in a black topcoat emerged. He descended the two steps and limped forward, squinting against the sun.

"Hello," he said from ten feet away, "if it isn't the beautiful Adelaide, either my eyes have called in sick or my memory has gone absent without leave."

She stopped and almost smiled. "Perhaps it's not your faulty memory, Mr. Kearney, but your judgment." Weathered face, sad brown eyes. He's seen a lot of pain, she thought.

"Always a pint short in the judgment department," he said.

He looked less gaunt than he had at the pharmacy. "Still, you had the good judgment not to call me again. Thank you for that, Mr. Kearney."

"Call me Joe, or Joseph if you must. Or call me late for my funeral. It was cowardice, not good judgment that stopped me. And Doc Elwood wouldn't give me the prescription."

"What?"

"The prescription for kisses."

Was the man dotty?

"Not from your son at the CVS," said Joe with a quick shake of his head. "I mean from the lovely young girls behind the counter. Doc said he'd give me a prescription for my gout, that kisses might be nice but they weren't approved as a treatment by the FDA. Is there any better proof that the medical system is broken?"

Total blarney, she thought, but she smiled anyway. "Broken or not, I do have an appointment with Dr. Elwood. Have a good day, Mr. – Joe. Now, if you'll excuse me – " She took a step forward.

He raised his hand. "It is a good day seeing you. You've put a spring in my step and a smile in my heart, so don't rush off. If you're here to see young Dr. Elwood, he's running an hour behind schedule. Poor lad's in terrible shape. Looks like he hasn't slept for a month of Sundays."

"Oh." Probably true what with his separation from Cheryl, his father's death. "Even doctors go through some very hard times."

"Murder makes for very hard times. A very sad affair it is. The father saved two of my teeth back when he was practicing in Worcester. Looking back, I probably didn't thank him enough."

"We all have regrets. I don't find them very useful unless you learn from them."

"And I have," he said. "One of my regrets is that I didn't call you again."

"I did ask you not to. What is it you want?"

"To meet for a cup of coffee and some civilized conversation, nothing more devious. I haven't met many people worth knowing since my boys buried me in senior housing. But when I met you, and knowing your son's kindness and sense of humor, I couldn't help but think we'd enjoy getting to know each other."

Not likely. She wrapped her arms around her chest and rubbed her shoulders. "Sorry, I'm getting chilled."

"Then I won't keep you. I'll try again as soon I can give my fingers the courage." Joe looked down at his hands and wiggled his fingers. "Cold fingers, cold feet." Offering a puckish smile, he took a step forward. "So would you care to save a man a crisis in confidence by going out sometime for a cup of coffee? Warm some appendages, so to speak?"

Appendages? Her eyes widened.

"Ah, I see in your lovely face that Joe Kearney has put a foot in his mouth again. It's a trick learned as a boy and unwittingly cultivated to a fine art. I apologize for the boy and the man he's become, but their invitation is still on the table."

"I don't drink coffee, but thank you. And I prefer to be called Addie."

"Is it the coffee, or could it be your lopsided view of me?"

"Neither one." There's no need to be hurtful, she told herself. But certainly no need to apologize. "I'm happy with my life and friends as they are. I'm not looking for any change."

"Then try to stay in this moment, for the next will be different."

"How unfortunate," she said.

"Perhaps. But as my old friend Henri once said, 'Almost all the misfortunes in life come from the wrong notions we have.' Might you be having a wrong notion about me, dear Addie?"

"Possibly. But I don't need – "

"Glory be to God, woman. Who's talking about need? Life should be more than that. A dollop of beauty and a daily dose of laughter to block out the pain, don't you think? And where are we old-timers to get that if not from each other while there's still a good story to tell and a friend left to share it with?"

Searching his features, she saw a guileless intensity, was touched by his loneliness. "I agree, but – "

He raised his hand to stop her. "No, you've done us a good turn. Imagine how awkward it might have been, having a date at our age." His forehead contracted as if he was having either a sobering vision or a migraine. "I mean we'd be wondering why did we ever get ourselves into this, what on earth do we have in common, where do we go from here – it would all have been very disturbing." He sighed, then slapped the side of his coat. "So. Thank you, dear Addie, for sparing us both."

Had he read her so easily? Was that why there was a twinkle in his eye? "You understand it's me, it's not about you?"

"Oh, yes. Truly the worst fear I had was that you'd say no in a very dismissive way. But I see that's not your style, so with the worst of it over, I think it's a big relief, don't you?"

"I suppose."

He grinned. "And with the worst of it over, I'll be able to call you tomorrow to chat and we won't have to worry about any of that adolescent foolishness, isn't that right?"

She couldn't keep from smiling. The man was a fox. "I suppose we'll have to see about that. I'm not making any promises."

"Nor would I ask for one. You and I, we're far too canny to believe them."

She nodded. "I think I'd better get to my appointment."

He stepped aside. "It's been a pleasure. And I hope you're in good health or will soon return to it."

"I'm okay." She started forward.

"I'm pleased to hear that. But look sharp in there. The good doctor's not in good shape."

"Don't you think it's because he's grieving for his father?"

"Maybe – but you're asking a recovering alcoholic, not a shrink. I can sure tell you he's not been drinking. But there are other ways to self-administer grief."

* * *

She sat on a chair in the cramped examining room, regretting she hadn't brought a book to block out her worries. The aide's assertion that "Dr. Elwood will be in a few minutes" had proved as flimsy as the paper jonnie still neatly folded on the examining table. Good thing she hadn't taken her clothes off, she thought. Without her sweater and woolen slacks, she'd be shivering her way into pneumonia. She rubbed her hands to warm them. Get her coat and gloves from the waiting room? Waiting room, indeed. Every room in this office seemed to be a waiting room. She scanned the walls for a thermostat, saw only cabinets, medical thingamajigs and a smoke detector.

So Joe Kearney was an alcoholic. Recovering or not, he was full of bull and she didn't need that in her life again. But could he be right about Larry Elwood? Was Larry on tranquilizers, on even worse drugs? That could explain why his wife asked him to leave but refused to give her reasons. Or why Leslie wanted George to check up on him.

A quick double rap on the door brought her head around. Larry barged in like a genie just released from a bottle, expanding over her as his white coat flapped open, his tie swayed, and his stethoscope clutched his neck for dear life. "Addie, Addie, sorry to keep you waiting. You of all people. Terrible of me, but it's been a hell of a day." There was a sheen of sweat on his forehead, but his eyes were alight with energy and a grin flourished below his thick moustache. "Hope we can make your day better. What's the problem? Back acting up again?"

"Some. It's cold in here."

"So they tell me. I've felt warm enough – running too fast." He retreated a step, plopped down onto a chrome stool and, with a touch, awakened a laptop from its sleep on a nearby stand. "I asked Judy to put up the heat. Anything to satisfy. Now what's the problem?" He glanced at the computer screen. "You told Judy 'back pain' when you called."

She felt tongue-tied. She hated meddling, but how could she turn her back on Delia? "It's not me. I came about someone else."

"Something else? Never a dull moment, right?" His right leg jiggled up and down. "Well, I'm sure we can handle it. What's up?"

Had he heard her correctly? She'd never seen him in such a rush, so overwrought. "*Someone* else," she said. "I'm worried about Cordelia Miggens. I know you're her doctor, too. Delia is – at least I think she is – very depressed."

He shook his head. "Sorry, Addie. I can't talk to you about another patient. You should know that." His eyelid twitched. "Can't do it. Now is there anything about you – "

"Of course, I know. I'm just asking you to listen."

"Listen? Sure." He clasped his hands in front of his chest. "I'm great at listening. It's just that I'm running late, today. But I don't want to shortchange you, so go ahead, tell me. Who is this you're concerned about?"

"To be honest, right now I'm more concerned about you."

He started, then quickly recovered. "Me?"

"Are you – feeling okay?"

"No, how could I be, with everything going on. What are you really asking?"

She bit her lip. Did she really want to know? She thought of Herbert, of Janet. "I think your mother would've wanted me to ask. Are you using drugs?"

His face got red, but he laughed. "What doctor doesn't?" His smile seemed forced. "I know, I know. You're asking about illicit drugs, and the answer is no. It's really none of your business, but I haven't done any illicit drugs since pot in college. But I am on an antidepressant, and it's jacked me too far up – I can't deny it. I'll be better tomorrow or the next day. Does that relieve your maternal concern?"

"Very much so."

"I guess my sister is still telling tall tales about me."

"No, I haven't spoken to Gloria since the funeral."

"I meant Leslie."

"Leslie?"

"It doesn't matter," said Larry. "The real damage was already done."

"Damage?"

"Who do you think planted that evil seed in my wife's head? And my father's? Look, I still have a practice to run. Anything else you're here for?"

"I really came about Cordelia Miggens. I know she hasn't come to you for a while. She tries to stay away from doctors because she's afraid they'll find something awful or send her to a mental hospital."

"If she needs a psychiatrist – " A facial muscle twitched; he rubbed his face. "Miggens – that guy across the street from you?"

"Yes, Delia's his mother. Haven't you ever met Raymond?"

"I might've seen him around when he was a kid." Larry leaned toward her. His eyes were bloodshot, his pupils large. "Does this have something to do with my father's murder?"

"I don't think so." She told him of Raymond's devotion to Delia, her depression, her fear of losing him. "Raymond may need to be away for a while. So if Raymond or I get Delia in to see you, would you be able to admit her to a hospital?"

"Not if there's nothing physically wrong with her."

"For her depression."

His leg began jiggling up and down again. He put a hand on his thigh. "I'm not a psychiatrist. You're better off taking her to an emergency room."

"She wouldn't go."

"Then I'm sorry. You'll have to let the chips fall where they may."

"Delia's not a chip, Larry, and I'm not a gambler. There must be something you can do."

He shrugged. "Mental health clinics have crisis teams. Call for a crisis team to come to her house."

"She wouldn't let them in."

"Then call the police."

"She's not threatening to kill anyone." She heard the frustration in her tone, tried to stay reasonable. "They couldn't go in without a warrant. Even if they did, she'd say everything was fine, they'd leave, and she'd starve herself to death."

"Maybe her son shouldn't go away. Or maybe he knows of some relative who'll come stay with her."

She stared at him. No, this whirligig wasn't Larry. "She still needs psychiatric help, maybe medical help."

His hands shot apart. "I can't help those who choose not to help themselves. I have too much on my plate already. Including the people out in that waiting room."

It's over, she thought. She'd accomplished nothing. "I'm sorry." She got up from her chair. "I didn't mean to take up so much time." She walked out stiffly, ignoring his parting words, willing herself not to cry. There was no help for Delia here. There was no doctor here any more.

CHAPTER 24

Tuesday Morning

"I think you should make an official complaint." Bella leaned forward in her desk chair, her floral blouse coming alive in the sunlight streaming through the office window. Her diamond ring sparkled as she framed her argument with her hands extended. "He's on drugs, with two little children at home and all those patients depending on him. The man doesn't have a conscience. It wouldn't surprise me one bit if Larry killed his father."

"It would me," said Addie. "But don't think I haven't considered it." Raised voices, electronic beeps and the clanking of a defective shopping cart floated up from the supermarket below. Addie used her feet to propel her chair backward until she could push their office door closed. "Believe me, I've questioned myself about each of Janet's kids." She rolled back to her desk. "I watched those kids grow up. I can't picture any one of them killing their father. Especially Larry. He's in the business of saving lives."

"Drugs can change anyone into a killer," said Bella. "You've seen those stories about parents murdering their children. You think it's any harder to murder your father?"

Addie's lips tightened. There were certainly times she'd wanted her step-father to die. Probably lots of people had such thoughts, but that didn't mean they'd commit murder. "Larry's not just anyone off the street. And he denied using illegal drugs. But I did look up the State Medical Board's complaint form on the Internet. It would be his word against mine. I don't have one whit of evidence."

"So you're going to let him get away with it?"

"No, that wouldn't be right. I'll tell George. He'll know what to do."

Bella grimaced. "With all due respect for your son, the police haven't done crap. They haven't found your housebreaker or Herbert's murderer, or even the pickup that tried to kill us."

"We can't be sure that wasn't an accident."

"Do we have to wait until they try again to be sure? No sooner does Dr. Wondernip tell us we're in danger from some Chinese mafia that listens in on his conversations, then bang – we're run off the road. Maybe he regretted telling us and got some other nutcase to drive the pickup."

"Just because two things happen close together, that doesn't mean one causes the other. But you may be right. I was racking my brain about why a Chinese group picked Millbrook, so I called Rona over the weekend to find out when they first contacted her. The initial call came from a Boston attorney two years ago. Rona is so tight-lipped about her clients, she wouldn't give me his name, but she did give his name to her nephew. She claimed he never specifically identified the group he represented, but they're Chinese and he's not."

"So?"

Addie locked her hands together behind her neck and stretched back in her chair. "Wouldn't you think that a Chinese-American spiritual group would use a Chinese-American attorney? But more important, going back to the timing of all this, Nascent Technologies moved to Millbrook three years ago. Marty says that Nascent has military contracts."

Bella's eyes widened. "Chinese spies want to kill us? I don't think so. Bring back the gypsies."

"I know it makes no sense. We don't know anything worth killing us for. And even if the Chinese want Herbert's land so they can spy on

Nascent, they wouldn't want to call attention to themselves."

"What about that guy I saw in Rona's car?"

"She told me he was from the spiritual group, but she wouldn't give his name. He wanted to see the land and the community. I also asked Rona how she intends to get the property rights away from Cletis. She said Cletis would sell his grandmother if the price was right."

"Then she doesn't really know Cletis."

"Neither do we, any more." Addie straightened in her chair. "Anyway, I told George and he'll talk with Detective Barker. They may call in the FBI."

"Oh, wow. I always wanted to meet a G-man."

"You could take this more seriously, you know. There is a murderer here, somewhere."

"What do you want me to do, tremble and cry? This whole thing has me more excited than anything I've been through since childbirth, and this is a hell of a lot less painful. If we can identify Herbert's killer before the police and the FBI, we'll be famous."

"Or dead," said Addie. "This is not a game. All I want is for someone to find Herbert's killer. The more people looking, the better. Still, if the FBI comes in, they'll be looking for industrial spies, not for the murderer. So kiss your G-man goodbye and let's do some work here." She awakened her computer.

"I hope you haven't kissed this new man in your life good-bye," said Bella.

Addie looked across the desk. "You just don't want to work."

"And you don't want to talk about Joe."

"I don't need a man in my life."

"So he didn't call again."

"No, he called."

"And he invited you out for coffee or tea, like he said he would?"

"Yes, but I said 'no, thank you.'"

Bella rolled her eyes. "How did he take being turned down this time?"

"He said he was disappointed but expected it. Then he said, 'Devil take the coffee. I've had enough to last a lifetime.'" Addie couldn't suppress a smile. "Then he asked me out to lunch again."

"There's a man for you. He's as stubborn as you are."

"I don't always like that in me, either."

"Did you accept?"

"Put it off, actually. It's hard enough I have to go out to dinner this week with Cletis."

Bella's jaw dropped. "Cletis? As in Cletis Desmond Adams?"

"He's sending surveyors and water engineers into the woods behind my house. I want to know what he's planning to build and how the deal with Herbert for land came about. I told you about the offer he made to Bess." She waved the image of Cletis away. "I certainly don't want *that* man in my life."

"But you're going out to dinner with him."

"I called to make an appointment with him at his office. He insisted on dinner. Believe me, it's not going to be a fun time for either one of us."

"I believe it. But I'd love to be a fly on the wall. You want my little tape recorder?"

"It won't be a meeting I'll want to remember."

"You never know. He's a bright man. Maybe he's a lot wiser than he was fifty years ago."

"You always did like him."

"So did you, as I recall." Bella raised her hand. "Not that I'm excusing what he did to you. It was a vile way to break off a relationship. I'm only saying, maybe – I mean it is remotely possible – he regrets how stupid and insensitive he was back then."

"A lot of good that does now."

"Maybe more than you think."

"What do you mean?"

Bella's grin turned sheepish. "I mean on this project behind your house. It can't hurt to be on good terms with the man in charge. So you're going to go out with Joe, too?"

"Why are you pushing me?" As well as changing the subject, thought Addie. "You're my best friend."

"You answered your own question. Maybe I should check Joe out for you. Life should be lived, not avoided."

"You think I'm going to find true romance at 70?"

"Find, rekindle, who knows? I leave such things in the capable hands of God. Pray and persevere and then let His will be done. God makes miracles happen."

"Oh," said Addie, deadpan. "So without a man, I need a miracle?"

"No, but think long and hard before you turn either one down."

CHAPTER 25

Tuesday Evening

She hadn't stepped into the Brookside Inn since the children took her there on her 65th birthday, but it seemed to have changed far less than she had in the past five years. The two young men on valet duty still wore white shirts and ties beneath their half-zipped ski jackets, and the carpet in the entry hall was the same tight-woven brown plaid, the dark paneling still festooned with framed awards, testimonials, and photos of Massachusetts politicians.

She paused to look at the faded 1884 photo of the original inn and an adjacent stable. Yes, that was a place she would've wanted to stay. The twentieth-century additions and remodelings had deprived the inn of charm and authenticity. It had survived because of its function rooms, its snob appeal to the business community, and the aggressively marketed image of quaint New England it sold to the tourists.

As Addie approached the reception stand, the white-jacketed greeter looked up from his reservation sheet. Like a Ken-doll, his lips offered a stenciled smile while his eyes stared beyond her as if awaiting the arrival of her escort, if not Barbie herself.

"Welcome to the Brookside. Do you have a reservation?"

Had Cletis made one? No matter. "I'm early. I'm waiting for a – " No, not a friend; certainly not an acquaintance after sixty-plus years. "Someone."

"I see," said Ken-doll.

Sure that he didn't, she nodded.

"If you're waiting – " He stepped around his lectern and extended a hand. "May I take your coat to the checkroom?"

What if she and Cletis fought? What if she couldn't bear his arrogance? She pressed the small evening bag she'd borrowed from Bess firmly against her black coat. "No, I'll keep my coat, thank you."

"Certainly." His hand flowed laterally, indicating a room to her left. "Perhaps you'd be more comfortable waiting in the Governor Peabody Parlor rather than the bar."

"Yes, I'd appreciate that." She thanked him with a smile. "If a Mr. Adams comes looking for me – my name is Carter – please tell him I'm there, will you?"

"Certainly. May I inquire if that's Mr. Cletis Adams?"

"He made a reservation?"

"No madam, he doesn't need to. He has his own table."

"His own table?"

"Yes, madam. He's co-owner of the Brookside."

"Oh." No way she'd surrender her coat.

Entering the parlor, she felt comforted by the fire on the brick hearth. She smiled at a young couple sitting thigh to thigh and holding hands on the sofa against the wall opposite the hearth, but they only had eyes for each other. She'd been that starry eyed with Cletis. Sure, they'd had some wonderful moments, otherwise the sight of young lovers like this wouldn't give her a twinge of what might've been. But that was a long time ago. She hoped these two youngsters would have better luck.

She sat down in a straight-backed chair close to the fireplace. Farther into the room, two businessmen in leather chairs were quietly discussing something over a loose-leaf binder and drinks. On the wall behind them, a painting of an old farmhouse in a bucolic valley. Life looked peaceful in landscapes, she thought. It was harder to find peace once people were involved. Well, with Cletis, she didn't need peace, she needed answers.

She was debating whether to shed her coat when Cletis entered the room and strode toward her, a smile lighting up his face. She clenched her teeth. She had to be civil and get through this. He had no power over her, any more.

Cletis carried himself well and appeared to be fit, she had to give him that. Still, what healthy, white-haired man wouldn't look good if he could afford custom-made suits, hundred dollar ties, personal trainers and a hair-stylist?

"Addie, how good to see you." His voice was deep, his tone sincere. "I'm so glad you called."

She forced herself to smile, to stand up and extend her hand as if her knees and back were twenty years younger and memory was no burden at all. "Hello, Cletis."

He took her hand between his and slowly shook his head. "Hard to believe."

"What is?" She extracted her hand.

"Aren't you hot in that coat?"

Vintage Cletis, she thought. Avoiding and misdirecting. "Yes," she said, slipping the coat off a shoulder.

"Here, let me." He stepped to her side, raised his hands to help.

"Thank you, but I'm perfectly capable."

He smiled. "That was never in doubt. Can we maintain your independence if we check your coat?"

"I don't know how long I'm staying."

"Nor do I. But I promise two things – "

"And I'm to believe your promises?" Damn! How did that slip out?

For a moment, his eyes closed, then a rueful smile broke through. "I still say all the wrong things when I'm with you. I'm sorry, Addie, sorry for so many things."

"I'm sorry, too. I didn't mean to – "

"I know."

She nodded. Neither of them wanted to rub salt on old wounds. "So your two promises?"

"Forget it."

"I'm curious."

He chuckled. "Some things never change... I promise you safe and silent passage out of here whenever you decide to leave. And I promise no one will hold your coat hostage. Fair enough?"

"Fair enough. And I promise to act like a lady instead of a rejected lover." She offered a tentative smile. "We'll get down to brass tacks after dinner, okay?" Oh, dear. She was such a blockhead with him.

"Brass tacks for dessert," he said. "I can't say I look forward to it. But a dinner with you will be worth it."

* * *

While a young waitress in a white blouse and black trousers cleared away their dinner plates, Addie noted the benign smile Cletis wore as he awaited whatever was to come next. Surely it was one of the most uncomfortable dinners she'd ever had. Not because of her Caesar salad, and not really because of the Cletis Adams who sat across from her, for he'd certainly tried his best to be pleasant, to show interest in her life, and to change the subject when she'd deflected his questions. He'd told amusing, often self-deprecating anecdotes of his foreign travels, updated her on classmates he'd heard from or seen in recent years, and discussed the Patriots' chances to get to the Super Bowl. Yes, the small-town boy had polished his act. And he was smart enough to avoid the minefields of their past.

She'd been equally careful, sitting on her anxiety and anger while politely fending off personal questions and keeping the focus on him and his business. What surprised her was that instead of coming on like Donald Trump, Cletis had played the modesty card. Oh yes, he'd profited in the boom years, but he'd taken his hits lately, both from the economy and from competitors underbidding him on more projects than ever before.

"Excuse me," said the waitress. Addie sat back as the girl ran a crumb sweeper over the tablecloth in front of her, then went to do the same for

Cletis. He smiled at the girl as if he were a patient grandfather.

No, thought Addie, there was no way she'd buy his pretense of sensitivity and benevolence. Successful developers weren't like that. Not that she was an expert on anything or a better human being. God knew her flaws all too well. Cletis probably saw right through her, too. If the land behind her house wasn't an issue, he'd leave her in the dust again in two seconds flat. He probably considered her a resentful, provincial and narrow-minded shrew. It was certainly a good thing they'd never married.

"Would you like an after-dinner drink or dessert?" the waitress asked.

"A double Grand Marnier, please," said Cletis. "You, Addie?"

"A cup of chamomile tea, please."

"Chamomile?" asked Cletis as the waitress carried off the tray of soiled plates. "You feeling okay?"

"No, but I'm not ill. A bit ill-tempered perhaps. What's happening with the land behind my house?"

He wiped his mouth with his linen napkin. She wondered if, behind it, he was collecting his thoughts or licking his lips.

"The Herbal Trust land?" He put the napkin on the table. "We're planning to develop it. I prom — I assure you, Addie, your house and land won't be threatened or diminished in value. I aim to keep a lot of open space but put up some luxury condos and town-houses for what we call 'active seniors' – with hiking and bike trails, a clubhouse with health club and swimming pool, and a separate assisted-living facility and nursing home."

She shook her head in disbelief. "My God, how can Millbrook afford that? I know you'll have private investors, but the traffic, the infrastructure, the loss of greenery – "

"How can they afford not to do it? We've lost our industrial base, the population is aging, the kids are going elsewhere for jobs. The tax revenues from this development will be substantial. Believe me, Addie, I don't live here any more, but I still consider this my home town. I wouldn't do anything to – mess it up." He picked up his unused teaspoon and turned it over in his hand. "The other truth is that I see my active days – even my life, coming to a close. I've had three wives but I have no close family."

"You have a stepson."

"Michael wouldn't take me in out of the rain if I wasn't his employer. For a smart man, I've been dumb when it comes to relationships.You know that better than anyone."

She felt sadness welling up, then anger, but she managed to keep her voice calm. "You chose the rich girl over the poor girl, Cletis. Did you get sincerity and love with her money?"

He put down the spoon, kept his gaze on the table. "What I got was opportunity, the right connections, and yes, a nice chunk of money – which greatly eased the path to earning my own." He looked up and met her gaze. "No matter who's in or out of my life, I can always depend on my money."

Under the table, her fingers dug into her thighs. What a stupid young girl she'd been. How could she have been so blind?

"Still," he said, his voice deepening, forming words slowly, "what I lost was incalculable. It took two days of marriage to my first wife to think that, and several years of growing up inside to believe it. That's why I called you after your husband ran off."

She grimaced. "Hardly the best timing for a 'kiss and make-up' reunion."

"I was divorced. I wanted to help."

"I wouldn't have taken a nickel from you."

"I believe your exact words were, 'I wouldn't take a nickel from you even if I have to go begging on the street.' Plus a few choice epithets." Cletis smiled. "You know I'd never heard you swear before? I thought 'oh crumb' was the best you could do."

Addie couldn't help but smile. Cletis had endured her stepfather's profanity enough to know she'd been exposed to a larger vocabulary. "I'm sorry if I went overboard, but I wasn't about to let another man abandon me – especially one who'd already done it. Some of what I said to you was rightfully deserved, but I know a lot of my ranting was meant for my husband and his floozy. I also think I hit you with some of the rage I couldn't ever express to my stepfather." She raised a finger. "But don't think this meeting is about making up. There's no way to do that, even if, as you say, life is coming to a close for both of us."

"There are no do-overs, but that doesn't mean – " He stopped abruptly as the waitress approached, put the teapot and fixings in front of Addie, then the glass of brandy in front of him. "Thank you," he said, taking a monogrammed billfold from his pocket. "We'll need some privacy after this." He extracted a fifty-dollar bill. "That's for your service and to make sure we're not disturbed."

The waitress offered a very appreciative smile. "Thank you, Mr. Adams."

Totally unnecessary, thought Addie. She put her teabag in the pot of hot water, waited until the waitress was out of earshot, then said, "I want to pay my half of the bill."

"I don't get a bill. I own half the restaurant."

"Then I'll figure out what I owe and pay it to the other half."

He took a sip of brandy and smiled. "Still the same Addie. Really, the last thing we should fight about is money. We have so many more important issues."

"Like the closing chapters of your life?"

"Certainly important to me." He put down his brandy glass. "I've really thought about where I want to end my days – that is, assuming I have some choice in the matter. I decided I wanted to go out in a place that I built, in a town where I grew up, played ball, had friends and, forgive me for this, but it's true – " His hand moved toward her, stopped well short of hers. " – where I first fell in love."

She hated the painful swelling in her chest. "You're getting maudlin, Cletis." She bowed her head and made a show of dunking her teabag in the pot of hot water.

His hand retreated. "It must be the Grand Marnier. Always makes me nostalgic. You want to try a little bit in your chamomile?"

She pushed her teacup and saucer away, put her forearms on the table in what her mother had called "a most unladylike manner" and leaned forward. "How is it you got the land from Herbert Elwood?"

A smile flitted across Cletis' face, then his expression turned serious. "He died – but you know. Must've been a terrible shock to discover the body."

"You didn't answer my question. How did you get the land?"

He sighed. "It's a long, unhappy story. The bottom line is that my company had a purchase and sale agreement on the land for two million dollars, signed by Elwood many years ago and registered in Probate Court. I – my company, that is – put down a healthy deposit, but I was sure the value of the land would increase. Elwood really didn't want to sell it – at least, not right away – so the expiration date was set thirty years from the date of signing. His death allowed us to move to execute the purchase. It's not a done deal, but his heirs would have a long legal battle if they tried to sell it to anyone else. And to put it succinctly, his kids want the money now."

She sank back in her chair, blew out a breath she'd held too long. Cletis had given her a lot to think about. Why would Herbert sign if he didn't want to sell? The deposit money? Why not get a bank loan? By his own admission, Cletis felt time was running out on his developing this multimillion dollar monument to himself. Then poof, Herbert is murdered. Coincidence? Unlikely. She looked up at him.

"No, I didn't kill him, Addie. I didn't plan or execute his murder."

"I didn't ask you that."

"It was going to be your next question, wasn't it?"

She nodded, then sat up straight again and reached for the teapot. Did it really matter to him whether she believed he had no hand in the murder? "Before his death, did you call him about the land?"

"No."

"Do you know that someone was calling him?"

"Rona Barker, but I wasn't aware of it. And perhaps other people called, too. Developers are always searching for prime land. Did you see or hear anything on the night of the murder?"

"You're the umpteenth person to ask me that. I was sound asleep." She poured a cupful of tea for herself. When she looked up, he was staring at her. "Really, I didn't hear a thing. I was of no use to the police – or to Herbert, for that matter. You were at a fundraiser for the governor?"

"I was. That obnoxious detective – Rona's nephew of all things – checked it out with the governor's aides."

"Then why did you tell Michael to say you were sleeping with me that night?"

He leaned back in his chair. "I told Michael what?"

"That you were sleeping with me."

He shook his head emphatically. "I never said that – never! Unfortunately, Michael's one of those grown-up children who love practical jokes. He once paid to have a circus elephant staked out on my lawn. He seems to get a kick out of other people's discomfort."

Which one was lying? Michael, probably. "Would Michael get a kick out of bashing someone's head in?"

"No, of course not. I've never known him to be violent. He's a good foreman, but a barely adequate project manager. I don't think he'd have the inclination or ability to think through how to get away with murder."

"No one's gotten away with it yet," she said.

"Does George say the police have some clues?"

"George never talks to me about his work."

"The self-reliant, self-disciplined Carters. You've raised your children well, Addie. I'll bet you're very proud of them."

"I am, but I don't take credit for who they are. In tough times, a family learns the importance of pulling together."

"Or falls apart. You held your family together."

"I only did what any caring mother would do. There's nothing special about me."

"If that were true, we wouldn't be having this conversation."

"Yes we would. I want to know why you've made Bess such a lucrative job offer."

He smiled. "She told you it was lucrative?"

"She's happy managing the branch bank. She wouldn't even consider leaving it unless something much bigger was offered." Addie raised her hand to stop him before he even opened his mouth. "And don't fob me off with what a good worker she is. You could have your pick of better qualified people."

"So what is it you suspect? That I have evil designs on your daughter?"

"It crossed my mind. Bess is a beautiful woman."

"Yes, I've noticed. But not up to what I saw in her mother."

She felt blood rush to her face. "Don't play with me. I know you too well."

His jaw tightened. "Do you? I think not. You know the 18 year-old kid who left this town, not the man who came back. I don't lust after your daughter. If I had any lust to satisfy – as you say, I'd have my pick of better qualified people." He cleared his throat, softened his tone. "Look, I want your daughter to work for me partly because of her banking skills, and partly because of her ability to recognize bullshit and call people on it – I know where that particular trait comes from and I admire it. We have a lot of bullshit in the development business. But mostly, Addie, I want Bess as a role model."

She was so startled, she couldn't suppress a laugh. "For you? Isn't it a bit late?"

He laughed, too. "You really are a goose, sometimes, you know? For my granddaughter. From my second wife, may she rest in peace, the gold-digging bitch."

"You said you had no close family."

"And that's true. Wife number two flitted off to Los Angeles when our child was barely three. Needless to say, we had a major legal battle, which I eventually won in principal, but she brain-washed my daughter so that visitation became unbearable for us both." Above his glass of brandy, his hands seemed to repel each other. "I backed off, but I kept tabs on what was happening to Barbara – my daughter – hoping that there'd be a place for me in her life after she grew up. Unfortunately, when she was sixteen, she ran off with a wanna-be actor who sold drugs. She only surfaced when she was frightened to death about delivering a baby." His hands found the brandy glass. "Social services stepped in and it was all quite a mess for a few years, with everyone involved, including the other grandparents, asserting that Barbara was an unfit mother and that they'd do better raising the child." Cletis sighed. "To make a long story short, my daughter prevailed in retaining custody, promising to put her life in order, but she didn't really want to give up the partying and the drugs to raise a child. I was invited to pay for boarding schools and did so in exchange for visitation. Fortunately, Cassie – my granddaughter – turned out to be a resilient and appreciative kid. So I paid for her four years at Mount Holyoke – and now that she'll graduate this May, I'm giving her a job." He shrugged. "Who knows where that will lead? She is my only true heir."

Addie put a hand on her cheek. Amazing how they'd been so close, only to live their adult lives in separate worlds. "What about your daughter?"

His face became grim. "Died of a drug overdose. That's one reason I want a different type of role model for Cassie."

"I'm really sorry for your loss. Cletis – "

"I know. Bess did drugs for a time. I want someone who's been there and come back stronger. Someone Cassie can look up to as a supervisor, and maybe come to see as more than that."

Addie frowned. "How did you know Bess used drugs? You weren't in town during those years."

"Even when I'm away, I keep my finger on the pulse of things here."

"Who did you talk to?"

"I can't betray people who tell me things in confidence."

No, she thought, just those who love you – loved you. Even as she corrected herself, she felt blood rush to her face. "I really don't like the way you're intruding in my life," she said.

"I think it's Bess' life. And she's an adult."

"It's more than Bess. It's my home, it's my privacy, it's my grandson Marty. It's too much out of the blue, without my consent."

Cletis looked puzzled. "Your grandson?"

"Don't pretend you didn't know."

He threw up his hands. "Know what? Damn it, I'm not all-knowing."

"You don't know that Marty's been seeing Cassie?"

"The *Millbrook Messenger* kid? I swear I didn't know." He started to laugh. "I don't even know how I feel about it."

"Then why are you laughing?"

"I had the crazy thought that we could wind up as great-grandparents in common."

"And that's funny?"

"No, it was the image – " He burst into laughter, wiped his eyes with his napkin. " – the image of you and me in our rocking chairs on the porch of my assisted living building, arguing over who should rock the baby."

She had to laugh. "There's no fool like an old fool. Only two old fools would be worse." She pushed back from the table, stood up and took her evening bag from the back of her chair.

He rose much more gracefully. "I take it you're ready for your coat."

"After I get a menu and see how much I owe for my Caesar salad."

"Addie, please – "

Oh crumb. Why was she being so stiff-necked? "No. I'm sorry. Thank you for dinner. I do appreciate your talking to me. I have a lot to think about, now. I hope you won't bother me while I do."

His face seemed to harden. "You called me."

"And I may again. Meanwhile, I'd appreciate it if you have Michael let me know whenever something is going to happen on the land behind my house. And tell him, no more jokes."

"I'll do that. It was good that we finally talked."

"Yes. It was."

She felt relieved that he made no move to show her out. By the time she retrieved her coat, she was scolding herself for the way she'd behaved, and even more for feeling annoyed that he hadn't walked her to the door.

CHAPTER 26

WEDNESDAY NIGHT

Paws scampering across her body awakened her instantly. "Flash?" She heard glass shatter downstairs and the electronic scream of the burglar alarm. She threw back her quilt and struggled out of bed in the dark, trying to make sense of it all. What broke? Who could be downstairs? She snatched her glasses from the bedside table, put them on and read 2:10 on the face of the clock-radio. Robber? Murderer? Call 911. She reached for the telephone, felt reassured by the dial tone. At least no one had cut the wires.

"Millbrook Police Department. Please state your emergency," said a woman.

"I think someone's broken into my house," Addie whispered.

"I'm having trouble hearing you."

Addie brought the receiver close to her lips and intensified her whisper. This time, the woman heard, asked for Addie's address and phone number, then told her to lock her door and stay on the line until the police arrived. The alarm's shriek made it hard to think. Nowhere to hide, nothing to defend herself with. She'd be an easy target standing by the telephone. Only the bathrooms had doors that locked, but neither door could withstand a good kick.

The woman's voice sounded too loud. "We received the alarm company's call. Officers should be arriving shortly. Are you still there?"

"Yes." She scanned the dark room by memory and focused on the metal lamp on her nightstand. Her knees hurt as she got down on the floor, followed the plug to the outlet and pulled the plug free.

No footsteps on the stairs, no more sounds from below. She pushed herself up, pulled off the lampshade and wound the cord around the base so she wouldn't trip over it. Not much of a defense, she thought as she gripped the cool metal, but damnation take her if she went without a fight. No one had a right to invade her home. Twice, no less. What was so vital they'd ignore the alarm company's signs?

She put the telephone receiver on her bed. Lamp in hand, she padded silently to her bedroom door, always left ajar for Flash. Would the intruder think twice about killing a cat? Her heart beat faster. She opened the door cautiously and slipped out into the hall. Her house seemed to quiver under the electronic shriek. Her hand found the banister, her bare feet the top step. She took a deep breath and started down...two...three... The fourth step creaked. Oh shit! She gripped the lamp with both hands, thought she heard a rustle below. Five...six...

* * *

"I wish I knew how you got so popular with the wrong people, Mrs. Carter," said Barker. "You must've done something for this guy to send you a message like this." He pointed to one of the three Zip-Loc bags that lay on the kitchen table around which they and young Officer Peterson were seated. One plastic bag contained the baseball-sized rock, the second enclosed the message -six separate words cut out of a magazine or newspaper and pasted onto a sheet of white paper. The third bag held the rubber bands that had bound paper and rock together.

Addie sniffed. "I could do without the sarcasm, Detective. If you think I did something knowingly to cause this, say it straight out. I'd love to know what it might be." She didn't like his insinuation, his attitude, or his forearms planted on top of her table. She refrained from looking for support from George, who was dumping a dustpan of window glass into the garbage pail.

"What makes you think it was a man?" she asked. "Women can throw rocks."

"I didn't mean it had to be a man," said Barker. "It's just more likely. It's a baseball thing."

Officer Peterson looked up from the report he was writing. "My cousin Tilda played Little League."

Addie rewarded Peterson with a smile, but the uniformed officer had gone back to writing. Peterson had been the first responder to her 911 call and she still felt like she wanted to hug him. Even though it'd been obvious that a rock had been flung through her living room window, Peterson had searched for an intruder in the house while a second officer had made sure no one was lurking outside. No doubt the young officers had been particularly thorough because George was on the way, but she'd never felt more relieved to have men with guns in her house.

Barker cast a baleful look at Peterson. "This isn't Little League. Leave it to us grown-ups, okay?"

Peterson kept his head down and continued writing.

Addie cut through the embarrassing silence. "Were you making a point for me, Detective?" Barker's arrival - so full of himself despite George having things well in hand - was only slightly more welcome than the rock itself. Not that she in her terrycloth robe, nightgown and cat-torn slippers presented a respectable image, but she didn't have to put up with his guff.

"The point is that days after your neighbor was murdered, someone ransacks your house. Then someone tries to run you off the road, then – "

"Did run us off the road. Have you found the pickup or the driver, yet?"

"It's hard to do without a license plate number. We'll keep checking the body shops. But now someone flings a rock through your living room window." Barker indicated the plastic bag containing the message. "I think we can safely assume that 'Stop meddling. You could be next.' refers to the murder next door, don't you?"

"I don't know what else it could mean," said Addie.

"So it would seem that this rock-thrower – female, male or transgendered – knows something of what you've been doing and doesn't like it. I, on the other hand, don't know what you've been doing, who you've talked to and what was said, and I would very much like you to tell me."

"Certainly. The problem is I talk to a lot of people in the course of a week, and at my age, I don't always remember what I said or they said to me. I did tell you after the accident about our visit to Dr. Warley. I don't think I've done anything unusual since."

"I went out there and talked to Warley. He doesn't own a pickup and he has solid alibis for the night Dr. Elwood was killed and the day your house was ransacked."

"What did you make of his conspiracy theory?"

The detective's hand brushed it away. "He's a good vet, but he's a fruitcake about other things. That's why I stopped – "

"Playing cards with him?"

"Seeing him altogether. But I don't think he threw this rock. He's too smart, and he certainly doesn't want to see me in an official capacity."

She offered as sweet a smile as she could muster. "Did he tell you Shot Glass is doing fine?"

"We didn't talk about that," said Barker.

"Shot Glass?" asked Officer Peterson.

"A parrot Detective Barker lost in a poker game – I should say 'allegedly lost.' He knows a lot of dirty words — I mean the parrot does. No telling who he learned them from."

Peterson's body shook. He hunched over his report and covered his mouth with his hand.

"Enough, Ma." George moved around the table to the empty chair, reversed and straddled it. "Sorry, Harris."

"Don't you have to get back on patrol?" Barker asked Peterson. "You can finish your report at the station."

"Sure, on my way, Detective." His chair scraped the floor as he got up. "I hope everything goes okay from here on out, Mrs. Carter. Oh, one more question for my report – " He wagged his notebook at them. "Is Shot Glass one word or two?"

"Get your ass out of here," Barker growled.

"Two words," said Addie, "and thank you again for responding so quickly."

"Don't hesitate to call," said Peterson. She heard him whistling his way to the front door.

"Okay, Ma, what makes you think Dr. Warley didn't throw the rock?"

Addie took off her glasses to rub her eyes, heard the front door open, then close. "Other than what Detective Barker said?" She put her glasses back on. "If Dr. Warley'd wanted to warn me to stop meddling, he wouldn't have waited a whole week. He certainly didn't want any attention from the police. And he wouldn't have done something that put glass on the floor because that could have hurt Flash. The man may be strange with people, but he really does love animals."

"So who else've you been talking to that was connected to Dr. Elwood?" asked Barker.

"I've spoken to his children, and George probably mentioned that Raymond Miggens came over soon after you talked with him." Better to hold off mentioning Delia until a plan could be devised to help her should Raymond be arrested. Joe Kearney? No, that was purely social. "Let me see – who else? My friend Bella Auterio. Then Cletis Adams, and briefly with his stepson Michael Planchette. And of course, your Aunt Rona."

Barker frowned. "Let's start with Adams. What did he tell you?"

"I'm sorry. It's very late, and it'll take time to tell you what I remember of each conversation. I'll remember more after I've gotten some sleep."

"Okay. Suppose you come down to the station at two this afternoon."

Addie yawned. She rubbed the back of her neck. "I'm supposed to work at Auterio's and I certainly will be late going in. How about four o'clock?"

"Alright. You going to camp out here tonight, George?"

"You bet. I'll vacuum up the living room and stay with her until she goes to work."

"Don't I have a say in this?" asked Addie.

"Sure," said George. "You can decide which glazier I call tomorrow morning."

"Did you know that men have thicker skulls and softer brains?" she asked.

"You talking about Elwood's murder?" asked Barker.

"No, just a mother's tired observation."

"Sorry, Ma. Is it okay if I sleep over tonight?"

She looked into her son's bloodshot blue eyes. "Yes, George. I'll feel a lot safer. Thank you."

"It's no big deal," he said.

"I think it is. When you give me a voice, you give me some hope for mankind."

CHAPTER 27

Thursday Morning

Bella sped by a pickup loaded with old furniture, then zipped the rented Cadillac back into the right lane only seconds before a minivan brushed by on her left, its driver laying on the horn. "I'm glad you had the alarm," she said. "You know how I love to say I told you so."

Addie eased her pressure on the dashboard. "Why is it your foresight doesn't help your driving?"

"Don't change the subject. The accident wasn't my fault. But thank you for your confidence in letting me drive again."

"Who says I'm confident?"

"You should be. I am." Bella looked over and grinned, then returned her attention to the road. "Have you considered moving out of your house for a while? Carlo and I could put you up."

"No, thank you. I'd be putting you in danger. And then, there's Flash – no one would be too happy with him as a boarder. My kids offered to let me move in with them, but that's even worse. At least you and Carlo wouldn't treat me like a child. But when would it be safe to go back home? Even if the murderer is found quickly, who's to say he doesn't have accomplices." Addie shook her head. "I'll do okay at home. The glazier came this morning, and George will be back to babysit me tonight There's just this last bit to take care of before I have to meet Detective Barker at four."

"I'm glad you asked me to come with you," said Bella. "Adventuring sure beats the hell out of standing behind a deli counter."

"It's not going to be much of an adventure. I'm only going to talk with Raymond for a few minutes, and I'd appreciate it if you stay in the car."

"You don't trust me?"

"I'd trust you with my life. I don't trust Raymond, any more. That's why we're going to give him a little surprise where he's not likely to make a scene. I want you and your cell phone in the car in case you have to dial 911."

"Or run the little bastard over. That would teach him not to throw rocks through your window."

"One rock. And I'm not certain it was him." It was hard to imagine Cletis or any of Herbert's sophisticated children using a rock to send her a warning.

Michael, the practical joker, was a possibility, but she'd hardly spoken to him, much less meddled in his affairs, and what would he have to gain by doing something that attracted attention? Ditto for Dr. Warley, although no way to know what his delusions might drive him to. "I just think Raymond's the most likely suspect." Throwing a rock through a window was usually a juvenile thing, and Raymond was an over-aged adolescent. And then when George had driven away after breakfast, the penny dropped – she'd realized she hadn't heard a car drive away after the stone crashed through the window. Either the rock thrower didn't need a car, or the car was parked some distance down the street.

Bella eased the Cadillac to a stop at a red light. "He's going to deny it, you know. The kids today have no sense of personal responsibility. Even my Anthony, when I try to talk with him about what he's not doing with his life – well, you've seen us get into it."

Addie nodded in sympathy, as much for Anthony as for her friend. "Either Raymond talks to me or he'll have to talk to Detective Barker – probably both, but he won't admit anything to Barker. I don't need him to confess he threw the rock. I want him to tell me where he goes Thursday nights, especially the night Herbert was murdered. And even if he won't tell me that, he'd better help me figure out what to do about his mother."

"But isn't that what he meant by 'stop meddling?'"

"I don't think so. I think he'd welcome help with his mother. But Delia must've let it slip that she told me about his being out Thursday nights. That ruined his alibi, and he panicked."

"Stupid kid, threatening the person who most wanted to help."

"It happens." She'd certainly alienated Cletis when he'd tried to reach out after Dave had run off. She'd been too proud. Too hurt. And she'd pushed him away again the other night. But how could she ever trust him? He was still shrewd and self-serving, still thought money was the solution to every problem – the stain-remover for the rare guilt-spot on his conscience.

"There it is," said Bella.

"Where?"

"Across from the Dunkin' Donuts." Bella pointed to the red on white Doyle's Autobody sign atop a one-story concrete building. Tapping her scarlet fingernails on the wheel, she waited for an oncoming school bus to pass, then turned the Cadillac through the open gate of a chain link fence and down a gauntlet of beat-up cars. She stopped the Cadillac a few feet in front of a large gray door, the middle one of three, all closed. "Get him to come out here. I'm going to back into that space next to the van, so I can run him down and we can make a quick getaway."

Addie clicked open her seatbelt. "Bella, this isn't a TV show. If I'm not out in a few minutes, look through the glass panel of one of those doors. And keep your cell phone handy."

The wind hit her as she got out of the car. She zipped her parka up to her neck. There was a worn sign that said OFFICE on a door at the end of the building, so Addie headed there, hoping Raymond wasn't out buying auto parts or having a late lunch. Opening the door, she recoiled from the sounds of metal being pounded, the stink of oil and paint, and the grimace from a stocky man in coveralls who, in looking up from his meal, dropped a piece of sushi from his chopsticks onto his littered desk.

"Damn," he said. His grizzled head bobbed down and then up. "Not you, lady, it's these." He waggled the chopsticks in a grimy hand, then dropped them into an empty take-out box.

"I'm not all that good with chopsticks myself," said Addie.

"My hands are too big," he said. "Ya'd think with all the brains at Toyota and Honda, they could come up with a better way to eat sushi." He studied the detritus on his desk for a few seconds, then brushed the fragments of rice and vegetables onto the back of an invoice pad and off into a wastebasket. "Name's Gary. Mr. Doyle's out right now. What can I do for ya?"

"I'd like to see Raymond Miggens for a few minutes, please."

"You his mother?"

"A friend of his mother."

"Your car get bashed?"

"No, it's a personal matter."

"Oh, per—son—al." Gary leaned back in his chair, turned his head toward an inner door and yelled, "Ray! Your parole officer's here!" In the shop, the pounding of metal stopped abruptly. Gary turned to Addie and winked. "Just kidding. He's a good kid, but I like to yank his chain."

Addie managed a small smile. "I see."

Raymond's "Fuck you, Gary," preceded his entry in dirty coveralls. Protective goggles dangled from his neck. He spotted Addie and his thick eyebrows rose, then fell as his facial muscles drew into a frown. "It's not my mother, is it?"

"No, but I do need to talk with you for a few minutes – privately."

"So come by the house after supper. I'm working."

"I don't think your mother needs to hear what I have to say."

"Uh-oh," said Gary.

Raymond shot an angry glance at Gary. "Give us a few minutes. This shouldn't take long."

"Sure, dude." Gary pushed back his chair and stood up. "Pleased t'meet ya. Come back when you've bashed your car." He started for the door.

Annoying man, thought Addie.

"Ignore him," said Raymond. "He can be a dickhead, sometimes." He folded his arms across his chest. "So, what did you come to say to me."

"You owe me the price of a window and a man's labor to fix it."

Raymond shook his head. "I told that fat detective like I'm telling you – I don't know what you're talking about."

"I think you do. Your mother told me about Thursday nights, and you were worried I'd tell the police. So you sent me a nasty message."

He thrust his face forward. "I didn't send you anything."

Too much anger, she thought. If he were innocent, wouldn't he be curious about the message? "Yes, you did. Airmail." No, not curious, but clever enough to be concerned about penmanship and fingerprints. "But you shouldn't have worn those gloves. The police say they leave traces you can see under a microscope," she fibbed.

"Bullshit! Latex gloves don't leave prints."

"Did I say they were latex?"

He looked away, then quickly back. "I just used that as an example."

"No, you tried to frighten me, and you did. I even thought you might be Herbert's murderer."

His hands shot out, grimy palms open to her. "I swear I never touched the old man. I've never even been in his house."

"I believe that, but I'm not sure that the police do. So I want to figure out how someone will care for your mother in the days or weeks it might take for you to sort it out with them."

"You going to sic the cops on me again?"

"I don't need to. Detective Barker will come to you for anything and everything until the real murderer is found. So you do the right thing and pay for fixing my window. And I want to know where you go Thursday nights."

"Barker said it was a rock. I didn't throw it. So why should I pay for your fucking window?"

No, he wasn't going to admit it, and her anger wouldn't help Delia. "Let's call it a Good Neighbor policy. You're going to pay for the window and guard my house against something like that happening again, and I'm going to help you get your mother into treatment."

He eyed her suspiciously. "How?"

She explained how he might check to see what her insurance would cover, how they would schedule a crisis team visit to his home when both of them were there with Delia, and how they'd both persuade her do whatever was recommended, with their support as the carrot and the threat of Raymond leaving to live elsewhere as the stick. "I've asked my friend Bella and a few friends from church to visit her regularly and to help get her to whatever appointments she needs. You'll have to make her agree to go with them and continue to see that she takes her medication."

Raymond pulled a rag from the pocket of his coveralls and wiped the back of his neck. His forehead was furrowed, his gaze steady.

"What's wrong?" asked Addie.

"Why are you doing this? And don't bullshit me with that 'good neighbor' crap."

Addie's eyes widened. Was helping your neighbor so foreign to young people? He'd never believe that seeing Delia so depressed had reminded her of her own dark days, and the very few people who'd reached out to her. "I'm offering to help your mother because I'm frightened that if we don't catch Herbert's murderer, I could be next. That's what the rock said, and if you didn't throw it, the murderer did. So I'm making a deal with you. To get my help, you have to tell me where you go Thursday nights, so then I have one less person to be frightened of."

"That's stupid."

"It may be. But that's the deal."

Raymond pocketed the rag. He turned toward the door that led to the shop, took two steps, then did an about face. "You can't tell the cops."

"I'll have to use my judgment on that."

He touched his chest. "I'm not worried because I'm doing anything wrong. But I don't want to get my girlfriend in trouble."

"Your girlfriend?"

"Yeah, she's illegal. If the cops go to question her, she could lose her job, or they could find out she and her family don't have papers and they all could be deported."

Addie pursed her lips. Raymond sounded sincere, but he also sounded sincere about not throwing the rock. "I want you to bring your girlfriend to meet me." She saw him bristle. "I promise I won't do anything to get her in trouble with the police or immigration people. But I still don't understand why you need to sneak out to see her."

"If I told my mother, she'd freak out I was going to leave her. She'd insist on meeting Yolanda, and I didn't want Yolanda to meet my mother like she is. If you tell the cops about Yolanda, I'll deny it."

"Like you would about the rock?"

"Rock? What rock?"

"But you will pay for my window?"

He put his hands on his head, inhaled the bad air and looked up as if seeking divine guidance. Finally, he met her gaze and offered a grudging smile. "Yeah, isn't that what a good neighbor does?"

CHAPTER 28

Thursday Afternoon

Detective Barker leaned forward in his chair, planted his hands on his desktop and scowled. "I've been in this business long enough to know when a witness is holding out on me," he said. With his jowls in five o'clock shadow, his shirt collar open, sleeves rolled up and tie knot at half mast, the man looked like he thrived on intimidation.

"I'm not a witness," said Addie. "I didn't see or hear anything the night of the murder." What more could she tell him without betraying Raymond and his girlfriend, without making statements about Larry using drugs or Leslie's bruises – statements which might lead to false impressions and accusations. Especially after the tactless way he'd used Gloria's concerns.

"I'm not talking only about that night."

"I'm trying to be cooperative." And civil, she thought, although that was more difficult after an hour in this chair. No wonder some people confessed quickly. She took a breath and wrinkled her nose at the cigarette stench.

"Trying to be cooperative isn't the same as being," he said.

"I've answered all your questions."

"Sure, if you count 'I don't know' and 'I don't remember' as answers. You report all of these conversations with persons of interest to this investigation, but what do you tell me?" He straightened in his chair and raised his right thumb. "Simon Warley must be innocent because he's a paranoid who loves cats but hates cops and politicians. Raymond – "

"I think Dr. Warley loves all animals," interjected Addie. "Remember how he treated Shot Glass?"

Barker flushed. "I stand corrected – he loves all animals." His index finger popped up alongside his thumb. "Raymond Miggens must be innocent because he shoveled your walk and he loves his depressed mother." The name of each suspect summoned up another finger. "You say Gloria Elwood didn't want revenge for being kicked out by her dad and she claims she doesn't care about money, she only wants justice and acceptance. But did she ever threaten anyone? You don't remember. Larry Elwood is a pillar of the community, and you and both of his sisters say he doesn't like violence, he's a good man. Yet he's not good enough for his wife. Why? You say you don't know."

Addie swallowed hard. Well, suspecting wasn't knowing. "My doctor doesn't talk to me about his marital problems. And I haven't talked to his wife. Why don't you ask her?"

"I did. She stonewalled me with 'personal issues.' She was another one that assured me Dr. Larry wouldn't kill anyone."

"Maybe if enough people tell you something, you'll believe it."

He glowered at her, then extended his fifth finger. "You tell me Leslie Elwood loved her mother, is concerned about her brother's separation and is pissed off at her sister, but she's too much of a caretaker to have killed her father, even though she'll benefit from the sale of his land."

Addie bit her lip. Every suspect was someone she really cared about. Maybe not every one. "I believe Cletis will stand to benefit even more."

"Yes, your charming dinner-date."

"He was not my date."

"Whatever." Barker's left thumb joined the finger parade. "Cletis D. Adams, the only person with an air-tight alibi for the night of the murder. Still, we can't exclude a man who'll earn a few million from developing property he got the victim to promise to him way back when. A strange deal, wouldn't you say?"

"Yes, definitely."

Barker spread his hands wide. "See, it's not so hard for us to agree on things." There was a bite beneath the smile on his face.

"We certainly agree that we want Herbert's murderer behind bars," she said.

"For that to happen, people like you have to cooperate with the police." Barker folded his hands on his desk. "So tell me, while you were out to dinner with Mr. Adams, did you ask him how he'd gotten Dr. Elwood to give up future rights to his land?"

"I did ask, but he wouldn't say. I guess he didn't tell you, either. Did you ask his stepson?"

"Michael Planchette? I forgot to mention him, didn't I. He said he didn't know why Elwood made that contract. I find that hard to believe. I mean the guy works for Adams and is presumably heir to his business and personal fortune. But Planchette denied ever contacting Elwood about the land, and Planchette's daughter and Leslie Elwood backed his alibi for the night of the murder."

"Didn't you think it strange that he had his eight-year old out to the movies on a school night?" asked Addie.

"Divorced fathers do a lot of things with their kids that the mothers wouldn't approve of," said Barker. "You say Planchette's a practical joker?"

"That's what Cletis told me. Cletis has a granddaughter, you know."

"Yup, but I really don't see her mixed up in this. Too young, too out-of-town, and not involved in the business up to now. But this joker is interesting."

"Michael said he never even met Herbert."

"So what? If old Cletis wanted to do away with Elwood, Michael Planchette would've been the logical choice, wouldn't you say?"

"I wouldn't say, because I don't know Michael well."

"But you know Adams. You grew up with him."

"I grew up with a lot of people. As far as I know, none of them turned out to be murderers. Are your Aunt Rona and her Chinese clients on your list?"

Barker grunted. "Believe me, I've talked with my aunt more in the past few weeks than I have in the rest of my life. She was bugging Elwood to find a legal way out of the contract with CDA, but his death put the kibosh on that."

"But that opened up going to Cletis directly. And she's handling the sale of Herbert's house."

"You really think she'd kill for a commission? Listen, my aunt may annoy people to death, but she'd no more bash someone's brains in than you would. And you didn't, right?"

"Certainly not. But what about the Chinese?"

"The FBI is looking into it. That's all I can say because that's all they'll tell me." Barker leaned back in his chair. "Anyone else you talked to that might be related to this case?"

Joe Kearney? She felt her heart sink. No, she couldn't drag him into this. The only way he was connected to Herbert was by two root canals, years ago. Was that the extent of it?

"I've spoken to my friend, Bella Auterio. She knew Herbert because he'd occasionally go into Auterio's for a bottle of milk or something he forgot from the big supermarkets. But no, no one else that knew Herbert personally." Lots of people besides Joe had known him professionally.

"So if all of the people you know here are innocent, what are we left with? Some opportunistic gang-bangers who thought a dentist's home might have drugs or money?"

"Gypsies," Addie muttered.

"What?"

"Never mind. It's a story from elementary school."

Barker's fist rapped the desktop. "This is not some elementary school story, this is a murder investigation. And you're holding out information."

"I'm quite aware that this is a very serious matter, Detective. Last week, I gave George the tape of the conversation we had with Simon Warley, and today I've answered your questions to the best of my ability. I think I've done all I can." She started to get up. "Am I free to leave now?"

"I'd like you to stay a little bit longer."

"And why is that?"

"Because I want your son to talk with you about the dangers of obstructing justice."

"George?" She sank back in her chair.

"Would you prefer a lawyer with George?"

Barker knew how she felt about lawyers. "I'd prefer to talk to George in private."

"You can, right here. But remember that he's an officer of the law and is sworn to uphold it." Barker pushed his chair back and stood up. "Anything else you'd like to tell me before I get him?"

Addie cocked her head. "Well – "

"Go ahead, say it. You're going to say it to George, so tell me to my face. You think I've been too hard on you?"

"I don't expect special treatment. I'm sure you're like this with everybody. But I do think I might have had a better attitude had you opened up a window to clear the air in here and offered me a cup of tea."

"I apologize. I was never good at social niceties. They hardly existed where I came from."

"We all come from somewhere. It's what we do now that counts."

"You mean like telling the whole truth?"

"I mean like catching a murderer – "

"I'm for that, too."

"– without hurting innocent people. I believe you were on your way to get George?"

"Yes. Maybe he'll remind you we're on the same side."

When the door clicked shut behind him, Addie closed her eyes, took a deep breath and tried to compose herself. Barker was right, they were on the same side, but the man was so insensitive, a fullback trying to steamroll his way to the goal instead of the nimble quarterback an investigative team needed. Maybe she'd missed her calling. Addie grunted and opened her eyes. How many women of her generation had made a career of police work, let alone had made it to Detective?

She stood up, jiggled each foot up and down a few times, then stepped over to the bird photos on the wall. Unlike Barker's desk and file cabinets, the simple black frames were free of dust. In the lower right corner of each picture, the tiny letters HLB appeared above a date. She liked that he'd caught the wild turkey emerging from an autumn thicket, head erect, seemingly oblivious to the camera and the man who lay behind it.

No, the patience and precision required for these photos didn't jibe with the fullback battering his way through a defensive line. There was more to Harris Barker than met the eye. She glanced over at his desk, at the back of the pewter frame placed so that only the person sitting behind the desk could see the photo. Wife and children? Another bird?

She was halfway to the desk when the door opened. "Hi, Ma. How're you holding up?" asked George.

She turned to face him. "You look good in your blues." She smiled. "I suppose you're the good cop, sent in after the bad cop has given me the third degree."

He came forward and kissed her on the cheek, then stepped back, making a show of surveying her for any damage. "He was that easy on you, was he? Harris offers six degrees of interrogation. He thinks each one gets him closer to the truth."

"I told him the truth."

"But not the whole truth. At least that's what he thinks."

She looked into his eyes. Between his blue uniform and the overhead light, they looked darker than usual. "And you, what do you think?"

He rubbed his temple with his middle three fingers. "I've never known you to not be a few thoughts ahead of the pack. Things you wouldn't share until you felt the time was right."

"And what if I feel the time isn't right?"

"We're running out of time, Ma. It's four weeks since the murder and we don't have a lot to go on. No witnesses, no murder weapon, no fingerprints, no DNA. And the suspects aren't the usual addicts and thugs we deal with. They're bright, educated people and now they're lawyered up. They all refuse polygraph tests." He raised open palms in obvious appeal. "I don't know if what you're holding onto will make a shred of difference, but we're down to looking at shreds."

With a sigh, Addie stepped over to her chair and reluctantly lowered herself into it. "When I told you about Gloria accusing her siblings of murder, you told Detective Barker, then he went right out to accuse and intimidate each of the three. What was worse, he told Leslie and Larry that Gloria was the source."

George pulled over a chair and sat down. "You're worried he'll do something like that again?"

"I don't want innocent people to get hurt."

"If they knew Herbert, they've already been hurt."

"Will Detective Barker be able to restrain himself?"

"I guess you'll have to ask him. He's not a stupid man."

"It's not his intelligence I'm worried about."

George leaned forward and put his hand lightly on hers. "Then tell him. You've never been shy."

"No, but I've always tried to be discrete. I'm not sure Detective Barker knows the meaning of that word."

"Then explain it to him. Look, I'm worried about you. Someone, most likely the killer, has already broken into your home. The more you go around talking to people about the murder, the greater the chance the killer will decide you have to die for him to be safe. You really need to let us do the job." George gave her hand a reassuring squeeze. "And if you insist on visiting crazy veterinarians or going out on a dinner date with a murder suspect, at least – "

She withdrew her hand. "It wasn't a date."

" – okay, any private meeting with a murder suspect, you have to let us know so we can back you up."

"I think I'd rather deal with the bad cop. Go get Barker."

"Ma – "

"That's enough, George. I got the message. Rather than say what I have to say twice, I'd appreciate you and Detective Barker hearing it together."

"Okay." His tone was submissive, as was his posture as he left, but she knew he hadn't given in any more than she would. They were too much alike, and they could work seamlessly. Barker was the one who needed coaching. Could he accept any suggestions, become a team player? Bird-watching required patience, but it wasn't a team sport.

She glanced at the door, then back at the pewter picture frame. Just a quick peek, she thought, leaning forward to turn it around. Yes, a family photo, Barker and his wife, with two adolescent boys in front of them. All in jeans and sweatshirts and seated on a large rock which projected out from a patch of autumn woodland. His wife, a willowy brunette with binoculars hanging from a strap around her neck, had a lovely, reassuring smile.

Addie turned the picture frame to its original position, then sat back in her chair and closed her eyes. Barker was right about Rona; she wouldn't commit murder. Larry, Leslie, and Cletis had the most to gain financially, so they were the prime suspects, but it was possible Raymond Miggens or Gloria Elwood killed Herbert for revenge. If Michael Planchette was involved, it was probably to help Cletis. And outside the box? Dr. Warley, the Chinese – Joe Kearney?

She heard the door open behind her and the men enter the room and approach her chair, but she didn't stir until George gently said, "Are you sleeping?"

"No, thinking." She opened her eyes and looked up. "Oh, my." Detective Barker was extending a Styrofoam cup from which the string of a teabag dangled. "Thank you."

"It's nothing fancy. It's the only kind we have."

Orange pekoe. Oh well, it was a peace offering. "It's fine."

George parked himself in the plastic seat next to her while Barker walked around the desk to reclaim his swivel chair. The big man settled in with a sigh. "George says I should ask you why you have reservations about telling me things."

"When George told you that Gloria had accused her brother and sister of murdering their father, you rushed right in to question them and told Leslie and Larry that Gloria was the accuser."

Barker's hands rose chest high. "I couldn't ignore that accusation, could I? In a murder investigation, you can't pussyfoot around. You have to go in and shake up the suspects and play one off against another."

"I'm not saying you should have ignored it. But the way you handled it made things much worse for Gloria and for me. And that's what I'm trying to avoid – getting innocent people hurt by passing on observations I may have misinterpreted or information that's told to me in confidence."

"Look, questioning people is part of my job. Sometimes I play it soft, other times I think I'll get more if I go in hard. If people feel intimidated, that's their problem. It's usually because they feel guilty."

"I'm talking about innocent people."

"Hey, everybody's guilty of something. Murder is an awful business for everyone involved, and I'm damn sure what's happened to your neighbor, to you and your house – even the injury to your cat – has been terribly upsetting and frightening. But we can't let people that kill and terrorize walk away to do it again. We need your full cooperation to catch these people."

"I agree, and I want to be as helpful as I can. Believe me, I certainly don't think I know more than you about crime and criminals. But I do know a fair amount about the people in this town and how they need to be treated to gain their cooperation."

"I can accept that."

"Then I hope you'll be open to accepting some suggestions."

"What suggestions?" His tone was wary.

"The information I have concerns Raymond Miggins, Larry Elwood, and Leslie Elwood and her husband. None of it proves anyone is a murderer. But George knows Raymond and Larry personally, and it might be better for him to take those issues up with them – at least initially – if you both don't have a good reason why not. As for Leslie and the others, you've already heard their stories and by now have a good handle on how to work with them. Clearly, it's your investigation, but I really think that would work best."

"I'll consider it once we've heard what you have to say."

"Good enough. Though I'm afraid there is one condition – a condition, not a suggestion."

"You really think you can lay down conditions for a police investigation?"

"Not at all. I'm laying down one condition for what I'll permit myself to say."

"What's the condition?" asked George.

"In the course of this investigation, you might run into some people who are illegal immigrants, but innocent of any other crime."

"Illegals?" said Barker. "Where the fuck do they come into this?"

"Only incidentally, I hope. But they'll be afraid to talk to the police. The condition is that, unless you believe they're involved in this murder or another crime – and I don't mean crossing the border to earn a livelihood – you don't inquire about citizenship."

Barker shook his head. "I don't know what you're getting us into, here. I can't promise you anything. On the other hand, I'm not a federal law enforcement officer. I just want to solve a murder. So you help us with that, and I won't come onto them hard, or like I'm the INS instead of a small town cop, okay?"

"I think we're beginning to see eye to eye." She took a sip of tea. As a peace offering, it was lukewarm but palatable.

Where to start? She sighed and set the cup down on the detective's desk. "I have no proof, but I think Larry Elwood is hooked on drugs."

Week Five

CHAPTER 29

FRIDAY, 7 A.M.

"You again?" said a bleary-eyed Ray Miggins. "You know it's fucking early for social visits. My mother isn't even out of bed yet." Wearing jeans and a muscle shirt, he stood barefoot in the half-open doorway of his house.

"I'm not here to visit your mother," said Addie. "I'm sorry it's so early, but I wanted to catch you before you went to work."

"We just talked yesterday. What do you want now?"

"I felt I needed to tell you personally. I told Detective Barker you lied to him – "

Raymond's head jerked. "You did what!"

" – about where you were the night of Herbert's murder."

He crossed the threshold onto the porch.

She backed away. "But I explained you had a good reason and your girlfriend would testify you were with her."

"You stupid bitch! Do you fucking know what you've done?"

Her stepfather was in Raymond's words and red face. She made herself stand straighter.

"I did the right thing," she said. "I know you don't agree, but Detective Barker assured me he wouldn't ask about your girlfriend's legal status or that of her family unless there was evidence of some crime – which I assume there isn't."

"And you trust that bastard? I can't even trust you. Get the fuck out of here!"

No, he wasn't going to hurt her. Her tension eased. "Whatever you feel about me, your mother still needs to get professional help."

"I'll get her help. I already called that crisis team, so we don't need you or your church ladies in our house or in our lives." He backed across his threshold "Get off our property! And don't ever speak to me or my mother again."

"I'll respect your wishes, Raymond, but you respect hers. If she wants to talk to me or wants some help, I'm right across the street."

"Stay over on your side." He slammed the door.

She let out a deep breath and waited a moment for her heart to slow down. At least that's over, she thought and started down the steps. Then she heard the door opening behind her. Did he have a gun? Don't look, keep going.

"And pay for your own fucking window!"

* * *

She threaded her way down the narrow aisle of the Valley Diner, passing between a line of strong male backs riding high on counter stools and a row of oak booths, their metal clothes posts overburdened with jackets and parkas. The booth occupants were wolfing down burgers and fries or so involved in conversation they didn't look up. Behind the counter, a waitress whose black locks had tumbled from her Red Sox cap called an order to the cook with a voice pitched to shatter glass. Addie wrinkled her nose at the odors of sizzling grease and meat. Oops! Joe Kearney was looking right at her, rising from the last booth to greet her.

"It's the kitchen smell," she said, "not you."

"That's a great relief, to be sure."

She flushed. "I never thought that – "

"Aye, and I never thought you thought whatever you thought." Joe's grin not only smoothed the lines in his face, it dissolved her discomfort.

"A great relief, to be sure," she echoed, then felt her smile slip away. How could she be sure about anything with this man? She knew so little about him.

"I'm very glad you're here," Joe said. "Perhaps you'd like to take off your coat and sit down?" He indicated the high-backed bench opposite his.

"Thank you." She put her purse down on the vinyl cushion. As she unbuttoned her woolen coat, she noted he'd had a haircut, looked rested and at ease in a blue turtle neck and pressed trousers. Clearly, he'd primped more than she had. Her only concession to appearance had been to brush her hair so it curved over her ears rather than keeping it pinned back. That and a touch of lipstick. She barely hesitated as he put a hand out for her coat, giving it up with a small smile before sliding into the booth. The chrome juke box under the window distorted her reflection terribly.

"I hope you don't mind lunching here," he said. "The food is good, and being I don't have a car – " A cup holding a smidgen of coffee sat on a saucer in front of him.

"It's fine." No doubt he had little money. Not that she'd let him pay for her, anyway.

"It's an historic place," he said. "One of the few remaining diners manufactured by the Worcester Lunch Car Company."

She glanced at the black and white wall panels below the window, remembered counting them as a child bored by adult conversation. "Yes, I know."

"You know?" He sounded a bit crestfallen.

"I've lived here all my life. There aren't many things in a small town you don't hear about over – " Seventy years, she thought. "– time."

"You come here often?"

"Mostly as a child." Until her stepfather had replaced church and pancake breakfasts with Bloody Marys. "Once I had children, eating out wasn't affordable. And luckily, food is not – well, it is important, but it's not something I crave."

His eyebrows rose, then the infectious grin reappeared. "Ah, if only I'd known. We could have skipped lunch and flown off to Tahiti."

She offered an obligatory smile. The man was a big talker, a dreamer offering pie-in-the-sky. "I doubt my cat would've approved."

"An elopement, then. Perhaps your cat could be the maid of honor."

Helen had been her maid of honor. She'd sat in the next booth with Helen and Bella planning her wedding. "His name is Flash and I doubt you could convince him to give me away."

"Stubborn fellow, is he? But lightning fast, I take it."

"Very fast. When I first let him out of the house after adopting him, he zipped off and was gone for two days. I thought 'My God, gone in a flash.' Since then, he's never left me. It's the months and years that flash by."

"I know the feeling," said Joe. His head inched upward. "Here comes Miss Pierced with some menus."

With plasticized menus tucked under her arm, a young waitress in jeans and a black tee shirt was bringing two glasses of water to the table. A small silver flower in each eyebrow and a nose ring overrode her perfunctory smile, while each ear sported a sparkly stud and dangling silver hoops. Addie winced at the thought of a needle piercing the fragile wall between her nostrils. So sad that some of these kids couldn't find better ways to express themselves.

The waitress carefully set a glass down before each of them and produced tableware in rolled paper napkins from a back pocket. "You guys need menus or you know what you want?"

"Menus, please," said Joe. "Half the fun is in the choosing."

Addie accepted the menu but declined the offer of a beverage. Joe asked for a refill of coffee. She watched the waitress bounce away. God, if only she could move that freely.

"Shaw was right," said Joe, "`youth is wasted on the young.'"

Surprised that he'd perceived her longing, Addie looked at him with renewed interest. "You've read Shaw?"

"I'm no scholar, but I did have a college education. Three colleges, in fact. And I did it in only ten years." His tone mocked his efforts.

This time her smile was genuine. "I'm impressed."

"Enough to fly off to Tahiti?"

"Not nearly. Tell me more."

"That I was a slow reader? No, dear Addie, it's better that you stay impressed, so let's order, eat a fine lunch and talk about the treasures of good health, better days and lasting friendships."

"Forgive me, Joe, but I'd be bored to tears. I want my friends to be direct, as I hope I am with them. I don't like flutterers or flatterers. I'm too old to waste my time with that."

He closed his mouth. She saw his upper lip bulge as his tongue passed over his teeth.

Was she being harsh? Yes, he was a blowhard, but smart and not egotistical. He was probably what he said he was, a lonely man looking for friendship. "I'm sorry. Sometimes I'm too much of a fault-finder."

"It's a common enough disease," he said. "I had a bad case of it when I was younger. Tell you what, let's order and then I'll answer your questions – and hopefully your doubts."

He ordered corned beef hash with eggs over easy, she a Cobb salad with a balsamic vinaigrette, and a cup of herbal tea with lemon. As the waitress walked away with the menus, Addie offered Joe a small smile and raised eyebrows.

"Ah, you want to know who this obnoxious fluttering fellow is, do you?" Joe sighed. "I was a Dorchester boy – no altar boy, but a spunky kid with big enough dreams. I can't blame what I did or didn't do in my life on any dark secrets from the past. The fact is, being the only boy with four sisters gave me some advantages – not that my parents didn't love us all, but overall, I got more attention and more forgiveness. There were higher expectations, too, but my three older sisters didn't see that part. Or maybe they did and resented that even more. Anyway, they seemed to get a kick out of putting me down when they weren't ignoring me." A smile flitted across his lips. "I simply refused to be ignored. Truth to tell, my sister Witchy used to call me a 'brassy-assed dwarf.'"

"Witchy?"

"Wanda. I called them Witchy, Bitchy and Barf. Barbara was the eldest, she had what they now call bulimia. I'll admit I wasn't sympathetic in those days, but I was too young for it to matter. The poor girl never had any luck that wasn't bad. She and her husband were at a meeting with their estate planner in the World Trade Center when it went down. So much for plans."

"I'm sorry," said Addie.

His eyes closed momentarily, then he nodded. "As we all are. Not that it does much to soothe the pain of their children. Ah, we had a less complicated growing up in our day. My fights were settled by fists. Not that there weren't neighborhood gangs, but by and large there was no wholesale killing of innocents, no drug dealers in the stairwells, no electronic cocoons deadening kids' feelings."

"Yes, life was simpler." Addie reached for her glass of water. "Did you get into many fights?"

"A few – because of my big mouth, mostly. But no physical nonsense at home. My mom ruled her roost with an iron will and a long wooden spoon." He chuckled. "She used to take that spoon to the school cafeteria where she worked." With the fingers of one hand, he rubbed the knuckles of the other. "I'm certain she used it much more vigorously at home."

"And your father?"

"He drove an MBTA trolley. He loved us, but he brought a lot of stress home with him and once he started drinking, he wasn't too pleasant to be around. You'd think I would've learned the right lesson from that." Joe's face became somber. "Anyway, he died of leukemia when I was 12. Cancer knocked the crap out of him, and nothing really helped, certainly not the priest or all our prayers. Long story short, the doctors sent him home to die. Watching him deteriorate, day after day – it killed what little faith I had. One night, one of the tubes in him came undone and he bled out. I suspect he disconnected it deliberately. You know, when you lose faith in everyone else, you also lose faith in yourself."

"That must have been so hard." We're so different, she thought. Without faith in God, without some faith in herself, she'd never have survived the bad times. Yet somehow Bess, like Joe, had come through a personal hell without either.

The waitress returned carrying their hot drinks on a small tray. "Your food'll be right up," she said.

"Thanks," said Joe. He waited until the waitress was out of earshot then cleared his throat.

"I want you to understand that I don't feel sorry for myself any more. And I've stopped blaming everyone else for my troubles. Plenty of other people have grown up with a lot worse, or never had the chance to grow up at all. My ma kept me on the straight and narrow, kept me running the rat race uphill – Boston Latin, a scholarship to Boston College. Truth to tell, I've only myself to blame for partying away my scholarship, for running off to the Navy and drowning my marriage in alcohol, and for two sons who don't respect or trust me – not to mention the decent jobs lost, and for God-knows-how-many other people and bridges I've burned." He gave an embarrassed smile. "So, have you heard enough yet to grant me a second date?"

She frowned. "When was the first?"

Over the restaurant din she'd blocked out, a child started crying. A woman's voice commanded, "Stop that!"

"Sure now, you don't consider this a business meeting, do you?" asked Joe.

She busied herself preparing her tea. "Not exactly." What really prompted his interest in her? Certainly not her looks at this age. More likely he was interested in Herbert's murder. "Honestly I don't know what it is – this get-together." He'd put his worst foot forward, daring her to accept him. Their waitress did it with her appearance, Joe with his candor – assuming everything he said was true. "I take it you've stopped drinking completely?"

"Every hour, every day. I've been sober 15 years, two months and – four days."

"Quite an accomplishment." She recognized the half-hearted tone of her compliment. "Really. My ex-husband was – is – alcoholic. According to my children, he's never stopped. How is it that you managed to?"

"A good detox program, AA, and a Higher Power."

"God?"

Joe chuckled. "No, my wife Ellen. Bless her heart, she was much more merciful." He shook his head. "Poor dear, she got no mercy at all from Above. She was diagnosed with ovarian cancer when she was 56. I was 59 at the time. Christ, I felt so awful – worse than in any detox – I mean I'd made her life so miserable for years before she threw me out. Not that I ever hit her, but I was unfaithful, unfair, a slobbering mess when I wasn't hopped up and angry." His face seemed to sag with regret.

"I said some really nasty things when I was drunk - accused her of planning to get pregnant to get me to marry her. I was a real shit, and a terrible example for our two boys. But she was a true Catholic – in it for the long haul, even if we couldn't live together. She'd be the one I'd call from a drunk tank or a detox. So when I found out she had cancer, I knew I couldn't let her down again; I couldn't let her die alone."

His hand gestured toward the window. "Our two boys live in California. They have their own families and their own share of troubles. She wouldn't go out there – said she didn't want to burden them further. Anyway, I swore to her I would go into detox the very next day, and I'd not take another drink until the day she died. I hoped that might give her more motivation to live. The cancer had spread so much that the doctors had given her a year, at best." He heaved a sigh. "I don't suppose God or the cancer cared what I did, but bless her heart, Ellen still did, and she fought the beast tooth and nail. After three months, she knew I meant what I said, and she let me come home to live. The next two years were the best and worst of my life."

He paused for a drink of coffee. Above the cup, his eyes seemed to search her face for reaction. "So – " He set the cup down. " – at the end, on her deathbed, she says, 'I know you'll want to drink again.' And I said, 'Christ, woman, I've wanted to drink every day for two years.' And she says, 'do me one last favor, Love, don't drink until the kids leave after the funeral.' See how smart she was? She knew that if she asked me never to drink again, I'd've said I couldn't make that kind of promise. But another week or two after two years? I could do that." His hands rose for a few seconds, then dropped softly to the table. "And I'm still doing it, one day at a time. But truth to tell, while AA helps a lot, it's a lonely life without Ellen, and it's doubly lonely without a barstool propping me up or a bottle to go home to." He grimaced. "Given what I've said, I suppose Tahiti is not in the cards for us."

She reached over and took his hand. "I'm touched by the offer, Joe." And by his pain. Yes, his needs were great, but so were his persistence, his determination, his love for his wife. "But – " She withdrew her hand. " – I think that – "

"So perhaps you'd consider Hawaii?"

She smiled. "It is closer to home. Which makes me ask when and how you came to live in Millbrook."

"Ah – " He seemed relieved to change the subject. "Many years ago, I consulted on a couple of projects for a local company and liked the area. I only came back to Millbrook six months ago." He picked up his coffee and took a healthy swallow. "After Ellen died, I tried to get back to work. I was a pretty good civil engineer as long as I was sober. But no one wanted to hire a man in his sixties, much less one with the patchy work history I'd rung up. So I sold our house, applied for Social Security, and ended up moving to Mexico. Living there was a lot cheaper." He set down his cup. "I came back because I needed a shoulder operation and because my younger sister and her family live here. She's a sweetheart; she still remembers the good Dorchester boy who protected her." Joe's hand flicked the air. "My two boys – they're happy to see the back of me after Christmas visits."

"You have a sister here?"

"Mary Ellen. She's married to a decent fellow, Martin Bouchard."

"The Postmaster?"

"You know him?"

"Only by sight. I rarely go to the Post Office. I don't believe I know your sister."

Joe smiled. "We'll have to fix that."

Her muscles tightened. "I don't believe anything's broken."

"No, no, I keep putting my foot – " He stopped as the waitress loomed over them with a serving tray. She placed a large salad in front of Addie. "Your Cobb, dressing on the side." She put the second plate down before Joe. "Your hash and eggs."

"I guess I am."

"Huh? You need anything else?" asked the waitress.

"Not right now," said Joe.

"No, thank you." Addie watched the girl's swaying hips as she moved away.

Joe put a hand up to explain. "Look, I'm sorry if I seem – "

"Don't worry about it. I can be a prickly pear when I'm – " Unsure of myself? " – haven't slept well," she said. "This whole murder thing – it's – please, let's eat." She picked up the tiny paper cup of vinaigrette and poured half the dressing on her salad.

He unwrapped his packet of silverware. "Aye, I'd have trouble sleeping, too, with a murder done next door."

"It's not just that." As she tossed her salad, she told him how her home had been ransacked, Flash injured, her mother's china destroyed.

He gripped his fork in one hand, the knife in the other, but made no move to eat. "No wonder you're not sleeping well. And you have no idea who did it?"

"There was a gang name – the Viper Kings – written on my bathroom mirror, but I think that was put there to throw us off the track. There's no reason a gang from Lowell would be interested in me." She put a forkful of salad in her mouth, then gestured that he should start eating.

"Bastards, whoever they are." Shaking his head, he plunged his fork into the corned beef hash. "Why would they wreck your home?"

"I wish I knew." Wait – she'd spoken to him that same morning. She managed to restrain herself while they ate, keeping the conversation light and her smile at the ready until he put down his fork and, with a sigh, pushed his plate an inch or two back.

"I seem to remember I spoke with you the morning of the break-in," she said.

"You did?"

"Yes, you invited me out to lunch and I said I had other engagements." She saw his face cloud over. "No, don't get me wrong. You're not the only person I talked to on the telephone that morning.

But is it possible you spoke to someone about my need to be elsewhere?"

"No. Not a chance. I'm not one to talk about my rejections by women – or my acceptances, for that matter."

"I like that, Joe."

"But you still have your doubts about me."

"Please don't be offended. I have doubts about everyone, including myself."

"Are you wondering whether I killed your next-door neighbor?"

"I really haven't considered that, but I doubt that you did. See, not all doubts are negative."

"Aye, but just so it's perfectly clear, I didn't kill him. He saved two of my teeth, but truth to tell, I haven't seen him in years."

"Did you know anything about his personal life?"

"You know I use his son as a doctor. I wasn't at all sure they were related until I asked Dr. Larry. I'd worked on a development project with the daughter many years before – she was the one that referred me to Dr. Herbert – and I had a good experience with him, so when I came here, I went for the Elwood name."

Addie leaned forward. "You worked with Leslie Elwood?"

He looked puzzled. "Oh, that's right – you probably knew her as a kid next door. I didn't work with her every day. I was a part-time consultant. She was coordinating a project team at CDA. I saw her at meetings until she left the company." He shook his head as if having an unpleasant memory. "Let me tell you, it was a real loss. She was a sharp young mind, and a treat for the eyes as well."

"Yes." Even in her forties, Leslie was both. Addie looked down at her aging hands. That Joe was connected to Herbert Elwood and his children troubled her, but not as much as his connection to CDA. "So you worked for Cletis Adams?"

"You know him?"

"Everybody in Millbrook either knows Cletis or knows of him. What did you do for him?"

"I consulted on a couple of CDA projects, planning access roads and sewage systems for large developments – nothing out of the ordinary."

"What did you think of him?"

Joe stroked his jaw as if a beard had once covered it. "He was a sharp enough businessman and he paid a decent wage but, to be honest, I never particularly liked the man. To be fair, my opinion is colored by the fact that he fired me – not that he didn't have good reason. I was hitting the bottle pretty hard at the time. But he was on a firing rampage, anyway. I got the ax a day after he fired Leslie Elwood and two other employees."

"He fired Leslie?" Hadn't Cletis said he attended Herbert's viewing out of respect for Leslie?

"Asked her to resign – it was the same thing. It shocked the hell out of people. She was a rising star in the company."

Addie grasped the edge of the tabletop. "So why did he fire her?"

"I don't know. Neither of them gave a reason. And you can't always believe office gossip."

"No. But there must've been some reasons bandied about. How did people explain it?"

Joe shrugged. "She didn't have access to the financial side of the operation, so no one thought she'd embezzled money. And she wasn't a slacker, that's for sure. So one rumor was that she'd sold information to CDA's competitors. The other was that she and Cletis were having an affair and she broke it off."

"Oh, my." Was that the affair Larry mentioned at the funeral lunch? she thought.

"What's the matter? You look like you swallowed a horsefly."

"No. It's that I – " Loved and hated, she thought. "– grew up with Cletis Adams, and I have a hard time stomaching what he did – what he appears to have done to Leslie." And did to me. She brought her fist up to her mouth. Now Cletis was going after Bess. Over this dead body!

"What stole you away from me?" asked Joe.

She lowered her fist. Could it be that Cletis' alibi wasn't as perfect as people thought?

"Gypsies," she said softly.

CHAPTER 30

MONDAY EVENING

Addie was crocheting a yellow afghan and half-listening to the talking heads on CNN when the headlights of a car coming up her driveway beamed through her front windows. Flash jumped down from the couch and ran to the front door.

Who now? Her rocking chair inched back as she stiffened. The reflection of her lamps made it impossible to see outside. No, no need to worry. Flash looked calm and the out-of-service police car was still parked in her driveway. Surely that would convince any would-be murderers that she was under 24-hour protection. Nice of Detective Barker to arrange that.

She tucked her crocheting materials into a canvas bag and set the bag on the TV where it would be safe from Flash. She clicked the mute button on the remote, made sure her VCR was set to record Monday Night Football, then headed for the door. Outside, there was a metallic creak from the storm door.

"Who is it?"

"Ma, it's George."

On Monday night? She unlocked the front door, opened it to see her son still in uniform. His face was grim.

"What's happened?"

"Let's go inside."

"Did something happen to your sisters? To Robert?"

"No. No family. But please go in and sit down."

"Come, Flash." As she walked back to the living room, she tightened the belt on her robe.

"Git!" said George from behind her. She heard a soft smack and a yelp from Flash, saw a blur of gray as he raced by her and sprang onto the sofa.

"He went for my shoelaces again," said George.

"Hitting him just antagonizes him." Her chair rocked forward, then back as she sat down.

Flash scratched angrily at the thick towel that covered his place, then circled and settled in with a resentful stare. With a sigh, George plopped down on the chair facing her and placed his police hat on the hassock.

He's very tired, thought Addie. "I'm ready," she said.

"Larry Elwood was found dead in his office a couple of hours ago."

She jerked back and grabbed the arms of her rocker. "Larry?"

"I didn't want you to hear it on the news tonight, or from Aunt Bella in the morning."

"Murdered?"

"Suicide, most likely."

"Dear God. Why?" He'd been so kind to her when she was ill, so concerned about her eating. She remembered the toddler so delighted to find worms in her garden, the little boy who'd pronounced her cupcakes 'best in the world.' She'd walked out of his office in anger, didn't recognize desperation when she saw it. Now there was no time to make amends, to say a proper good-bye. She fought back her tears, then gave up the struggle. George was a battle-hardened adult, not the adolescent who couldn't bear watching her cry. Why was she still trying to protect him? Why couldn't anyone protect Larry?

She blotted her face on her sleeve. "Tell me – "

George rubbed his temple. "Nothing more than the fact of his death goes outside this room. Promise?"

"Yes, of course."

"Okay. Larry called his receptionist and nurse yesterday evening and told them to take a day off today, that he had the flu and wouldn't be coming in. He said he had his schedule on his laptop and would cancel his appointments himself. When the cleaning lady let herself into the office at six tonight, she found him dead. There was no sign of forced entry. Empty pill bottles and a suicide note were right there on the desk. So was his laptop." George heaved a sigh. "The medical examiner thinks he died around midnight last night."

"Cheryl, who's told Cheryl?"

"I did. I just came from there. That was tough. She has a couple of friends with her now. She was really torn up." He shook his head. "Fucking drugs. That's what caused the separation."

"Maybe if I hadn't accused him..."

"You?" George uttered a sound that was half growl, half groan. "I confronted him Saturday. He denied it. Denied and denied it. Looked like hell. I told him I knew him well enough to know that he was lying, and that he'd better report himself to the Medical Board by today. Barker was going to ask Judge Potter for an order to examine Larry's records of drug samples and prescriptions." He hit his thigh. "Big mistake."

Addie got up and went to his side. She gently squeezed his shoulder, then straightened his collar. "George, I feel responsible, you feel responsible, I'm sure Cheryl feels responsible. All of us wanted to help. He turned away from help. It's not our fault he chose to die."

George put his hand over hers. "And here I came to comfort you."

"We all need comforting when something like this happens."

"Thanks." He moved her hand away, rose from his chair and hugged her tightly. "I have to go back."

She patted his back a few times, then released him. "Did Larry confess to anything in his suicide note? Did he say anything about his father's murder?"

"Nothing so straight-forward. He apologized to Cheryl and his kids, told them he loved them, and gave her the name and phone number of his life insurance guy. He said the insurance and their share from the sale of Herbert's land would make them financially secure. The only eye-opener was a line saying, 'Forgive me for lacking the courage to deal with the consequences of what I did.' It's anybody's guess whether he meant drugs or his dad's murder or both."

"It's the drug addiction and having his medical license taken," said Addie. "If he was the murderer, there'd be no reason not to say it before he died. Larry wouldn't want his sisters or another innocent person to be blamed."

"Yeah." George reached down for his cap. "But there's a possibility he wasn't completely sure his cocktail would kill him. Maybe he worried that someone might accidentally find him too soon, or that he'd vomit up half the pills and wake up in the hospital. He wouldn't want a murder charge added to his problems."

Addie shook her head. "He was too smart to underestimate the dose."

"You sure? He certainly wasn't smart enough to stay away from self-prescribing." George kissed her on the cheek, then put on his cap. "You want me to send Bess or Joanne over?"

"No. I need to do some thinking." And crying, she thought. "Besides, you won't let me talk to them about this."

"No, not until it comes out publicly or you hear it from Cheryl. I take it you'll be in touch with her?"

"Tomorrow. Flash and I are going straight to bed."

He started for the door, then stopped and turned back. "You sure you're okay? I mean as okay as you can be, given the – "

"Yes, yes. Go on." No need to burden him further. "I'll lock the door after you, then I'm going to bed."

With George out the door, she felt the weight of grief dragging her downward. She turned off the outside light and returned to the living room. Using the remote, she clicked off the record button and then the television. "I'm cancelling tonight's game," she told Flash.

CHAPTER 31

Tuesday Afternoon

A maroon sedan and a black SUV were parked in the driveway of Larry Elwood's farmhouse, so Addie parked on the grassy shoulder outside the low stone wall. She locked the Corolla and got the pan of foil-wrapped chicken pot pies from the trunk.

In front of the large porch, a Dora the Explorer tricycle and a pink scooter had been left overturned. Addie rang the doorbell and heard a female voice yell, "Just a minute!"

Life inside this house would never be the same, thought Addie. Terrible that Larry did this to his children, to Cheryl. Not all that different than what Dave did to her and their four kids. What was it about men that they could bear any sacrifice for their brothers in war, but not have the same willingness to give of themselves at home?

The inner door opened and Cheryl was looking at her as though she were a complete stranger. Cheryl's face was pale and etched with grief, but her dark hair was neatly gathered into a ponytail and her chunky body was well served by a black blouse and skirt. Before Addie could say a word, Cheryl's head twitched, recognition softened her expression, and she hastily opened the door.

"Addie, I'm so sorry. I'm so – I don't know." Her large nose looked chafed, her brown eyes brimmed with tears.

"No need to apologize. Everyone who knew Larry is so sorry, but no one has more sorrow to bear than you." Addie stepped inside, spotted a small bench in the entryway, shoes and boots beneath it, coats and children's jackets hooked above. "Here, let me put this down so I can give you a proper hug."

Cheryl's body was warm and welcoming, her grasp firm, then prolonged by a spasm of tears. With her face partially buried against Cheryl's shoulder, Addie reached up to stroke Cheryl's hair. So sadly different from their embrace at Cheryl and Larry's wedding. So beautiful in her enthusiasm, so in love with her young doctor. And all of them in the church choir singing their hearts out for the bouncy young girl who'd been adopted as a niece or granddaughter by everyone over 40. There'd be no singing without tears at Larry's funeral.

"Thank you, Addie." Cheryl's arms released her. "I haven't been able to do that in front of the kids." She took a step back, pulled a clump of tissues from her pocket and used one to wipe her eyes.

"Where are the girls?"

"My mother has them upstairs in my bedroom watching a DVD. I needed some time to get my head together."

"Then I won't stay but a minute. I thought you might be able to use some ready-to-eats, so I cooked up a few chicken pot pies."

"No, no. It's okay. I mean thank you – that's so thoughtful. Why don't you take off your coat and bring those into the kitchen."

"No, you have enough to deal with. You don't need visitors before you're ready."

Cheryl shook her head. "You're no visitor. You're Larry's Aunt Addie, and you're my old choir buddy, right? Please, please come on in."

"For a few minutes, then." Addie hung her coat on a hook, picked up the pan of pies and followed Cheryl past the staircase and into the kitchen. She never ceased to be surprised at how this old farm kitchen had been so completely rehabbed. There were two frying pans on the cooking stove and a few dirty dishes next to the sink, but the white cabinets and stainless steel appliances gleamed under recessed lights, and fire flickered in the ceramic wood stove. A Cheerios box stood lonely vigil atop the kitchen's center island.

Addie bit her lip. All this, she thought, Cheryl, the two little girls upstairs – Larry, Larry, other parents sacrifice and die to protect their children. "Where shall I put this?" she said.

"Anywhere," said Cheryl. "We'll probably eat some of it for dinner – those that are hungry, anyway. Gloria and April are coming over."

Addie placed the baking pan on the island's granite top. "Your father upstairs, too?"

"He's at Larry's office. There's so much to do there, and I'm not up to it. My brother's flying in tonight on the red-eye." She pulled a high-backed stool out from under the island's overhang and tapped the seat. "Come sit."

Before Addie could decide to stay or to go, Cheryl headed for the counter next to the sink, where a half-filled wineglass and an open bottle stood in front of a coffee machine. "You want a glass of Chardonnay or some cof – no, you're a tea person. All those rehearsals, how could I forget?" She rapped her head lightly with her knuckles.

Addie moved toward the stool. "Please don't bother. I've already had more than enough tea today. And choir practice was years ago. This is certainly no time to be hard on yourself." Cheryl was surely blaming herself for a lot more than a slip of memory. "I truly hope you're not blaming yourself for what Larry did – chose to do."

Cheryl expelled a harsh breath. "How can I not blame myself? I told him to leave, didn't I?" She transferred the bottle of wine and her glass to the island. "I wouldn't let him come back until he got some help for his – problems. I know that hurt him."

"He wasn't even ready to admit he had a drug problem."

"You knew?" Cheryl stiffened. "George told you?"

"Actually, I told George. What I suspected, anyway. I asked Larry whether he was using drugs. I went to his office a week ago. He was acting so – peculiar. Of course, he denied it. He certainly wasn't ready to go for help."

Cheryl sagged against the island. "I should've forced him to. I could've reported him to the licensing Board, to the hospital, to that detective. I mean I had so many opportunities – " She groaned, then reached for her wineglass.

Talk about something else? No, let Cheryl lead the way. "It must've hurt even to think about reporting him."

Cheryl swallowed a mouthful of wine. "Oh, I thought about it. And now I've asked myself at least a hundred times why I didn't." She pulled out a stool to sit down, then noticed Addie still standing. "Please sit down. You look like you have one foot out the door."

"I wonder if I'm not – "

"No, you asked me a question – didn't you?" She set down her wineglass, bowed her head and took a deep breath.

What question? No, she hadn't asked anything. Cheryl needed to get some things off her chest. Addie hiked herself onto the stool.

"I knew I couldn't let him back in the house – to live, I mean." Cheryl's eyes appealed for understanding. "I couldn't let him drive the kids anywhere, Addie. I couldn't even trust his judgment with them if I went out. He'd be hyper sometimes, completely in his own world or almost comatose at others." She pressed her fists against the granite surface. "Like you say, he wouldn't admit he overused the pills, but I'd find empty prescription bottles in the trash – bottles with other people's names on the labels. I suppose he convinced his patients to turn in medicines they didn't like or need any more. When I'd ask him about the bottles, he'd claim he threw the pills down the toilet. And of course, he always had a stash of samples at the office."

Cheryl bowed her head. "I didn't report him for a lot of reasons – bad ones, obviously, but they seemed right at the time. I thought that no treatment would work if he was forced into it. And I certainly didn't want him to lose his license – he was so invested in his career, and he cared so much and so well for his patients." She swallowed hard. "To be honest, I was also being selfish. We live very comfortably, you can see that. What would happen if we suddenly didn't have any income? Who'd hire him to do anything if he was thrown out of Medicine because of drug addiction?" She looked up and extended a hand. "You know I would've worked to help out, but what could I bring in as an office worker?"

Addie reached for Cheryl's hand, gently squeezed it and brought it to rest on the island's countertop. "You were trying to do what was best for your family. God knows I've made decisions that were followed by bad things happening – who hasn't? None of us see the future clearly enough to always do the right thing. Especially as there often is no right thing."

Cheryl withdrew her hand. "No, I never should've gone to my father-in-law."

"You went to Herbert?"

"I thought as a dentist, he'd know about addiction programs for medical people. I knew he loved Larry, and he was always good to me and the children. Maybe he wasn't a very understanding father, but he loved being a grandfather. He never came over without a present for the girls. He made them a beautiful wooden doll house last winter."

"Did he say anything about making bird houses for them?"

"He showed them to you?"

The memory of Herbert's battered head tore a grunt from Addie's throat. She cleared it, then said, "I saw them."

"I'm sorry. I forgot. It must've been awful to find him like that. I can't imagine feeling worse than I've felt since yesterday, but if I had found Larry – "

"I'm sure he didn't want you to find him like that. Were the bird houses for your children?"

"What? Oh. One was for our backyard. Herbert wanted it to be a surprise for the girls. He called that Thursday to see whether it would be more convenient to bring the birdhouse here on Saturday or on Sunday afternoon. He said he had one for Leslie, too, but I shouldn't say anything about the bird houses if I spoke to her. He was going to surprise her with it on her birthday." With one long swallow, Cheryl emptied her wineglass. "Like I told Detective Barker the day after Herbert was found, that was the last time I spoke to my father-in-law. It was a brief conversation – with Herbert, I mean. Barker was here for almost an hour, questioning me about Larry and his family and the reasons Larry and I separated. He was really obnoxious."

"Detective Barker?"

"Yes. He was so negative about Larry. He even had the nerve to say that Larry might have murdered his father. I wasn't about to tell him Larry was using drugs. That would've convinced him that Larry was the killer. Even my parents would've had their doubts about Larry if they knew." Cheryl glanced toward the ceiling. "I told them he overdosed on medicine from the office, which is mostly true. They knew he was depressed because of our separation and his practice not doing well."

Addie rubbed her chin. "Do you have any idea why Detective Barker's attitude toward Larry was so negative?"

"Probably because Gloria told him that Larry had a big argument with his father a few days before the murder. Gloria thought the argument was about our separation or about money, but it wasn't. It was because Larry wouldn't admit he had a drug problem. Herbert got mad and threatened to call the Board of Registration if Larry didn't call them the next day. He even threatened to cut Larry out of the will. He finally gave Larry thirty days to transfer his patients before calling the Board." Cheryl's eyes brimmed with tears. "I know Larry would've made the call himself. He just needed more time."

"But once Herbert was dead, Larry didn't call."

Cheryl poured herself another glass of wine. "I should've recognized how desperate he was. The drugs, our separation, his practice going down the tubes – then his father's death – Larry was getting hit from all sides."

"Gloria told me Larry didn't answer his cell phone the night his father was killed."

Cheryl gulped her wine. The glass clinked as she set it down on the countertop. "Larry slept in his office that night. I didn't blame Gloria for reporting that – she had no way of knowing he was addicted. It was blaming him for Janet's death that was so unfair. He'd only refilled the antidepressant prescription because Janet's doctor was on vacation. Larry never dreamed she'd overdose on them. He was devastated. He freaked out and got rid of the vial." Cheryl thrust her hand forward as if to forestall any judgment. "Herbert and Leslie knew it wasn't his fault. They both told him that. I think it was his guilt about Janet's suicide that pushed Larry into overusing drugs."

"I remember Gloria telling me how upset she was when the vial disappeared. Why didn't they tell her the truth?"

"Because Gloria has a big mouth. She's a great person but she takes some weird pleasure in 'outing' everyone about everything. Who am I to talk? I'm being just as big a blabbermouth." She pushed her wineglass away. "I don't usually do this. Too much in my head – not a minute's peace."

"Grief does that to people. It doesn't mean you're not discrete in normal circumstances."

"Gloria's grieving, too."

"I'm sure. They're coming to dinner tonight?"

"She and April wanted to help. They were going to bring food – but now I can tell them not to bother – we have some home-made pot pies." Her face suddenly contorted as she tried to hold back tears.

"What?" Addie asked gently.

"He'll never taste anything ever again."

Addie's throat tightened. "No, not in this life." As if there were another – well, she'd keep hoping and praying there was. "Have you heard from Leslie?"

"Not yet. I'm sure she'll call. She's probably as overwhelmed by this as I am. She's another one being hit from all sides."

"Oh?"

"Yes. She's been having marital problems for quite a while – at least since Todd lost his shirt in this last recession. And of course, Gloria had to go and 'out' her, too. You'd think sisters would have a better relationship."

"She 'outed' Leslie about what? To whom?"

"I shouldn't really talk about it. Oh Christ! I still can't believe Larry's gone." Cheryl reached into her pocket for tissues and wiped her eyes. "My mother is so angry with him. I'm sorry. I'm such a mess since this happened. What was I saying?"

"How Gloria outed Leslie."

"Yes, right. Gloria went to Herbert and told him his precious daughter was having an affair. She called Larry, too. Gloria said Todd had lost everything, including – you know how Gloria talks – including his 'pecker-power' in this latest market fiasco."

Dear God, thought Addie. Worse and worse. "I remember Larry mentioning that affair after Herbert's funeral, but he said it happened before she married Todd."

"No, this was a more recent one. Larry thought the guy Leslie was involved with was a turd."

"He knew the man?"

"Larry confronted her and Leslie finally told him who it was. But neither of them would tell Gloria, or even tell me. I asked Larry, but he said Leslie had made him promise to not tell anyone. Still, whoever the man was, he had the nerve to call Larry a few days after his father's death to ask permission for people to come in to survey Herbert's land. Larry sounded off about that after a visit with the kids. I remember him saying, "The slimy bastard isn't satisfied with fucking my sister, he wants to fuck both of us."

Cletis! Addie felt the breath go out of her. With Leslie again. For the land? How could Leslie be so stupid? 'Slimy bastard' fit Cletis to a tee. He'd almost succeeded in charming her over dinner at the Inn. "If Leslie's lover called about surveying, he must've been associated with the developer."

"Yes, Cletis Adams. You remember him?"

"Yes, I do," said Addie. All too well, she thought.

CHAPTER 32

Wednesday Morning

Addie hated to drive into Boston, but Bella's uncharacteristic refusal to go adventuring had left her little choice. Mid-morning traffic on I-95 and I-93 hadn't been bad, but the crazy-quilt of streets and aggressive drivers around South Station had stressed her to the point of white knuckles, tense arms and an ache between her shoulders. The discomfort had lasted through her walk from the overpriced parking garage to the black-marbled foyer of the skyscraper in which CDA International had its offices. Now, sitting on the edge of a plush brown chair in the waiting room, she felt very much out of her element. As if the framed photos of fancy hotels and skyscrapers and the two beautiful scale models of resorts in Culebra and Manama – places she'd never heard of – weren't enough to convince her she lived in a cloistered world, the blonde glamour-girl at the desk had received her as if she were Granny Greenpea, in from the farm.

"You're sure Mr. Adams said today?" Glamour-Girl had asked.

"He said anytime this morning," Addie had replied. Whereupon Glamour-Girl had looked at her computer monitor, tsked twice down into her cleavage, and reported that no Ms. Carter appeared on Mr. Adams' schedule, but surely if she wished to hang her coat in the closet, use the ladies' room out the door and to the right to "freshen up" and return to sit down "for a very little bit," everything could be worked out "serendipiciously."

What fun she and Bella would've had dissecting this girl, thought Addie as she watched the receptionist from her chair. Far more interesting than the jacket-and-tie man that had carried a scowl and a computer printout out of one office and into another. Trust Cletis to hire beautiful women, with or without brains. No matter what he'd said about a role model for his granddaughter, Cletis never would've considered Bess for a job had she not been a treat for his eyes and his fantasies – hopefully, only that.

It was bad enough that Cletis was having a second go-round with Leslie. Why else had he come to the funeral home? Surely he'd lured Leslie back to preserve his deal on the land. No wonder Larry had been so upset about his sister's liaison. But Leslie wasn't stupid. Was she so blindly in love, or desperate – or did she demand a fortune? How could she not realize Cletis' goal had always been money – women were to be used and tossed off while the great man built his empire.

"Where is Manama?" asked Addie.

Glamour-Girl looked up from filing her fingernails. "Bahrain."

"Thank you." Did Bella know Cletis' reach stretched to Bahrain? Too bad Bella hadn't wanted to come. She would've loved those models. But she probably didn't want to see her hero's clay feet.

"Addie, so good to see you," said Cletis.

He'd come into the waiting room so quietly, he'd caught her lost in thought. Her gaze traveled up the pin-striped suit to his welcoming smile, his tanned face, green eyes and white hair.

"You look well, Cletis." Teeth clamped into a smile, she rose from her chair and hastily smoothed her wool dress. Even if his welcome had been sincere, it wouldn't last for long. "Thank you for making time for me."

"My pleasure." With a slightly mocking smile, he indicated she should precede him to an office door that was now open. "At least for the moment," he added.

"For the moment," she said, moving past him.

His office was large and shaped like an inverted L. She didn't care for the modern abstracts on the sand-colored walls, but she had to admit the room was tastefully furnished. A lovely floral centerpiece topped the mahogany conference table in the center of the room. The table was flanked by four straight-backed chairs on each side. A matching desk and two chairs were highlighted back by the windows. The carpeting was a weave of variegated browns – soft on the eyes as well as the feet.

"Back there," he said. "It's more comfortable."

She thought he meant the desk, but once she neared that, she saw that the short arm of the L was furnished as a sitting area, with a small rust-colored sofa, a glass coffee table and two upholstered armchairs on the other side of the table. She used the arms of the nearer chair to keep her from sinking too deeply into the seat.

Cletis stood in front of the sofa. "Would you like some tea?"

"No, thank you. I won't take much of your time."

"A pity," he said, sitting down. He placed his hands on his thighs. "I suppose you're still concerned about Bess."

She gripped the arms of her chair. "Do I have reason to be? I understand she won't be starting with you until the first of December."

"True. I can honestly say you have no reason to worry."

"Plenty of reasons. Start with a murder next door, a rock through my window, my house trashed by someone leaving a calling card from a Latino gang, and now Larry Elwood's suicide."

Cletis didn't even blink. "Look, I'm very sorry all this has happened to you, but what does it have to do with Bess working for me? That's a whole different issue." His facial expression softened. "So is our history. And I heard about young Elwood's suicide. It's a family tragedy and a terrible waste of a decent man. But bad things are bound to happen once someone gets hooked on drugs." Cletis' hands rose, then fell in a gesture of futility. "Tell me, how did you get embroiled in all these horrible situations?"

"I suppose you could say my cat dragged me into it."

"I'd get a different cat."

"I'm sure *you* would."

"Touché." He offered a tight smile. "I've also heard that young Elwood left a suicide note. I suppose if it was a confession of murder we would have heard that on the news."

"I doubt Larry had anything to do with his father's murder. Maybe it's you that needs to confess your role in it." She scrutinized his face for guilt, saw only anger.

"Don't be ridiculous. You know me better than – Damn! You know I'd never do anything like that."

"I don't know what you're capable of. Case in point, your affair with Leslie."

Cletis looked stunned. His mouth opened, closed, opened again. "How the hell did you find out about that?"

"So it's true."

His right hand shot up to swipe away her accusation. "It's really none of your business, but fucking yes, it's true, except – "

"Except Herbert found out about it. So he was killed to keep him quiet and get the land, isn't that right?"

His apparent astonishment gave way to gruff laughter. "Oh God. For a smart woman, Addie, you really can be a dunce sometimes. The land was Herbert's idea."

"Herbert's idea?" She sank back into her chair. Bullshit! she thought.

"Yes," said Cletis. "Herbert came to me and insisted I break off my affair with Leslie. I told him she was an adult and quite able to make her own decisions, and if he had a problem with that, he should talk to her. He said he had. He offered me money." Cletis raised his hands a few inches off his lap, then dropped them back. "I didn't know whether to laugh out loud or to cry – the angry father putting a price on his daughter's honor after she told him to go fly his own kite. For Pete's sake, I had more money even at that time than the good Dr. Elwood could ever put together – so I told him to get out of my office. It was then that he offered me the land deal."

"But that was twenty-five years ago."

"That's what I'm talking about."

Addie shook her head. "No, I'm talking about you getting back together with her recently. That's what Larry was disturbed about."

"No. If he implicated me, he was misinformed. For Christ's sake, Addie, I swear to you that over the past twenty-five years, I've only seen Leslie now and then in the course of business. After I ended the affair, she went to work for one of my competitors. That first couple of years, I got a few 'ha-ha' calls from her after her company underbid us for projects, but then she got married and stopped calling. I assumed she was happy with her new life. Believe me, I had no desire to stir things up again. I haven't seen her or spoken with her since her father's funeral."

"Why did you even bother to go?"

"To pay my respects. I think I told you that in the funeral home. Leslie and I worked together –

and we cared deeply for each other – for a while, anyway."

"Wake up, Cletis, you traded her for fifty acres of land. What does that say about how deeply you feel? How was trading her for Herbert's land any different than selling her for cash?"

"You don't get it, do you. That parcel of land is a unique opportunity for me. You of all people should understand. That land is where I walked – we walked – when all we had were dreams." He bit his lip, then continued. "Leslie and I weren't a good fit. She was in her twenties and on the rise. I was in my forties, between wives, feeling down about things. And Leslie was smart, beautiful, understood my business. After the first few months, I was still flattered but knew it wasn't going to last. To be crude, I ditched her for something I really wanted before she ditched me for some young stud on the way up. Why did I go to the viewing?" Cletis ran a hand through his hair. "Remember *Ripley's Believe it or Not?* Well here's a little nugget for you. It's never taken me long to stop caring for my wives, but I've never stopped caring for my girlfriends. In some cases, I felt I went wrong – "

Addie sniffed. "Sounds like you're chasing might-have-beens, Cletis."

His head jerked. He glared at her for a few seconds, then looked out the window, as if appraising the skyscraper across the street. When he turned his attention back to her, he wore a mocking smile again. "Looks like you can still see through a man darkly."

"I'm sorry. It's hard for me to lighten up – and not only with you. It's difficult enough to feel safe in this world when nothing big's going wrong. But lately – "

"Yes, the murder. I'm sure that's been hard for you – and Herbert's family." He pointed his thumb back over his shoulder. "As for that land, it will be my legacy to Millbrook." His hand came forward to indicate her. "And preserving the privacy of your lot will be my final gift to you."

She grit her teeth. Final gift? Leaving her privacy hers? "Don't expect any thanks from me, Cletis. And I'm not going to feel sorry for you if the town turns thumbs down on your project."

"I never did anything to solicit either thanks or sorrow, Addie. But that doesn't mean I can't sometimes help my friends."

"Well, if you didn't call Larry after his father's funeral to ask permission for the surveyors, some man from your office did. Larry Elwood thought that person was having an affair with Leslie. If that's true, the person who called him might have his own plans for the land, with or without Leslie's blessing. And perhaps there's some connection there to Herbert's murder."

Cletis' face turned grim. "I doubt that. But I'll certainly look into this end of it."

"Who called Larry from here?"

"I'm not sure anyone did. I said I'll look into it." He rose from the sofa. "I think it's time for you to go home."

She stood to face him. "And I think it's time for you to tell all you know."

"And have you tell George? I don't want the police involved until I know what's going on in my own shop. As painful as it is for you, you'll have to count on me to do this."

She couldn't keep a lid on her sarcasm. "Count on *you*?"

"Yes. This time, I won't let you down."

CHAPTER 33

Wednesday Evening

Addie sat at her kitchen table, cordless phone in hand. She'd found Joe Kearney's telephone number by calling Information, but now hesitated. Joe was bound to think she was calling for personal reasons. She'd have to make it very clear this was not about their relationship – not that they really had one – no, this was entirely about finding Herbert's murderer. Probably Michael Planchette. Who would Cletis protect other than his stepson? Himself, of course. Unfaithful, devious, yes – but Cletis a murderer? Hard to believe. Still, she had to examine every possibility. Then she'd be able to go to Barker and George with a sound theory and a clear conscience.

Bowing her head over the envelope on which she'd jotted Joe's number, she inched her bifocals a bit higher, then made the call.

"Addie, what a pleasure it is," he said before she'd uttered a word.

"How did you know it was me?" she asked, then remembered George's smart phone.

"Telepathy," said Joe. "The good vibrations come right through the phone."

"I'm not calling about personal issues. I want to ask you a question about Herbert's murder."

"I didn't do it, Addie." His tone went from facetious to somber. "I take it you've heard about young Larry."

"Yes, that was a shock. I've really felt awful. I – "

"No, don't blame yourself," he said, as if truly telepathic. "Every addict has his chances to choose between drugs and real life. Sad as it is, Dr. Larry chose to end the pain of both."

"It's not that simple."

"Life never is. So when can I take you out for another lunch, dear Addie?"

"Back when you worked with Leslie Elwood at CDA, who else had a crush on her besides Cletis?"

"Ah, shrewd lady – you traded a question for a question. Will you trade an answer for an answer?"

"If it's a serious answer."

"Other than me?"

"What?"

"I gather you're asking who was on the lust-line for Leslie other than Cletis and yours truly?"

She touched her forehead. How could she not have thought of Joe? "Yes, other than you two."

"Probably most of the men who worked with her. Not that she was promiscuous. Nor would anyone who worked for Cletis try to steal his candy. But I'd bet every man-jack who wasn't a –you know, the other way – had his hots for Leslie."

"Was there anyone in particular who stood out that way – someone who still works for Cletis?"

"No one who worked there dared to stand out in that way. Not that my memory of that time is so great. I can sooner recall the bars I got drunk in than the people who worked in that office."

"What about Michael Planchette?"

"Cletis' stepson? He wasn't around back then, that's for certain. Cletis didn't marry Michael's mother until way after Leslie and I were both gone. You think Michael is involved in Herbert's murder?"

"It's possible."

"Almost everything is possible. Including lunch together. How about this weekend?"

Should she? Maybe he could remember more about Cletis and Leslie. Oh, God, who was she fooling? She liked this man. His enthusiasm, his humor – yes, he made her laugh.

"I'll take your silence for a yes," said Joe. "Lunch at your home or mine?"

She lowered her fist. "My silence means I'm thinking. Larry's funeral is on Saturday. Will you be there?"

"No. Funerals tell me life is too short, so they get me thinking 'what the hell' and make me want to raise some again. How about a small Sunday brunch at your place?"

"No. I go to church on Sundays. One o'clock at the Valley Diner?"

"I'll be there. Although I was really looking forward to some good home cooking." His tone made him sound like a starving urchin.

"I'll send you a cookbook for Christmas," she said.

CHAPTER 34

Thursday Morning

Addie had barely walked through Auterio's automatic front door when Bella, in a black blouse and oversized jeans, came at her through a register aisle like an offensive lineman. "How did it go with Cletis?" she demanded.

"Let me get my coat off," said Addie. She smiled at Eunice, the new cashier, then glanced around as she undid her rain bonnet. Only a few customers shopping this early, and they were prowling the food aisles. Paula was opening up a second cash station, but she'd experienced Bella's enthusiasms enough to turn away so her toothy grin wouldn't be obvious.

Droplets of water fell to the floor as Addie shed her raincoat. "You really shouldn't rush around today," she told Bella. The floor's going to be slippery."

"Not as slippery as my best friend. You here to do a day's work or do you just want to get more chicken and another day off?"

Eunice was eyeing them with obvious curiosity. Addie lowered her voice. "I'll fill you in upstairs." She hiked her purse up on her shoulder, draped the raincoat inside-out over her arm and moved to pass through the next register aisle.

"But you're working today?" Bella said as she followed Addie to the stairs.

"Yes, I have to get the payroll checks ready for tomorrow."

"Good thing. I was ready to turn the job over to ADP."

Bella had reason to be miffed, thought Addie as she went up the steps. Not only had she taken two consecutive personal days for visits to Cheryl and Cletis, but she hadn't picked up the phone to share what she'd learned. The last thing she wanted to do was jeopardize her friendship with Bella, but there were times when solitude and peace trumped everything and everyone. Behind her, she heard Bella breathing heavily as she clomped up the stairs. Short of a heart attack, what would convince her to lose weight? Devastating to lose her, too. Surely the only reason Carlo hadn't signed up with a payroll service like ADP was that Bella had put her foot down to protect her best friend's hours. It would be much tougher to make ends meet with Social Security alone.

Despite her wool cardigan and slacks, the brightly lit office seemed cool and she still felt damp. She turned as Bella came through the door behind her. "I'm sorry for keeping things from you. At first, George wouldn't let me talk to anyone about Larry's – suicide – until the media reported it."

Bella closed the door. "They made such a big deal of it, connecting it to Herbert's murder. Even your grandson was trying to dig up some dirt."

"I know." Addie hung her coat in the closet. "He left three messages on my machine." She turned on her space heater and then settled into her desk chair.

"You didn't want to talk to him, either?"

"I would've called both of you, but I needed to burrow in with Flash and think. I've been letting the messages pile up."

Bella grunted as she plopped into the chair behind her desk and swiveled it around to make eye contact. "It's not even eight, and my knees hurt."

"It's your weight."

"It's the rain. They say after this clears out, a big nor'easter is coming. You couldn't think while you talked to me?"

"It's not personal, Bella."

"So now it's all public. Why did Larry kill himself? The drugs?"

"Along with everything else. The public exposure and removal of his license, his separation from Cheryl, the death of his parents – too many things he didn't want to face."

"So no balls and not enough religion," said Bella. "Bad combination."

"Bella! He was my doctor – he cared about me. He grew up next door and I cared about him. God, I'll bet you'd be great cooking corned beef and cabbage."

"For Italians?" Bella rolled her eyes."Never in my lifetime – and what's that got to do with anything?"

"You have this great talent for boiling things down to the tasteless."

"What've you got to be crabby about?" Bella touched her brow; her fingers rebounded above her head. "I got it." Her facial expression turned serious. "I'm sorry for your loss – really. I know you've had a shitty month." She pointed a finger at Addie. "But you insult my tortellini salad today, you better start looking for another job."

"Your salads are wonderful, Bella."

"You don't have to tell me. But you do have to tell me about your visit to Cletis. Did you kiss and make up?"

"As you said, 'not in my lifetime.' He's so conniving and self-centered. He did have an affair with Leslie when she was in her twenties, but he dumped her for the option on Herbert's land. He told himself she'd soon leave him for a younger man, anyway."

"Maybe he was right."

"It wasn't right he dumped her for a piece of property, and it wasn't right he fired her." Addie's hands rose from her lap, then fell back. "And he won't tell me who in his office called Larry to ask about surveyors going onto the land after Herbert's death."

"Why does that matter?"

"Because Larry believed the caller is having an affair with Leslie and using her to get the land, maybe even by murdering Herbert. I think it's Michael Planchette."

Bella's eyes lit up. "His stepson? Wow! You think Leslie is involved in the murder?"

"God, I hope not. I really don't know. Cletis wouldn't get specific about anyone – all he'd say was that he'd 'look into it.' I didn't specifically bring up Michael's name because I knew Cletis would protect him."

"You think Cletis would out-and-out lie to you?"

Addie laughed sharply. "His business was built on lies. Lying to the banks, to the contractors, to the people who buy condos in his developments. For God's sake, he said he loved me and he lied to me; didn't he ever lie to you?"

Bella thought for a minute, then shook her head. "No, I can't say that he did."

"I guess you didn't know him well enough. The man is so false; you know what he said? That he still cared for his girlfriends – and being as he was talking to me, I'm sure he was including me – but he said he had no trouble losing all concern for his ex-wives."

"Maybe he – "

"No!"Addie's hand swept away any retort. "Cletis is as phony as a three-dollar bill. He told me he was going to protect my lot's privacy as his 'final gift' to me. What bullshit. He gave me precious little before he broke up with me – what in God's name did he ever give me since?"

"You turned his offers down."

"Of course I did. What kind of woman takes money from a man after he's rejected and embarrassed the hell out of her?"

"A smart one?"

"Don't be a wise-ass."

"Sorry. I just mean you and your kids were almost destitute at times and he wanted to help. Is pride worth making your kids go hungry?"

"It's self-respect, Bella. And my kids never went hungry. Thanks to you and Carlo, they didn't."

"Yeah." Her tone was flat.

Addie frowned, then realization struck like a migraine. It bored into her brain, then twisted her gut so hard she bent over in her chair and clutched her abdomen.

"What's wrong?" Bella pushed up from her chair.

With a groan, Addie reached desperately for the waste basket. "*His* money," she gasped before the burning in her throat erupted and she spewed vomit into the basket.

* * *

She'd cleaned up the best she could in the restroom, with Bella alternating between anxious hovering and forays down the market aisles to bring back a clean dish towel, a bottle of mouthwash, a can of ginger ale. Now back in her office chair, she felt drained of energy, her anger flattened by sorrow. She shook her head at the large woman sitting across from her, arms folded defensively across her chest, face screwed tight to suppress her tears. Yes, as if she were the victim rather than one of the perpetrators. "How could you do it? How could you betray my trust like that?"

"I'm sorry, Addie. I felt I was doing the right thing. You wouldn't take his money because you were too damn proud, yet you had four kids to feed."

"It was my choice Bella. My kids, my choice – *my* life. Who gave you the right to interfere."

"It wasn't about rights, it was about putting food on the table. And it was about more than you. It was about your kids. And me, and Carlo. How do you think we got the down-payment on this store. You think a worker in the fruit markets makes that kind of money? Cletis called me to see what he could do for you. It was an afterthought to chat with me about my life, my plans – or come to think of it, maybe it wasn't – maybe he really was concerned about both his childhood friends. He gave us fifty thousand dollars at 5 percent interest on a handshake, Addie. A handshake and one condition. He said he knew that Carlo was a stand-up guy, and he knew I'd kick ass if things weren't run right."

She felt her gut churning again. She pressed both hands against her abdomen. "The condition was that he'd give you money for me but you couldn't tell me."

"No, that came later. And he told me I could say no if it put me in too bad a spot with you." Bella unfolded her arms, brought her hands to her lap. "The original condition was that I call him once a month and let him know what was happening in Millbrook."

"With me?"

"You and your kids most of all, but he was really interested in the whole town. If he was away, I had to leave a message so he could get back to me. I got calls from him from Belize, from Kenya, from Jordan, from – "

Addie raised her hand. "Wait a minute! You've been talking to him once a month for – "

"Almost fifty years."

Addie's eyes seemed to squeeze shut of their own volition. How could she have been so blind? Humiliation and anger engulfed her. She saw herself cowering before her drunken stepfather, shrinking into nothingness as Cletis' girlfriend flaunted her engagement ring, cringing each time she had to tell a friend that Dave had run off with his secretary. How could she tell her children that she'd been such a fool? How could she ever again face Cletis, or work for Bella? She opened her eyes and saw the hangdog expression on Bella's face. "And I said you didn't know Cletis well-enough. The joke's on me, isn't it – I didn't know you well-enough."

Bella put her hands up to her mouth, then dropped them. "You still going to be my best friend?" she whispered.

Addie rose from her chair. "I don't know." She took her coat from the closet. "I don't know anything for sure, any more. Except that I'm going home. Please don't call me. I have to get away from everyone."

Week Six

CHAPTER 35

Saturday Morning

The graveside service concluded with the singing of *Amazing Grace*. Standing on a grassy rise twenty feet from Larry Elwood's open grave, Addie joined in song with more than a hundred mourners, including her children, son-in-law and grandson. Despite the bright sunshine, her feet were icy and her face tingled from the wind that whipped dead leaves into flight. She felt very sad for the Elwoods, especially Cheryl and her two little girls. Bundled up in their parkas, the children seemed secure in the arms of their aunts, the two-year old nuzzling between the lapels of Gloria's heavy black coat. Gloria's face was grim, Leslie's tearful above her fur collar, but neither of Larry's sisters was as ravaged as his widow, thought Addie. Cheryl's face was a death mask leaking tears. She'd refused to wear a coat over her long-sleeved black dress but finally had consented to drape her brother's topcoat around her shoulders and take his arm for support. Their mother clasped Cheryl's other arm, and their father stood a step in back of them, perhaps worried his daughter might collapse. As the hymn ended, Addie silently thanked God for the health and safety of her own family. Still, even with His blessing, how long could it be before they were singing over her grave?

Reverend Carlton's final benediction was brief.

"Thank God. I'm freezing," muttered Bess instead of "amen."

Addie turned to stare.

"Well, I am," said Bess.

"That's not the point," said Addie. She was distracted by people working their way by them, greeting her in low tones or just nodding sadly before joining a line to pay their respects to Larry's widow and his two sisters. Addie scanned the crowd once again for Bella or Carlo. Her disappointment in not seeing them was tempered by relief. Several tombstones away, three gravediggers stood waiting to bury Larry. And there stood Detective Barker, observing everyone. What did he expect to discover here? she wondered.

"You want to get in line, Ma?" asked Joanne.

"You all go ahead. I'll be right along." She walked over to stand before Janet's headstone. She pictured her friend vibrant with life, then offered a silent prayer that mother and son were with Jesus in Heaven, or at least joined in complete peace.

"She was a good woman," said George from behind her.

"I miss her," said Addie. "She died too soon. But I can't help but feel it's better that she didn't have to endure this." She glanced toward the open grave.

"Not better for Larry," said George.

"Nothing is better for – " She looked at him sharply. Beneath the brim of his policeman's cap, his face showed more anger than sadness. "What do you mean?"

"Janet committed suicide. She may have given Larry the green light."

Addie felt chilled. She crossed her arms over her chest and clutched the rough fabric of her coat. "I didn't think about that. Cheryl told you Larry's part in it?"

"Day before yesterday."

"God knows what kind of state Janet was in when she did it." Addie took a deep breath, fought back her tears. "Didn't the autopsy show how much drugs she'd taken?"

"Uh-uh. Herbert refused to give consent. Everyone knew she was terminal with cancer. She was pronounced dead by one of Larry's buddies from medical school."

"And they didn't tell Gloria."

"They were worried about her big mouth getting Larry in trouble. You know Gloria. She couldn't keep a secret if her life depended on it."

"Are you going to – "

George shook his head. "What would be the point of trying to prove it now?"

Joanne, bulked up in her brown parka, was heading toward them. Addie nodded. "I agree," she told George. "Let's keep it between us, okay?"

"Never any intention otherwise," he said.

"Hey, folks, how about we get moving," said Joanne. "There are warmer places to talk."

"Okay," said Addie. She tilted her head toward the dwindling line of people offering condolences to the family. "But I want to go over there for a minute or two. You going back to Cheryl's?"

Joanne nodded. "She needs all the support she can get. How about you, bro?"

"I have to get back to work," said George. "Robert, too. Women do better at these things, anyway."

"At all things, bro, at all things."

"Where's Bess?" Addie scanned what was left of the crowd. "Has she gone already?"

Joanne inclined her head toward the road. "She's over there by the hearse, talking to Charlie Rendell."

Addie turned to look. Yes, Bess and Charlie.

"I thought she didn't like him," said George.

"She's weirded out by the work he does," said Joanne. "I mean how cool is it to say 'my boyfriend, the mortician.'"

"He's a Funeral Director," said Addie. "And he's always been in love with her."

"Which is why she's run the other way," said Joanne. "Scared stiff she'd end up as Mrs. Mortician."

"Oh, Jesus," said George.

"They're only talking," said Addie. "But as far as I'm concerned, Charlie's grown up to be a very good man and I'd not be the least bit sorry if something more came of it." No, not likely Bess would trust a man after that abusive pig she divorced. Still, Charlie Rendell... "Come on, let's go," she said, starting off toward the Elwoods. She heard George and Joanne fall into step behind her. Cheryl's parents had taken the children to their car and other people were hurrying to their own vehicles. A gray SUV and several sedans were already moving slowly toward the cemetery exit.

The Elwoods receiving line had split into small groups, with a cluster of people around Cheryl, her brother and Reverend Carlton, and smaller clusters around each of Larry's sisters. Addie headed toward the small group that surrounded

Gloria. As she waited her turn to offer her condolences, Addie offered a sympathetic nod to April, who stood shoulder to shoulder with her wife. April offered a sad smile in return.

Gloria freed herself from the attentions of a young woman Addie didn't know and stepped forward for a hug. "I'm just devastated." Gloria's eyes welled with tears. "We never thought he'd do something like that."

"I never would've imagined it either," said Addie. "I don't have the words to tell you how badly I feel. Your family has been through so much, lately."

"God, I wish it was over." Gloria seemed reluctant to let go. Her face expressed grief, her eyes appealed for understanding.

"At least this part will be over in a few minutes," said Addie. "You and April will be going back to Cheryl's, won't you?"

Out of the corner of her eye, Addie saw April nod. But Gloria shook her head.

"I don't mean this," she said softly. "I mean everything that's still tearing this family apart. You've heard about Leslie and Todd?"

Addie glanced at the group that surrounded Leslie. Yes, there was Todd. She looked back at Gloria. "No, I haven't heard."

"Oh crap!" Gloria whispered. She covered her mouth with both hands. With an angry shake of her head, she dropped her hands to her sides. "I thought Leslie or Cheryl would've told you."

"What's happened to – "

"No, no. It's really for Leslie or Todd to tell people. I'm sorry. I keep opening my mouth before I put my brain in gear."

Addie tried to look sympathetic. Gloria was a bright woman – was it possible she could be so unintentionally indiscrete? "You know that I only wish the best for you and April, and for Leslie and Todd, too."

"I know that. But please don't mention I said anything about – "

"Of course not. I'll see you at Cheryl's." As Addie stepped aside, Joanne moved in to hug Gloria. George was looking away – no, he was looking at Barker. She saw her son nod and the detective start toward them. Addie tensed. This wasn't the time or place for police business. She moved quickly to join the half-dozen people surrounding Leslie and Todd, scrutinizing the grieving couple carefully. Was the arm's length gap between them indicative of emotional separation? Or was Todd, looking every bit the gentleman in his topcoat and fedora, standing a bit apart merely to permit the mourners access to his tearful wife? One look at Leslie and there could be no doubt about the enormity of her loss. But Todd? Addie worked her way around a burly man in a tweed topcoat. No, no way to tell if the sadness on Todd's face was inscribed in his heart, much less how much of it might be due to the possible death of his marriage rather than the death of his brother-in-law.

"I feel terrible about Larry's death," she told Todd, offering her hand.

He took her right hand and reached down for her left, completely enveloping them between his large palms. His touch was surprisingly warm and tender. "As we all do," he said. "Larry was the pride and joy of this family."

"Leslie looks distraught."

Todd glanced over at his wife, sandwiched between a bearded man and a woman in a pill-box hat. "She'll be okay. She's stronger than she looks right now. A lot stronger."

Addie withdrew her hands gently from his. "I'm glad to hear it. I – " Did she really want to open the can of worms Gloria had pointed to? "I heard – "

"No, I'm not leaving right away," said Todd. "I mean with this – " He looked toward the grave. "I'll stay through Christmas, if she wants me to."

Addie blinked. Oh, crumb. "I – well – that's good." Was it? Who'd decided that he should leave? And why? Was there a connection between their separation and Herbert's murder? So many questions she couldn't ask here. "I hope things get much better for both — for each of you."

"Time heals all wounds," he said.

No, she thought. Not Larry's suicide, not Herbert's murder. She managed a tight smile. "I hope so."

She was aware of Detective Barker shadowing her as she moved to offer her condolences to Leslie, and then to Cheryl. Although she offered the women hugs and words she hoped were soothing, she felt less than helpful because she couldn't keep from wondering why Leslie and Todd were splitting up, why Gloria had put that bug in her ear, what Detective Barker wanted, and what all of that had to do with Larry's suicide and Herbert's murder. She figured that George must have tipped off Joanne, for neither one was present when Barker caught up with her on the way to Joanne's car.

"Mrs. Carter – "

She stopped short and turned on him. "I don't like you shadowing me, Detective. Especially at funerals."

"Forgive me. I was here to observe, and not specifically you."

"Who then?"

"The family. And everyone who attended."

"I didn't see you talk to anyone else. Why me?"

"I wanted to tell you a couple of things. The opportunity presented itself here."

"Not a very appropriate time or place."

"Agreed. Would you prefer to come to my office?"

"Don't be absurd. Please make it brief. I'm cold."

"Sorry," he said. "First, it looks like we found the pickup that ran you off the road. It was brought into a body shop up in Nashua two days ago. The owner thought he'd be safe if he lay low for a couple of weeks and then brought the pickup in for repairs out of state. Of course, the jerk now denies driving it that evening, but he didn't report it stolen and we're in the process of getting a paint match with your friend's Cadillac and verifying this guy's movements that day."

"Who's the owner?"

"A carpenter named Victor Ostman. Lives in Pepperell. His name ring any bells?"

"No. Should it?"

"No. I raked him over a few coals, but I don't think he's involved in Elwood's murder. My guess is that he stopped off at a bar before he drove home that night. Once I get the paint match, I'll do a little bar hopping myself."

"Thank you, Detective. Any word from the FBI?"

"I don't think we're high on their list of concerns. But I did check out Raymond Miggens' Latina girlfriend. She backed up his story about being with her the night of the murder."

"And you believed her?"

"Let's say I can't prove otherwise." He raised his hand to prevent questions. "No, I didn't ask specifically where she was from or whether she was illegal. She was quaking in her shoes to be talking to a policeman. The interpreter who questioned her in Spanish thought she was honest. Either that or she's a very good actress."

"I'm relieved," said Addie. "I thought Raymond was telling the truth."

"Well, maybe you were right on that one."

"Meaning I'm wrong on something else?"

"Not exactly. Sort of – for not telling me."

"Telling you? What?"

"George said you've been going out with this Joe Kearney guy."

She felt a rush of warmth to her face. "I'm not going out with him. I met him at the CVS, we got to talking, and we had lunch together once. What's wrong with that?"

"Did you know Joe Kearney served time for assault and battery with a dangerous weapon?"

Oh God! She tried to keep her distress from showing. "No. When was that?"

"Over twenty years ago."

"So how is that relevant now?"

"You mean aside from the fact that Herbert Elwood's head was bashed in?"

No, Joe wouldn't have done that. Unless – "Apparently there's more?"

"With my job, there's always more. Guess who Joe Kearney managed to assault back then?"

"I haven't the foggiest."

"Your other gentleman friend, Cletis Adams.

"Oh crumb!"

"Yeah. Like it or not, Mrs. Carter, I think you're in the middle of a love triangle that could turn ugly."

She had to restrain herself from slapping him. Then the absurdity of his words struck her and she laughed, and kept laughing. "Thank you for your concern, Detective," she finally said. She knew she was grieving Larry and should be worried, but she was still chuckling when she climbed into the front passenger seat of Joanne's car. Joanne had the motor running, the heater on max.

"What's with you?" asked Joanne.

"It seems I'm still desirable," said Addie. "By all the wrong men." And she laughed again.

CHAPTER 36

SUNDAY AFTERNOON

As she picked at her salad and listened to Joe Kearney's funny, probably exaggerated tales of his past misadventures in Mexico, Addie became increasingly restless. The noise level and meat odors in the crowded diner were not nearly as oppressive as the questions she hesitated to ask.

Not like me, she thought, to be timid with a man. Surely Joe must've been provoked by Cletis to get to the point of assaulting him. Cletis could be very provocative, and he had no qualms about rewriting facts to suit his needs. But what if Joe had lied, or lied now? She'd end their relationship – no great loss, really. Not like losing Bella. Closer than sisters. Each woven into the fabric of the other's life. To rip the pattern any further would be unthinkable. Especially after Reverend

James' sermon this morning. Oh crumb. Why wasn't it as easy to forgive as to pray?

"Ah, dear Tinker Bell, will you ever return from NeverNeverLand?" asked Joe.

Embarrassed, she looked up. "I'm sorry. My mind was wandering." She smiled. "I'm afraid my Tink's been grounded by age."

"Nonsense. Pixie minds stay young forever. You've just got too much weight on yours." He set his fork down on the remnants of his omelet. "You care to unload some of it?"

She dabbed at her lips with a napkin. "I met Detective Barker at Larry Elwood's funeral. I never mentioned you to him, but he knows we've met."

"Does he? The long nose of the law, I suppose." The creases in Joe's brow deepened with his frown. "You know, Barker questioned me a couple of weeks after your neighbor was murdered. He said he was going through the patient list. I told him the truth. That night, I was trying to get a friend admitted to a hospital before the DTs could do him in. I thought I'd satisfied Barker's curiosity."

"George must've told him about our first lunch together. I'm sorry about that."

Joe's hand waved away her apology. "No need. This is a small town. Secrets are open, hearts are broken, and the chickens always come home to roost – it goes something like that, doesn't it?"

"Detective Barker told me you assaulted Cletis Adams with a dangerous weapon."

Joe's head and eyebrows inched up, then came down as his strong jaw was softened by an embarrassed smile. "Indeed I did. Were you shocked?"

"I was surprised. It would take more than that to shock me."

"Then you should see my prison tattoos." He laughed at her expression. "Don't worry, I don't have any. I never show anyone my scrapbook of prison memories."

"It was hard?"

Joe shrugged. "It's in the past. The present is much better. I just take one day at a time."

That old refrain again, she thought, hearing echoes of her ex-husband and of her helpmates at Al-Anon. At least Joe sounded like it was heartfelt. "That may be best for you," she said. "It may not be so great for – for the other people in your life."

"I'm trying to do the best I can for me without hurting anyone else. Is that wrong?"

"No, that's not wrong. But secrets can hurt other people."

"That's usually their problem, not mine. You think I should've told you I was an ex-con before that detective did?"

"You told me a lot of other things about your life."

"Look, my saying that I knocked out one of the boss' teeth with a desk stapler never impressed anyone – especially in prison." He offered a thin smile. "Big Olaf told me breaking a jaw or a head might have been acceptable – knocking out one tooth indicated a definite lack of effort and enthusiasm."

"I don't mean to be critical. I'm sorry if I come across that way. I have no right to tell you what you should reveal about your life. In fact, I'm just as – "

"Would you like me to clear some of this away?" The voice was female, the tone intrusive.

Addie looked up, saw the waitress Joe called Miss Pierced.

"Not now," said Joe. "We're fine."

Not really, thought Addie as she watched the girl walk away. She turned back to Joe. Yes, they'd come too far in life to play games. "In high school and the summer after graduation, I was in love with Cletis. He talked of marrying me. We got rather intimate."

The muscles in his face tightened. "You didn't need to tell me that. Cletis probably slept with every pretty girl in town."

She struggled to keep her composure. "I hope not. That would've made me a bigger fool than I was."

"I'm sorry. That wasn't a kind thing to say."

"No harm done. But I did have to tell you enough so that you'll understand where I'm coming from about Cletis."

"You still in love with him?"

"I hope I'm not that big a fool. No, I need to learn more about his relationship with the Elwoods. Do you know Herbert had signed a purchase and sale agreement with CDA for fifty acres of land he owned behind our houses?"

"No, but so what? Cletis is a developer. If the old doc hadn't been murdered, who'd have been surprised if Cletis bought a big parcel of land in his home town?"

"But the purchase and sale agreement was signed in exchange for Cletis firing Leslie Elwood."

Joe's eyes went wide. "That son-of-a bitch."

"But you didn't know anything about the land deal back then. So, forgive me for asking, but why did you hit him?"

"Because I was drunk. Probably wouldn't've sober."

"He'd fired you?"

Joe shook his head. "Not until I used his stapler. I went to his office to register my opinion about how shabbily he treated his workers."

"His workers? I thought you were a part-time consultant."

"Yes, which was why I could risk telling him off. I didn't need to suck up to him to keep a regular paycheck. Truth to tell, I thought I'd be next out the door, anyway. The day before, he'd fired three members of our team and cancelled our mall project without any notice."

"And Leslie was one of those people?"

"She was project coordinator." Joe's fist thumped the table. "Now I understand it!" A woman in the booth in front of them turned her head to look. "Sorry," he told her. "Light just dawned on Marble-head." He leaned forward toward Addie and lowered his voice. "I always thought maybe the financing fell through or maybe Cletis realized that there were too many big shopping malls already built or under construction. Boy, was I blind. The prick – sorry Addie – was badmouthing all of us to cover up his own skuzzy deal."

"What did Cletis say?"

Joe's hand rose in a dismissive gesture. "It was the usual bullshit you hear when a boss wants to get rid of people. Our architect didn't have enough vision, I was too rigid about drainage and sewage systems, the environmental geek was literally for the birds – Cletis gave us no warning at all. Probably didn't want any questions."

"And for that you hit him?"

"No, it was some other things he said."

"You mean about Leslie."

"More about me." Joe's tone had become hard, his face taut.

"What did Cletis say?"

"No secrets with you, huh?"

"One of the problems with a pixie mind."

He winked. "It could be a burden to those around you. But then I suppose it's their problem, right?" His face turned grim. "The son-of-a-bitch said that Leslie hadn't moved the project along effectively, which was even less true than the other crap. So I said, 'Well, now you've fucked her in more ways than one. You satisfied?' And Cletis, the smooth bastard, said 'More satisfied than you'll ever be. A woman like that would never give you the time of day – you don't have the money and you certainly don't have the balls.' So I bashed him with his Swingline. 'Now I'm satisfied, too,' I told him and walked out. Of course, I really wasn't satisfied until I got to the nearest bar and knocked back a few. But even then, I knew it was going to be my very last party."

CHAPTER 37

Sunday Afternoon

Marty was there with a welcoming smile when Addie parked at the top of her driveway. Despite the November chill, her grandson was wearing only jeans and a flannel shirt. Was he looking to get sick again? Don't be a nag, she thought, and managed to smile.

Dragging her purse behind her, she eased herself out of the car. The wind had picked up and dark clouds had moved in. If they were going to walk, they'd better start soon.

"Hi, Granny." He gave her a hug and planted a kiss on her cheek.

"What a lovely welcome." She disengaged from him. "I'm sorry I kept you waiting."

"No problem. I always have my Blackberry with me. I used the time to catch up with Cassie."

So he was still seeing Cletis' granddaughter. And she'd promised not to pry. "Cassie Adams?"

"Uh-huh. She's been real busy since she started working for CDA, but we call or text each other at least twice a day. You said you had a story for me?"

"Yes, but not the one you're probably thinking about. Did you find out any more about the Viper Kings?"

"I didn't have any luck with the gang-bangers. The last guy I talked to told me they didn't publish membership lists and I'd better stop asking questions and get out of Lowell before something bad happened to me. But I finally located Pedro Serrano's sister – she goes by her married name, Torres. She said Pedro wasn't gang connected, but I'm not sure she would've told me if he was."

"I don't want you going back to Lowell," said Addie. "Detective Barker has cleared Raymond as a suspect, so the whole Pedro Serrano connection is out the window. The Viper Kings had no reason to come to Millbrook or to kill Herbert. Nor did Rona Barker's Chinese clients. But I want you to check out a Pepperell man named Victor Ostman. Detective Barker thinks he's the fellow who ran us off the road. He's a carpenter, so see if you can find any work connections to Cletis or to Michael Planchette, or other connections to Dr. Warley or Herbert's children."

"Barker cleared Ray Miggins? You get more out of that guy than I do. All he says to me is 'no comment.'"

"You're a reporter. He knows you'll print whatever he says. By the way, I thought that story you wrote about what Larry Elwood meant to this town was excellent."

"Thanks, Granny. What's the story you want me to write now?"

"Come inside. I want to get out of these church clothes so we can take a walk out back. Then, if you feel it's the right thing to do, I'd like you to do a story on how Cletis Adams will turn those beautiful woods into condos and parking lots."

"You're going to fight him?"

"No, my fight with Cletis is over. But we're going to fight for this town."

* * *

The clouds looked ominous as they headed back through the woods toward her house. Like the birds, she and Marty had become silent, hearing only their breathing above the crackle of leaves and twigs underfoot. She was pleased Marty had agreed to write a story for *The Millbrook Messenger* and to seek support from conservationists via Facebook and Twitter, but she couldn't help but wonder whether she'd have been so concerned about the development of this land had she lived on the other side of town. What if Cletis hadn't been the developer, or if Herbert hadn't been murdered?

She pushed aside a thin branch that threatened her face, then jammed her hands into the warmth of her coat pockets. No, she thought, as Coach Belichick had often said after Patriots' games, "it is what it is." She had to face facts. More than anything, she missed Bella Auterio. Bella was the sister she'd always wanted, the soul-mate she'd not had in her marriage. So easy to take intimacy for granted until it was no longer there. Holding on to the illusion of being so strong and independent wasn't worth the price of their friendship. False pride had to go – especially the belief that she could see all things clearly. Everyone was blind in one direction or another, but her arrogance had kept her believing other people never saw anything better than she did.

"Look at Flash," said Marty.

Her eyes followed his pointing finger. Flash was strutting across her back lawn, clearly on the way to her house. Addie put her hand on Marty's arm. "Don't move for a minute," she whispered. "What's he got in his mouth?"

"Hard to tell from here, but it looks like a bird."

She thrust her hands back into her pockets. It wasn't that Flash couldn't learn – he didn't want to. Like Rona Barker when she shopped at the store. "He always kills them before he brings them home."

"Well," said Marty, "at least you know the identity of one murderer."

"Not the one I want." She watched Flash reach the back steps, look up at the door, then turn and scamper around to the side of the wooden steps and disappear behind the overgrown yew that filled the right angle between the steps and the back of the house.

"Keep your young eyes on where Flash disappeared." Addie strode toward that spot and was thirty feet away when Flash bolted from behind the yew and raced around the side of the house.

"He doesn't have it now." She felt excited. "That must be his hidey-hole."

"Better than in your house."

"Not if it rots. And who knows what else "he's dragged back there." She reached the bush, forced her way around to the back, knelt and pushed branches aside, wincing as the evergreen needles prickled her hands. "I don't see the bird." A pain down her thigh told her to bend no further. "Please Marty, it's hard for me. I'll get out and you get in here." She used the side of the house for support as she rose.

"I'm glad I wore my best jeans," he said, as he got down on his knees behind the bush.

"You can do them in my washing machine." She saw the lower branches moving.

"I don't see the bird under here," he said

"Look closer to the steps." She saw Marty's head and shoulders move in that direction, then almost disappear amidst a flurry of branches.

"Oh!" he said.

"You found it?"

"No, not the bird. You have a hole under here in the lattice work. This could be Flash's hidey-hole."

Her heart quickened. "What's inside?"

A branch snapped and the bush seemed to convulse. "Shit," said Marty. "The bush doesn't give me enough room to get down far enough – okay, that's better. No, I'll need a flashlight."

"Can you put your hand in?"

"Not for a dead bird." He put his hands on the top step and struggled upward. "Who knows what germs it's carrying? There could be a rat or a snake in there, too."

"No. Flash would've killed anything smaller than he is. But you're right about the germs."

"So we're done?" he said hopefully.

"Not yet. Be a dear and get a pair of rubber gloves from my kitchen. They're under the sink.

And also the long barbeque tongs hanging in the pantry. Oh, and a garbage bag."

"You going to clean everything out?"

"I would if my back would let me. As it is, I'll look around for a volunteer."

"Ohhh."

She rewarded him with a smile. "I'm sorry, dear. But I don't want things rotting under there. We'll find something solid to put in front of the hole tonight and I'll have one of your uncles seal it up first chance they get."

"Won't Flash just bring dead birds into the house?"

"Please Marty, get the things I asked for."

"Sure, but don't be shocked if he does." He started up the steps.

"I'm not shocked by anything Flash does, any more."

Five minutes later, she had to take back her words. Not because of the dead crow, tarnished charm bracelet or rodent skeletons, but because of the black leather glove with a red stain.

CHAPTER 38

MONDAY, 8:15 A.M.

"Of course it's not blood," said Addie. Did Barker think she was a dimwit? The Zip-Loc bag containing the glove now lay on the desk in front of him. From where she sat, the glove's small button blended in with the black leather – not so, the stain. "I didn't need a microscope to tell me it's red paint." She glanced at George, sitting next to her. "Or anyone to tell me it's a woman's glove. What I hope you gentlemen would agree with is that a woman was down in Herbert's basement when he was painting those bird houses, or not long after, and that this glove is what she – or the people she sent – were trying to find in my house."

"Maybe, maybe not," said Barker. "We'll send it to the state lab to see if the paint on the glove matches the paint on the bird houses, or whether we can identify the owner by DNA. And we'll check out who sells this style glove. But maybe I can save us all that work by calling all the women involved in this case to ask whether they lost a glove. At least I can get their glove sizes. Still none of that can prove – "

"I don't think you should – "

"Ma, let him finish!" said George.

"I'm sorry, Detective."

"No problem." Barker's tone belied his words. "As I was saying, no matter who owned this glove, we can't be sure that's what the people who trashed your house were looking for, nor can we prove the glove was connected to the murder next door. Even if the glove came from Elwood's house, your cat might have stolen it a week before the murder."

Just what she'd thought he'd say. "So it doesn't help at all?"

"No, I'm not saying that. I can't predict what we'll learn from it. And you and your grandson did well not to handle it, although judging from the tooth marks, I can't say the same for your cat. He should've left it at the crime scene, if that's where he found it." Barker lips twitched as he glanced up at the wall clock. Apparently satisfied that he had more time, he focused his attention back on Addie. "Look, even if someone admits owning this glove, they'll say they touched Elwood's bird houses two days before he was killed, or they were painting an old cabinet at home – and we can't prove any different." He extended his hand airily in her direction. "Could you testify your cat only steals from your next-door neighbor?"

"Of course not."

"So much for the glove. Let me know when your cat brings home the murder weapon with blood on it."

"May I make a suggestion?" said Addie.

"Sure. I'd welcome anything constructive at this point."

"If we assume that glove didn't belong to a stranger, when you call Herbert's daughters about the glove – and Gloria's wife, April, I should think – whichever one of them owned that glove could deny it."

"Let me guess, you think they won't deny it to you? That glove could belong to any woman in the neighborhood. What makes you think it's one of those three?"

"Herbert's cleaning lady wouldn't bring a fancy glove like that to work, and I don't know of any other woman who had access to his house. The paint indicates that's where it came from."

"Look," said Barker, "for all we know, the paint could've – "

"Could've been from somewhere else," Addie said quickly. "But I doubt that the timing of the break-in to my house so soon after the murder was a coincidence. And only a very few people could be sure I'd be out that morning."

"It would be easy for someone to learn your work schedule," said George. "Or call on the telephone or knock on the door pretending to collect for some charity."

Addie sighed. "That's possible, but don't you think it's better to go with what's probable. If the glove is what the woman is searching for, she had to be very worried about anyone finding it. So if I call to ask what she wants me to do with it, she might say she wants it back."

"Wait a second," said George. "If this woman's the murderer and thinks you have incriminating evidence, she might come after you."

Barker grimaced. "Hang on, George. Don't jump the gun. Mrs. Carter, I thought I made it clear that establishing who the owner is doesn't prove anything."

"You need proof, Detective. I just want answers. And these women might tell me more than they'd tell you. I mean, starting with Gloria, they have already. You can worry about how to prove things once we have more information." Addie managed a thin smile. "Of course, if George is right and the owner tries to kill me, that should be proof enough for you."

"Proof you are going dotty," said George. "I won't let you do it."

"It's not up to you – " She turned to Barker. "– is it, Detective?"

"Technically, no, but – but George is right. We can't allow you to set yourself up like that."

"And how do you gentlemen propose to stop me?"

"I can lock you up," said Barker.

"On what charge?" asked George, his voice betraying his irritation.

"Obstructing justice."

"I know from TV I'm entitled to one phone call," said Addie. "I'll call Gloria and ask her to ask Leslie and April about the glove."

"Stop!"demanded George. "We're not going to arrest you, Ma, but you have to be sensible."

"I'm being very sensible. And I'm not trying to be stubborn. I know this might not work, but if you two have a plan that has a greater chance of success, just tell me."

George looked at Barker.

Barker gave a small shrug. "We need more time."

"To do what?" said Addie.

"To check alibis again," said George.

"You said all of them were at work during the break-in. Verified by at least two people."

Barker looked sharply at George. "You told her that?"

"It was her house that got trashed. It supported the gang theory."

Barker shook his head. "I hate mothers getting involved in my work."

"Believe me," said Addie, "I never planned to be involved in a murder investigation. But here we are – it is what it is. So, gentlemen, how are we going to keep me safe after I make those calls?"

CHAPTER 39

MONDAY, 9 A.M.

No busier than usual, thought Addie as she entered Auterio's through the sliding doors. The possibility of a nor'easter later in the week hadn't hit home yet. Carlo's favorite Sinatra album was being played through the speakers and a few customers with shopping carts or plastic baskets were in the food aisles. Paula's register was beeping as she scanned the items for a mom toting an infant in a front baby carrier. In the other open check-out aisle, Anthony was chatting up Eunice. Addie braced herself as Carlo strode toward her from the service desk, his face that of a schoolmaster who has to discipline his favorite pupil.

"So, do we have a bookkeeper or not?"

"Hello, Carlo. I'm glad to see you. I'm really sorry for leaving you and Bella in the lurch."

Carlo looked around to make sure no one was listening. "Save your apologies for upstairs. The accountant finished the payroll. What bothers me more is that my wife did the right thing and her best friend has made her a basket case."

No, he'd never understand. "I'm sorry. I owe both of you a major apology. And whether you have this bookkeeper is up to you and Bella. I certainly would appreciate being taken back."

His stern expression softened. "So when did we ever let you go? I understand you've been through this murder thing, and then a suicide – so you act a little irrationally, why not? Go upstairs and talk to Bella. And then try to catch up with the important bills. My wonderful wife has sixty-seven virtues, but a math brain she's not."

Addie let out a deep breath, then smiled. "You've counted her virtues?"

"It's an estimate. I'm sure she'll tell you she has more."

"Thank you, Carlo. It's good to be back."

Bella must have heard her climbing the stairs, for she'd swung her swivel chair around to face the open doorway. Her black trousers were overlapped by a Millbrook High sweatshirt, the faded gold letters crossing twin mountains of faded green. Bella's smile was cautious, her eyes hopeful. "You forget something?" she asked.

Addie nodded. "I forgot to apologize. I forgot to say thank you." Tears blurred her vision. "The only thing I couldn't forget was you."

"God, I am so sorry." Bella struggled up from her chair, her face contorted by a sob. "I was so worried you wouldn't come back." She blotted her tears with a forearm, then rushed forward.

Still in her coat, Addie stepped into the charge, surrendering to the large arms that wrapped around her. She hugged Bella as if they'd been separated for decades, regret, relief and joy spilling out with her tears. She stroked Bella's back, felt a protective hand settle on her head. Bella's other arm still held her tight. Yes, thought Addie, she felt safer now than at any time since she'd found Herbert's body. The cocoon that she and Bella had spun together throughout their lives was stronger than ever. And she needed it. "Bella, let me breathe. We have a lot to talk about."

Bella eased her grip, but did not let go. She looked Addie straight in the eyes. "I never meant to hurt you."

"I never doubted that." Without breaking eye contact, Addie took half a step back. "But stupid me, I was too proud for my own good – and the good of my children – and my friends. I'm very sorry."

"It's okay," said Bella. "I knew you were a jerk ever since you said gypsies stole your homework."

"Thanks for sticking with me anyway." Addie smiled and took off her glasses. She pulled a wad of tissues from her coat pocket and wiped her eyes. "So can I take my coat off and get to work? Carlo said there are bills that need to be paid."

"Aha!" Bella flung her arms upward in mock exasperation. "Now the truth comes out. Carlo called you to come back because he thought I couldn't handle your job."

"Peace, Bella, peace. Carlo didn't call me. I saw him downstairs. He thinks you've done fine. In fact, he told me you had sixty-seven virtues."

"Sixty-seven? Last week he said sixty-four. I definitely don't like the direction he's heading. He's buttering me up, and now you are, too. I know what he wants from me – that hasn't changed – at least not much. What do you want from me?"

"I already have it. But after I get some bills out, I need to make some telephone calls."

"So? You want a personal secretary?"

"No, I need you to help me prepare a very short message and to be a witness to what I say."

"You're not breaking up with Joe, are you?"

"There's nothing to break up. No, I'm calling three women we know."

"You planning a party?"

"No, a surprise. I think one of the three is a murderer."

* * *

Leslie's voicemail clicked in after four rings.

Addie flashed a thumbs up sign to Bella, who'd moved her chair to the side of Addie's desk. "Machine," said Addie. She looked at the brief script she and Bella had devised and waited for Leslie's greeting to end.

"Leslie, this is Addie. I found that glove you've been looking for. We need to talk very soon. Please call me at Auterio's between eight and four. You can't reach me at home for a few days. I've been drafted to babysit with my grandchildren." She hung up the telephone. "How'd I do?"

"We forgot to put in the telephone number," said Bella.

"Doesn't matter. She'll call the store's main number and they'll put her through." She looked down at the slip of paper for Gloria's home number, then tapped the corresponding buttons on her telephone. She heard the phone ring twice, then someone pick up. Oh crumb!

"Hello," a woman said.

"April?" Addie saw Bella's lips form an O.

"Yes. Who's this?"

"It's Addie. Good morning. Listen, I found that glove that you or Gloria lost."

"I didn't lose a glove. I don't think Gloria did either."

"I'm sorry, I was under the impression that one of you had, and wanted it back. Is Gloria at home?"

"She's at work. I don't go in until three today. How are you, Addie?"

"I'm fine. Ask Gloria about the glove tonight, okay? Just to make sure. If she wants it, she can call me tomorrow at Auterio's. I won't be at home for a few days – I have to babysit for my grandchildren. Do you need Auterio's number? "

"No, we have it. What made you think we lost a glove? Has Gloria been over to see you?"

"No. It's from her father's house. But if it's not hers, she doesn't have to get back to me."

"Is it connected to the murder investigation?"

Normal curiosity? Addie looked over at Bella and shrugged. "I think the police will have to decide that."

"Gloria would've told me if she lost a glove. But I'll let her know you have it. If it's hers, I'm sure she'll get back to you. It may not be tonight. I don't get home until midnight."

"That's okay. I'm sure you two have bigger things to worry about than a glove."

"Wha – we are very busy."

"Of course, dear. Take care. And have a nice day."

CHAPTER 40

MONDAY, 10:30 A.M.

Addie was finalizing her list of accounts payable when the office telephone rang. She looked at her desk phone. Leslie, already? More likely some vendor asking for an overdue check. She clicked the "save" command and picked up the telephone.

"Auterio's Supermarket. How can I help you?"

"Addie? Good morning. It's Cletis. I tried to get you at home. I'm glad you're back at the store."

She'd recognized his voice the instant he'd said her name. She cast an accusing look at Bella's empty chair. Still reporting to Cletis? Was that why she'd gone down to the deli counter?

"I hope it's still a good morning," she said. "When did Bella last talk with you?"

"Thursday, after you walked out. She was very upset. I'm sorry you got so angry with her; she was trying to help – as I was."

Addie exhaled softly, felt inner knots ease. "I know. I've apologized to her for my reaction. I guess I owe you an even bigger apology."

"King-sized." He laughed. "The size of my ego. But I'll tell you what, you never have to say another word about it if you take me out to dinner. We don't have to go to the Inn again. I'm told it's horribly expensive. You pick the restaurant."

Oh, crumb. No way to refuse, might as well be gracious. "Thank you, Cletis. I appreciate your thoughtfulness. I really do. Does Domino's Pizza take reservations? No, I'm sorry, I really will do better than that."

He chuckled. "I look forward to it. Tomorrow night?"

"No, I'm sorry." God, apologizing twice to Cletis within a minute? "I'm expecting – " A housebreaker? A murderer? "– company this week. I'll call you next week so we can set a date." Damn! Why did she say 'date'? "Thanks for calling. I hope your good morning lasts all day."

"Wait! The main reason I called was to get back to you about Michael. You were right about his calling the Elwoods about Herbert's land. But really, there's nothing to worry about. It was partly my fault, and I've taken care of it."

"How so?"

"For years I've been holding out this Millbrook project as an incentive for him to improve his management skills, both on the financial end and with people. I'd told him that if he met certain criteria, I'd appoint him project manager. Frankly, I never thought we'd get the land this soon. Hell, even though I'm younger than Herbert, there was a chance I might've died first." He grunted as if the possibility was painful. "Anyhow, when I confronted Michael about the calls, he freely admitted he'd been trying to hurry this project along. He said he wanted to prove himself capable – both to himself and to me."

"Hurry – it – along?" she said.

"For God's sake, not by murdering Elwood. Michael might do a lot of stupid things – like parking that elephant on my lawn, for example – but don't think the kid is a complete idiot – or a murderer."

"I wasn't accusing him of either. But sometimes I can't turn my mind off to the impossible, much less to what's possible."

"You must waste a lot of time worrying." Cletis uttered a brusque sigh. "To be honest, the thought crossed my mind, too, so I asked him again where he was the night of the murder. He insisted he'd taken his daughter to the movies in Worcester. Not only did she back him up, he happened to run into Leslie Elwood there – seeing another movie in the same Multiplex. Of all people, Leslie Elwood. So I grilled him about whether he had or was having an affair with Leslie. He vehemently denied that, too."

"Of course." Addie took off her glasses and rubbed her eyes. Would Michael be risking more by lying or by telling the truth? Cletis might find it amusing that his stepson was enjoying his former mistress. He was equally capable of firing Michael. It could be that the land was Michael's only interest. Larry or Cheryl could've misheard or misunderstood about the affair. "So you sanctioned Michael's calls?" Addie said as she put her glasses back on.

"No, I didn't know what he was doing until I talked with him this morning. Believe me, I busted his you know whats for jumping the gun. At the same time, I know where he's coming from. The kid fancies himself the heir to my company. Not that I ever gave him the slightest hint of that. He's a capable foreman, but I've told him several times I had reservations about him moving into management. It seems he's been even more worried since I took my granddaughter into the business. But who knows what she'll be capable of? I certainly don't. Still, Michael was trying to increase his head start."

"I see. Thank you for the information."

"Does it put your mind at rest about Michael?"

"It should. But I wonder if it should worry you a bit more."

"Why's that?"

How could such a smart man fail to see what was beneath his nose? No, not her business to point it out. But hadn't he made her hardships his concern? "You're kind of setting up a competition between your stepson and granddaughter. Someone seems bound to lose – even you."

"Competition breeds winners. You should understand that. Bella told me you've stayed a football fan. I guess I had some lasting influence on you."

"You certainly did. I learned life isn't a game. In life, when you fumble the ball, you lose a lot more than yardage. But aside from that, don't you think it's a major coincidence that Michael and Leslie were in the same theater at the same time the night of the murder?"

He was silent for several seconds, then said, "Coincidences happen."

Yes, now he was thinking. "Certainly." She offered a grim smile to the telephone. "You know, I remember Gloria telling me that Leslie didn't even like movies. I suppose I can ask Leslie about that the next time I talk with her."

"You're planning to see her?"

"Not specifically. But she may be planning to see me."

CHAPTER 41

WEDNESDAY, 7:30 A.M.

Addie felt tired and achy as she stepped down from George's SUV into the parking lot in back of Auterio's. Dark, thick clouds had moved in again and the wind came in gusts. Yawning, she used one hand to cover her mouth, the other to retrieve her purse from the car's floor. How many more restless nights would she have to spend in George and Margie's guestroom before they decided she wasn't in danger? Not good to leave Flash alone so much, especially with a nor'easter coming.

George came around from the driver's side. "You going to be okay?" His head turned this way and that as he scanned the cars in the lot and then the sidewalks beyond.

"I'll be fine here," she said. George's ski jacket and blue jeans would draw less attention than his uniform. Still, she didn't need protection here. "No one's going to try anything rash in a store full of people – maybe Bella would, but we're used to that."

"Just be sure *you* don't do anything rash," he said. "I'll see you in. Call me when you're ready to leave. Otherwise, I'll come pick you up at four. If I can't come, I'll send Peterson."

"Fine." Was meeting Leslie very rash? Leslie could be a murderer, but she certainly wasn't a lunatic. On the phone, she'd been cagey, asking for a description of the glove, then saying she had several pairs of black gloves and didn't remember losing one. George would definitely forbid a meeting – or insist on being there. Well, she'd tell him afterwards. "Come on, I'm cold." She started for the store but had to give way as he moved in front of her. My God, the way he watched over her, you'd think she was the President – or a four-year old.

As they passed through the automatic doors, Bella came toward them wearing a fresh white apron over her dark skirt and red blouse. "Good-morning, George. Morning, Addie." Behind Bella, Eunice and Paula already had lines of customers waiting to check out, while other shoppers maneuvered full baskets around each other in the aisles. Anthony and Lily were bagging to speed up checkouts and Karen was opening up a third register. Sinatra's *My Way* was competing with a medley of chatter, thumps, beeps and rattles, as items went from conveyer belts into paper bags.

"Good morning," said Addie. She unzipped her parka.

"Hi, Aunt Bella." George scanned the store. "Busy this morning, huh?"

"Because of the storm. The weatherman said it'll track west of Boston."

"Take good care of Ma," said George. "I'll pick her up at four, or sooner if the storm hits earlier than expected."

"He's checking me into daycare," said Addie.

"What time does she nap?" asked Bella.

"Easy, ladies. I'm just doing my job."

Addie sniffed. "Thank you, officer, for helping us old folks out. Now go and do your day job. And while you're at it, see if you can catch a murderer."

"Good idea." George leaned over and pecked her on the cheek. "See you later."

Bella waited until George was out the door, then said, "I take it you haven't told him Leslie's going to meet you here."

"He'd never let me do it, Bella. I'm not even sure I should. Leslie's only coming because I threatened her."

"You threatened Leslie?"

"Sort of. I said, 'I know about you and Michael.'"

"That must have gotten her attention."

Addie nodded. "She wanted to know what I knew, but I insisted on this meeting. I don't know whether she's afraid I'll tell Cletis or Barker, or both."

"I'd love to be a fly on the wall," said Bella.

"No way. It has to look like a regular workday. You need to be working somewhere other than the office – somewhere where you won't bump into Leslie."

"Rats." Bella saw Addie's frown. "Okay, I'll be behind the deli counter with Anthony. But things could get out of hand upstairs. I'll have Carlo stand behind the service desk. He can listen for the buzzer from upstairs while he's watching the front. And he has all the extension numbers right there – "

"Good."

" – with his gun," said Bella.

"His gun!" Her voice was loud enough to get Eunice and Paula's attention. Even a customer on his way out the door looked back. Addie lowered her voice to a whisper."You want a shoot-out in your supermarket?"

"Of course not. Hey, these are my customers. I don't want any violence. That would be stupid. That's why I told Carlo not to put any bullets in the gun."

Addie glared at her. "Lock the gun in the safe. If it gets bad enough we even think we need a gun, one of us will call the police. Really, Bella, I want you and Carlo to swear you won't take that gun out today, no matter what happens."

"Okay," said Bella. "But I hope you realize that you're violating our Second Amendment rights."

"So report me to the NRA."

"I think I'll do that. The publicity will be good for business."

* * *

With the office door open, Addie had no difficulty hearing footsteps on the stairs, then Bella's voice saying, "She's up here, Leslie."

Addie looked up from her computer screen as Bella clomped into the office followed by Leslie Elwood. Leslie's face looked almost as pale as the high-necked blouse she wore under her unbuttoned car coat.

"Hello, Leslie."

"Hello, Addie." Leslie looked around the small office. Her angular features looked strained, her eyes wary.

"I have to get back to the deli counter," said Bella, heading for the large purse on her desk. "I just need to get my tissues."

Oh, no, thought Addie. Bella's tape recorder! Leslie wouldn't know Bella kept a box of tissues under the deli counter, but she couldn't fail to realize there were shelves of tissues downstairs. Hoping to distract Leslie, Addie rose from her chair. "Let me hang your coat in the closet."

"No, I'd rather keep it on. I'm not planning to stay long."

Bella brandished a packet of tissues. "I got 'em. You can sit here, Leslie." She pulled her chair out from the desk and headed toward the door, flashing Addie a smug smile Leslie couldn't see. "Ciao."

Addie rubbed the back of her neck. "Ciao." Should she maneuver around Leslie to close Bella's purse? No, it'd look odd. Tell Leslie? She'd clam up or walk out. Oh crumb. With a sigh, Addie sank into her chair. "How are you, Leslie?" Yes, her own fault for forgetting about the recorder, and for underestimating Bella's need to hear every word.

"So-so." Leslie perched herself on the edge of Bella's chair. "I must admit I was surprised by your call."

"Because I found the glove or because I said I knew about you and Michael?"

Leslie offered the ghost of a smile. "Mostly because you were so tight-lipped. Exactly what do you know about me and Michael?"

Addie took a deep breath, then exhaled slowly. God, she hated to get down in the dirt like this. Janet would turn over in her grave if she knew her daughter was an adulterer, maybe even a murderer. Well, it is what it is. But not yet time to put her few cards on the table. "You know, the police will match the paint on the glove to the birdhouse paint, and DNA from little hairs left inside the glove can identify the owner."

"You gave the glove to the police?"

"I had to, didn't I? It – " No, saying it was found in the basement might not hold up. "It was crime scene evidence."

"Oh." Leslie's expression was grim.

Addie waited for more. Leslie remained silent.

Addie pursed her lips. Leslie wasn't going to ask why she'd been singled out. "You thought Flash took it," said Addie. "And you knew I was going to be out, the day my house got broken into."

"I'm sure other people knew." Her tone was defiant.

"Yes, because you told them. At least, that's what you said when we met in the coffee shop."

"Addie, I'm truly sorry about what happened to your house, but that wasn't me. I mean houses get broken into every day. The timing between my father's murder and the break-in could've been random."

"But it wasn't. Nothing was taken. Do you have another explanation?"

Leslie offered the petulant pout Addie recalled her parading in as a child. "How should I know? Sometimes these Latino gangs vandalize for the fun of it, sometimes they rob or kill. Who knows why they do what they do?"

"Really." Addie nodded as if she'd learned an interesting fact. "Did I mention a Latino gang?"

"Yes – not today, but another time."

"I guess you'll have to refresh my memory. I do remember George taught me never to reveal what I saw at a crime scene, because then only the criminals and the police know the details." Addie shook her head sadly. "Forgive me, dear, but as George is fond of saying, when you're knee deep in shit and sinking, you'd better start swimming in truth."

Leslie leaned forward, clearly indignant. "You saying I'm lying? Who the fuck are you to question me!"

Addie recoiled. Her jaw muscles worked. "I'll tell you who. I'm your mother's friend. I care about her kids. Many's the time I cleaned your butt, and right now I'm trying to save it. If it's worth saving. You sure don't have to answer to me – you'll answer to the police. But if you do decide to talk to me, do it with some respect." She got up from her chair.

"Addie – " Leslie face was flushed. "Don't go."

"I'm not leaving." Addie moved around her own desk to Bella's. "Speaking of respect, I owe you the same." She extracted Bella's recorder from the purse. "Bella set this going without talking with me first. I'm sorry, I should've told you right away." She clicked the off button, extracted the cassette and handed it to Leslie. "When you get home, listen to how you sounded there before you destroy the tape."

Leslie looked down at the cassette. Her shoulders rose with an audible inspiration, then fell as the breath came out of her. "I'm sorry," she said softly. "I was out of line. But I'm also angry about being set-up. I mean, do you really think I killed my father?"

"No." Addie moved back toward her chair. "But did I have any notion your brother would kill himself? That you'd split up with Todd? That my Bess would go to work for Cletis? Life is full of unpleasant surprises." With a sigh, she lowered herself into her chair. "I'm just trying to find out why my house was trashed. Is that so unreasonable?" A very reasonable lie, she thought. Was there any special place in Heaven or Hell for people who lied to get at the truth?

Leslie sank back in Bella's chair. "No, not unreasonable. But whatever I say, you'll tell George. How unreasonable is that?"

"I would hope you'll tell him first. And I would hope that Michael will tell Cletis, being that you work for one of his competitors." Addie rubbed her forehead. "I really don't want to be in the middle of all this. I keep thinking of your mother and how hurt she would feel about what's happened to her family."

Leslie's eyes glistened. "I miss her, I really do. Mom always saw me as better than I was. She was one of those mothers who really deserved better children... Addie, I was stupid, but I didn't kill my father – that's the God's honest truth."

"You'll have to convince Detective Barker of that. You want to tell me about my house?"

"Excuse me a minute." Leslie opened her purse, extracted some tissues, wiped a few tears away, then blew her nose.

She's considering what to say, thought Addie. Wait her out.

Leslie finally dropped the soiled tissues into the waste basket next to the desk. "It was all a mistake," she said. "A seven-layer shit-cake of mistakes. I'd stopped at my father's house the day he was murdered. He was fit and feisty as ever. So when Detective Barker later told me he was dead, I was in shock. And Barker came at me like a backhoe digging up dirt, so I panicked – I lied. I said I hadn't seen my father for two days. Then, after Barker left, I remembered the glove. But he hadn't said a word about it. Over the next few days, I kept expecting he'd bring it up, but he didn't, and I certainly didn't want to."

"Why not? Why didn't you tell him you'd forgotten about visiting your father that morning?"

"You think he would've believed that? How would it've looked – changing my story like that?"

"A lot better than if you remained silent and he found the glove."

"Yes, but he hadn't found it, and I would've had to have lied about why I was at my father's house in the first place. I could never have gotten through a lie detector test, and once it came out I was at our father's house, Larry would know why and might even have blamed me for the murder."

"Now you've lost me," said Addie. "Why were you at your father's house?"

"That's really none of your business." Leslie thrust out her chin. "I need to talk to a lawyer."

"Yes, you do. But I want to know about *my* house. Once you learned that Flash brought home the pipe, you thought it was likely he took the glove, too. Am I right?"

Leslie's nod was barely perceptible.

"You were there that morning and were wearing your gloves when you touched the bird house?"

Leslie looked down and picked at a fingernail. When she looked up, her face spoke of sorrow, and of resignation. "I was getting ready to leave when he told me to come down to the basement and see what he was making – something for me and for his grandchildren. I was already late, but I had to humor him. I thought I'd go out through the bulkhead to my car. I didn't realize the paint was still wet." Leslie shook her head. "That was my first mistake. My second was leaving the glove there on the workbench. He said he'd clean it and get it back to me as good as new. I didn't have time to fool with it, and I certainly wasn't going to put a glove with wet paint in my pocket."

"So you hired someone to break into my house to look for it."

"No. Another mistake." Leslie's lips parted, then closed, then opened again, the public face of private debate. "I didn't hire anyone. I – asked – someone to look around your house for it. Breaking in was that person's idea. If Flash went down the bulkhead into the basement to steal the pipe and maybe the glove from my father, then it followed he could have gone down your bulkhead to hide the glove."

"So why was it necessary to trash the whole house?" Leslie shrugged. "It wasn't necessary. I felt terrible when I heard what – that person did. Ridiculous as it sounds, my – person said Flash started it."

"Wait – " Addie's voice rose in anger. "He ransacked my house, emptied every drawer, broke all my dishes and my mother's china – and all that is Flash's fault?"

"Yes – no – but Flash attacked him." Leslie winced as she heard what she'd given away, but she wasn't about to stop. "The stupid cat went after his shoelaces, bit him when he tried to pick him up in the kitchen. Some things got knocked about and broken. My friend lost his temper." Leslie's hand made a dismissive gesture. "Anyway, he had the idea to make it look like a gang had vandalized the place. That was his idea. I never wanted your cat or any of your things harmed." She reached out to Addie. "I certainly will pay for everything that was damaged."

"That's fine and dandy, isn't it. What price do I put on the shock of coming home to find Flash trapped and hurt? How much do I charge for the last tea cups my mother left me? Never mind the weekend of labor it took my girls and me to clean up the mess, you think money can make up for the violation of my home, my privacy?"

Leslie bowed her head. "I'm sorry. I didn't mean for any of that to happen."

"Then you shouldn't've asked Michael Planchette to do your dirty work."

Leslie's head jerked upward. "You knew?"

Not until now. "Of course," said Addie. So Michael was the elephant in the room. "Tell him he shouldn't go around leaving elephants on other people's property."

"You mean what he did to Cletis?" Leslie looked distraught. "You're not going to tell Cletis he broke in, are you? He'll fire Michael."

"For trashing my house? Or for having an affair with you and giving you company information? Or perhaps for murdering your father? I wonder which of those things Cletis might find most objectionable."

"Michael had nothing to do with my father's murder – "

"As far as you know."

"– nor did I," said Leslie. "Yes, we're having an affair. So what? Michael's divorced and my marriage was on the rocks long ago. Sure, he did a terrible thing to your house and your cat, but Michael's only motive was to help me, not to hurt you. I love him, Addie. I know he made a major mistake, but I don't want him to be put in jail or lose his job because of my stupidity. I asked him to look for that glove."

Addie frowned. What parts of Leslie's story were true? If Michael had acted on his own in the break-in, couldn't he have murdered Herbert without telling her? No, as each other's alibi for that night, collusion was more likely. "I guess I'm old-fashioned. I don't approve of people having affairs, but I certainly understand there are lots of reasons they do. Still, I don't get it, Leslie – now you love the stepson of a man you loved twenty-five years ago?"

"What can I say – tastes change?" Leslie's grunt made a mockery of her words. "No, since I have to swim in the truth here, I'll be candid about this. I didn't start out loving Michael – I was just hating Cletis. See, when my mother was ill, she gave me the combination to the safe in my parents' room. Her jewelry and my father's rarest coins were in there, and there were some documents. I didn't take a thing, but I had plenty of time to examine it all. It blew my mind when I found the purchase and sale agreement that my father signed with Cletis. The date made it clear that I'd been traded for land. Do you have any idea how it feels to be a rising star in the company, and the next day to be out on your ass? And to be fired by the man you love?"

Cletis dumped me before you were even born, thought Addie. Then Dave did. "I have some idea."

"I doubt it," said Leslie. "I was like one of those promising young ballplayers who gets traded away. Except I didn't have another team that wanted me. I was sent packing for a fucking fifty acres and a mistress to be named later – boom!" Her hand cut a horizontal strip of air. "So when I met Michael at a business meeting, I imagined how it would burn Cletis' ass to know I'd taken up with his stepson. If I cozied up to Michael, maybe I could even find a way to hurt Cletis in his business."

Addie recalled Cletis talking about his contracts being underbid. "So you got very cozy."

Leslie's cheeks flushed. She closed her eyes and nodded. "At first I only wanted revenge. And there was definitely an ego-boost that I could attract a man ten years my junior." Her eyes opened, her face pled for understanding. "But the more I got to know Michael, the more I really liked him. He has an energy and a wild sense of humor that Todd never had. I mean Todd's a nice guy, but he's dull as a doorknob. Michael is passionate. All Todd thinks about is the stock market and investments."

Addie took a deep breath, then let it out slowly. "I hesitate to ask – but you know my husband left me for someone else – how do you handle your guilt about deceiving Todd?"

"I didn't do Todd a favor by letting him pick me up on the rebound, but I really tried to be good for him. I came home from my job and cooked and cleaned, and I supported him emotionally through a lot of crap – he's a compulsive worrier. When he gets very worried, he gets irritable and yells about stupid little things. I just take a good book and hide out in another room."

"So why didn't you divorce him years ago?"

Leslie uttered a rueful chuckle. "Don't think I haven't asked myself that over and over." A hurt child took over her face. "The truth is I didn't think anyone else would ever want me."

CHAPTER 42

Wednesday, 9:30 a.m.

"You gave her the tape?" Bella's scowl and voice expressed her dismay. She snatched up the cassette recorder from her desk and thrust it into her purse. "Why on earth did you do that?"

"Please sit down," said Addie. "Believe me, it wasn't to leave you out. I need you to think with me."

"Yeah, you and the Pope." She lowered herself into her chair, tugged an apron end from beneath her thigh, and swiveled around to face Addie. "You mad I didn't tell you I was going to tape it?"

"I was annoyed. Please don't do that again. But I must admit the tape came in handy."

"So why did you give it to her?"

"It wasn't fair that she was being taped without her knowledge. In some states, unless you get a warrant, it's a crime to do that. You could've gotten both of us in trouble."

"That's not very likely," said Bella.

"Why take the chance?" Addie poked her glasses a bit higher on her nose. "I remember on *Law and Order*, a tape made without consent wasn't even allowed in as evidence in Court. Besides, Leslie didn't confess to any crime. All she'd admit was that she was having an affair with Michael and asked him to look for her glove. She put all the blame for the break-in on Michael, and on Flash for attacking him."

"So that's who put Flash in the dryer? In my book, anyone who tortures a pet should be put in a cage in a public square," said Bella. "Still, I would've liked to hear what she had to say."

"I needed to win her confidence."

Bella raised both hands as stop signs. "Wait, let me see if I got this straight. She denied everything, blamed her own lover and your beloved cat – and you won her confidence? You're telling me that's worth the price of my cassette?"

"No, I traded your cassette for an hour of talk. And Leslie did own up to some things. She told me that Todd had lost his temper and hit her when she admitted she'd been having an affair. It seems Larry had been told of the affair by one of his patients, a desk clerk at a Worcester motel, so he called Leslie. She told him it was none of his business, but he wormed the name out of her. When she wouldn't promise to end it, Larry went ahead and told Herbert. That's why she was there the day of the murder. Herbert was giving her an ultimatum – if she didn't give up Michael, he'd write her out of his will."

Bella put a hand to her forehead. "Addie, Addie. She admits she was there and gives you the reason she might have killed Herbert, and you could've had it on tape. Do you realize what you did?"

Addie's lips tightened. Hard not to have doubts. No, Leslie wasn't going to open up to threats alone. She had to feel she could trust someone. That's why Leslie couldn't tell Barker – he made trust into a foreign language. "I know exactly what I did. I gave Leslie a chance to consult her lawyer. I gave Michael Planchette a chance to tell Cletis before I do. If he's going to lose his job or be arrested, he'll have a few hours to get himself and his daughter prepared."

Bella snorted. "Or time to cross the border to Canada or hop on a plane to Whicheverstan. Don't you see? Whether Herbert's murderer is Leslie or Michael or both together, you've given them time to get away."

"No, I think Leslie and Michael had their hungry eyes focused on Cletis' wealth and each other. Not that they didn't benefit from Herbert's death, but I doubt they wanted to kill him."

"But Herbert told her he was going to cut her out of the will."

"Yes. But even if that made Leslie want to kill him, she's not the kind of person to act impulsively. She's more of a schemer. Look how long she waited to get back at Cletis. As it is, with Herbert dead, she has a million dollars or more coming to her in Millbrook. She's not going to run away. And Michael has his daughter to consider."

"Your ex-husband had four children to consider."

Addie felt her muscles go tight. "I know. To most men, money means more. Michael can share Leslie's inheritance – if she's telling the truth about how much she loves him. But I believe she told the truth when she said she didn't murder Herbert, and that she never wanted to, despite his threats."

"And I suppose you know who did want to?" Bella challenged.

"Of course not. If I did, I'd tell you." Addie rubbed her forehead. Who wanted to murder Herbert? Michael? Gloria? April? Cletis? Or – no one?

"Bella, it just occurred to me – what if no one really wanted to murder Herbert. What if it started out as an accident?"

CHAPTER 43

WEDNESDAY, 2 P.M.

By the time Addie pulled into her driveway, Bella's windshield wipers were losing the battle against the rain. She stopped the Cadillac behind her own Corolla, turned all the dials to "off," and put Bella's car keys into her purse. She'd have to make a run for it. Her umbrella wouldn't survive ten seconds in this wind.

Maybe Bella and Carlo would be smart enough to close the store early and go home together to wait out the storm. She'd wait it out with Flash, snug in her own home again. She'd call George around three-thirty – by that time, he'd be too busy helping other people to bother with her.

The wind almost tore the Cadillac's door from her grasp as she struggled out into an icy rain. Her glasses fogged up but she kept hold of the door and used her body to force it closed. By the time she reached her front porch, she was waterlogged and chilled.

Flash was sitting in the hallway, waiting for her. "Hello, sweetie. I'm home."

Flash lifted his head, turned his back and padded away.

Payback, thought Addie. "I'll be home with you tonight. Isn't that good?" But Flash was already out of sight.

* * *

She'd put up the thermostat, changed into her favorite overalls and turtleneck, put on a warm pair of socks and brewed a cup of tea before she found the remains of her slippers in the living room. "Bad, Flash," she said, turning her MAHIB face to the couch. Yes, the monarch of all he surveys. Too bad there were no anger management classes for cats – or kings.

Outside, the trees and bushes were bending and twisting as sheets of rain flew by. She got down on her knees and gathered up the beige and white scraps of material that once were slippers. As she rose, she noticed the telephone message light blinking rapidly. That could wait until she put on her tennis shoes and checked the basement for leaks. Yes, and filled some pots with water. What else? A flashlight or candles and matches in every room.

She'd just tossed the scraps of her slippers into the garbage pail in the kitchen when she heard the doorbell.

"Who on earth?" she muttered. "In this weather?"

She kept the chain on as she opened the front door and peered out. It took her a moment to recognize the face under the hood of the yellow rainsuit. "Gloria? What are you doing out on a day like this?" Addie fumbled with the chain to buy a few extra seconds. The murderer? No, if Gloria had killed her father, she wouldn't've opened up the family can of worms at the funeral luncheon. And how could she turn Gloria away in this storm? "Flash, get back."

"I was going home from the hospital." The storm door jerked against Gloria's grip. "All my afternoon PT patients cancelled. Then my car broke down two blocks away."

Addie opened the door. "Come on in before you drown out there. Do you have Triple A?" She stepped back to let Gloria enter and pull the storm door closed. Water ran from the rain suit onto the welcome mat.

Gloria pushed back her hood and set her black purse on the floor. "I called them from my car, but they said in this weather it would be a few hours unless I was blocking a road or in a dangerous situation with downed wires or trees. And I had to pee, so I came here. I'm sorry to impose on you. I don't have the keys to next door."

"It's not an imposition," said Addie. "Take off your wet things. I'll hang them up while you use the powder room. You'll find clean towels on the shelf."

Gloria's smile seemed wistful. "I remember." She bent over to take off her boots. "It feels like I was here studying for the S.A.T. exam with Bess only a few weeks ago. Okay if I leave my boots here?"

"Sure, you make yourself at home again." Addie waited as Gloria shed her rain gear, revealing a dark brown sweat suit. Did Gloria go to work in that? Still, her explanation for intruding seemed reasonable. The glove was Leslie's, so that wouldn't've prompted Gloria to come. "I hope this storm isn't as big as the forecasters predicted," said Addie.

"It's wild out there – it's supposed to last until midnight." Gloria handed over the wet garments, then ran a hand through her hair. "I'm a mess. I'll need more than my brush to put myself together." She bent and scooped up her purse. Flash came to Addie to investigate the rubberized yellow trousers dangling from her hands, then sprang back as drops of water hit him.

"You go on in and take care of yourself," said Addie. She let Gloria go by, then gently shook the rain suit over the mat. "How about a cup of tea?"

"No, thanks." Gloria kept walking toward the bathroom but raised her voice. "Too much coffee, today. That's why I couldn't wait."

Addie watched the bathroom door close, then went through the kitchen to the mud room. She hung the rain suit on a peg near the back door. Call George? Yes, better safe than sorry. She had to tell him she was at home, anyway. She went to the kitchen and speed-dialed his cell phone. After two rings, his recorded greeting came on. Oh, crumb. As she waited for George's message to end, she heard the toilet flush, the sink faucet go on. "George, I want to let you know that I'm at home and safe. Gloria's car broke down on her way home – "

Purse in hand, Gloria entered the kitchen. Her short blonde hair glistened, her cheeks were rosy from the wind. "You calling George?"

Addie nodded. "She's having trouble getting Triple A to come out right away, so we'll just stay cozy together. I'm sure you have plenty to do, so don't feel you have to come until things quiet down." She hung up the phone and smiled. "Shall we sit here or go into the living room."

"We can sit here while you have your tea." Gloria pulled out a kitchen chair and sat down. "So, was the mystery of the lost glove solved?"

Addie took her mug of tea from the counter and put it into the microwave. "Yes. It turned out to be Leslie's. Didn't she tell you?" She pressed a button and the microwave hummed.

"No, I haven't spoken to her since you called. By the way, April thought that was an odd call."

Addie shrugged. "I told her you didn't have to get back to me if the glove wasn't yours."

"You said something else that puzzled her – something about us having bigger things to worry about?"

"Oh." So this was more than idle conversation. "It was just a casual remark."

Gloria smiled. "Good to know. Being that neither of us had been in your house or in Auterio's, we had no idea why you called us. Did you find the glove at my father's?"

"Flash found it there and hid it away. I didn't discover his hidey-hole until Sunday."

"First the pipe, now the glove. You have a real klepto cat. Do you know when Leslie lost it?"

The microwave beeped. Addie popped open the door, took out the mug and headed for the table. "She said she left it there the day your father was murdered."

Gloria looked stunned. "My God! She confessed being there that day? Then I was right! She did kill him."

"Perhaps." Addie sat down opposite Gloria. "There are other possibilities."

"Like what? The killer presumably wore gloves, that's why there were no fingerprints. Leslie was there and Flash took one of her gloves from the basement – it all adds up."

The basement? Addie tensed in her chair. No, not proof. It was possible Gloria just assumed that Flash took the glove from the same place he'd taken Herbert's pipe. "Except Flash didn't take the glove from the basement," she said. "Leslie told me she left it in the kitchen."

"She's lying. She left it on – in the basement." Gloria's face turned red. "She must have, for Flash to have grabbed it."

Gloria saw it on the workbench! Addie's face paled. No, not Bess' best friend. Murdered her father? And now? "You may be right. So let's talk about something more cheerful."

"You don't believe that I – "

The door bell rang. Addie sprang from her chair. "That must be George." She hurried to the door. The chain was hanging free. She whipped open the door and gasped at the man in the dripping black raincoat and hat.

"God, woman. Why don't you answer your messages?" said Joe Kearney. "How's a friend to know whether you drowned in your bathtub or out on your lawn?"

"Joe!" A gust of wind drove rain into the entryway.

"Didn't your mother ever teach you it's rude to gape like a fish in a hurricane?" he said. "Either move aside, dear Addie, or bar the door and let me swim home."

She stepped back hastily. "Come in, come in. You didn't walk here, did you?"

"Taxi. As a man without wheels, I've done my best to cultivate drivers. Still, I had to pay a premium to get one out this afternoon. May I take off my coat and stay a few days?"

Addie laughed. What a relief! "Yes to the first request, and no to the second. But your taxi driver – "

"Safely on his way. Once I saw your car and another in the driveway, I knew you'd be here. And, if truth be told, I didn't want to chance your turning me around to go home." He looked beyond Addie. "Well look who's here, the princess of PT."

Addie did an about-face. Gloria looked amused. A worm of fear crawled up Addie's spine. She turned back to Joe. "You two know each other?"

"Hello, Joe." Gloria's tone was friendly. "How's the shoulder?"

"I'd say ninety percent." He looked at Addie. "What's wrong?"

"I'm surprised you know each other."

Joe started unbuttoning his raincoat. "This glorious Gloria helped me get my arm back in shape after my shoulder surgery. Couldn't lift my hand higher than my belt when I met her. Now I can do this." He made a show of taking off his hat. "Notice my head stayed in place. So how is it that you two ladies come to share this lovely day?" He offered a summer smile.

"I grew up next door," said Gloria.

A puzzled expression replaced Joe's smile. "You mean – "

"You didn't know Gloria's last name is Elwood?" asked Addie.

Joe shook his head. "Her nametag only said 'Gloria.'" He looked beyond Addie. "I'm sorry for your losses, Ms. Elwood. I didn't realize – "

Addie's heart sank. What a convincing liar he was. Hospital nametags would have both names – wouldn't they?

"That's okay," said Gloria. "I'm glad you're here – to see you again."

Too many coincidences, thought Addie. Come on, George, get over here. She tried to rub the prickles from the back of her neck. Better not leave these two alone together. "Joe, why don't you hang up your wet things in the mud room – it's through the kitchen and to the right." The cruiser will come up the driveway, she thought. "Gloria, why don't we go sit in the living room? It's more comfortable."

"Fine," said Gloria. But she didn't move.

"Excuse me." Joe squeezed by them both. "Out of my way, beastie." With narrowed eyes, ears laid back and whiskers fanned out over his snarl, Flash crouched in the center of the hallway. His body was arched, his tail swished back and forth.

"Don't mind Flash," said Addie. "He doesn't appreciate people visiting me." She patted her pocket. Yes, Dr. Warley's Wondernip. "Flash, come!" Flash cocked his head, then sprang forward, dodging Joe, then Gloria, to pluck the nugget cleanly from Addie's fingers and saunter off to the living room.

"Thank you for paying the toll, dear Addie." Joe walked toward the kitchen.

Did he mean the nugget or the toll to come? Addie cleared her throat, called out. "On your way back, you can pour yourself a mug of tea. The teapot's on the stove, mugs are on hooks over the counter. Milk's in the refrigerator. Use the microwave if it's easier."

"Home, sweet home," said Joe.

"Oh, I forgot my tea in the kitchen. Silly of me." She smiled at Gloria. "Why don't you go sit in the living room, and I'll be right in."

Gloria shook her head. "I need to talk to you before he comes back."

Maybe they weren't in cahoots, thought Addie. "I suppose my tea can wait. Come inside."

Addie seated herself in her rocking chair, where she faced the windows. Rain smacked against the glass as if desperate to break through. Outside, the bushes and trees were in frenetic movement. She was about to utter a warning about not sitting on the couch when Flash leaped onto her lap and began nosing her pocket for more Wondernip. "No, Flash. You've had your treat for this afternoon." She embraced Flash with one arm and shielded her pocket with the other.

Gloria had chosen the arm chair close to her rocker. She spoke in a hushed tone. "What have you told George about April and me?"

"Are you here for a nice visit, or are you interrogating me?"

"Look, if there are any suspicions about us, I want them put to rest." Gloria's tone was pleasant but her gaze was piercing.

Put to rest? "You're talking to the wrong person, Gloria. You need to talk to the police."

"I have, to that idiot detective. I expect I will again. I just need to be sure we're on the same page."

"And what page is that?"

"That it's most likely Leslie killed Herbert. She wanted the land and the money. You say she was at our father's house that day and the glove proves it. I know she and Michael are lovers. Maybe he was there, too. Their alibi is just each other."

Addie heard the microwave beep. "Michael's daughter was there."

Gloria snorted. "She's only eight. Obviously, Michael coached her on what to say. Their whole alibi depends on the kid's story."

"And each other. The way your account of that night depends entirely on April." Who belied it in the Emergency Room, thought Addie.

Feeling Flash start to squirm, Addie reached into her pocket for another nugget of Wondernip. Flash gobbled it down. "There may not be a gun, but there is a murder weapon somewhere," she said. "And missing gardening shoes and socks."

"So what?"

"So Michael's too big a man to literally fit into Herbert's shoes. It was either a small man or a woman who didn't want to leave footprints." Oh crumb! She'd said too much.

"Is that what you meant when you said I had bigger things to worry about?"

Addie thought she heard the microwave start up again. "Not at all. It was a chance remark."

"Don't lie to me. You could get me in serious trouble. If that stupid detective arrests me, the hospital will suspend me – even though I'm innocent. Maybe April, too." Gloria's eyes narrowed. "Our future depends on you remaining silent."

How ironic, thought Addie. The family blabbermouth demands silence. Yes, Gloria would kill her without shedding a tear. Fear twisted into Addie's gut like a corkscrew. She heard the microwave beep again. What was Joe doing out there? Was he her friend or her enemy? She'd been so wrong about everyone – oh God, it hurt. Can't count on George coming in time. Bet her life on Joe?

"Will you and your partner – " Addie inclined her head toward the kitchen. "– push me down the stairs, too?"

Gloria's eyes grew wide, her expression grim. She licked her lips nervously. "I don't know what you're talking about."

"Don't *you* lie to me. Doesn't it work both ways? You two are going to kill me, aren't you? Like the two of you killed your father."

"No. April wasn't involved. She didn't even know that I was going to visit him."

Relief flooded her. Not Joe! Thank God. "Whatever happened, April lied for you afterwards. That makes her an accomplice."

"She was just trying to protect me, to protect our life together. She's the only person in my life who's loved me more than herself." Gloria's eyes teared up. She leaned forward and scooped her purse off the rug.

"Your mother loved you."

"Not enough to go against my father and tell him to leave me be or get the hell out himself. Not even enough to visit me openly, or to say good-bye and give me her wedding ring before she died. That's why I went over to have it out with him. He was still stringing me along about it, and I'd had enough."

"So you killed him?"

She put her hand into a purse and extracted a handgun. "You ask too many questions, Addie. I'm really sorry, but you're old, and April and I still have our lives ahead of us."

Addie felt herself turn cold. You little turd. Time – play for time. "How about satisfying my curiosity this one last time. After all, I did a lot for you way back when."

"Yes, but it was Bess who got you to do it. I'm mostly sorry I have to cause her such pain."

"Don't forget to send her a sympathy card." She saw Gloria flush. Stupid! Another wisecrack and she'd end up dead sooner rather than later. "So you simply reached out and pushed your father down the steps?"

Gloria looked toward the kitchen, then lowered her gun hand so the weapon was hidden by her thigh. "I didn't go over there to kill him. But he was walking away from me again. Walking off to finish his fucking bird houses after telling me he'd never had the slightest intention of putting me in the will, and that my sinful hands would never touch my mother's ring. The man was a monster."

No, but he'd created one. "Don't you have a shred of guilt?"

Gloria's eyelid twitched. "Not about him. I'm glad he's dead."

"Who's dead?" Joe asked as he stepped into the room carrying a mug in each hand. He looked at Addie. "I heated your tea up, too."

"Thank you." Addie looked at Gloria. "Will I have time to drink it?"

"Why on earth not?" Joe's head turned as if he were following a tennis match.

Gloria raised the handgun. "Because you're going to kill her."

Addie tensed. Flash squirmed. She wrapped her arms around him.

Joe gaped. "Me?"

"Poor Joe," said Addie. She felt sadder for him than for herself.

"If this is a joke, it's not funny," he said.

Gloria rose to her feet. "Put the mugs on top of the TV."

"What is this, Addie?"

"Do as she says. She's going to kill me and blame it on you."

"But I'll — Ah! I'll die in the struggle for the gun."

"If it's any comfort, I'll have to get shot, too," said Gloria.

"Try the shoulder," said Joe. "It hurts like a bitch."

Get the gun, thought Addie. Or get her onto the couch. "Gloria, if you and I were having tea when Joe burst into the room, you'd have your fingerprints on one of the mugs, and Joe wouldn't."

"You're right." Gloria pointed the gun at Joe. Her hand was trembling. "Put the mugs on an end table next to the couch. Then take that afghan from the piano bench and wipe off the mugs real well."

Addie watched Joe's reluctant movements. No, even without the gun, they were no match for Gloria in a brawl. Get Gloria to sit down on the couch. "Put the mugs on the end table closest to where I sit, Joe." She tried to sound casual. "Oh, and bring the TV remote. It's a Swingline." Would he understand? And keep his mouth shut? "I'd like to put the TV on for Flash."

"Television?" Gloria looked puzzled.

With the remote tucked under his arm, Joe looked up from wiping the mugs. "Does *One Life to Live* have reruns?"

"TV calms Flash down," said Addie. "Otherwise he'll go crazy at the gun shots. He bit Robert and Michael. And Joe shouldn't have his fingerprints on my cup of tea. Will you hand it to me?" she asked Gloria.

"Get up and get it yourself. Back away from the table, Joe."

Addie managed to keep her arms around Flash while she got to her feet, took three steps to the end table, and picked up a mug. She glanced out the window at the driving rain. George, please come now, please come.

"Now put the cat down," said Gloria.

"Sure, I don't want Flash to get hurt. I just want to give him one last treat and a hug. Let me get back to my chair. And you should really leave an impression of your body or a hair or two on the couch next to the end table. On CSI, they'd see you never sat there."

"Why are you being so goddamn helpful?" asked Gloria.

"Believe me, I'm not trying to help. I'm playing for time, hoping George will get here. But I've known you since you were born, and I admire your courage. So I'll warn you, this is a tragic mistake. You have absolutely no chance of getting away with it."

"Why not?" Gloria's tone was laden with suspicion.

Get her to the couch! "Well, if you go back and sit in your chair for thirty seconds, I'll tell you."

"No way," said Gloria. "I'll sit here. You have thirty seconds." She perched on the arm of the couch.

"Joe, the Swingline, please. And here's your treat, Flash." She dug her nails into his belly, then flung the enraged cat at Gloria's face, jumped aside and ducked. Gloria screamed as her gun went off. A lamp shattered and Addie felt pain slice from her back to her thigh. She forced herself to straighten and rush toward the couch, where Gloria had fallen back screaming, both hands trying to fend off sharp teeth and claws.

Joe whacked the remote down on Gloria's wrist, once, twice. Gloria shrieked as she dropped the gun. Joe was looking at the shattered plastic in his hand. Addie smashed the mug into the side of Gloria's face and felt the impact up to her elbow as tea flew everywhere, the mug shattered against bone and Gloria's head recoiled, blood running down her cheek.

"Don't just stand there," Addie yelled at Joe. "Get the gun!"

"You mean this little piggy?" Joe raised his hand high enough to show the gun, but his attention had flown out the window.

Gloria moaned and clutched a pillow to her face. Flash was nowhere to be seen.

Then Addie saw the flashing blue lights coming up the driveway. She felt Joe put an arm gently around her shoulder.

"You throw one hell of a party, Addie."

CHAPTER 44

Thursday Afternoon

Addie was winding up her account of Gloria's visit when she heard footsteps coming up the steps to the supermarket office. She raised her eyebrows at Bella, who replied with a shrug from her seat at her desk.

"Maybe another problem downstairs," Carlo said. Adjusting his spectacles, he rose from the folding chair he'd been sitting on and hiked up his beige Levi's.

"George!" Addie got up as he came through the doorway. His cap and uniform were spotted with moisture. "Why aren't you wearing your raincoat?"

"It's letting up," he said. "We ran in from the cruiser. Hi Aunt Bella, hello Uncle Carlo." George stepped aside. "I don't believe you two have met Detective Barker."

Barker had to duck as he came through the doorway. "Hello again, Mrs. Carter." His bulk filled the office. "Pleased to meet you, sir," he said, offering his hand to Carlo. "I've heard about this place from my Aunt Rona."

Carlo shook Barker's hand. "Good to meet you, too."

"And we've heard a lot about you from your parrot," said Bella. "Were you the one who named him Shot Glass?"

Barker's face reddened. "In my younger days." He moved to shake Bella's hand. "Pleased to meet you, Mrs. Auterio. Actually, I found less talkative birds more appealing."

"The dumber the better," said Bella. "A lot of men think that way."

No need to be rude, thought Addie. "What can we do for you, Detective?"

Barker turned back to Addie. "I know I gave you a tough time at the station this morning. George and I were very concerned about your safety and I felt you'd made a few really bad choices, but I think I went over the line a bit."

Way over, thought Addie. "Do you mean in calling what I did 'idiotic' or was it in labeling me a 'know-it-all broad'?"

"Is that what he called you?" asked Bella

"I suppose either one wasn't a good choice of words," said Barker. "So I'm here to apologize – and to ask you not to do it again."

"That's a real man's apology," said Bella.

Barker frowned at her. Bella smiled and batted her eyelashes.

"Not to do what again?" asked Addie.

"Not to interfere in police business. We're perfectly capable of doing our own work. We don't need vigilantes, nor do we need a senior citizen going rogue."

Addie tried not to smile. "I wasn't dishonest with you, Detective, and I certainly don't intend to get involved in any murder ever again. And your apology?"

"Yes, I'm sorry." Barker looked at George, who nodded.

"I appreciate your coming over here to do that, Detective." She looked at her son. Clearly, he'd had his say in private.

"I agree with his point," said George. "You should let us do the police work."

"I also wanted to tell you the crime scene people are done with your house," said Barker. "You can go home any time you want to. The only problem is that you have a bunch of reporters in cars and vans out front. Please be careful what you say to them. They're good at twisting things around."

"I don't plan to say anything to them," said Addie. "My grandson is the only reporter I'll talk to. I'll give the police department credit for coming up with such a good plan to trap the murderer."

"I appreciate that," said Barker. "And you'll be glad to know we arrested Victor Ostman for driving to endanger and leaving the scene of an accident."

"Did you ever hear back from the FBI?" asked Addie.

"Yes," said Barker. "Some wealthy businessmen wanted to build what they call The Academy of Learning and Cultural Values. It was to be a private school for Chinese-Americans or kids who wanted to learn Chinese, as well as a retreat for families. It checked out as legit, but wherever it's built, I think the Bureau will keep an eye on it because of the potential for industrial espionage. Both our department and the Boston FBI appreciates everyone's cooperation."

"Yeah," said Bella. "We appreciate you, too. Have a donut on your way out."

"And a coffee," said Carlo as he sat down.

"Thanks, but I'm not a moocher." Barker smiled. "Not when I'm on a diet, anyway." He turned to leave. "I'll wait downstairs," he told George.

Hearing the Detective descend the steps, Addie allowed herself a sigh of relief. "So the reporters are waiting outside my house?" she asked George.

"In force. Eyewitness News has already interviewed Ray Miggens, who told all of Massachusetts what a good neighbor you are. You may want to stay an extra night or two at my house."

Would this never end? thought Addie. "How's Flash?"

"Ornery as ever. I had him in the basement until the photographer and tech people left. When I let him out, he headed straight for the bathroom. Unfortunately, I forgot to remove the toilet paper, so it quickly became confetti city."

"You might have had a few other things on your mind," said Bella.

"Don't worry, Ma, I cleaned it up. And I left Flash food and water like you said."

"What happens to Gloria?" asked Carlo.

"Now that we got signed statements from Ma and Mr. Kearney this morning, Gloria'll be taken to District Court tomorrow for arraignment on two counts of attempted murder. The D.A.'s office wants us to do a little more work before they charge her with Herbert's murder." George's expression turned sour. "She's still insisting Herbert's murder was an accident, and of course April backs her up on that. The prosecutor is going to have some serious talks with April about her options before the list of charges is completed." George shook his head. "No jury is going to believe a sledge hammer accidentally fell on Herbert's head."

"And Gloria never called for help," said Bella.

"Gloria did call," said Addie, easing herself back into her chair. "She put calls in to Leslie and Larry, but they didn't answer. She must have panicked after she pushed Herbert down the stairs and he didn't die."

"If it was really an accident, she would've called 911," said Carlo.

"She should've," said Addie. "But maybe she was afraid of what Herbert was saying, or would have said. He was so homophobic, chances are he would've involved April."

George waved her argument away. "Don't make excuses for her. She killed her father in cold blood and then tried to make it look like a robbery."

"I'm not excusing anything." Except you, Addie thought. So much easier to think in black and white than to work at perceiving colors. "Did you find Michael Planchette?"

"He surrendered himself to the Worcester Police this morning. He came in with a Boston lawyer." George winked. "Your old friend Cletis protecting his own?"

Addie bristled. "He's not my friend." She looked at Bella. "Have you spoken with him?"

"This morning." She caught Addie's look. "No, he called me. He is paying for Michael's defense, but he said that Michael would have to find himself another job. Michael did take the blame for what happened to your house. Cletis said that if Michael couldn't pay damages, he would."

"I don't want his money," said Addie.

"Here we go again," said Bella. "Didn't you learn anything?"

Addie sighed. "I learned much too much. I'll thank him for his offer. But I'm so upset that he's going to ruin those woods."

"It'll take him a year or two to get a proposal together that will satisfy the Planning Board and the Selectmen," said George.

"Longer, if I can help it," said Addie.

"I hate to remind you all," said Carlo, "but this is a place of business."

George smiled. "Sorry, Carlo. Can we expect you for dinner, Ma?"

"Yes, thank you." She couldn't go home yet. She'd have to ask Marty to check on Flash.

"Great," said George. "Luisa wants to show you the new songs she's learned on the keyboard. See you later."

As George closed the door behind him, Addie looked at Bella. "What other choice do I have for tonight?"

"Carlo and I are here until late. But you could call up your boyfriend and invite him out."

"Joe's not my boyfriend."

"Didn't he save your life?" asked Carlo.

"Flash saved my life."

"Oh, Addie," said Bella. "You're not even going to give Joe a call?"

"Certainly not. I saw him yesterday at my house and this morning at the police station. I need my life to settle down a little before I decide anything about Joe."

"I suppose you think you're being perfectly reasonable," said Bella.

"No. I'm being totally unreasonable. But I feel I'm being pushed into a relationship before I'm ready."

"Who's pushing you?"

"You are for one – calling Joe my 'boyfriend.' And George, too."

Bella cocked her head. "George? He didn't say a word about Joe."

"Not here," said Addie. "But this morning he invited Joe to our Thanksgiving. I mean I am thankful for what Joe did and otherwise he'd be alone – his sister is going to her in-laws in Ohio –but it puts him right in with my whole family."

"I think he's already in right with the whole family," said Carlo. "They're all grateful he was there for you. So don't be a turkey."

Addie laughed. "I suppose I am sometimes. Thank you for pointing out when I act like one." Suddenly, she felt sad. "This whole murder thing has been a nightmare."

Carlo got up and folded the metal chair he'd been sitting on. "I think it all goes to prove one thing."

Addie braced herself. No way would she invite one more male platitude.

"What does it prove?" asked Bella. She winked at Addie, then leaned forward in her chair. "Speak up, dear."

Carlo kept his gaze focused on Addie. "It proves a burglar alarm is worthless if you let bad people in."

"Truer words were never spoken." Bella had a glint in her eye and a quiver in her jaw.

"Right," said Addie. God bless her, Bella never stopped trying to lighten them up.

"Go ahead and laugh," said Carlo, carrying his chair to the closet and setting it down inside. "But mark my words, you two keep opening the door to danger, I'll live to regret it." He shut the closet door firmly. "And I'll hold both of you responsible."

"Don't worry," said Addie. "I want to get back to my house and my music and football games. I'm done with danger. All I want is peace and quiet. I'm really going to lay down the law to Flash."

"Really?" said Bella.

And Addie laughed.